CONDITION ZERO

A NULL
&
BOYD NOIR

GARY S. KADET

Melange Books, LLC
White Bear Lake, MN 55110
www.melange-books.com

Published in the United States of America.

Cover Design by Caroline Andrus

"Sunlight doesn't enter eyes that are closed," I answered the old man. "But we will cut open those closed eyes…"

—ISAAC BABEL, "GEDALI"

"Condition One is cocked and locked; Condition Two is hammer down with a round in the chamber; Condition Three is with a loaded magazine, empty chamber; Condition Zero is with a round in the chamber, hammer cocked, safety disengaged."

—JAN LIBOUREL, "HANDGUNNER'S GLOSSARY"

For Maxwell Davis, grandfather and scourge of villainy, and for Nancy Pepin, née Durocher, who handles just about everything else.

ONE

The eyes tell the whole story, even if you can't believe it.

Even if it makes no sense.

The eyes have a history in them, if you just take a moment to cut through all the useless junk, focus and read.

It's hard in the dark to read the fine print of the soul in the eye —true. Not so hard at all for someone like Malek the Mallet Turbot. Truer still.

Malek just drew a bead on his target to point of penetration then *fired and fired and fired.*

Everything was a target to Malek the Mallet.

A wiry, anxious man whose hair was wirier and even more anxious than he was, Malek affected wraparound sunglasses round the clock to cover his untreated amblyopia. He looked emotionless, but beneath was a taut, roiling jumble of paranoia. Even outside of the Ork, he was a legend on the street.

Ork was for Orchestra—a reference to the old T stop by Symphony Hall where back in the seventies the first few cops were laid out dead on the tracks as a warning to the old gangs—The Patriarca's, The Flemmi's, The O'Doyles—to show that patronage was just as cheap as Slavic blood.

During the last gang war that bloodied up I-93 all the way to Brockton, Malek found himself on the spot. Next in line not to be promoted.

So, he met with his predecessor in a bid for mercy.

He has been known ever since as the Mallet for the most uncomplicated of reasons: he caved in his predecessor's head with one forty-five times before taking his place.

"Don't fuck with me!" he drawled at the big man sweating terrified before him. "Don't fuck around." The big man was losing it, honest-to-God trembling before him! This he'd seen before, okay, but it wasn't from The Mallet this time—oh no—that much was clear. The clarity of it pissed him off. "You bring me fucking fairy stories for business and I shouldn't burn you down now without a thought? You think this is comedy? I should have Abbott and Costello here show you who's on first."

Nobody laughed.

In fact, the big man in the debased and sweat-disheveled Ermenegildo Zegna cloth suit seemed to be holding back actual tears.

His eyes swelled wide devouring all scant light of the room.

Tears welled.

The story was there alright, but the eyes didn't tell it so much as they bemoaned it. His thick chest heaving deep and fast, Nadio "Fester" Solecise," mad *starets* and *caporegime* of the most aggressive crime crew in Boston known simply as "The Family"—not for old-time Mafia ties, but for something else—went and begged. Pathetic, amateur night stuff.

Malek was almost too repulsed to act.

It was like this guy was one of the local deadbeats from the track making the usual mercy stop on the way to receiving his own personal beatdown. He was fucking pleading right there in the cramped basement of Armenian Specialties down on South Street where Malek liked to take his more serious meets. This was supposed to be serious?

Doing the song and dance before the fists of the inevitable came spinning down in his face?

The Mallet was perplexed. 'This guy had whacked out too many mooks to just be written off as a pussy.' The Mallet remembered the big man bearing down on him in a deal gone wrong once—just with his fists—and he knuckled, cringing, terrified.

But this whole thing before him now—a pussy move!

He nodded at the men flanking him.

Their names were not Abbott and Costello. Whatever their names were, you did not want to know them. You did not want to see them up close. You did not want them at all, nor did you want them to ever, ever want you. They stood thick and imposing like some great gutter Praetorian Guard—mottled, gristled, muscles and guns poised tight under the kind of baggy suits that did not impede movement.

They were the muscle of the Ork.

"Well, I got Martin and Lewis behind me says you'll listen," Fester countered.

Two other shadows moved behind Fester. Pockmarked, semi-shaven faces came into the light. Huge men yet again.

"Well, well," croaked the Mallet. "What do we do now, Dean?"

"I'll pay you, Malek. Name me a price."

"For what? One guy? One fucking amateur? Jesus fucking Christ, Fester, what are you setting me up for? You jerkin' me off and I can't come!"

Uncle Fester "The Confessor" pounded the card table hard in response without rising from his chair. "It's not a fucking set-up, *strunz!* You ain't got word shit went down? You ain't got no fucking street-briefing or what?"

"I hear all kinds of shit. So?"

At first, The Mallet had been interested, but now that he had at last penetrated the target, he was bored. He got up and paced in the darkness, wondering if and when to blow this particular target to pieces.

The eyes told the whole story to a slice of light from a passing car coming in from the dingy street-level window. The words backed it up.

"I—I'm—afraid." It sounded weak and vulnerable—a blood-call in this world. Malek licked his lips without knowing it.

"Fester. Fester, my buddy—"

"I don't care how it sounds. I'll pay."

Malek went for him out of the shadows, grabbed his collar and smacked him again and again, smiling. "You'll pay, that's guaranteed."

Looking unmoved, almost bored, Fester leveled a gut punch from where he sat that sent Malek the Mallet across the room and knocked the wind out of him.

The Mallet fought for gulps of inarticulateness rather than let dead air count him out. No, not a pussy at that.

Red-faced, Fester got up and braced Abbot and Costello, breathing in their faces.

"You think it's funny? That I'm terrified like a punk? Fucking Hilarious, huh? You wanna laugh?"

Abbott grinned and Fester easily creased his neck with his elbow just as Costello pistol-whipped him from behind, cool and jerky as some makeshift louver in a Rube Goldberg machine.

The Mallet rose coughing, still doubling over. He signaled to his guard to stand down just as Fester did to his own men while struggling up against the concrete wall just to sit.

"Keep your dicks in your pockets, boys. We're dealin' here." Fester was being optimistic, and they all knew it.

"Fuck you. This is your own game, Fes. You got juice enough. You don't need Ork juice or Mallet juice, or anything you say. You just need a shrink. A blowjob, maybe. A lay." He made his way back to his seat, playing with a fish-gutting knife in his hand as he did, as if for luck. "Fuck all, Fes. I'd kill your ass now, if a war with your friggin' Family didn't cost so damn much."

And maybe I don't need a war, he didn't say.

Fester stood up rubbing blood from the back of his head with a silk handkerchief.

"But you know it would."

"Which is why you get to leave here walkin' with your two girl-friends there."

Fester kicked the table and made his plea. "I need muscle out the ass, Mal. A fucking army, if I can get one. I mean it. This is no grift. I'll pay, up front!" He nodded to Lewis who produced a cheap metal strongbox with the stationery store tag still stuck on it. He unlocked it and shoved it across the table to where the Mallet now sat. He opened it with a single finger.

"Fifty large, fuckwad. Now, tell me I'm jokin'. Tell me it's pussy fucking shit, asswipe."

The Mallet's eyes were slits. The play had been made and the trump was his.

"Sorry, Charlie. The tuna stays off the hook."

The eyes told the whole story all over again: weakness, desperation—hopelessness.

Terror.

"You fucking have to take it! It's free Goddamn money!"

"Go get laid, Fester. Better yet, go get fucked."

He slid the money back across the table without a second thought.

Fester stood. He was slow, imposing, and despite his huge size it seemed he was carrying a weight he could barely handle.

"We were friends once, Malek. Back in the day."

"Ya. We were."

"For the old times. Help me out here. Please. I'm bein' genuine."

"I believe you. I really do"

"I'm afraid. *Afraid…!*" His eyes were tearing. Malek could see that he had been without sleep; he knew this from his own sleeplessness, the result of doing what had to be done. Small price.

"Okay. Let me get this right. One fucking guy?"

"Yeah."

"A degenerate fucking gambler, a low life non-member, a douchebag, right?"

"That's him."

"And you need an army for that? For this one little racing form dipshit *maricon* thinks he can bet on the ponies legit and win? Stick yourself with a fork, Fester. See about gettin' out before you can't. You feelin' me?"

Now it was Fester's turn to get up and pace back and forth before his protectors in the shadows.

"I feel you. It ain't just one guy. He's not—just a guy."

"Well, he ain't a chick, that's for sure. Or is he?"

"He ain't fucking human. He's not like anything you ever seen. You can't stop him. I couldn't stop him. He's like the boogie man. He's like fucking Dracula, this guy—"

Fester stopped at this point as all the guns in the room were now drawn but his, the black eye of each barrel staring him down.

"I don't fucking care he's Ozzy fucking Osborne with his own fucking family sitcom. When it's like this, you know it's over."

"Yeah. I do." Fester sighed and let his shoulders slump.

Change up—disinterest. "Usual stalemate, Fes'. Crawl out now and don't be coming back."

"I gotta know why ya wouldn't do it. Why you wouldn't help an old-time guy like me who you came up with?"

"Simple Fester. Simple."

"Ya. I'm stupid, so I gotta ask."

"You-gotta-ask." Sneering.

"So what?"

"So this. You're definitely worth more than 50k to me, sure—" Mallet cut himself off here to chuckle and shake his head. Then, breaking the silence of Fester's perplexity, he added two words.

"—But dead."

———

They knew they were being followed down Prince Street, so Fester had to walk between Martin and Lewis, whose respective Magnum and Glock were both drawn and cocked. Footsteps clacked loudly on the pavement. Fester crouched down when both fired.

Nothing.

They hurried him into an apartment building for which they had the keys and hustled the big man up six flights to the roof. There was a peace garden of Christ on the roof and a number of satellite dishes for pirate TV signals. Fester was pushed flat by his men against a dormer while the two bodyguards did perimeter surveillance of the entire roof to secure it.

Fester was breathing hard.

He closed his eyes and prayed.

He entered a dark space.

Time in terror becomes another thing; fear compresses the moment and can make hours the single skip of a heartbeat.

"Got a match?" said a voice.

It was the wrong voice.

Fester slid down the side of the dormer, not looking up. "Please, God. Please God. No." Eyes closed, trembling, hands held up to his face but weakly.

"Let's not bring God into it. Yet."

"I'll pay you! Anything. Anything…anything—please!" Fester, a thug, a career criminal with the Family who had beaten perhaps ten men to death in his career with a grin on his face, who had tortured, disfigured and raped countless others, was whining and blubbering curled into a ball like a small child.

Standing over him was a stooped, dry little man half his size. A nervous type appearing slack and relaxed. His expression was as colorless as his skin, as blank as his deep-set eyes. He didn't look sick, and he didn't look well. He didn't look sane, and he didn't look crazy. In fact, he didn't look like much of anything at all.

He was, beneath his unfastened overcoat and in the shadow of his pork pie hat, in every way a man in between.

"I don't need any money, Fester. I don't even need a match, really." The voice was toneless, mechanical, yet not dead. "But I'm trying, you know, to remember. What it was like? So, I might still smoke now and again. Even though I lack the habit. The need."

Fester eyed him from where he sat slumped. Could he rush him? He was a light guy, small like a bird. He could take him. No, he couldn't. He knew. Where were Martin and Lewis? Where the fuck were they?

"So. If you could help me out?" The voice was even, without depth, had less charm to it than a prerecorded message.

"S-s-sure." Fester stood up, shaking and fumbled to light a match. He failed, and the smaller man nimbly grabbed the book from him and lit a filter-tip smoke.

"I remember this was good. Doesn't do anything for me now, though. No, not a thing."

He reached up in a relaxed motion and put the cigarette out hard on Fester's cheek, forcing his head into it with his other hand.

Fester let out a cry, charged him, swung and missed. It didn't stop him from keeping it up.

The lighter man made a startled sound when he finally managed to connect.

Nevertheless, Fester kept pounding him, grunting and growling, "Take that you fucker, take that you piece of shit! Take it! Take it! Take it!" He powered triumphant relief into his blows, landed them all with the full fury of his weight.

It went wrong too fast to control.

From the corner of the eye, like fugitive mercury loosed from the glass of a shattered thermometer, the smaller, lighter man flipped on him from behind, unfazed and deliberate, strangling him with one arm while pounding his bull-neck with the other. His motion was measured, precise.

Even calm.

He kept at it, machine-like, his legs hard around the barrel torso, squeezing. Fester made moans of pain and sank down. His ribs cracked.

The smaller man breathed steady breaths despite the beating he had just taken. He kept attacking without letup, brutal, precise, untiring.

Fester at last collapsed under the rain of blows and the persistent leg-squeeze.

The smaller man kept it up anyway, giving Fester no recovery time. After he lay sprawled panting on the tar of the roof, he lifted Fester high by the collar and began to smash his face again and again with his knee. It was as routine-seeming and repetitive as automated metal stamping in a factory. Fester went limp, flopped his arms about in weak, token gestures of defense.

Slurred, drowsy, he said, "Don't…kill me…Please…"

Not breathing hard, emotionless, a rote response, "No. Not yet. I won't."

"Th-thank you."

"Don't mention it. We have a few months left to go Fester, you and I. Remember? Three I think it was for me, right? You lose track of time when they're pulling your fingernails off one by one, smashing your knuckles, pouring vinegar in your eyes."

A blubbering whine, "No…please…I…"

"Come and stand up, Fester. Come and have a visit with your friends."

He dragged Fester up as if his immense weight were no trouble at all, smashed his face to get his full attention.

It was a grotesque cartoon.

Martin and Lewis hung like bloody scarecrows from a huge TV antenna fallen into bent and mutilated disuse. Just like them. The man held Fester up by the collar so that he could see them all the better.

Whatever the man had done to them—and Fester's vision was far too blurred to tell—it was bloody. The faces of the bodyguards were contorted with anguish and gore. It looked like a horror movie make up job done on two movie extras.

They might have been extras, but it was no make-up that marked their faces.

"Now, tell me, Fester, please, are their expressions funny, sad or both? I can't tell. And I honestly want to know which."

"You…sick…fuck!" A sob more than a statement.

The man smacked him back down to the rough tar of the roof with a stiff wave of his arm, dragged him to the ledge, holding him up by his hair, forcing him to look down.

"Wouldn't it be agonizing to fall from here and hit the bricks? To be smashed and torn apart, inside out? I suppose it would. I wish I knew for sure. But I never could know, could I? Even if I did it myself? Right? Isn't that funny, Fester?"

Thick and wet. "No! No! You're insane, you freak!"

"It's okay if it is, Fester. If it's funny, then go ahead and laugh. Hearing you laugh might help me…remember."

"Fuck you!"

"In time, Fester. In time. I think maybe a great fall would be a nice option for you, don't you think?" When Fester didn't answer, without any indication he was going to do so at all, no change in expression, breathing, stance, nothing to telegraph it at all, he shot his fist right into Fester's face in a calculated move to break his nose.

It worked and bright blood spouted down like a torrent of face paint

"God help me!" A wanton scream.

Null dragged him further forward from the edge, holding him up by his hair as he screamed. More than half of Fester's body was now off the ledge. If the man were to let go of Fester's scalp, down he would plummet.

"Fester, Fester, Fester. When you and the guys worked on me for three months, steady, I wanted to die. I went beyond death, and when I got there, in this place, I saw the face of God."

"Help me!"

"No really. I did."

Screaming: "Help!"

He whispered into Fester's ear even as his arm trembled holding him up.

"I am helping you, Fester. This is what God looks like. This is the face of God, and this is his mercy." He jerked Fester forward another crucial inch.

"No!"

Fester felt a terrific blow connect with his head from behind, which blackened even the world behind his closed eyes. He soon awoke to heavy droplets of moisture splashing on his face.

Hot droplets.

When he looked up, he found he was lying right beneath Martin and Lewis, who were hanging—hanging! And bleeding all over him.

The man was gone.

In despair and disgust Fester gulped a single word as he recoiled from the two corpses and their rivulets of blood.

He said it like a curse.

"Null."

TWO

Dark dawning on a rooftop

A mob of professional activity overtook the shadows as two obscene scarecrows hung in wretched silhouette against the gunmetal gray and wounded orange light of a Boston sky.

A five-story building on crabbed, narrow Prince Street shunted hard against others just like it—soot-smudged, ruddy, the color of old, dried blood. Despite the hour, the building and the street buzzed with life. Uniforms, frazzled grannies in robes, house-coated mothers hemorrhaging youth, screaming kids, scattered ape-neck types in overalls, sleazy skater teens in cable TV punk-wear of the moment shoved against each other, got in each other's way. They clambered to the roof, wandered about outside, mingled in sub-groups, jabbered. Cop cars and EMS trucks clotted the narrow street. Sawhorse barricades were placed off a truck. Despite the hour, off-street onlookers collected as fast as urban dirt, as did the uniforms necessary to hold them back.

Their echoes mixed with the cries of the gulls falling down to the harbor.

In the street was the managed, slow-motion chaos of the canvassing. On the roof was the unbalanced shambling of the criminalists, the detectives and the senior politicos in thick suited mufti.

"We got names yet?" said a husky woman, smoking a long

cigarette and jotting notes into a tablet with a stylus. She wore a not inconspicuous cell phone headset."

"Yeah, Dean Martin and Jerry Lewis."

"That's as funny as the wallet photos on the IDs in their pockets." She used a dry laugh to mask a wince at this. Detective Specialist Kay Boyd was nothing if not disgusted by the staged bodies on the roof, and, hung as they were, calling it "staging" was putting it mildly.

They were an unfunny message meant to mock.

And what they mocked was pure juice. Family juice.

They had OC Task Force written all over them, which is why she was there.

A stomach cramp stabbed her in half, and she fought hard not to go down with it. She wanted to go home. She wanted to cry. She did not want to be here.

Memories were what kept her here.

Her daughter's face—what was left of it—in the morgue.

Her husband, no face left at all.

The baby crushed to nothing.

They made her identify them all anyway.

Though she couldn't.

And she did.

God damn them.

500 drunks too many.

The AA meetings.

The Decision.

The Comeback.

Flashes of past emotion kept her looking tough and unemotional when in reality she was next to crumbling.

The purpose would take her through it, she reminded herself. The purpose.

Scarecrow corpses dangled like broken puppets from a huge, disused building TV antenna—rusted out and bent to hell as if the freakish skeleton of a hunchback mounted against the clouds. She might have even said they were sad, these two fleshy ghosts of evil men—and they were evil, right out of her OC book—and would have done so loudly as a former wife and mother. But as the holder of an MSW and a relinquisher of the soft-science human-service ethic of the liberally blamed victim, it was now the time for such "victims" to be stopped, and if not locked away…

Well then, blown away.

Prophylaxis long since having given way in her mind to cauterization, preferably with the hottest iron available—preferably with a forty-four.

It's amazing how easy it is to watch bad men die, once you're past a certain point.

It's amazing how truly easy it is to make death your friend.

The only drawback though is that death never leaves you.

Her body reminded her of this once again with a stabbing cramp of revulsion and a gag in the back of the throat as she took in the full measure of the suspended corpses before Yonah Shimmel and his criminalist team babied them down.

"Usual stonewalling shit-on a-stick, Kay. Nobody knows from nothin'." This from Sergeant Grant Monad. The only thing saving Monad from being another department night school lifer with no chance of making detective was that he not only knew it but knew how to use it. He preferred wielding power with brutality from the street, rather than with glad-handing savvy from a division desk. And even within the subtle twists of department politics, brutality was still king. He knew when to punch, when to kick and when to schmooze, even though of course every move he made was awkward, whether it worked or not.

A stand-up cop, they all said of him; ultra-deep code for a certified pain in the ass.

Boyd was competent, which was code for being on the outs, surviving every professional day at sufferance. She knew this and flipped them all off in her mind with a smile.

"The fucks that did this were smooth. We won't nail 'em."

"We'll see just how smooth." She made a sly one eighty to take in the scene, survey the team. "So, what do you think they saw?"

"Some nurses and interns busy scoring some of the local product at the time said they saw a skinny guy doin' the pimp roll down Prince. Struttin' loose without a care. I buy this."

"Strutting? As in a funny walk?" This went right into the tablet.

"That's what they said, pupils dilated and about as defensive as my daughter caught with her boyfriend's hand up her shirt."

There was a sound like a watermelon dropping off the back of a truck. Boyd didn't have to turn around to know what it was. Her stomach contracted and her skin went clammy.

"Kay—this guy's clothes—his skin—holy fucking Christ!" This from a thin, nervous lab geek criminalist. He jumped back nervously as if the corpse would actually splatter when it landed.

Thick wet stains coming through the deceased's overcoat made this threat credible.

"Yonah, what is it? We haven't started yet and already this whole investigation is going to hell!"

"Lieutenant I—" Yonah Shimmel was aware of the standing he had amongst the Boston cops—or lack thereof—so he covered for himself carefully. "It's just that this is a first for me. Maybe even for you."

"I doubt that." She did her expert grunt to cover the gag reflex when she looked where Yonah was looking.

"Looks to me," drawled Shimmel, commanding the moment, "that the only thing keeping these guys together is cloth and skin."

"I don't see what you mean."

"They're like mush. These bodies were battered to mush by whatever was used. And when they stopped breathing the beating didn't stop. You can tell from cyanosis on the faces that a lot of the blows came posthumous. Gross lividity could tell the rest."

Her eyes were dry and her cigarette stuck to her lower lip.

"Could?"

"These bodies. They're—let me find the right word. Unstable?"

This was new. "You're saying the corpses are going to come apart?"

Yonah gave a nervous grin showing recent dental work, white-capped teeth. "I think they could burst like water balloons if we don't proceed with extreme care."

"Water balloons?"

"I don't know how else to describe it. The only thing holding these men together is skin and cloth and whatever bones weren't smashed by whoever did this."

Boyd narrowed her eyes, and her long filter-tipped cigarette still stuck to her lower lip when she spoke. "The evidence must be preserved."

"My team is packing and bagging one of them now."

"What about the other one?"

Yonah sighed. "You saw what happened. His dead weight shifted when we were cutting him down. He fell to the roof."

"So?"

"What can I say?" Yonah gave a grim smile, somewhat mischievous. "The guy's all over the place."

Out the corner of her eye she could see it. The remains of a Family button man, half liquid and spilling out of the sleeves of his jacket and cuffs of his pants, seeping through the material like some revolting human stew. Once a man, now a splatter on the roof. The criminalists—all of them—were huddled about the more intact corpse, taking pains to keep it that way, leaving the other a semi-puddle, lying there as grotesque and odd-looking as a defunct comic book villain.

Boyd bit the back of her tongue then clicked it.

"Do whatever you can with it, Yonah. I know you. You live for challenges like this."

"Yes. Puree of Mafioso is my life."

"I need every little strand you can get me to build this case. And I'm not so sure this is OC at all, so start with that in mind."

"Well, if it isn't, what the hell are you doing here and why the hell am I not back in bed with my wife?" Politics reared its ugly head, not so bright, but early. Inspector Phil LaCuna was looming over them. LaCuna was an old-time BC bully boy, favored on the force from uncles, brothers, cousins and extra accounts down at the favor bank. His father was a career lower city official, which made him a high-ranking behind-the-scenes baggage handler and hatchet man for the illustrious. He had done favors for Kennedys, O'Neills, Kerrys and Welds. He had been the man in the shadows cleaning up the tough messes and confusing the evidence that could not be covered up. If ever a man was said to be "on the city," in the way they mean it when they rush you through some licensing procedure at City Hall because you dropped the right name, that man was Phillip LaCuna Sr. Phil Jr. was the same, but tougher. Harder.

He had the brutality down pat.

What's more, he had a taste for using it.

Six-six, sandy haired with silver through it, thick and beefy, with a respectable Boston pub gut clad in the best of what Brooks Brothers had off the rack, Phil was there to keep the power moving squarely in his old crony fashion one way, while Detective Specialist Kay Boyd was moving another.

He sipped an extra-large "regular" Dunkin' Donuts coffee with a rueful expression, cautiously scalding his thin lips to get some of the creamy liquid into him as quickly as possible.

"Shimmel, you have the scene secured, do you?"

Looking up and nervous again. (How could he not be?) "In the works. I was just conferring with the Lieutenant—"

"Shimmel, this is OC till I say otherwise. That being the case, this is a huge department priority. See to it personally, won't you?"

Yonah giggled with nervous hysteria and swallowed it fast as he could. "I-I'll just go bag and pack now."

He slinked back to the criminalist crew before Boyd could stop him.

"Isn't this overkill for two guys, Kay? Expensive, if it ain't OC like you say." He took a series of tiny sips after this, then chugged.

"It's still OC officially, and that being the case, full discretion is mine, Phil. If you guys want to do a commission study on it, you're welcome."

"Thanks for reminding me of the scope of my powers, Boyd. You are a pip, I'll grant ya that. Yes, you are." He laughed without malice.

"Phil, you, your cronies, the mayor gave me OC to run because you knew it was impossible to do yet important enough to draw fire. It keeps me on the outside yet on the PR radar. Best of all, it gets you off the PC hook without really having to have a woman in a key position and privy to the power."

"You always recite your lessons this early?"

She wanted to paste him one and she did. "So, fine. I'm on the outside. But since you made OC my turf and let me have all the rope in the world to hang myself with, guess where that leaves you, bucko?" Roped off, she was ready to say.

"Now Kay. Nobody's politicking here. I'm just askin' yez as to this bein' OC or not?"

"You know it's OC, but these guys weren't the perps, they're the vic's. So, it's also not."

"But just like every street bum was some mother's darlin', these boys was definitely somebody's perp. Let us let the corpses grow cold and not waste any further department money on 'em. Whoever dispatched these boys took out the city's garbage for free."

Can I log that in my OC book?"

"You most certainly may not."

I will anyway, you sonofabitch, she thought, covering her smile as she lit another cigarette.

The crew of criminalists just about had the entire roof secured. Even the second, less stable corpse had been spirited away by hefty, uniformed EMTs on a Stryker under Yonah's austere direction. He spied them eyeing him and jogged back over to break the news.

"I got somethin' for ya, if you don't mind a grossly unqualified prelim' from a science guy."

"We should wait to hear from the M.E.," Phil said stiffly, as he wiped milky coffee from his sallow cheek with the edge of his shirt cuff.

Boyd countering, "Nothing that comes out of Yonah's mouth is ever grossly unqualified." She turned to him. "What have you got?"

"The weapon."

"Well show us and be done with it."

"This," said Yonah, solemn and composed, holding up a single fist.

"Christ, why the fuck do we hire these guys?"

"Wait. Hear him out, Phil. Yonah's not fucking around. He never fucks around."

She ignored Phil and turned her attention straight onto the criminalists. "You're saying they were beaten to death with naked fists."

"Exactly, yes. To death and beyond. Gloved fists, judging from scrapes and marks. Likely weighted. No evidence of anything else whatsoever."

Phil cleared his throat. "Well then. That's OC plain and simple. Gang beatings are a hallmark. Not stopping after they died sent a message, as did the staging."

"Yeah, sure, Inspector. You got it. One thing though."

It's never really one thing with Yonah, Boyd remembered. No, not really. She let Phil be the one to bite at it.

"Oh? Missed something, did I?"

"Yes sir. You did."

"What then?"

"From all appearances—from everything we could examine fresh on the scene, well—umm." Yonah was having trouble keeping his cool as the six-six departmental upper-echelon hatchetman glowered down fiercely upon him.

"Spit it out now, won't you? Christ almighty!"

"One guy!" he blurted, swallowing hard, watching Boyd's face go slack and the crags on LaCuna's become harder.

"One guy did this."

THREE

Boyd lit up a cigarette blank-eyed as Nadio "Fester" Solecise's face slammed into the table in conference B-2.

They called all the interrogation suites "conference rooms."

Detective Sergeant Bim Hundertwasser, sucking on an unlit cigar, looking benign and jovial with his hapless, jowly face, was the one doing the slamming. Hundertwasser had worked it all and he had worked it from the gutter up, a detective with no college who made detective on toughness alone. He was there now to keep Fester in line, keep him mindful of the facts of the situation. Keep him focused.

He was there to drive home Boyd's interrogation with his fists.

He was one of the many happy sadists the Boston Police released into the streets to keep the rabid dogs at bay.

Fester was there to give up someone he should want to give up, being that the guy was wiping out The Family by degrees, but despite the almost total anarchy of the street one last rule held: We take care of our own.

"I hope the cameras—up there—get all—of this!" Grunting and sweating, Fester groped for the chair when Hundertwasser let his face off the table.

The bloody impression of his cheek remained.

"We lost the tapes, I'm afraid," said Boyd more weary than sarcastic. She would suck it up however and get through this no

19

matter how detestable it was, and it was detestable. It was enough to make her as woozy as that morning's find had made her. It was just enough to bring back the pain. You never get used to this. No, not if you're human you don't.

Not like....him.

"They ain't finished recording yet," Fester whined.

"Doesn't matter." Cold shrug. "When they're lost, they're lost." She swallowed back bile on that one. God knows this man was sewage, but she hated doing it, nonetheless. "Shit happens."

Hundertwasser lit a cigarette and slipped it into the mouth of the heaving, slumped-shouldered Fester. He laughed from the throat. "Don't look like you can take much more, do it, Fester? No, you got beat up pretty good while your two guys got waxed last night. Now, you're gonna sit still for the full boat and take the beating I'm next gonna throw ya just to protect the asswipe who's doin in ya whole crew. Does this compute?"

Fester was greedily sucking on his cigarette as his thick shoulders rose up and down, laughing and crying, a series of mirthful hiccupping sobs. "I wanna give him up. I'd do it this second. You can have him. Nobody'll bitch, but—" Now he was overcome and sank into his beefy arms. "But—"

"But what?" asked Boyd, mopping her face with a handkerchief while Hundertwasser looked on with a dark expression. She almost pitied Fester until her mind went over again just who and what he really was: Torturer, murderer, pimp, white slaver, defiler of little children.

And Fester enjoyed it—she had seen him smile over his grisly handiwork once up close—once too damn often.

Fester's was a sick, persistent sort of lust, the kind she might once have helped to treat in vain a lifetime ago.

Before the death-time.

Not that Fester was a pervert. He was a pole dancer patron with a fat wad in his pocket for private dances. Not that it mattered since he was one of the many bosses the young women had to pony up to for mere survival. He was one of a succession of big old greasy guys they had to get down on their knees for to stay in the game, to be permitted to swing from a pole onstage, let alone do the high-end lap dance. Fester paid for the implants, kept them protected, set up the outside gigs, dried their tears and tucked them in at night.

Before and after raping them.

This was how he got his other name: Fester the confessor.

Well, he was confessing now, wasn't he? And that's what she wanted.

"But what?!" Boyd screamed into his face with a blind rage that surprised them both.

Choking on his laughter, face wet with blood and sweat, eyes watering.

"But—" And now he seemed pathetic, almost small as he coughed, trembled, sniveled. "But it would be just like giving up Santa Claus."

———

"There ain't no Sanity Clause for this guy!"

"Cute, captain, really." This was Boyd, perfunctory but shining them on with a sly smile and precise femininity, the doublethink double standard of a doubled up double-dealing department. And thanks to all that, she had achieved a warped sort of double indemnity through the city politics of gender.

And she was determined to use it.

"Yeah. Chico Marx—always a favorite. Marx Brothers marathon on cable. Helps me when I lie awake at night wondering what the fuck to do with you."

"Captain Parseeman, you already know what the fuck to do with me. Just let me run the OC task force."

"The special task force that can be disbanded at any time for any reason."

"That's the one."

"Fine. You'll run it. These slayings go on to homicide though—"

"Who I'll need to liaise with—"

"As they see fit, Lieutenant. Not as you do."

"This could be a gang war."

"Yes, and I could be mayor. But we both know neither is the case. It's a vendetta, a revenge grab. The Targets may be OC, but the perps are not. They do nothing but whack out soldiers of the Family —damn near a public service!"

"Captain that's outrageous!"

"Don't pull your sanctimonious shit on me, Boyd. You know just what these vic's are, you know just what they do. You have their histories tacked up on your wall in little Family trees. We all know it's not OC. This has been going on for weeks and the only bodies piling up are The Family's, and that's not a terrible thing."

"Of course, it is."

"But not in the economies of scale out on the street. This investigation has shifted over to Homicide, period. You want to help, fine and dandy. Come on down, take a backseat and consult. Do your human services thing—"

"Captain we're treading—"

"Fuck we, Boyd. You're treading. Or you were. But this little street-sweeping vigilante thing is now in homicide territory. You've been benched on it. So, go back to your crime crew anthropology seminar, or whatever the hell it is you do over there down at division 16."

Boyd sighed and decided not to slug it out in the game of politics for inches. She'd play it honest. "Captain, this is still OC in principle because the perp is actually known out of OC files. He was a CI."

"Jesus fucking Christ, woman," Parseeman laughed to near choking, sat down with blazing chilblains and rum blossoms in his cheeks, his red eyebrows whitening with the skin beneath them. "When you turn a man, you turn him, doncha?"

"I feel responsible, Captain. I'm to blame."

"You know this how?"

"I know this because the perp is Joseph X. Null."

"Joey X? DQ Null? The racehorse tout? The low-level mope?"

"That's him."

A coffee mug, not an entirely empty one, went flying past her head and smashed to bits against the bookcase. The coffee might have scalded her face when it hit her, except for the fact that it was yesterday's.

"Get the fuck out of my office."

Dignified, coffee tears crying down the side of her face: "There are disciplinary proceedings for this."

Parseeman looked up and grinned with wide-eyed sarcastic innocence. "Oh, by all means initiate them. You can fit it in with all the rest of the paperwork you have to do, along with the papers for leave while they sort out the complaint, maybe for transfer reassignment—""

"You're out of line."

"And don't I know it. But I have faith that justice will prevail through sheer force of your formidable paperwork skills. That should expedite things. And I could use a vacation pretty soon, I think, you know, while IA drills down to the inevitable conclusion —'unfounded.'" He blinked, stared at her, smiling.

"He's still alive, Captain. And he's behind it. You know it!"

"As you so aptly communicate to anyone who'll listen, "I don't know dick.""

"I never—"

"Lieutenant, kindly blow it out your derriere, and please shut the door on your way out."

She slammed it just as he knew she would, and he laughed out loud at the timing of it.

———

The day ended with a punishing rain.

The day ended with Ignatzio "Cousin It" Cavilli pounding thick practiced fists into the belly of one of the faithful. Cousin It liked to make sure any new hirelings could take it as well as dish it out, and he also liked to dish it out.

Besides, this guy was on a Family track, being that he came from the right beginnings, and though he thought he was tough, he needed some tenderizing first, so there would be no mistake just as to who was whom—who was God and who was not. The right toughness had to be instilled to accomplish this conversion. None of this barroom show-stopping, beer bottle over the head stuff. It had to be final. It had to go as far as it could. It had to be at least heading toward fatal.

That far and no further.

Each thudding contact of his fist was accompanied by a deep, jarring grunt.

"That good for you. Vitty? You like that, huh? You think you tough enough for the full boat, or ah we throwin' you back to ya mutha?"

Nick Andromeda, known as "Vitty" Vittorio, the guy strapped in a chair, blindfolded and gagged, moaned through the rag and duct tape over his mouth. A hulking assistant looked on jovially, brandishing a 45 Ruger Redhawk, traditional but rock-solid reliable.

It was in the insulated library of the soundproofed townhouse of some yuppie investment banker gone belly up, courtesy of the recent downturn and the terms of the Family's friendly loan sharking business. Now it was a Family safe house and Cousin It's preferred residence. His "playpen," he liked to call it.

Cousin It especially liked the ambience of the library for such solemn occasions as the toughness induction of the newly come-to-Jesus.

A shadow moved across the room from the high oriel at the top of the elegantly sloping gambrel roof. Pigeons or a cat.

At last, blood foamed at the corner of the tape on his face. This meant Cousin It would ratchet it down a little bit.

Dead assistants are of no assistance at all.

He went at him with an open hand to the face to breathe a little life into him.

Cousin It was in the full stride of his enjoyment. "Come on, Vittorio, come on Vitty baby, be a man here for me. Don't tap out so easy."

"He's soft as a melon, Cuz. Wants some toughening up, know what I'm sayin'?

"Oh, I do know exactly what you're saying," he affirmed.

Cousin It leveled one to Andromeda's solar plexus, nearly removing the tape from his face with the accompanying muffled bark. He loved this, and the rest of the Family knew he loved it. More than any of them, Cousin It headed up the muscle for the dirty jobs, the enforcements, torturing and executions. Sure, they could all handle it, but not with as much enthusiasm, interest or volume as Cousin It. He brought élan to pain, a sort of landscape architect of agony. And he produced.

Supposedly under Uncle Fester Solecise, he had personally gone at a guy for over three months nonstop, treating his subject to heretofore unknown vistas of anguish.

But these were the dark myths and exaggerations of the street.

They served the muscle of The Family well.

The soldier laughed, cocked the Ruger, put it to Andromeda's head as Cousin It punched away.

A shadow passed over his face as Andromeda murmured an incomprehensible prayer.

There was a crashing, like a heavy object smashing through glass. The soldier fired into it as he would into a flash of light.

Glass, in fact, did rain down from the ruined oriel.

A wounded man sat on the floor covered in a thick, rain-drenched trench coat, rocking back and forth. The soldier extended his arm with the Ruger, somewhat shakily, amazed. The man was bleeding and hurt from the fall. He was, from the look of his pale eyes, by no means incapacitated.

"What the fuck have we got here?"

Cousin It turned and smiled, showing only one row of stained teeth. "What we have here is an alumnus of our little training course. Mah-rone!"

Andromeda was wild-eyed with relief, which he utterly failed to conceal.

He had wet his pants.

"You can go, soldier. I don't have any interest in you." The voice was affable though devoid of warmth. Even, unconcerned—relaxed as a commercial voice over.

The soldier wasn't moving but for his slightly wavering arm.

Cousin It gave the soldier an approving nod.

The man took this as his answer. From where he was sitting, he instantly sprayed a line of shots straight through the soldier's neck almost severing his head before he hit the ruined rug on the hard-wood floor. Andromeda and Cousin It were both spattered with bright arterial blood.

"Untie him, Cousin It."

This was done quickly with almost avuncular care. "You know, if you came here to save this mook, ya wastin' ya time pally. He's already saved—the fact is he works for me as of next week. I mean, after he recovers." He smacked and pinched Andromeda's face, giving a throaty chuckle, abusing the flesh as if it were rubber.

"You can go," the man on the floor said softly. He paused to process, seeming frozen in time for a moment. "Unless you want to start working for Cousin It right this second. Looks like he needs a replacement." No humor, no anger, nothing but even.

Andromeda grabbed his belly with both hands, doubled over and threw himself from the room, leaving the two bloody men facing each other, one standing and one sitting like a Buddhist monk on the floor in a pile of glass and debris, his head bowed slightly. He slid along the wall hoping for the nearest exit, with zero desire to go back and see just who this man was and with how much a degree of sadism Cousin It would finish him.

Andromeda tried to dial his cell phone when he reached an alcove by the stairwell at the end of the narrow, rococo frescoed hallway. He tried punching numbers with a sense of victory after being waved on by the Uzi-toting soldier barring his progress. He tried to hit redial, sliding down against the smooth plaster coolness of the wall, slumping to the floor just moments after his cell phone clattered to his feet. He tried to hold on to the world, but it let him down hard and fast, as it eventually must to all.

The last thing he heard before he went out was the screaming.

FOUR

"You want a drink, or what, DQ?"

"Don't call me that."

Bloody, chuckling, forcing himself to feel as relaxed as he was nervous, Cousin It stalled for a time until he could find an opening to whack out the mope. "Fine. Null then." He poured himself a scotch in a wide tumbler and offered one to Null who gave him no reaction at all.

Cousin It drained both glasses.

"Ya come a long way, Joey X," he said, stepping over the soldier's corpse and getting too close to where Null sat on the floor. "What, like half a year ago, youse was in fear of ever seein' this place. Now you break in and call the friggin' shots. Who friggin' knew?"

"That's close enough," said Null, the Glock pointed precisely between Cousin It's crinkly pale blue eyes at the bridge of his tortuous nose.

"Okay, okay. I do believe you're not a pussy with that thing. You'd take the shot. You still might miss though, being new to this end of the game, and then I could rush you." His face was bathed in mirth.

Null answered that with a nine-millimeter round that blew out the bottom seam of Cousin It's Versace blazer. Cousin It put both hands over his heart and shut his eyes for just that second, then blasted them both open like a drowning man bursting to the surface for air. He recovered quickly.

"I stand corrected. You won't miss, will ya? Still, you counting those bullets or what? That one only takes fourteen to a clip, ya know, plus one in the chamber."

"I have an extra clip in my breast pocket. It loads fast. Two moves, then I shoot."

"I could whack you out in two moves."

"Why not try it then?"

Cousin It wasn't getting any less nervous, but his laughter was genuine. "I friggin' love this guy! What have you been takin', DQ— I really gotta know! I wanna steady supply of it for the boys. You're a fuckin' pistol, you are."

Totally flat, an echo of real speech: "I'm not taking anything anymore."

"Ha! Well, DQ, when you next see your supplier hook me up."

"When I find him, he won't be able to." Crypt-like, he added, "When I find him."

"Where's your sense of humor, Null? Christ in a crapshoot!"

"Trouble is, I don't know what's funny anymore. Really."

"How's this for funny, then? Why not come work for me? I could use someone like you. Someone doesn't rattle. Someone with initiative who ain't no pussy." Now he began to relax. Propositions to the low and needy always put him in control. And that's what this guy had to be. After all, why risk your life to be here holding The Family's chief enforcer at gunpoint? Not much else made sense.

And if it were just a vendetta, wouldn't he be dead by now?

No, no, the mope needed something. Need was always the escape clause, the safety catch. He'd play it out, see where his opening might be. Then, once found, he'd kick right through it. Who knows? It could even prove to be another three-month's diversion. Just like last time.

"Just put the guns on the table, It. First the one in your waistband, then the magnum mini in the ankle holster. Please."

Almost impressed and with a shrug of agreement, Cousin It reached around for the first weapon and lay it dully on the sideboard where the liquor decanters and silver ice bucket sat in casual disarray.

Every torture suite needs a well-stocked bar—all the comforts necessary for a good, long stay. At least in Cousin It's world it did. He made an old man's grunt of effort going down by his ankle for the magnum, but came up in a fierce charge instead, lunging for Null.

Two moves and the gun was reloaded, but Null didn't bother to stick the barrel in Cousin It's face. Instead, from his position on the floor, he swung his arm out then back in a stiff arc, connected with Cousin It's right cheekbone, breaking it with a crisp snap. The pure force of the blow laid him out on his back in the gore of the fallen soldier, arms and legs splayed apart.

Cousin It bubbled up blood from his mouth, not from crying or pleas, but from belly laughter. He laughed as Null stood over him, the Glock aimed straight for his throat, looking as if he were deciding something. He seemed perplexed. Well, that wouldn't last.

Nunzio would be in there soon enough.

He heard the welcome footsteps coming down the hall, felt them vibrate with new hope through the aged dryness of the hardwood floor.

Goodnight, sweetheart.

The soldier from the hall kicked the door open and simply had no time to strafe the room with fire from his Uzi. He had to take one fatal second to size up the scene to make his move.

But Null had no need to size up anything.

Nunzio's head exploded with a vicious pop, as if he were a prop in a bad horror movie.

"Fuck. Me," said Cousin It as if waking from a dream, or sinking further into one.

"Copper stoppers," said Null. "Dum-dum hollow points, copper coated and filled with Teflon, guaranteed to blow apart just when you breach the skull. Want one?"

Cousin It coughed blood, loving this guy, despite the fact he might very well soon be killing him. Still, this was a problem that could be handled. "I'm gonna remember that and outfit the boys accordingly. So, you wanna help or not, Null? Fuck, as far as I'm concerned you already made your bones wit' this. Don't be fuckin' stupid. Guys wait a lifetime for this."

"Sorry, It, but I have other plans."

"You're saying no to a golden opportunity, a once in a lifetime shot at the real money mopes like you only get to dream about!"

"That's right. I am."

"So, what do you want, then? What's your score here?"

"No score. Not really."

"Then what the fuck are you doing this for? It makes no sense! You can't whack us all out!"

Null stared at him with vacant intent plain in his eyes. There was no need to answer that.

"You think you'll get your three months back whackin' me out? Forget it, they'll gun you down in the street like a dog."

"I don't want them back. And what I might want I can't have."

"So be smart for once in your life and take the money. You could play your no-win pony system down at the track and still come out ahead."

"I don't gamble anymore. Lost the drive."

This was going nowhere fast. He'd keep him talking so he could make his play. "This is a waste of time. Do me and go or don't, already. I'm sick of this shit."

"Do you think the three months you worked on me was a waste?"

Almost reverently, almost contented, lying on the floor, he said, "Oh no. No. Not at all, Null. You tortured up so beautiful, I popped a woody every time I came into the room to see you. You played it like a man right to the end, too, never gave up nothin', which made it even better. What a shock! We had you made for a pussy then you go and stick it out like a for real guy. Course, it wasn't too long under the knife before you lost it totally and couldn't give up nothin anyway."

Cousin It croaked laughter. Even in this position, he was savoring the memory. "Oh, but we kept at you just to see how far it could go. You know, for the science of the thing. You took a lickin' and kept on tickin', but let's flash forward a little. Here you are standing over me with a Glock up my ass on top of your game. You're beatin' the house, in fact. So, I can't say in all honesty it didn't do you no good what happened. Seems to have straightened you right out." That ought to do it. He knew this game by heart. He knew exactly the buttons to press, and he had pressed them good and hard.

Yes, that's right.

Null looked blank, distracted. Yes, the memories must be pouring back to affect him. Look at him—so angry he can't move! He doesn't even know he's here anymore. This is the moment. This is the time to hit it.

Cousin It rose to his feet as Null stood motionless and blank-faced. Ha! The fucker had short-circuited! The mobster began his confident approach, only to have both legs shot out from under him in nothing flat, one exploding bullet for each thigh.

Great. Now he was going to bleed to death.

Shock set in and put him under.

When he awoke, he was strapped in the chair where before he had been torturing Nicky Andromeda a little less than an hour ago. All the doors to the cabinets were open and the twisted panoply of his favorite tools were on display. Null seemed oddly distracted, indecisive. It just didn't fit. He looked down and both his damaged thighs were tied off with rope.

"Tourniquets on both," said Null. "It won't stop the bleeding, but it should slow it."

"Get me to a hospital or finish me off, already." Stall for time. Stall!

"How about both?"

"Fuck you, Null."

"The tourniquets are only a stopgap measure. You're going to bleed out over time, maybe by morning. Since that's the case, we're going to have to hurry." He paused without a change in his facial expression. "I guess I'm just going to have to cram your three months into just a few hours."

This can't be happening. No, this is DQ Null—degenerate gambler and sometime junkie we're dealing with here. This is one of the all-time lost-cause mooks! So, it must be a money dodge. He's going for a score. He's got to be going for a score!

"How much, Null? Go ahead. Tell me. We can pay it."

"But they always told me that the best things in life are free. Maybe they were wrong. I just wish I knew such things could be true. I really wish I knew. But I don't connect." His eyes narrowed with focus. "Anymore."

"This ain't you, Null. You ain't like me—you don't want to be like me." This time it was a plea, a piteous whine—the torture victim's fruitless bid for mercy and reason in the face of the golem of inquisition. He shook his head. No, this ain't you! Null."

"I know," said Null dully. "But even I ain't me."

Null had gone over to the cabinets and come back with a few handheld tools.

"These look good. What do you think, It?"

"I think it's amateur hour if you think play actin's cuttin' you any ice here. You can't press my buttons, pally."

"No, I suppose I can't. So, I guess I'll just have to go through with whatever it is. Threats don't really work with guys like you, do they?"

"Put those friggin' things away, for Christ's sake! "Don't you have any human feeling?"

That stopped him. "Good question," Null sighed thoughtfully. He was honestly considering this. "You know, this has been on my mind a lot. I've been mulling it over for a while, and I think I finally have the answer."

Cousin It was poised to continue pressing any button he could, maybe string the guy along until another opportunity arose—he felt he was making headway. And he knew more soldiers would be on their way sometime soon. Besides, Null really didn't have the heart for this. And for that, he'd grab him by the balls and squeeze. Then tear out the heart he did have.

That pleasant thought ended at the exact moment the ice pick went through his pharynx.

The story was there in his eyes, and his eyes betrayed the scream that the voice could not.

"I don't think I have any human feeling at all," said Null.

Then he went to work.

Dawn.

Kay Boyd was sprawled on the floor, passed out in her Fenway condo amid OC paperwork, aborted IA complaint forms and the now thick CI file on Joseph Xavier Null, Jr. She was clutching an empty pint bottle of Gilbey's gin in her left hand, lying on the rug and snoring loud enough to frighten Mudgett, her cat. Boyd was always a cheap drunk, and it didn't take much to lay her out. Problem was, she got that way night after night, then first thing in the morning. In her right hand, she still clasped the number of her AA sponsor. She had yet to make the call.

This was occasion number ten of her AA clean and sober short-fall—a reason to celebrate.

That and insomnia.

It was getting harder and harder to sleep with the sense of the shadow that passed over her windows each night. She knew it was a shadow of the mind but felt nevertheless that it was real. So, she drank for this too, only to discover that for tonight at least, the shadow had gone.

She killed the bottle anyway.

She killed it in hopes of the bottle killing the spirits of the murdered who came for her in her dreams. She wanted blank dreams. Blank, but not too blank. Oh no, because if they were completely blank, if they were like a vacuum…

Then Null would come.

And Null, she knew, was the final nightmare.

———

Dawn found Null working diligently.

You could barely hear Null talking over the keening bleat of the electric drill as it sank in and out of Cousin It's chest.

That he couldn't be heard, or could barely hear himself, didn't dampen his enthusiasm for talking, if it could be called that. Maybe it was simply momentum. There was no tone to it, no urgency in the voice, just an outpouring of monotonous observations.

"I'm here on the other end trying to understand you, Cousin It, and I just can't. I get neither pain nor pleasure nor anything really, but a mild strain of effort doing this to you. And the strain isn't so bad that I couldn't keep doing this for a few days without stopping."

Cousin It's only response was a hissing.

Null thought it curious until he realized that this was just the sound of Cousin It's punctured left lung deflating. His eyes may have been frozen open, and every muscle wrenched hard and tight, but Cousin It had lost consciousness hours ago. Null didn't realize this, so he kept talking, the way he used to when he was at the track, to calm his nerves, only now there were no nerves to calm. It was autonomic, a body reflex like the blinking of the eyes in a dust storm.

"No, I don't get it. I don't connect. I'm sure it's just me, but the value of spending so much time and effort just to achieve agony escapes me. I mean, I don't think you could tell me the time of day, even when I put the drill into your abdomen—like this. Can you tell me the time of day, It? Take a guess. Come on, take a stab. If you come close, I'll stop doing this. How's that?"

All that escaped from Cousin It's lips was a wet sigh.

So, Null put the drill even deeper into his abdomen.

"What use is torture if the victim is rendered unable to tell you what you want to know? That happened to me, I think. I mean, when I was sitting where you're sitting. Yet you continued. You said something about it advancing the science of the thing, can you tell me what you discovered?"

Null thought he heard something, so he cut the drill, watched the slowing red swirl of the blackened bloody bit spiral to a stop.

It was just the groan of the ancient steam pipes deep in the walls.

Null blinked. "I was really looking to get something from this, Cousin It, at least learn, maybe. But since the flattening of my affect, I don't even care enough to be mildly disappointed. So, if it's all the same to you, we can stop now anyway. That would be okay with you, wouldn't it?"

No answer from the mortified face, white lips and bulging eyes of Cousin It, the enforcer.

Null noticed an unpleasant odor, put his fingers to the blood clotted neck.

Though still warm, Cousin It was no longer alive. He had probably expired somewhere during Null's ongoing, extended monologue.

"Oh. Well, you're probably feeling better now and at least that's something. Not feeling at all! What a relief, you'd think. But the joke's on us both, isn't it? No laughter for either of us, is there? No."

His face smoothed back to its former nondescript expression. "You know, you were right. Your tools really do quite a job. They take pain and injury to a whole new level."

He held up a pair of tongs with razored spikes welded onto the ends. "Clappers, huh? For castration, I see. This might have been interesting to try. But not postmortem." He let them fall to the floor with a hollow clatter. "Nothing that you have here, in fact, is really of much use outside this room. But it's all balanced out now, isn't it? Since you're of no use either, I mean. Not that you were before, but you had so many choices you could have made, other things you could have done. Now there's only this."

He patted the dead flesh of Cousin It's face. "So, you can have it all."

As Null was walking over to the corpse of the soldier to get to the door, a wall mirror in an ornate gilt frame caught his eye. He went toward it and adjusted his overcoat and clothing, dapping gobs of blood and fluid away with his handkerchief, mopping the sweat off his face with it. He smiled, he frowned, he made a funny face, then let his face snap back to its constant grave emptiness.

"What really worries me is that nothing worries me. I don't know how long someone can survive who doesn't care about anything, even his own being. I really don't know. But I should thank you, Cousin It. I really owe you. Oh."

He stared back at the dead man's staring, sightless eyes.

"I guess I just did."

Null was still talking full-voiced as he went out into the hallway and walked toward the stairs, as if a companion were walking along with him who was simpatico with his line of discourse.

Fighting to get a hold on his consciousness, Nick Andromeda heard him in the hallway as he grabbed for his cell phone and struggled to push himself up. He wound up vomiting blood on his knees instead.

Null went on talking—walking down the corridor.

"Victims in your chair really despise you, don't they? Up until the time they die or lose their minds. I can only imagine what a victim might be like who spent months with you that way. Oh wait. That was me. But I don't really feel it anymore. Not since therapy, but I have one last thing. It's like a neural snapshot, a biochemical souvenir: Hatred. Against you, Fester, Gomez, Morticia, Thing, Lurch, all of you. This is the last feeling I have, though it's dead. But it's—"

Something punched Null hard enough in the rear shoulder to body check him against the wall of the corridor. He let out a gasp.

Nick Andromeda had stopped vomiting long enough to pull up a number on his cell phone, connect, and bark two words into it. He stood, trembling, and made the effort to step forward.

Null had been shot in the rear left shoulder by what he guessed was a thirty-eight. It was a hard punch, granted, but not so hard that his shoulder process had been shattered. He was in shock so that the blood was now flowing slowly. Null turned around just in time to see a thickset Family soldier bearing down on him full speed. Null didn't react much more than that. He paused, weighing matters.

The soldier collided against him hard, smacked him full in the face with the butt of his thirty-eight-Chief's Special, police issue, obviously a clean piece taken off a cop. Null dropped to his knees from the force of the blow, panting.

"What did you do?!" screamed the soldier. "What did you *do*?!"

"Just business as usual," Null said thickly, heaving. "Just things you do here." The voice was still even, unbroken.

The soldier extended his arm and cocked the special. "You're dead."

"Yes, I know," said Null, unaffected.

———

Now was the time! Nick Andromeda stepped out from his alcove stiffly, calling to his fellow soldier. "Arno—what the fuck is going on? Who is this guy?"

"Fucker's killing everyone! That's what!"

Null took a breath, spoke well-enunciated syllables to compensate for the swelling of his jaw. "I may be dead—"

Arno turned his head.

"—But you're much deader." Then Null put a copper stopper in the soldier's brain, which subsequently put his brain on the walls and his body in an awkward heap next to him on the floor.

Null stood up dizzily and faced Andromeda. He was ready with his gun before Andromeda could even realize that he had left his on the table back in the torture suite.

"Do you want to die?"

Andromeda felt caught. Had he blown it? "I don't. No."

"You don't look well. You need a hospital."

"You're the one who's been shot." Andromeda was frantically, and obviously, looking for something he could do. Anything! The pain and weakness seriously impeded this effort, and it frustrated him to know this.

"Yes, but I don't really feel it, so don't worry. You on the other hand were worked over by Cousin It. He did internal damage, I'm sure, always does. So, if you want to live, you can take the door at the opposite end of the hall, open the laundry chute and jump down it. Good way to avoid the greeting committee that will soon be on its way here. Then you can probably walk west to Mass General Hospital. You should make it before you bleed out. Or you could stand there and—"

"And what?" coughed Andromeda, thinking he was buying time.

"Let me take care of you."

Null held the gun with Andromeda's bruised face in the crosshairs of its site, staring. He blinked once and caught Andromeda lunging off to the laundry chute, no doubt expecting a bullet to hit him in the back of the head as he went down.

None did.

But Andromeda did hear more explosions going off as he slid down the chute.

More copper stoppers.

He knew what it was as he hit the concrete and scraped his chin. It was the wounded man in the hall taking out some more soldiers before making good his escape.

Andromeda knew this guy would get away. It was just how it worked in this town.

Cold blooded killers always did.

FIVE

As the elevator door closed, so closed her eyes.

Flashes of the dream played in hangover time.

The junkie, trembling, helpless—black, savvy and disenfranchised. A clue about everything except how not to be a street-crime smash and grab junkie. Typical. Boyd kept giving him a leg up, got personally involved, because there was such hope in his eyes.

Such intelligence.

A hint of wounded sensitivity behind the street bravado made her smile.

And the eyes always told the story. You could see it right there.

The story was still being told by his eyes when she awoke at home in bed to stare back into them as his spatulate, dry skinned right hand clapped over her mouth to stifle her screams.

His eyes told her eyes everything at that moment.

Then, with the lights on in the living room of her apartment, his two friends told the rest.

Her husband, Ted, told them where everything valuable was without a fight. There was a knife at his wife's throat and one that played lightly across the region of his daughter's carotid. He was in Med School. He knew these things.

They got it all with nervous efficiency, then gutted him the same way.

Without a fight.

Kay Boyd, MSW, shrieked and bit into the dirty palm of the long, flat hand of her most promising case.

Where was the baby?

Her daughter, who neither screamed nor cried, kept her mind alert, the physical reactions to a minimum. She was a calm, shy, intelligent girl. The intelligence shone even in terror. And Kay Boyd had such high regard for intelligence.

There was a deal to be struck. She was a handsome, pretty lady, yes? So, it might be nice if the three hungry studs there with her could have their way with her, one after the other. If she didn't struggle too much, why, they'd let her daughter live. Without so much as a scratch. Otherwise…

Everything would be everything.

She might even like it.

Her daughter didn't scream, but her eyes told a story that said they would meet in heaven soon.

This wasn't something for Kay Boyd to see or read. She was a good mother.

Good mothers will do anything for their children, even as the bad mothers will.

In this, it's almost impossible to tell them apart.

Where was the baby?

So, they had Kay Boyd, MSW, one at a time, in jerks and fits and grunts. Kay didn't struggle, didn't cry, didn't react, but she went away for a little while and let them do whatever they wanted to her.

Then she came back.

When she got back, it was just in time to watch her daughter smoothly decapitated by a K-Bar Military knife as long as her fore-arm. She saw it go into the sensitive neck like butter. Then, her most promising case reared back his head, holding the blade slicked red with the bright blood of her daughter, laughing like a carrion crow, hunching his shoulder blades up like wings.

He held up her head like a trophy.

One of them standing opposite held up a small bloody thing. The baby.

It had been through the trash masher in the kitchenette.

That's when the good mother grew deadly calm.

Or was it the bad mother?

The world shrunk down and became very basic and slow—a dwarf star of reality.

Kay charged her promising client.

He stabbed her in the kidney with the K-Bar knife without a thought.

It didn't matter. She kept coming, hard and fast.

Momentum was on her side, and they both went crashing through the bay windows together and out into the dank night air in a shower of glass. When they hit the ground, her client was dead, and she was beyond caring, the knife deep in her side. She was busily groping for her daughter's body, still held in her attacker's arms, floating in front of her, just slightly out of reach.

Then she was too high to reach for.

A leaf in the wind, like her baby.

Though the ME's report didn't show it, her client had died before the impact of their five-flight descent.

Kay had torn open his throat with fingernails that had been freshly manicured just that afternoon. She had savaged her way through his carotid artery and beyond.

Of course, the other two got away, as they so often do.

But, in the dream, she gets up from the concrete, pulls the knife from her side, spits down on the bastard, pursues the other two, her headless daughter watching her sadly from afar.

When she finally finds them in an alley, she corners them. And they turn on her. They both have Null's face. Surprisingly, they do nothing when she cuts out their hearts with the knife ripped out of her side. When she comes back to herself at the scene, lying next to her mutilated former favorite case, she looks at his face and of course it was Null all the time.

She clutches the knife with relief until the EMTs come to collect her.

They are Null, and the police are Null, and she turns the knife upon herself and can only wake up—to find herself gasping for air in a cold sweat.

To find herself in desperate need and fresh out of Gilbeys.

"This your floor?" some young intern asked, nudging her. She said yes and left the elevator, even though it wasn't.

The intern winced at the alcohol fumes, always worse when processed through the human body, aren't they?

———

"Helluva job you did for your first time out, Nick. Helluva job. You'll get a jacket citation for this minimum."

Nick Andromeda was woozy, propped up in a hospital bed in a private room at Mass. General, saline and morphine dripping into his IV line and the television oozing images mutely above him and his superior, Detective Kay Boyd. He had a ruptured spleen and partial renal failure, cracked ribs and a huge hematoma above his chest cavity that was slowly draining red into a plastic cylinder by the bed. His lips smacked drily as he spoke.

"Citation? For what, Lieutenant? And I'm not crackin' wise wit ya, or anything."

"Isn't it obvious? I thought you did first-rate undercover work."

"Yeah, so great, I'll never get to do it again. I'm the survivor other than the hitter, which makes me in with him. Not only that, but I might as well have never been there for all the good it did."

"Still, you infiltrated The Family."

"I did, and I would have gone all the way—I paid the entry fee with my guts."

"The department knows this. We can still use this."

"Use it how? They're all being whacked out by one fuck of a pro hitter. A bad one."

"So, you saw him."

"Ya, the guy was something. Scared the shit out of me. I've never seen anything like it. If I heard this from anybody else, I'd swear it was a fairy story."

"None of the kills were yours, then?"

"Ballistics will tell you whose they were. I don't use a Glock."

"Tell me about the guy."

"Not much to tell." He started coughing, reached for an oxygen mask, and sucked in deeply. "Bruises to the chest muscles make it hard to breathe," he wheezed. "This is supposed to help."

"Take your time, Nick. I can come back."

"No, it was fucking freaky. This little guy, maybe half my size, gray face, scars everywhere, crashes through a skylight, must of fallen twenty feet, takes out one soldier without blinking, braces Cousin It like he wasn't the psychotic monster he was, but some mook. He releases me nice as you please then turns around and gives Cousin It a taste of his own medicine. Took his time, knew what he was doing. It was fucked up."

"He didn't want you? Why? Were you made?"

"I don't think so. It was more like—like he knew I wasn't a threat. That I wasn't involved in his thing, whatever it was, so he had no interest in me. I was irrelevant."

"You could have whacked him out."

"No. He knew the shape I was in. I was apt to look after myself. He had it all covered."

"Nicky, when you get released, you're going hunting for this hitter. He's the worst mob figure I've come across yet. We're making him an OC hot file."

"He's not exactly Whitey Bulger, whoever he is, LT I don't get that he's OC."

"No. He's worse."

Sucking on the oxygen cleared his head while intensifying the morphine high.

"Hey, how bad could he be if he's just gonna wipe out The Family. He'll probably just get himself killed anyway. Why not leave bad enough alone?"

"Because I'm in a position where I don't have to. Rest up, Nicky. You're going to need it."

———

"You what?"

"We kicked him." Byron Wurdalaka, homicide detective second grade, was working the Martin/Lewis slayings. He had volunteered to do liaison with OC.

Boyd sat back in her chair and sipped a forgotten cup of yesterday's coffee without making a face, savoring the rank sweetness. "You guys in homicide really are the highflyers, aren't you?"

Byron was an aging pretty boy with rum blossoms and age creases that spidered across sallow, drooping cheeks. He had jowls and wattles, though he had yet to break out of his thirties. Sandy haired, lantern jawed, standard athletic physique ruined by the usual debauches of leading a double life, urban versus suburban, cop versus work-a-daddy, he played his politics to lose like a degenerate gambler. This made him play all the harder.

"Judgment call. These fucks want you to lock 'em up, you kick 'em, give 'em a couple a hidden playmates in the street, let 'em hang themselves from the end of a long tether, ya know? That's how we do it in the big leagues, baby."

"You're watching Kojak? You want a tootsie pop? Or something else to suck on?"

"Hey, LT, watching TV is the only way any of us ever get to sleep around here." He cast both eyes ruefully down at Boyd's desk to preface his point. "That and paperwork."

Boyd was unfazed by the hulking detective. They were all hulking here, she had learned early on, a prerequisite for the job as crucial as an account at the favor bank. She counted it all off merrily on chipped fingernails—she had long since given up getting manicures—"Racketeering, pandering, white slavery, kidnapping, assault with intent, bail and parole violations, three out of state warrants—and you in your infinite wisdom kick the son of a bitch!"

"Where's he gonna go?"

"Straight to Logan, if I were him."

"Let him. They all have his face and ID in the system. No one will issue a ticket. Even if he tries the fake ID and proxy ticket deal, his face is on all the hot screens. He'll be detained. Besides, he's one fucked up dude. Sloppy as hell these days."

"Aren't they all?"

"Sure. But he's so fucked up and rattled by this hitter they got on his ass, I don't think he's got it together enough to make the planes it would take to leave the country, let alone get himself the clean paper."

"First rule is you put nothing past these thugs," she said, standing primly, glowering at him. "Second rule is that you keep them on a very short leash."

"Ya got that wrong LT. First rule is that you see to your own investigation before doing a liaison."

"So, it's going to be like that?"

Byron laughed genially, coughing and lighting up a smoke in front of the No Smoking sign in Boyd's office, flouting the scowl on her face as he did. "Of course, it's going to be like that. It's always like that and you can't change it."

"But I did change it, Detective." She presented a letter from the mayor's office extolling cooperation with the task force. Wurdalaka scanned it, nodded, then tore it into quarters and let them flutter to the ground.

"I hate politics. So does Captain Parseeman."

"And I fart nickels."

"Look, we caught the case, and you didn't."

"Fine. Be that way. I'm picking up Fester on the BOP violation then. With or without you."

"Cool, LT. You go do that."

He was getting itchy under his suit. The broad wouldn't quit.

"Know what happens then? We'll pick him up again on the homicide and kick him loose. We can play perp badminton with him for a few days, if you're up for it."

"What do you want, Wurdalaka?"

"Detective first grade and a crack at Demi Moore. What else would I want?"

"What you'll get is a suspension and a crack at a can of Dinty Moore's, if I have anything to do with it."

"I'm glad we understand each other so thoroughly, LT."

"We don't at all, you stupid infighting lummox—"

Wurdalaka laughed a staged laugh and dismissed her. He put his hand on her shoulder and she knocked it off. "They told me you were like this down at Schroeder Plaza. You keep forgetting we're all rootin' for you, LT. We really are. Women got it tough, ya know—"

"If you kick him, Null will whack him out."

"The dead guy? Your old CI? Joey X?"

"He's not dead. He's scamming us all."

"Maybe I should try that scam if I don't get the Christmas slot for my vacation bid. My wife won't have to kill me if she thinks I'm already dead."

"But the hitter will kill Fester as soon as he gets a chance, you know this, and you're in homicide for God's sake!"

"And this would be a bad thing? Besides, I investigate homicides. I don't prevent them. Hell, in this case, I might pitch right in and help."

"Wurdalaka, I'm in on this investigation whether you like it or not."

"I know. I heard that too. But don't worry, LT."

"I always worry when hacks like you are involved."

The detective laughed a staged laugh at that while his rum blossoms went purple. He fired back, "Don't worry. I'll make sure you get all the paperwork."

He walked out on her, smirking the same way he did at age eighteen, when he was picked up for loitering, let off and first got the idea of becoming a cop. He was the right kind of guy to be let off, then let in. Boyd knew it too and it galled her. So, as he left, she gave him her customary gesture of dismissal.

She flipped him the finger.

SIX

Boyd came home with a bottle of Gilbeys. She could afford better, but the roughness of the cheap stuff made the taste so much more vivid – so much more low and real. What was the point of downing a well-made martini as subtle as a baby's breath? She wanted to feel it ripping her throat, tearing up her guts. She wanted to smell the fumes coming out of her as offensive as if they were not from her but from some other lowlife drunk. She wanted to wallow in her drunkenness, embrace and accept it, not deny it with Tic-Tac pocket mints and fumbling apologies.

Before she had the light on, she had the cap off, the neck between her lips and the gin rolling furiously over her tongue.

She was still sensitive it knocked the wind out of her and she gasped for air switching on the light.

He was sitting there, crumpled and pale in the bentwood rocker.

"Turn it off," he whispered. But it was a loud whisper.

The bottle dropped to the floor, did not break but burbled out gin in puddles sucked up by a throw rug. She hesitated, thinking, but letting him believe he had caught her in a weak moment as her fingers inched to her overstuffed handbag where she kept an unholstered Sig-Sauer.

"I have the wrong bullets in this gun." The voice—empty and plain. The machine approximation of a stock analyst. "If I try to make my point by hitting something near you, you'll still get hit by bits of shrapnel and debris. I could blow off some digits too in the field of impact. So, I'm really not set up to make an impression. Just kill you or not. Right now, killing you doesn't make too much sense. But if you want me to, I will. I have the idea I owe you something. Maybe that." He stared with the dead eyes of a shark. "I owe a lot of that."

She grabbed the handle of her gun and Null shot out the lights.

The phone went next, exploding into shards.

"Does the darkness make you feel calmer? They say it does. Breathing helps too."

"Joseph—"

"Why not DQ like on my CI jacket, or Joey X?"

"You need help."

"I'm beyond help, and your help is spilling out there on the floor by your feet."

"It's not too late—"

"Neither of us believes that. Go ahead. Go kneel and get it. I know you need it. And it'll calm you down. I think it would serve me best if you were calm. Don't get me wrong—a common drunk would get all bold and sloppy on the stuff. But a rock-ribbed practiced alcoholic? The first few jolts have a steadying effect."

Boyd obliged him, slowly, her eyes stabbing into the sliver of streetlight through the window, illuminating Null's scarred face and serene features. Half the bottle was left, having reached a level too shallow to run out of the neck. She rescued it gingerly, then slowly rose, drinking it down.

"You should be feeling fine in no time."

"They heard the shots. You don't have much time before the cops come." She lowered her voice to approximate coolness.

"They know you in this building. You popped off your gun before, remember? If they can hear it, they won't report it. Boston is busybody town, sure. But it's also a do-nothing leave ill-enough-alone-town too. No one will knock, no one will call. You're a cop—it's your business."

"Sure enough to risk it all?"

"What 'all'? If they come, I'll just hold court here. You will die and they will die and I won't."

"Why not you?"

"You haven't figured it out by now?"

"No. You'll die just like me." A win/win, she thought, for one glum beat.

"Not really."

"Why not?"

"Because I really don't care. And the rule of this world is you only lose what you care about. I get to keep it all because I care about nothing."

"That and the flak jacket you're wearing, you mean."

"High caliber round wounds are inconvenient. I'm recovering from two of them right now and it's best not to compound things."

"You're bleeding on my bentwood."

"Just a little."

"Don't tell me what you want, Null, because I'm not giving it to you."

"I came to warn you off me. That won't work, will it?"

"They called you DQ for a reason—didn't they?"

"Drop the cell phone on the floor now and step on it."

"You didn't answer me."

"Drop the phone on the floor and stomp it to pieces—now. Do it, or most of my decisions will have been made for me. You don't want that. Not really."

The phone clattered to the floor, lit and open. The ring tones were audible. Null blasted it to pieces before Boyd's foot could descend on it.

"Just in case." Null said, leaning back in the shadows.

"DQ," Boyd seethed.

"It wasn't for Dairy Queen."

"No. It was how they knew you. Your associates."

"I was a fool. I was betting legit in a world of fixes. They kept teaching me a lesson I wouldn't learn. Inside joke if I bet too heavy and too long on the fix favorite. The horse would wind up DQ."

"Disqualified."

"Just like me."

"Seems now you're in the game."

"Yes. But with no stakes. No winning, no losing. No joy in playing. Nothing from nothing."

"So why do it, Joey X?"

"Honor."

"Whose honor—yours?"

"No. I'm nothing. It's in honor of the death of the angry soul of Joseph Xavier Null."

"That's you."

"No, I'm just his remains."

"If nothing can matter to you, you can't feel and you can't care, then why are you doing this? It makes no sense."

"I'm honoring a dead man's last request."

"Bullshit!" She was feeling about in her bag again for the Sig-Sauer.

"No, really. I found you can't live if you feel no purpose. I don't even have the basic drive to stay alive—taste food, have sex. I feel none of it. But my mind works. If I can construct a purpose, that will drive me. Then I can and will follow it out. To the end."

"Like a bad computer virus?"

"Like the Golem, a clay man of biblical revenge with life breathed into him by a dying rabbi, a holy man."

"It's absurd."

"No argument there, but absurdity is no disqualification for seriousness."

"You can't kill everyone."

"Only if I'm dead."

"So, you're here to kill me?"

"If I have to. The jury's out on that, and the late Joey X wouldn't have minded seeing you die slowly and horribly. But that's off the table for now because I think you can help me."

"That's how I got into this."

"Joey X's dying dream as they tore out his fingernails and drilled holes in his skull and shot high voltage through his testicles was to see every last one of the Family members die suffering. You can help with that—arrest them, bring them to me and I'll execute them. One-by-one."

"You want me to face murder charges too?"

"What "too"? They can't charge a dead man."

"But you can bury and cremate one. I think that's next up for you."

"Too bad you spilled half that bottle. You need a bracer. No, next up for me is dispensing with you." He seemed paralyzed for a moment, as if in the throes of a silent seizure or stroke. It was like he was a machine set on "pause." She took one step toward him and heard a soft click, the bullet entering the chamber of the Glock. "You're a problem."

"I was only trying to help."

"Joey X knew that. He also knew that's how you managed your life's greatest harm, the baby in the trash masher and whatnot—"

"Shut up!"

"I know. I lack human feeling. I don't deny it. Now, killing you would be at cross purposes with my goal. But slowing you up some wouldn't be. Perhaps a wound? Nothing permanent—just something to keep you deskbound and demure for a few months?"

"It won't matter. I won't stop coming for you. Every second I'm back on the street will be devoted to putting you away."

"This is good. Point in your favor. My purpose in living after the last sibling of the Family meets his reward was up in the air until now. After the last one goes down, I will dedicate myself to staying out of jail. Congratulations. You have now become my reason for living." No humor, no change, no nothing. "This solves a problem for me so let me solve one for you. Would you like me to kill them for you?"

"Kill who?"

"The two that got away, of course. From that night."

"I don't know—"

"Sure you do. Right after you tore Anselm's larynx to bits on the way down to the sidewalk. One of them must have done your baby. Anselm was too busy holding a long blade to your daughter's throat at the time, right?"

She forced herself to speak, though her throat clenched shut against the morass of rage and sorrow. It was like a burp: "You—"

"I know who they are. I can get to them. I can bring you their heads, if you want. Just tell me."

Tearing only partially from the harsh gin, she nodded her head an emphatic "no." The gun was stuck in her handbag. She'd have to make a big move to yank it out. The only question was when.

"It's up to you. I thought if I could remove old distractions from your mind, you could better concentrate on the matter at hand—"

"Which is wiping out the Family."

"From Gomez on down. We both want the same thing."

"No, I think I've shifted my attention to you." Get ready.

"Oh, you want them all as badly as I do. But I can see you only want to help me through hindrance. Just like in the old days."

"I didn't know this is what would happen!"

"That isn't what the chart said. That isn't what Dr. Frankenstein said, although no one, including you, was very much interested in thinking how real it would be. How damning. For you the logic had a convenient dead end, but for me it was self-replicating, a geometric regression down to the final zero." His voice was almost electronic—a robotic parody.

"I was only trying to help."

"No. Joey X was a martyr to your guilt. Helping was where you met Anselm."

Boyd saw the gun go down in the half-light and Null now slumped in the chair, on "pause." He was in his catatonic thought state again, she decided, and quickly fumbled for the Sig-Sauer. She heard two mechanical clicks as she dragged it from the tangle in her bag. Her left ear suddenly hurt.

When she looked up, Null was standing so close to her she could feel his breath on the fine hairs of her neck. The barrel of his Glock was thrust hard into her ear canal; the sight on the barrel drew a bit of blood where it was pressed into her skin. She could smell the oil, almost taste the metal. "I changed the clip so we just have good old nine-millimeter slugs in it. Nothing fancy, no dum-dum effect. Do you think knee-capping you would be too severe? I might need you back on the street sooner than that."

She let out a growl and brought the Sig-Sauer up hard, but before she could use it she saw it skittering by the baseboard. Something hit her and stunned her so fast there was no pain.

Null made one more move that blackened her vision with

shadow and laid her out for good and all on the rug in the wet spot of spilled gin.

He had smacked her in the face with the butt of the Glock.

"Concussion," he observed, looking down on her and pocketing the gun into the lining of his open topcoat. "That'll have to do."

SEVEN

"What the fuck did he say?"

"I am in the service of madness and chaos."

Lupo "Lurch" Luchese, a six-foot nine hulk of aging, decayed yet hardened flesh, played sausage fingers into a church steeple sitting in a heap. His lips were parted like those of a fish, which added further humor to an already benignly wide and comic face, though nothing about him was ever comic. Malice and terror had forever exiled comedy from his life. Lurch was not a man for laughter.

"This is the bullshit he had to say after you beat him for three fucking hours?" Lurch sat in a thickly tacked massive leather uphol-stered lounger in the center of a hollowed-out trailer on a waterfront construction site off Rowes Wharf. His outsized lips were wet with spittle and his eyes were slit with suspicion.

"It's all he said, like he was givin' us the time of day. No cryin', no beggin', nothin' else."

"This worries me. It's abnormal."

"Tell me about it."

"Where's the mutt now?"

The soldier shrugged, lit a cigarette. "Outside. I got two guys holdin' the fucker up to keep him from fallin'. We threw him a pretty good beatin' there, ya know."

"No smoking."

"But you just stubbed out a big fat cigar, for cryin' out loud!"

"You're not me," Lurch seethed. "You're lucky I even let you exist. Your second-hand smoke is gutter garbage I don't want in my face, never mind my lungs. When you earn for us at captain level, I might let you share a cigar from my humidor. But for right now, fuck all, would ya please?"

"I don't get it."

"Deaf or stupid guys in our thing don't live so long. Get that."

The soldier took the cigarette and crushed it out coolly with mock obedience in the palm of his left hand as the fingers closed about it like the petals of a carnivorous plant

"Good. Toss that shit out the door when you bring the mutt in. Now." The stubbed-out cigar was still smoldering away in the thick tinted glass ashtray.

"He hasn't said anything in three hours. What makes you think he'll talk to you?"

Lurch sighed, hefted himself up from his chair, towering over the soldier. He put his arm around him in friendly fashion only to crush him down to the floor and level a single hammer blow of a punch to his breadbasket, underscoring the point. "That's what makes me think that, ya fuckin' mook."

He dragged the soldier up from the floor with one arm and pushed him hard toward the door. The soldier left and returned with two associates, a bleeding, battered Null hanging limp from their arms as if dead. Lurch recoiled, his suit billowing purple in the shadows.

"Shit, this jamoke is bleedin' all over my good carpet! Oh, for Christ's sake."

"Cold water'll get that out, Lurch. I'll do it right now for, yez," said the soldier to redeem himself. Lurch nodded snidely as his man went obsequiously over to the sink.

"So, this mostly dead sad-sack is the guy what offed Cousin It and gives Uncle Fester the heebie-jeebies? This little freakin' thing?" He smacked the unresponsive face and wound up with blood on his fingers for his trouble.

"Shit!" Lurch wiped the palm on the Armani jacket of the soldier holding Null up on the right, who spoke as if prompted.

"He took out like five guys down at It's place. But when we get to him, he's a creampuff. No problem. Takes a beating though and doesn't give."

"Yeah," said the other. "Takes a lickin' and keeps on tickin'."

Lurch knelt down a bit and lifted Null's chin with a turgid index finger. Blood streamed down in a slow ooze from the nose and mouth, slick upon caked, dried rivulets and bruised skin scraped raw.

"Well, he's gonna take some more before he dies. What is he—insane? Trying to whack out the entire Family? Where do we get these idiots from? He's fuckin' lucky he offed Cousin It cause that guy woulda partied with him for a month at least."

"So, what now? He's trunk music?"

With a nervous look, Lurch touched Null's neck gently with his fingers and smiled.

"He's gettin' heavy, ya know. This guy's like dead weight."

"No, I wanna hear his little story. Then we can make a nice example out of him. You don't go round whackin' Family soldiers and then hittin' on a freakin' Captain without makin' a show to keep the peanut gallery on the street in line."

"So what then?"

The first of the three soldiers was on his hands and knees with wet paper towel carefully working blood stains out of Lurch's carpet, too fearful to curse. Lurch moved aside a little to allow him access to another spot.

"Bring him around."

"We tried, Lurch," said the guy at his feet, "but he wasn't givin' us nothin' from nothin'."

"Do it again. Try spirits of ammonia or some shit like that. I wanna have a little palaver with our guest."

The voice was soft, like the whisper of an air conditioner kicking in. "You don't have to bring me around. I've been right here all along."

The head was up, the eyes open, white, wide and clear.

The two soldiers jerked back. Null remained slack in their grip without a struggle.

"You won't be here for long, kid, that much is for sure. You're one lone guy tryin' to kill off an army. You should be in a mental hospital."

"I was, but they released me. Said I was cured."

"Pally, you're gonna wish you were back there before I'm through with you."

"Cousin It had similar ideas. They didn't quite work out."

"Okay, Maverick. Tell me why and I won't draw it out. I'll kill ya good 'n' fast."

"Sure. I am in the service—"

Lurch smashed a terrible blow to Null's face, breaking his nose.

"Now, tell me again."

"Come closer."

Lurch obliged and Null spat a gob of blood in his face.

"These guys," sighed Lurch, wiping the blood off with an expensive handkerchief and letting it fall on the freshly dabbed out blood stains that the soldier was still finishing with, despite Null's apparent resurrection. "Get up, mook!" belched Lurch and the man at his feet obliged. "Ya know, I could beat you to death right now, for that. Have you got any idea about the germs, you fuck? But you're gonna have at least a few hours to repent and beg, to cry and plead before you get the long, hard killing. We may freeze you, we may bleed you. I haven't decided yet."

"Don't hurry on my account."

Lurch coughed a guffaw. "He's got balls. No brains, but a lotta balls. You guys can let him go. He's runnin' on empty as it is."

The soldiers released their arm locks and took one step back in unison. Null teetered, obviously woozy, threatened to fall over but didn't. The two behind him moved to catch him and stopped short, just shy of doing so.

"That's better. Now take a breath and tell me why."

"This is the last request of a dying man. Dead man now. Joey X, the gambler. You had him strapped in a special chair with feeding tubes and saline bags as you cut him apart in slow motion. Tortured him to death—well you had Cousin It do it, but you watched and gloated. Your face is forever in my brain. I think you even took a piss on Joey X, right? Right into the open wounds. Well, this is his dying wish. This is the last shadow of a fire of emotion I have like a snap-shot imprinted in my brain. This is the wish. This is what I hold to."

"The fuck? You're saying you're that piece of shit DQ—the fucking CI? The rat?"

"No. I'm saying I'm his corpse."

"You can't be him. He wasn't no hard guy. He was just a degen-erate gambler, a mope. He couldn't do these things. He was a pussy. DQ fucking Null. The name says it all.

"I'm here to carry out his death wish." Null stepped toward the huge man and the soldiers reached for their weapons. Lurch laughed and waved them to stand down.

"Wanna take a poke at me, little man?"

"Exactly."

Lurch cracked his knuckles. "I think I'll oblige you."

"You beat Joey X half to death. Does it feel good to beat up on smaller, lighter men? I'd really like to know?"

"Sure, it feels good, but not quite as good as beating a man like that to death. Now *that's* a rush."

"I wish I could experience that—feel what you feel, but that's all over."

Feeling smug and drunk with vengeance, Lurch bent down and looked Null in the eye. "Losers like you talk pretty tough, pally, but when it comes down to the actual kill, well, you just don't have it. You're—"

He never finished the sentence. It happened too fast for the soldiers to respond to it, almost too fast to see.

In the space of a single unhesitating thought, Null had poked both fingers deep into Lurch's eye-sockets, palm up, gouging straight through the eyes, the aqueous humor and blood, curled his fingers up into his brain and squeezed back over the bone shelf and orbits to the front of the skull. Lurch never saw it coming and was frozen in space like a morbid cartoon.

Instantly dead, Lurch stood there rigid for a moment; the body simply couldn't register so fast a death. While the nerves and synapses were busy processing their end, Null dropped down to the newly cleaned rug, unsnapped the ankle holster just above Lurch's sock, drew out the magnum mini and shot both soldiers square in the neck, causing unrestrained arterial spray about the room. Kill-shots both. They fell one by one, just a second or two apart into a heap on the rug as Null rose weakly.

The third soldier came screaming at him with a long kitchen knife.

He didn't last long.

A few minutes later, walking his funny, damaged walk along the waterfront, blood on his face glistening in the streetlight, he asked the greasy harbor itself a pointed question: "Are we having fun yet? I really wish I knew."

EIGHT

There was an electric saw cutting through her skull.

Was it the door buzzer of her apartment where she was supposed to be?

No.

Chatter.

It was the voices, the laughter, the political hubbub of the lunch crowd at the Fill-A-Buster.

Boyd was on medical leave, having been given a moderately severe concussion by a burglar—ironic for a cop, they said. If it weren't for an anonymous 911 dial-in, she might have lain there bleeding for another day or so.

The dial in wasn't so anonymous to her.

Her hands shook as she downed her coffee and lost a stare-down contest with a corned beef sandwich sitting before her insolently on a plate.

A hand touched her shoulder, and she flinched. This time, the Sig-Sauer was ready and waiting within the pocket of her overcoat. Her fingers squeezed the grip tightly, then released it.

Yonah.

Dressed smartly as usual; even his little knit yarmulke was taste-fully bobby pinned back in such a way as to be barely noticeable.

"Jumpy, today are we, Kay?"

"Just look at the bandage on my head and think why."

He ordered coffee from the waitress covering the counter—another young thing from Northeastern who gave him back the fisheye to counter his fleeting interest.

"You're off your game, Kay. You should be home in bed."

"You don't know what my game is."

"Maybe not, but I know enough from doing the cleanup on it." He passed her an envelope under the counter. Boyd grabbed it and brought it up to the counter to read it.

"You don't have to be so obvious."

She laughed a brittle laugh. "What's obvious here is considered discreet. This is Boston's original don't ask/don't tell bistro. Everybody on the state is passing things back and forth they shouldn't. This is just a death certificate, for Christ's sake."

"Okay. But I don't know why you needed it. There was a whole file on this guy, Null, I mean one with guts to it. The file tells the whole story. I think the mystery isn't so much how he died, but how he lived at all after the Family got their hands on him."

"You mean before he was admitted to Boston City?"

"You know what happened. I'm not that forgetful, Kay. This man—they put him through a Khmer Rouge-style reeducation program. They burned him with acid, pulled out his fingernails, sliced him up and down slowly in every non-fatal way, burned him, broke his teeth, his tibia, electrocuted him scrotally, stuck a power-drill in his abdomen, hamstrung his left leg—from the post snaps, it had to have been over a long period. Months maybe. But the million-dollar question is, How did he ever make it even just to die at Boston City?"

"He's not dead."

"You have the certificate right there signed by the ME."

"Sure, a sign off on an indigent at Southern Mortuary by a volunteer dermatologist from Wellesley."

"Urologist," said Shimmel. "From Newton."

"Null is smart. He knew how to fake it somehow. He's smart and he's a sociopath."

"Boyd, the dead lack affect because they're dead. Not for any other reason."

Kay's eyes never left the certificate once as she spoke. "Sure, and

Null was pretty much dead before he was dead so he could fake his death pretty easily, I think."

Shimmel's eyes showed disappointment in Boyd's acumen. She had been drifting before this—the alcoholism was an open secret—but now she had gone off into some grim fantasy. He had the sinking feeling that she was not long for the job, which meant one less ally for him in an already shaky arrangement of criminalists, hack trainees and politicos.

"How do you fake complete arrest? How do you fake pneumonia?"

That's what I want to know from you, Yonah. You're the MIT guy, you're the best we've got."

Shimmel blushed. "In everything but name."

"How could you do it?"

"You couldn't. I'm telling you from the photos and the chart, this character is as dead as a Pet Rock."

"Yonah, I've seen you tackle tougher problems without batting an eye. Just because I sustained a grade two concussion doesn't mean I'm losing it, and stop thinking about the AA thing. Just because I'm through with those sanctimonious bastards doesn't mean I'm sinking into an alcoholic wallow. You've never seen me take a drink on the job and you never will. Higher power my ass."

"You're rationalizing."

"So what? It's how we all get through the day. Even you, Yonah."

"I'm not gay, Kay."

"That's another conversation. Now tell me, how would you do it?"

"Ask a Fakir, one of those magic trick beggars of India."

"I don't get it. You mean like a Buddhist monk?"

"Not Buddhist, Hindu. They can will their bodies to do almost anything. Control autonomic nervous system functions of the medulla oblongata just by will."

"Heart rate, respiration, you mean."

"Yeah."

"Enough to fake death? Enough for an overworked part-time volunteer to buy it?"

"Enough for an attentive physician, too, I think. But Null isn't a Fakir, Yogi or anything else like it. He's just a dead guy."

Boyd took him by the shoulders and looked gravely into his eyes. "No, Yonah. He's the guy who gave me the concussion."

———

Giorgio "Gomez" Gomelsky reclined in a smoking jacket on a Louis Quinze daybed with a cliché stripper blonde bodybuilder type massaging his withered shoulders. He was dragging on a Monte Cristo Cubano and smiling up at a lurid looking woman with large breast implants, dressed in leather. She was smiling back, fire-engine-red lips against milky pale skin, black crepe de chine blouse show-casing her jutting chest, tight leather pants accenting a figure hard-ened by genetics, drugs and persistent attention at a private gym.

She was Maureen "Morticia" O'Doyle, the only female captain of the Family but one of the shrewdest and most ruthless—Gomez's right-hand woman. It was uncertain if there was anything sexual between them as was Gomez's sexuality itself—whether he liked girls, men, boys, women, sheep or transsexuals was up in the air. The strangeness of whatever his orientation was, compounded by Gomez's absolute stranglehold on power within the Family, made it a speculation that was squarely off the table for reasons of health and safety.

Morticia, like the blonde, tightly spandex-clad bodybuilder, was massaging someone's shoulders, who also puffed steadily on a Monte Cristo.

Null.

"Harder, Gomez?"

"Mia, cara, you're as hard as they come, but don't break anything."

"I'll be careful." Her powerful deltoids and thick veined biceps bulged beneath smooth tanned skin as she went to work.

"Good. Mr. Null, delighted you could see me."

"I had every intention of seeing you."

"I know, but these circumstances are better, yes?"

"They're probably good. For now."

"You always play it close to the vest, don't you?"

"When that's how life is lived, that's how you play it."

"We should have had you deeper-in a long time ago, Joey. Included you more on the better end. Bad mistake on our part. Cousin It saw this, I think, but too late."

"It was an afterthought," said Null almost seeming amused while puffing. It took extreme effort for him to emulate this sort of warmth.

"You had no choice but to kill him—I know this. Otherwise, I'd have soldiers and gypsy talent beating the streets for you hard."

"You still can. Maybe you have Morticia here all set to off me." Null stiffened visibly.

"I might try to off you, sure, but I think that effort has already presented too many repercussions. You might survive. Then I'm back with a worse version of my original problem. Sure, we'll ultimately kill you, but I might be a casualty on the way. We're making a deal here, and you got safe passage until we do it."

"Your word is as good as a bet tip from the late Joey X."

"Maybe. It's a rough world."

"I like it rough," purred Morticia, squeezing his shoulders hard with her nails clawing to zero effect but unacknowledged blood.

"What's this late stuff? You're alive and kickin'. That's the friggin' problem. You bein' dead would be a relief."

"I am dead. I'm just a ghost of flesh."

"You always were a sucker for the poetry, Joey. Better be careful or that shit'll kill ya."

"I don't think I'm walking out of here alive, Gomez, or maybe you don't think I am."

"Nobody's unarmed, Null. You want we should hold court here and get it done?"

"No Gomez, I think I'd like to sleep on your proposal."

"Sleep could be permanent."

"It's an expression—I don't need much sleep. Maybe what little I do need I can take out in trade—with Morticia."

Gomez coughed and spat a fleck of tobacco in the air. "You always did like her, but you couldn't get close. Now she wants it more than you do, don't you, *mia cara?*

64

She leaned over Null from behind and let her vermillion taloned nails ride up and down his torso, reaching down for his crotch until she grabbed it. "Null's an exciting man when you get to know him, I bet."

"The ones got to know him recently got to visit the morgue to recoup. But that's your thing, Maureen, ain't it? You two are a match made in hell." He chuckled. Morticia looked serene, still grabbing Null's crotch.

"Why I don't think that's a knife in your pocket and you are glad to see me."

"If it's not too much trouble, I think we should get a room."

Gomez was drooling just a little out of the corner of his mouth. He was a dry, bony man with hungry eyes, rat brown hair, and sunken cheeks, yet his attitude and carriage was that of a fat man. "And then what?"

"Then you'll know."

Gomez squinted up at the bodybuilder massaging his shoulders and neck. "Helle, take them up to my suite on the fourth, would you please?"

"Why don't I just break his back instead?" She flexed vascular biceps and inflated her ribcage, still giving Gomez a controlled massage. A thick, brown medically marked bottle was on the floor in front of Gomez—veterinary grade Winstrol V suspended in alcohol. Obviously a tip.

"Because, my darling, Helle, I don't think all the weights and human growth hormone you do could save you."

———

She put on Type O as she undressed, and the body was impressive—the hard, lean curves of a Goth Girl workout chick. At her age, she was going for the ageless look, which was a good call, being that she was pushing forty. She exuded a sort of depraved health, an exuberant, cold-bloodedness; a lust of the laissez-faire.

She did a teasing dance for Null, who nodded as appreciatively as a plastic Halloween skull in the back window of a car. The attraction was in earnest and no sham for some other effect. Maureen

"Morticia" O'Doyle was a power junkie and she sensed that the power was shifting to this strange, broken little man who was once the butt of her jokes. It didn't upset her—this too carried an excitement, an enticement: that someone could turn things around so extremely and set them on their ear. The runt of litter who now would run the pack.

It wasn't the look, the charm, or even the lack thereof, of the man. It was, for her, always the power. The power and what it would bring her.

Null sat still, frozen, as if in deep meditation.

Morticia squirmed toward him and captured his legs between hers, kneeling on the cushions of the sofa on which he sat and gazing into his glassy eyes. "Let me undress you."

"You might not like what you see."

"I'll like it."

Null jerkily cooperated with Morticia as she stripped him down, setting the Glock on the sofa so it would remain within easy reach. It was a body of scars and disproportioned muscle, lean and rippling with suppressed energy.

It was a broken body, with some freshly healing bullet wounds on the left shoulder, dressed with hastily taped pads of gauze. He stood lopsided and you could see why; the huge, snaking gash scar on the back of his thigh. The place where he had been hamstrung.

Morticia thought of the pain and licked her lips.

Null blinked, and sat back down, watching Morticia's approach, her teasing mannerisms that to him amounted to little more than the jerky spasms of a victim, although these usually occurred after the encounter, not before.

The sight of his drying blood only seemed to warm Morticia to him more and Null faked a grisly smile.

"You always wanted me, and I tortured you."

"Funny how that works, torture. Made me what I am today."

"I heard."

"You tasted it."

"Did I?"

"You lapped the blood off my chest for fun. You laughed."

"I was made to. I didn't really feel that way. I started out as an actress, you know."

"I know. You were always putting mooks like Joey X on."

"But you're Joey X."

Null let the smile evaporate. "Not anymore."

"You're so scarred."

"I needed to save money on plastic surgery."

"And ripped."

"I don't like food very much so I keep that budget low too."

"What do you like? Do you like this?" She was lilting, expert.

"I would have once, but now it doesn't matter."

Morticia gave a throaty laugh, forcing him down on the sofa, grabbing him firmly, straddling him as she did before. "I think it does. You know if I'd have known you were really big, I wouldn't have waited till now."

"You almost cut it off when I was on Cousin It's table." He pointed to the thick scar on the underside of his member.

"I don't remember. You know the world as well as I do, Joey. Let's not pretend."

"Let's not."

"Just fuck me."

"I will."

Morticia, one silver tear streaming down her powdered cheek, kissed two fingers with swollen bee-stung, lipid-enhanced lips and placed them to Null's slit mouth, raised herself up on the cushion until her vulva was at the level of his eyes, dismounted with a smirk of triumph.

It was always this way.

She went into the bathroom to take precautions.

Null began patiently rooting around for something in the armoire, the closet, and dresser. He found what he was looking for before Morticia was finished in the bathroom.

A toy.

Morticia emerged, having added little sparkles to her skin, makeup on the nipples. She was going for a look. What she saw didn't faze her.

The set-up by the bed, the crooked, naked Null making adjustments.

"I knew you liked it this way—I do too."

"Get on."

"You have to be nimble to do this, you know. Good thing I was a dancer."

"I'll help you."

She demonstrated a deft back flip, rubbed up against him, feeling the coarseness of his scars, the hardness of his half-starved form. "Do I look like I need help?"

She mounted the thing and Null strapped her waist and ankles into it. She grunted when the rubber coated rod in its penile molding was inserted into her, took it with a defiant smile.

"I have been paid thousands—ugh."

"Yes?" queried Null.

"—Thousands of dollars to do this, and best of all I loved doing it for those impotent slobs."

"Tell me how it felt."

"You'll see, but I don't understand why you need this? From what I can see, you're far from impotent. In fact, it's surprising."

"It's like the twitching limb of an insect after it's been crushed. Don't pay any attention to it."

"It's hard not to."

She spoke as Null finished lacing up the leather bondage sleeve behind her back, which both her arms had been gracefully extended into backwards. They were now being forced together as he finished, and she made it all look comfortable and alluring.

He stood as proudly as his damaged spine and hamstrung leg would allow him, examining his handiwork.

"All I have to do is lower this seat, and your weight pushes it in further, as far as I like. Maybe too far."

"Easy, baby."

"This pedal at the base fucks you hydraulically, up and down, when I put my foot on it."

"Yes, it feels really good baby, but not so hard." This had the taint of a growing desperation in it.

Null stamped down on it abruptly and she shrieked, then

laughed. "Well—that was—a surprise." Sweat beaded on her brow and above her exaggerated lips. A rivulet trickled between the implant ridges of her breasts.

Null stamped on the pedal again, both feet hard. Her body went rigid, legs strained and her scream was guttural.

Morticia, panting, believed she was still in control. She could take sexual pain anytime and never forget where a mark kept his wallet. "You can be my machine. I don't need this piece of junk. Unstrap me?"

Null knelt down, examined the point of entry.

"What are you doing?" She was playful in the wake of the subsiding wave of pain."

Null reached under the bed and produced a Phillips-head screwdriver. "Making an adjustment."

"You're removing the seat."

"Yes."

"But it's supporting me so the center part doesn't penetrate—"

Null punched the pedal to quiet her down and as the rod went up, her face clenched and her throat constricted.

"You mean fuck you all the way up through your mouth."

"This isn't funny! Let me out!"

"Well, if it were funny, I'd never know it. I suppose it could be, though. You know, 'live by the sword, die by the sword?'"

She added, screaming, "Gino, Alf, get the fuck in here!"

"Soundproofed for privacy. I rerouted the cameras earlier." Null tugged hard and the plastic seat came off in his hands. "That's better."

"Better?" Frantic: "Do you realize that when the muscles of my legs give out, I'll be dead?"

"Maybe before, if I do things right!"

"You're a sick, dweeby, little asshole, fucking DQ!"

Null stomped the pedal hard. The rod forced up further.

"God help me!"

"He's going to," said Null. "Rest assured."

Null began dancing a weird repetitive jig in the nude, hitting the pedal with both feet again and again.

Morticia gave out with a desperate growl, her body jerking, the bondage sleeve with both arms securely in it swinging to and fro. "God—help—"

He knelt down again, punching the pedal with one hand and helping the central rod move up and down with the other.

"Me!"

"He will. I'm going to introduce you."

One last articulate rumbling: "You're—killing—me!"

"Yes. I am, which is good, because you probably wouldn't want to live anyway when I'm finished."

She screamed; Null pumped.

At last when he stood up, she had relaxed entirely into the machine, her body somewhat slumped, her eyes and her mouth wide open, and the black rubber dildo end of the rod, now a slick red, sticking up out of her mouth like a rude joke.

Null licked some of the blood off her face, wiped his chin with his wrist and said, shaking his head, "I don't get it."

He dressed quickly then went to work on Helle in the hall, who was waiting for him there as he was leaving.

No one was as surprised as the once-champion bodybuilder from Venice, California, when her jaw was broken, her left shoulder dislocated and her entire body went tumbling in an angry confusion down three flights of stairs. Null thought about killing her but came to a decision to kick her unconscious instead.

Null met Gino on the way out and put his nose bone through his brain in a single move. Alf was pistol whipped before he could run, Null slamming the outside security door into his face.

"Tell Gomez his deal with me is still good."

"Then why the fuck—?"

Null bent down and elbowed him in the neck. "But the bill he owes Joey X is way past due. And I'm coming back to collect on it."

He left Alf just alive enough to convey the message.

NINE

"Go home, Boyd," Captain Parseeman said, as though delivering a cheery good morning. She had called to meet him in his office to see about coming back early. He had told her she had no chance, but he penciled her in anyway. Cross-agendas must be met. Parseeman bore no malice toward Boyd—thought she was cute in her prim stubby way. From the face, he could tell that at one time she was a babe in anybody's book, but guilt, alcohol, and poor diet had dampened it all with lines and puffiness. As a cop, he hated her bureaucratic stiffness and refusal to play it loose and ride with the complex currents of the Boston Police world.

She wasn't going to be one of those female officers who was in any way "just another one of the guys."

"She's on leave, right?" Phil LaCuna hulked in a corner of Parseeman's non-smoking office, smoking a filterless Pall Mall.

"She's not on the roster for today."

"She's right here in front of you," Boyd reminded sweetly.

A grunt from LaCuna. "Well, she fucking shouldn't be."

"The body count is getting higher, and no one is listening to me. I ought to change my name to Cassandra." Her hands were trembling, she had lipstick on her teeth, she felt ill-dressed in both her clothes and her skin, but she'd be Goddamned if these lifer politicking hacks were going to get the best of her. Not a chance.

"Call yourself Sybil—same difference."

"It's just a mild concussion."

"So what? You got leave comin' and you're gonna use it so we don't have to bear the insurance liability and a lawsuit when you stroke out."

"Look Phil—"

"No, you look. I fixed you up with OC for a reason—to keep your soft liberal yack and MSW feminism out of the main of department life. You empowered women are like a—a—hey Cap, what's the mayor's word for it? Cuntocracy?"

"Gynocracy." Parseeman whistled a single high note.

"That's it, and believe me, this is the wrong ideology to have around here. You're better off with communism."

"Kay, there's no reason for you to be here. Just go home before we all have to do more paperwork."

"I'm shocked at you guys. What do I have to do to get you to listen, get a sex change?"

"I'd say it would help, but we're still smarting from that last class action suit, so please, for heaven's sake, don't do that."

"It's probably an option on her health plan, for Christ's sake. They offer Life Extension and Yoga too," Parseeman added.

"If so, then it's an option for you too, Captain."

"Don't go there, Lieutenant."

"Okay, I'll just go through medical, have an exam and be recertified for active duty."

Parseeman spat coffee, laughing as he sat at his desk leaning forward in his chair. "You go do that, Kay. But you'll have to stop drinking first for a few days, you know, let some of the physiological effects subside. We don't want to have you diagnosed an alcoholic, because that'll open a whole new can of recertifications all its own. Could take months to untangle, maybe even a little trip to the vacation home in Concord?"

"The Wendigo Falls Substance Abuse Treatment Center."

"A little trip to Wendy's—they got a drive-up window for cases like yours."

"All this for me? Gee thanks, Phil."

"Just work with Wurdalaka, Kay—he leads, you follow."

"Phil, she needs go-along/get-along lessons and I don't intend to send her to school. I'd send her back to the beat if I could."

Boyd smiled, sat down on the edge of Parseeman's desk, picked up his coffee mug by the handle and smashed it, held the broken handle in front of his face and said, "I'm still here, handsome." She let it drop in front of him.

"No, she stays in OC to make what's-his-face ArtyMarty down at city hall look good, keep his track record with the gynocracy all straight.

"Cunt-*ocracy!*" coughed Parseeman.

"You want me to work second with Wurdalaka, fine. But as soon as he makes an ID that looks anything like an OC perp, it winds up in my backyard. And he can pound sand."

"Nobody cares, Kay. Even you're happy the Family's being whacked out, and so far, only the Family, no civilians. Unlax yourself about it. You got a whole family tree of crews and gangs and posses that need tidying up. This is a gift horse you should just ride off into the sunset on and not invite to bite you in the ass."

"Corpses aren't a gift."

"Well, this time they are—tied up pretty with a bow like Morticia O' Doyle on the fuck machine. We're happy to see Gomez, Fester and his family of thugs brought low."

"I'm never happy about murder, even when the worst of the murderers happen to be the victims."

"Let the serpent eat its tail for Christ's sake."

"Serpent? You don't get it, Phil. It's Null, my former C.I."

"You got a concussion, Kay, and it's putting bad thoughts in your head."

"We don't care Shimmel says it's one guy—he's a fruit loop lost in the test tubes."

"One guy couldn't whack out a whole crime dynasty, for cryin' out loud. It's impossible no matter what forensics reports. It's impossible."

"That's the thing you don't get and won't listen to me about," Boyd said, hefting herself off Parseeman's desk and added while exiting, "Null's impossible."

———

"Five bodies, Byron, five. Maybe more, presuming the family crew dragged some away in time before we got there. You working some kind of death toll quota before you come around to the facts?"

"You're on fucking leave, LT. You don't come busting in here directing my investigation."

"Won't be yours too soon if I can show an OC perp."

"But you claim it isn't. You gonna switch and say changing your mind is a woman's prerogative?"

Boyd shrugged. "I'll do what I have to, Byron. Get used to that."

"Cold bitch."

"Just where you're concerned."

"Like it or not, I'm the primary and you're in for a consult. So, consult already and fuck off."

"Nice."

"Hey, we don't have to pretend to be in love. So, let's not."

"Here's the ME's report—says it's just one guy did all of them. You deny it?"

"Of course I do. So, which proctologist did this one? The guy from Weston?"

"Shimmel wrote it up."

"Shimmel's a freak—good science, bad imagination, worse conclusions. He's testing out another screenplay idea and you know it."

"I don't know any of that, but I know you're at a dead end here and have no clue how to proceed. Anyone can see that."

"We're interviewing past family victims, reviewing Family-related cold case files, canvassing the scene, bracing all the CI's a little bit extra."

"And it's not a gang war, is it? It's not Malek the Mallet or Shlomo the schmoe, not New England La Cosa Nostra, nor Altneuschul. It's not an internal power grab, not a disgruntled captain, no, not at all."

"Then it's not OC."

"It's a victim."

"Gotta be."

"You think someone outside."

"So do you."

"Find any that survived?"

"Not any that are talking. Or who can talk."

She leaned into him and narrowed her eyes. "What about the ones who can't talk then?"

"Suck my dick."

"Isn't that normally your job description?"

"You got a mouth—"

"And a brain, and a few more degrees than you. So, shut up and listen. This isn't OC, yet it is. You're right, it's a vic, but the vic is a mass murderer, a serial killer who won't stop. Shimmel's the best. If he signs off on it being one guy, then it's one guy. And I say DQ Null doing the whacking makes it OC. Gonna work with me, or do we have a turf war which I will win just for the fun of emasculating you before the other would-be Neanderthals?"

Wurdalaka rose wearily, shaking his head and snickering. "Bull-fucking-shit. I'll clear this eventually without you—I have a few more pressing cases. And this guy, or guys, only wants his OC targets. He takes great care not to clip even one citizen bystander. I should sweat this?"

"Yes, Goddamn it, because it won't stop with the Family!" She slammed both hands on his desk to wake him up.

"I hope not. They keep at it, whoever they are, and you're gonna be out of a job, Ms. Special Task Force."

Wurdalaka smiled right on psychological cue.

It split his face in two almost exactly the way Boyd would have liked to have split it.

———

Gomez was freaking out, popping tab after tab of something black and shiny, shooting looks that said come close to my stash and I'll rip out your trachea. Helle stood there looking like a hermaphroditic sex statue, all muscles, hardness and stripper femininity, her arm in a sling and anger set in ice behind the colored contact lenses of her eyes. She smiled viciously and said nothing.

The veins on her biceps bulged like tumescent sex organs due to a recent draught of Winstrol V in alcohol.

Her jaw had been wired shut.

Pugsley and Wednesday, the thin/fat husband and wife team of Family hitters were there—Wanda and Peter Impetigo —as was Grandmama, a sleazy-seeming senior brothel madam sort chain-sucking brown cigarettes in a rhinestone holder, wearing a platinum wig and taking Gomez's place, reclining sloppily on his favorite daybed. This was Gomez's soul and inspiration, his mother, Kostianaya Noga. Wednesday sat limp and giving in to gravity in a straight back chair that seemed as if it might at any time be completely sucked up between her thighs like inoculum into an amoeba. Pugsley, nervous and slight, fidgeted.

Gomez, hitching up his smoking jacket, paced about, kicking furniture and looking for objects it might be safe to throw.

Helle stood as relaxed as if she had just been called out in a bodybuilding lineup onstage.

"He fucked me, that mutt."

"You were stupidly good-hearted, Go-Go," said his mother. You should have had Helle break him in two."

"Jesus, Granny, she's just for show—a set piece. Damaged too! Who do you think broke her arm?"

"That putz?"

Helle stood and flexed silently in rebuttal and Gomez stroked the curve of her right biceps as he paced past her.

"*Pezzonovante* psychopath—I don't get why he's doing it. Not money, not power, not sex—why the fuck bother?"

"Revenge, sonny boy?" Grandmama hacked into her hands, sniffled then lit another cigarillo, which she immediately began sucking on as violently as a slapstick comic sucking soup. "And he got a sex buzz off fucking Morticia to death with that pump get-up, probably."

"Don't seem like it, Ma. No semen, condoms or nothing to show for it. Just blood."

"My son, the sex world isn't always about an orgasm. If it were, you wouldn't be here."

"I keep you around for morale, right?"

"Wisdom, little boy. Wisdom."

"All this whackin' for revenge—that's like for teenagers, movie-goers and Walter Mitty citizens. Maybe for Islamic fundamentalists, some Jihad deal—but Null ain't got no religion."

"Since when was he ever one of us?"

"Since never."

"You don't need a why, a when or a how, Go-Go—you just need a who!"

"A who? Well, isn't that just so fucking helpful. We already know who. That freaking disease named DQ Null."

Wednesday was so astonished by this statement that she nearly rose to her feet. "You're sayin' all this is because of Joey X? Disqualified Null? The only track player with a losing streak on inside bets?"

"That's it, pudding," soothed the tense, high-strung and wire-voiced Pugsley.

Wednesday broke into hysterical, uncontrolled cacophonies of laughter.

Pugsley got up, faced her and, as she was inhaling for another peal of mirth, punched his fist hard into the center of her doughy face. She mimicked death in the chair, which miraculously enough still held her without collapsing, as she began coming around slowly with much drama.

"Sorry, Boss," said Pugsley meekly, and sat back down.

"Who doesn't necessarily mean Null—he's a dead man any way you slice it. My darling boy, who means just who's going to make trunk music out of this mope."

"That's why we're here, honey, pay attention. We're going to finish what dear departed Cousin It started."

"We'll demolish him," Wednesday said weeping. Pugsley handed her a handkerchief.

"Here pumpkin…blow!"

"Is that all we got from Alf before he croaked?"

"Boss, we almost didn't get that. If he hadn't memorized it to the point of being able to say it semiconscious, we'd be shit out of luck."

"Memorized?"

"From terror."

"He's gonna die, and die bad, Pugsley, that Null fuck. It's gotten round: Malek, Shlomo, Pat the Arachnid, they all see it coming—enforcers and captains gettin' picked off along with choice soldiers. This keeps up, only the ghetto gangs will have the guts for it. No one wants that. There's enough gang-bangers stealin' the business as it is. Imagine them gettin' our piece of the KP."

"And making their own shipments to Dhubai and Abu Dhabi."

"Fuck me, mother! They take over filming the little girls with the logboys and lipstick trannies, ship the remains off to the feebs in the tunics for a double-dip." He punched his shallow chest with defiant passion. "It's my fucking business model and I'll be reamed through the pupik out my mouth before I let them take charge of it, abo-fucking gangsters."

"You mean like Morticia?" She coughed, cackled and sucked juicily on the cigarette holder. "Not like you're doing much of that business anyway lately, being under indictment for kidnapping, white slaving and umpteen counts of the sexual abuse of a minor." Grandmama went off on a hacking jag then relit her cigarillo.

For the first time that afternoon, Gomez cracked a smile. "We'll beat it on probable cause and evidence mishandling issues as always, on appeal. This is Boston, remember?"

"We might bring in Fester on this."

"And then again you might not. This mope's got him so spooked he's ready for the mattress factory. Fester's loose as a goose."

"Thing then."

"I've sent word. That guy lives in the shadows, but he's got to be at least twice as bad as this Null twerp. Only problem is, he's twice as unpredictable.

"Wanda and I don't mind if he helps, as long as we get paid no matter who kills the screw-job mutt. All the other crews got paper out on him, so odds are we won't get there first."

"Just pitch in proper, as I know you will, and you'll get your end. Get there first and pick up a fat bonus."

Pugsley made a silent, easy move and suddenly Grandmama's still smoldering cigarillo and its holder were now neatly stabbed against the wall behind Gomez and Helle by a palm-sized, obviously ultra-sharp solid steel throwing knife. Gomez had trouble exhaling; the thing had flickered past his left eye.

"It's a fair deal." Pugsley grinned displaying brown and rotted teeth that resembled the rind of a pineapple. He retrieved the knife and politely lit another cigarillo for Grandmama, placed it in the holder, then in her waiting mouth. "We get our end, he gets his."

TEN

He came out of the shadows by the emergency room cul-de-sac outside Mt. Auburn hospital, where the ambulances were parked and grabbed her, silencing the scream with a glove in her mouth.

Despite the trembling, he was strong, and she knew how to go with it. He dragged her around the building, bounced her once against the wall both to scramble her brain and to jar her ear. She pulled a knife and right then he thought of wishing to God for humor to laugh, because certainly this must have been funny.

"I don't need to scream to cut you, fucker!" she hissed.

"You don't need to cut me. I'm dying as it is."

He moved into the light and he didn't look good—wan, scarred, fresh wounds, old wounds, swollen mouth and eyes—like some kind of tortured monster with a latex mask for a face, but all the e-room experience with trauma taught her the difference.

"Well, go sit in the E.R. like the rest then. You don't need to brace me. All you need is insurance."

She tried to move, but the knife wound up in his hand and she wound up sitting uncomfortably on the grass. She looked around quickly for help but saw none coming. They were ignored as if just another arguing couple. People in Cambridge were used to that— the spectacle of bad relationships expressing themselves. Really, even when imported to Harvard or MIT high tech, New Englanders minded their own business with the fierce aggression of New Yorkers.

"I can't and you might know why. Think about your husband, Missy."

"Do I fucking know you?"

"You know the Family. You know Uncle Fester."

She lunged at him and he kicked her back down hard.

"I should have killed you when I had the chance."

"I think so. But don't worry. You may get another chance soon. Or you may do nothing and get your way anyway."

"Best of both worlds then." She shot him a winsome look for sympathy, but none was coming. "Can I get up?"

"Do it slowly. If you go too fast, you won't go at all. I'm too sick to take chances."

Sneering: "Awww, poor baby, what's wrong?"

"We'll get to that. First, let's talk about Nat Crocus."

"If you're Family, you know, if you're not, screw you."

"How far is your apartment from here?"

Missy shrugged, no longer really afraid. Her assailant was right. He looked sick, on his last legs. It was a matter of time. She'd lead him around for a while, let some time pass, and that would be that.

"'Bout a mile down the road in Watertown."

"I can make it. We'll start walking now." Null retracted the knife and put it in his pocket. "If you know anything, Missy, you know that I don't need this to kill you. If you don't know anything, know that."

"Fine. You wanna escort me home? Do it and shut up about it."

He took her arm and she could feel him shaking, smell his dank sweat. No, it wasn't going to be long for this guy. She smirked, swallowed it so he wouldn't see. Her assailant walked with uneasy steps and a stooped gait—pain cramps, no doubt. What puzzled her was the force with which he did it, as if it were all only a physical hurdle, a practical encumbrance that he didn't feel, that didn't even register in the voice, the attitude or affect the speed with which he acted.

Weird. But then Family types were always weird.

"You're getting checks from Fester, yes?"

"From his accountant. I doubt that fucker can either add or write."

"If he could before, he can't now."

"So what?"

"The checks should stop soon."

"No, the Family takes care of their own."

"But Nat wasn't made. He was just a mope got jammed up in a task force sting."

"Sure. They gave him a paid vacation until the machine finds other grist, and they help out now that he can't earn."

"Condos go high in Watertown, don't they?"

"Tell me who the fuck you are or I'll kick you into the street."

They were in front of Mount Auburn Cemetery, the imposing beauty of which went unnoticed by either of them.

"Joey X."

"The fuck you are. He's dead. Nat told me."

"Well, he's dead, but not buried." He tightened his grip on her arm. "I'm him."

"Loser made Nat look like a winner, and I married the biggest mook of them all! You should have pretended to be some Family big shot 'stead a local joke."

"I wish I could appreciate irony so then I could laugh."

"Couldn't we all."

"He's rumored to be alive, I'm rumored to be dead, both cases exaggerated. Isn't that funny?"

"Not at all."

"I'll take your word for it."

"Nat's coming back, then I'll divorce him, that prick."

"No, you love him. That was Nat's pride and joy, his citizen nurse wife he could always come home to. He didn't even cheat on you." He forgot to add "though he tried." This way was better for effect.

"Really? I assumed he did. I wish he had. Would have made it all easier."

"His only mistress was the ponies, just like Joey X."

"Made them asshole buddies, or something. Mostly just assholes."

"Maybe, but you love him. And since you love him, I know I'm in good hands."

She laughed at this, gauging the right time to toss him into the street in front of a passing car and run like hell. It was coming. This guy could barely walk. She'd run now, but the only thing was, well, he might be able to tell her something real about Nat. And she had been nursing a growing worry as to whether she would ever see him again—that prick!

"Mister, you're in no hands at all. You're about done as far as I can see. So, you better tell me something straight, or I'll just leave you here."

"You can try to leave. It won't work. I don't mind going out and taking you along. Honest."

"I'd like to see that."

"You only think you would."

"Who sent you?"

"Joey X. That's it. I'm honoring his last will and testament and you're going to help me."

"Why the fuck should I?"

Null lunged at her for that and Missy jumped back. She needn't have. He was only pitching forward as his equilibrium had just left him, his fever having spiked and he could no longer force himself to remain standing. He fell hard to the pavement, and she knelt down next to him and took his pulse by rote. It fluttered like a moth.

"I should leave you here to die."

Null coughed, his voice more of a whisper now. "But you won't. Nat said you were standup, so you won't put me in that e-room either—"

Missy grimaced. "Fuck! You're bloody!"

"I think the bullet wounds are infected. Septicemia, right?"

"You need a hospital."

"I need you to rig something up at home, like you did for Thing that time, with the armor piercing bullets that ripped him up that way."

She screamed, "What the fuck do you know about Natty?!"

Null put a quavering index finger to his lips. "Shhhhh. If you want to attract attention, flag a cab or call one on your cell."

"Where's Natty! Where did they hide him?"

"I said I'm here to execute Joey X's last will and testament and you want to help me do it."

"No I don't! Why the fuck should I?"

"Because it's his last will and testament too, only—" Null struggled for clarity.

"Only what?"

"Only he's not around to do anything about it anymore."

Then he was out.

———

"Arrest them all? Are you fucking nuts? They're all out on probation, got about four mill in bail and legal fees ante'd up and a full roster of pretrials."

"Byron, I don't want them rearrested on the outstanding charges. I want something new."

"Being killed off ain't a crime as far as I know, Kay. What's your point?"

"Gin, Byron? It's all I have here to drink."

Wurdalaka made a face and waved his hand. "No thanks. I don't share pint bottles, besides, I'd have to stand your disgusting kickback."

"Suit yourself." She sucked greedily from the neck of the bottle and welcomed the illusory warmth as her blood temperature cooled.

"You'd think you could afford a maid on your salary. This place is a sty."

"I've been meaning to get to it. I just want to clean up this Null business first."

"There is no Null. Get with that, already!"

"Okay. Your super victim vigilante avenger then, the one you haven't got anything on yet."

"I'll find him."

"You always do, Byron. That's why ArtyMarty loves your ass. Problem is, it's never the right guy. But we all know that kind of stuff doesn't even make back page at the Herald, never mind the Globe."

"You're calling me a hack?"

"You don't miss a trick, do you, Byron?"

"You said you had something for me, LT. I didn't come here to dick around."

"Why not? Everywhere else you go, you dick around. Why not here?"

"If you were a man, I'd fucking paste you one for that."

"Go ahead and do it, fucknuts, because I'm sure as shit more of a man than you are."

"I don't hit drunks."

"Since when? This some radically new policy or something?"

Canny restraint belied rage. "Okay LT, I'll leave you to your private party. Good to see you're enjoying your leave."

Boyd got up and barred his path. "You're not going anywhere yet, Byron."

"Look, don't think about getting physical, Kay. I'm in no mood."

"Byron, either way, you don't stand a chance. So, sit down and shut up."

Wurdalaka did neither but stood and glowered down at her.

"Okay handsome. Chew on this. I can have every one of the key Family members hauled in by uniforms and keep them in lockup until I feel like doing otherwise."

"Not on their current charges you can't. Not on RICO or anything else, that's all bundled in the prosecution."

"True enough. Can't touch 'em on any of that, though they should each be tortured for three months like Joey X for the shit that they did to those kids and their whole scummy operation."

"If wishes were horses—"

"Yeah, well drunks ride fine, according to legend." She brightened. "So, how's this one for you? 'Stead of locking them up to punish them we do it for their own good?"

"How drunk are you?"

"Not nearly enough."

"Work on it and get back to me."

"Get Phil to reinstate me or your investigation is over."

"That would just be terrible. That way, I could kill two birds with one stone. A dog shit investigation ends and you stay on indefinite leave. Jesus, Kay, the only reason they don't rehab your ass is because the Globe would shit on the entire department and make ArtyMarty look like an even bigger asshole than he is for backing a drunk bitch for the Organized Crime Task Force."

"You mean the Herald. The Globe would never want to make Boston's first woman OC Task Force chief look like an incompetent drunk."

"They'd get it wrong, per usual. "You're actually a very competent drunk."

"That hurt, Byron It almost felt like a compliment. Anyway—" She killed the pint and threw the bottle in an unkempt corner of the den of her apartment where she sat while Wurdalaka shifted restively from side to side. "How do you think they'll like this headline: 'Key Mob Figures Put In Protective Custody To Thwart Assassin'? Catchy, yeah? Or is it too long? Either way, could be a career maker for some, and a breaker for some others, ya think?"

Wurdalaka sat down, looking weary.

He cleared his throat and popped the question steadily. "Tell me what you want again?"

———

"You got enough Epi in you to shock a moose, mook! Now tell me about Nat Crocus or I'll make your heart stop!"

Null reached consciousness like an injured swimmer clawing his way to the surface.

"Where is he? And don't tell me he's dead, because I keep getting postcards from him, postmarked from Europe, recent."

Null tried to speak, but his voice box fought him. Missy gave him ice chips to suck. She had him on a cot, already had put a line-in with a saline/ringers/antibiotic/morphine drip coming at him from the bags that dangled off the two steel trees on either side of him.

Null coughed the words in a monotone, "Nat's dead."

"Fuck you, he is."

"Think, Missy. He was a witness to the kiddie porn setup, the white slaving, he was a low-level bagman in deeper than even Joey X was."

"So, you aren't Joey X then."

"That's right. I'm not." He gave her a stony look, unaffected by drugs or pain. "I'm his corpse."

"Pick your daydream of choice, doesn't matter. Nat's not dead, I'm telling you!"

"Of course he is. They'll get round to you too. Only reason you're still here is your bullet removal service, and for the occasional drug swap, scrip laundering or pharmaceutical shipment log misdirect."

Her throat constricted.

"The Post Cards!"

"All written with the help of Cousin It. Nat wrote one, he got to keep a finger, another, maybe a toe, a foot. Eventually he couldn't write no more—couldn't make anything up, got sick of it, so Cousin It just cut him apart, once piece at a time, all with medical equipment handy to keep him stabilized. I think they used stuff funneled through you, you know—amputation/cauterization kit, surgical trays, bags and tubes. Just like this set up. You were a silent partner in the deal."

Tears of belief began streaming down Missy's face.

"Don't worry, though. I killed Cousin It as slowly as possible. I say that because the old fucker couldn't hold on very long. Turned out at the end he was nothing but a pussy after all. Nat died a lot more bravely. I mean, if there's any way to do that with a sadistic maniac cutting you to pieces, and without anesthesia."

"You're a pig," she said and spat in his face.

With a cold expression, she pressed hard on Null's shoulder where one particularly hideous infection of a bullet-entry wound had been laid bare. "That hurt?"

"Of course it does. Would you like to do it again? Keeps me awake."

She did it again and Null lay there breathing keenly.

"Who are you?"

"I am your salvation, so do your best to fix me up."

"Well, it's going to be a hard road—you were right. You have septicemia, some tissue necrosis that I'm going to have to cut away. I'm going to have to reset your nose too – it's badly broken. You have a fever of one hundred and four and climbing. I might have to dunk you."

"Do what's necessary."

"You're a mass of infected wounds. You know that. You may not make it."

"Make sure I do."

"Why the fuck should I? Why should I give a shit?"

"Because I'm the one who's going to crush the Family down to the last man. In memory of two useless mooks, that's why."

ELEVEN

Why didn't Boyd do it?

Let Null have his way, let him off them all—he'd only likely die himself.

His batting average so far had been too good. He was riding for a fall that would come soon anyway. Let him take them out on his way out.

So, she should have let him do it, if he really knew who they were, as he said he did—their names, how to get at them.

But of course she couldn't. She couldn't let him.

They were hers.

Ever since the night they took everything she had, ever since a gutted husband, decapitated daughter, crushed infant, they were hers and hers alone.

To kill.

Her empty glass hit the long bar hard.

"I'll make 'em kneel and cry!" she shouted amid the crowded confusion, all but engulfed by the television and slurred, "Beg the way I begged, fuckers!"

Then a calm voice to her left. "That's enough, don't you think, LT?"

It was Andromeda, looking tanned and fit and only somewhat leaner from his recent hospitalization. Some people were like that. The vain pretty ones. Recovery looked good on them. She had been in recovery for years, but all it did for her was to add a gaping gray burden to her flesh. All recovery did for her was to add years.

Fuck recovery.

"No more of that, LT."

She gave him the fisheye, looking up from the tremulous jigger of gin.

"Oh, I think there's a lot more. You come to join me on my leave, now that you're out on one too?"

"Something like that LT. But I'm not actually on leave right now. I'm here as sort of a baggage handler, an errand boy. "

"Doesn't that bother you?"

"No more than wearing a uniform did. It's just how it's done."

The grumbling, guttural, smoke-dried voices of the Penalty Box —a dive sports bar near the TD Garden—were a screaming in her ears. So, she shouted over them. Nick Andromeda squinted from the smoke hanging in the air and from the jarring peal of her voice.

"Oh goody, looks like they got my message. Did you communicate through all that mutual cocksucking? How could you understand each other through all the gurgling?"

She killed the gin and waved for another.

"Maybe it's like ants exchanging formic acid."

Andromeda grabbed her arm and she went for the Sig Sauer, this time smooth and knowing, not fumbling in her handbag at all. She had it up and under his gut before he could let go. Isn't that always the way, though? When you truly don't need something, it happens without a hitch.

She loaded the chamber and poked him hard with the barrel.

"You don't ever want to take that kind of liberty with me, Nicky boy."

"Put that away."

"Go back and tell the boys in the band to play me a new tune."

"I'm on your side first and foremost, LT. If I'm sucking anybody's cock, it's yours."

"Bad time to make jokes, Nicky."

"Worse time to point a gun. You're drunk."

"I can still shoot the eyes off a fly if I have to." She smirked. "Maybe your fly."

"Sure, but you can't judge when the gun should be cocked, or locked. Better ease off, LT. A drunken accident won't help you or me. But I bet they'd love it down at Post Office Square. If you squeeze the trigger, consider it an eject button."

The Sig went back in the bag as quickly as it had emerged with a brisk clicking of the safety. It had been held so low to Andromeda's gut that almost no one noticed it and those who did, made it their conversation of tobacco stanched whispers for the rest of the night.

"Now I remember why I requested you for OC. Tough, with at least half a brain and standard Boston high ward macho inbreeding. How many generations of baggage transport and dumping for you, Nicky?"

"We're all baggage handlers in Boston, even the Brahma bullshit artists with family townhouses on Beacon hill. This isn't the cradle of liberty. It's the freakin' incubator of politics."

"The ex-governor writes crime novels, ya know?"

"Ya, ya. John Harvard by way of New York with the summer house in Cambridge. He's the only one who *doesn't* know where the bodies are buried."

"Sure. That and Harvard Law, perfect requirements for the crime novelist."

"That and the fact nobody reads anymore so any trashed-out pol' can write 'em. You wanna sit here and swap ironies all night or what? 'Cause we're sure as hell not swapping spit. Have a drink, Nicky. Unlax, like LaCuna says."

"I can't, Kay—I'm recovering."

"What, you too? Great. Take a drink to celebrate then." She slammed down the new round like it was nothing. "Recover with me."

"That's not what I meant. I'm on too much medication for that."

"Pain meds?" she brightened.

"Just for the infection. And some enzyme boosters for my liver. Hence no cocktails."

"Sucks to be you, doesn't it?"

"I try not to think that way."

She gestured again for a drink, and the bartender nodded no, so she flashed her badge, which got her service right away.

"Is she for real?" the aging ponytail behind the bar sneered.

"She's a nightmare I keep having."

"You'd think they'd know the fucking drill by now." She took the first sip very slowly.

"Sometimes it's better to pretend not to know."

"But you know for a fact, so spill it already before I get dizzy and puke all over you."

"You're such a lady, Kay."

Boyd barked out a short burst of laughter. "Oh, I'm way beyond being that, Nicky. I'm way beyond even being a bitch from hell, which is what they think I am downtown, anyway."

"If they didn't I wouldn't be here. Anyway, they got your message from Wurdalaka, and LaCuna doesn't think it's worth fighting that fight."

"So, I'm in?"

"Not exactly."

"Then what the fuck are you here for?"

"I'm the message they sent in response."

"Yah? So, stand and deliver, messenger boy."

"I can't. That would mean cold cocking you with my Smith, dragging you outside and leaving you to get rolled and raped."

"Try that again, cuddles?"

Nick sidled up next to her, leaning in close against her barstool.

"They're ready to reinstate you and remove the mandatory leave as early as tomorrow, if you want."

"Halla-fucking-loolya"

"But there's one catch, LT, and it's a deal breaker."

"Here it comes." She snapped her fingers. "They're going to demand celibacy!" She leaned over and pinched Andromeda's cheek. "How could I ever undertake the challenge with such irresistible hunks as you and LaCuna lumbering about?"

He pushed her hand away in disgust, then let her have it. "You have to go into detox, LT. The party's over."

"I liked your first message better."

Andromeda sighed and shook his head, looked straight into his debauched supervisor's alcohol-glazed eyes. "At this point I think I liked it better too."

Theron "Thing" LeCoeur was impeccably attired in a black, Gianfranco Ferre linen suit, tailored with great care to flatter his stubby twisted physique. He sat at the bar at the Waldorf Astoria in New York City, nursing a clean, icy Absolut martini with a twist. He was scoping the pros, who weren't scoping him back. And why should they? Looking the way he looked.

It was also the way he came off—meek, docile, a definite sense of absence, vacancy and shell-shocked disinterest.

If Thing realized he came off this way, he would have laughed his thin wheezy laugh that ended in a gurgle. He had always assumed he came off arrogant, superior—a man nearly over-confident in the full knowledge of his freedoms. A man who knew he was bound by constraint of practical logic and expediency and very little else.

His face was a ruin—bloated, askew and scarred from a lifetime of violence interrupted only by quiet necessities of stalking and biding his time until the next event. His face was a life museum. There were burns from service in Kuwait, scars from youth home knife fights, juvie blanket parties. He was missing an ear, bitten off in lockup doing a stretch for attempted murder. An ex-Navy Seal washout, Thing was a combat junkie, hence his enlistment in Operation Iraqi Freedom, where he was decorated with the bronze star for fragging his CO, who was about to recommend his discharge owing to the identity fraud that allowed him to be mustered-in in the first place. Thing's quick fix was to take out some surrendering Iraqis, then cut down the CO who was accepting their surrender, with a quick burst of a round from a confiscated outmoded burp gun that happened to be handy.

Never waste any opportunity, Thing would say.

Nevertheless, one of the dying Iraqis got at him anyway with a field knife—sank it straight through his face under the cheek bone, permanently severing the right mandibular, so that now the lower half of his face hung slack and uncontrolled, perpetually dampened with drool, making him look as idiotic as he was savvy and slick.

Keeping his cool and mastering the situation (as he inevitably did), Thing experimented with slow death on the Iraqi soldier, who would have been a hero by any standard, save the taint of Saddam Hussein, as he died without begging and pleading while Thing systematically broke him to bits in a desert tent.

Theron LeCoeur won the purple heart for that.

All throughout these life incidents, Thing's face projected a sad, open sort of innocence, like the face of a Down syndrome idiot in the care of the state, always lit with dead hope. This innocence, which might have been compelling if not for the slack mouth, gnarled face and twisted drooling lip, was both real and palpable. Thing had never managed an intimate connection with anyone. He was entirely innocent of human bonding. He was entirely innocent of love. Not only the act of love—if one can be said to be distinguishable from sex—but from love itself, either being loved or simply loving anything. He had tortured small animals to fit in and be tough, he had tormented the weak with the strong, and he had seriously wounded any detractor, always striking first. He was never again going to be anybody's bitch; this he learned the hard way.

Love had never been a factor in Thing's life and now, by design, could never be.

His prostitute mother sold him to a pedophile for one hundred dollars when he was five.

He had been tied naked like a dog for two years in his own filth until authorities at last arrested "Uncle Jimmy."

His teen years were spent in foster homes and juvenile facilities riddled with violence, injury, threat and betrayal.

No girl would touch him, and somehow within him was a shame too profound to even allow him rape, much less the charms of a prostitute like his mother. He was ashamed to remove his clothes, to be seen and touched in a nonviolent way up close.

Yet he had normal heterosexual needs, as one boy who tried to seduce him at a foster home found out while drowning in a nearby lake.

Thing was no homosexual, he just was very private about his normal needs; very wary, very secretive.

Maturity, and position within The Family, brought a solution, simple and broad.

You can have any sort of fulfillment or release you want as long as you can pay for it in cash. Nobody asks, nobody tells, nobody whispers, nobody even glimpses if the price is high enough, and if you know where to go.

Thing had been doing this for years. He knew exactly where to go.

Tonight was his night.

He knew he was something of a repugnant freak, at least by appearance. He was resigned that the world of manners, protocol and rudimentary transactions would have to fight to surmount this perception as long as he performed rightly. It neither nettled him nor gave him cause for mirth; it was just another encumbrance of a well-regretted humanity.

No action at the bar—there never would be for him. He knew this too, but always liked to put in an appearance. And then there was the reason he was there, the passive action staged just for him at the slowly approaching, appointed time. The special reason he was at this hotel sitting in that exact stool at the bar in the center of New York City.

The catalog of flesh.

It had all been arranged with a few secure e-mails, a veiled phone discussion, an ICQ exchange; it was part of a prior understanding done many times throughout the past few years. Thing was, in this one sense, "a regular."

He was a special repeat customer of the nameless referral agency, the high-priced enabler of secret lust.

Thing sat drooling into his empty martini glass as they came in one by one in a stop action time-delay parade of sexual array.

There was the creamy blonde lemon tart in the backless black cocktail dress, willowy and tight.

She was followed by the buxom Mediterranean seductress in tightly shining PVC, eyes liquid with hunger, heaving chest and sinuous legs.

Thing sweated perceptibly and kept drooling.

Next came the tall, buttermilk Texan, on whom everything was outsized, save stomach, waist and shanks. It all settled in a strained and nervous near perfection with a high gloss polish on the lips and nails.

The cocoa crème oozing beauty from Haiti sashayed in, modeled her legs for him, sipping Perrier and lime, pirouetted coquettishly and flitted off like the frustrated stage dancer she was.

Thing didn't bother to wipe away his drool anymore.

The Asian from Chinatown, the Russian from Brighton Beach, The WASP from Connecticut, the Jewess from Long Island—they all came and strutted and minced and made way for the next candidate.

The French Canadian flashed her pussy at him in a fetchingly coquettish motion at the end of her modeling routine.

Distractedly, Thing flipped open his cell phone and spoke two words in lisping sibilance. "Number seven."

Then he retired to his suite.

———

"You're even more beautiful in this light." This came out at first as a series of slurps, so Thing repeated himself.

Despite her being yet another aspiring actress, she was repulsed and could only cover her disgust clumsily. Jesus... Face like warped putty, like a clown whose makeup turned out to be permanent deformity. Face like childhood pathos grown large to freakish maturity.

She shuddered at his touch and did mental calmness exercises to fight it off.

This was a high money gig, and if she did well, there would be a huge tip and a good chance of repeat business.

Thing came close to experience the pheromones, the skin, subtle breathing and heat. He took her by the wrist to feel her pulse, which was fast and feathery, as he expected. He knew her loathing for him, and this aroused him.

That he could have her anyway.

That he was going to have her.

He ran quaking hands all over her, the cool, tall, buxom Icelandic beauty queen he had chosen, and she was in fact a beauty queen, the reigning Nordic Miss from New Ulm, Minnesota. She was a newly hardened, newly disabused milkmaid from the

Midwest, only recently brought under the first hard rungs of disappointment and exploitation for brute survival amid glamorous dreams.

In some ways, she remained very fresh.

Thing could taste this when he stood close to her.

Her sweat was delicate, perfumed by youth's best bloom; his was thick and rode across his shaved head and down his face in heavy rivulets like runaway microbes.

She yielded to him like a dancer miming a resistance that happened to be real.

He was clumsy and jerky in his motions, and as he drew her into him, her pink, smooth flesh next to his mottled skin, his repulsive slurp of excitation increased. She had changed him with her presence, invoked something long buried. He no longer moved with a fierce economy of motion, directness, and surety. He no longer held bellicose arrogance as a shield.

He had been transformed and remade by her scent and breath.

To a horny, inexperienced boy.

In the realization of this, she pushed him back to free herself from his clamminess and stench, and anger became the flash point to the defects of his face.

Before he could move, her dress was on the floor.

"Let me," she said gently. "It's what I'm here for. It's what I do."

Her undergarments slid off and her motions were both liquid and undulous.

She was a slick men's magazine spread come to life for Thing, but with enough of a hint of the amateur approachable tart to efface the knowledge of the enormous professional payout, of the gross expense of having her as he was about to have her. She led him to a chair as if in a ballet, and he followed her lead. Drool ran down the front of his collar, glistening in the light as the sweat glistened on her breasts.

She gave him the dance, gave him the show.

She teased perfectly, her genitals a weapon against the mind, swallowing Thing's senses with grinding precision, her perfume heady and dizzying, her breasts jutting and taunting.

He had no choice but to give in to the pleasure of it, the pleasure of her sumptuous body.

At first, she had been disgusted and afraid, but she was in possession of newly won experience. She knew from this that she had him, not the other way around.

She was in control.

All she had to do now, was control her reflexes, her gag reflex in particular, her nausea, the urge to cringe, and then take him. Wring him dry, and then, in his moist-eyed satiation, seduce the huge tip.

She concluded her dance on her back in a writhing autoerotic finale flung dramatically across the bed.

Both legs kicked with enthusiasm.

"I want you," she said. "I know what you need."

The twisted lips smiled, looking like a sideways pucker. "No one knows that."

"I do," she mouthed, licking glossed and sensuous lips.

"You shouldn't though. It's bad if you do."

She gestured for him, and he mounted her on the bed, still fully dressed.

"Take your clothes off."

"I will. But you shouldn't know what I need, and I don't think you do."

She pouted, stroked the ruined face. "I'll show you."

He settled into her, let his body soak in her warmth, his ears full with the beating of her heart. "Okay," he breathed against her breasts.

Her arms reached around him, her face radiated a sultry bliss, both eyes closed, a consummate performance and sheer act of will. She began to skillfully undo his pants. He removed her hands with equal skill.

He kissed her cheek chastely with the slurping, contorted lips.

"Just one thing before we start, okay?"

She didn't answer, but lay there, suddenly going limp as if a narcoleptic falling into a spontaneous nap. Her eyes opened and she let out a long sigh.

Thing withdrew his arm from the tender place between her legs.

Her blood poured down like sloe syrup from the bed and pooled on the rug as it sank in.

A long blade rode up Thing's arm in a spring-release mechanism, which was now fully extended and held over his head, spotting his naked scalp with red.

"I have to make you go away first. I'm sorry that I have to, but, you see, you just—"

He kissed her again tearfully and whispered, "Can't know!"

Thing carefully removed his clothes, hurriedly leaving his shirt in the sink in cold water to soak out the blood and leapt upon her with abandon. He fucked her hard, came screaming as he rolled about in her blood, covering himself with it, pumping the deep wound in her vagina until he could pump no more.

Had he seen himself, he would have been ashamed and revolted, but in the act itself he was comfortable, at ease with the gore like a warm familiar bath of acceptance and intimacy, which is what it was to him. When he was done, he would, of course, be sick, full of self-loathing. That was all a natural part of sex, as was the release and freedom from urges until they built up again.

He would be himself again when the cleanup crew came; how he had paid through the nose for that! All in all, though, it was worth the price every time. This is what made him a repeat customer.

And now there were SMS messages crawling all over his cell phone screen.

More text about Null. Well, now the pleasure was over, it was time for business. He was the type who liked to reward himself before the job, not after. Life, as he knew too well, was disastrously short, so it was best to get your nut in first, collect up front. Less chance of missing out that way.

But Null wouldn't miss out.

Not this time.

He smiled as he cleaned and retracted the blade, which made a sound that seemed to say, Next!

TWELVE

Null had entered fever and delirium without feeling, without suffering.

The world was swimming in his head as his body slowly drowned within it, having no other effect on Null than creating the outward tics of trembling and muttering and the inward tic of remembrance.

But to Missy, who knew suffering the way one knows a favorite doddering old uncle, was sure he suffered as his fever climbed and his shakes were so severe she had to check and recheck to make sure they weren't convulsions. She was at the point of dragging his slight frame into the bathroom, where she had a full tub of water already waiting. If he spiked past 105, she would have.

She wished she had the resolve to simply kill him, let him die, call his bluff and treat him like the lowest form of DNR.

No one would miss the creep.

It would be easy, just pump in a nice, sustained overdose of morphine through the line-in, and that would be that.

Who was she kidding?

She was that tough, sure. Tough enough to survive the whore world, the stripper world, the gangster crime-crew world, make RN secretly while seeming to be everybody's bitch, everyone's disposable skank and then walk away, taking the one good man she knew with her.

Well, almost.

They never really let you walk away, just find a new and different way to use you.

And Nat Crocus could never have walked away, besides Missy's heart he had nothing else, no way to make it like John Q. Pissant in the pissant world of the office cubicle sitting in front of a dumb terminal getting dumber all the time. Be another installment plan Stan? No fucking thanks.

Some people were just born to be bitches to the world, at the mercy and pleasure of the vile and mechanically brutish. Well, that was the fate for her and Nat. But at least she could see it and make defiant choices within it.

At least they could hope for better.

And now this creepy fucker bullied then guilted her into saving his ass at the risk of her license, if not her life, as if he really was some Family button man gone renegade. If this hit the street, so would her corpse not long after. But this fuck said her man was dead, and what would life be without Natty?

More of what it was now?

Cold, methodical, plodding as close to dead as a woman in the prime of life would ever want to get, that's how it would be.

What if what creepo had said was true?

Christ, let's not think of that.

But he was right; if they killed Nat, before she died herself, she would take as many of them out as she could.

And if this motherfucker wanted to hold court and thought he was bad enough to do it, she'd better help him get well enough to do it as quickly as possible.

It occurred to her that even if Natty was all in one piece, somewhere in Florida or Bimini, hidden away until total need for his testimony blew over, what was the harm in setting the fucker after them all anyway?

After all they did to her, did to Natty, did to her friends, surviving and not, they all deserved what they got: Fester The Confessor, compulsive rapist, Cousin It The Shit, the torturing moron, king of pain who cried the tears of a child when she stitched up a minor knife wound for him once, Gomez, Morticia—and

Thing! Oh, she had seen Thing just once; she was the one who had to keep his latest victim alive long enough for him to find out where some package of horse was headed.

Thing broke all the guy's digits, while he was slowly dying of damaged organs, a ruptured spleen from hammer punches and multiple gunshot wounds, without breaking a sweat.

The dying man's screams gave her the dry heaves, but all it did to Thing was prompt him to ask her out for coffee. She was too terrified to refuse.

Then he did the unthinkable!

He planted that disgusting sideways sucker mouth right on her cheek and had those sausage-fingered hands right on her. If it wasn't for an attempted shooting nearby it turned out had nothing to do with Family business (directly anyway), she'd have wound up another of Thing's conquests.

And after he had you, no one else would want you.

So, you ran away and disappeared.

Like Natty.

Null moaned, or perhaps was speaking. Anyway, the fever was high enough to hurt, but not high enough to kill him yet.

A hot tear splashed off Null's stony cheek.

"Suffer, motherfucker," she said, adjusting the drip on the line. "Suffer for us all."

———

If Null could have suffered, he would have.

The best he could do was have the kaleidoscopic cross-fade of incidents and events that brought him to the condo in Watertown flood through him in a dreamscape to tease him with former feeling, and the promise of suffering. The former self alive to every second now dead to him, even as he somehow considered in some way there would be something left that might make him stay alive.

Something hit him as hard as the crack of a bat across his head.

The sound of a pistol.

The hand clapped on his back.

The crowd.

He was in the moment, right there.

Smelling sweat.

Chasing his own heartbeat, the run of the horses vibrating long, hard, high and thin like a wire in his blood.

Back at Suffolk Downs, laying a bet, feeling pretty good, cigarette dangling from his lip and the old tension humming sweet as a new machine. Nat Crocus was bracing him from behind. Always a pest Crocus, but also his savior ready to supply him with the special inside tip to offset the constant string of losses from his pet system. The inside tip on which of the races were fixed.

They might all have been fixed, and Joseph X. Null was closing in on the system that would either reduce the odds of loss in an honest race or crack the methodology of the scam.

Crocus broke his concentration as he jotted down probabilities in a smeared notebook

"What, you're bettin' the Perfecta?"

"Exacta, schmuck. Only in fucking Boston do they call the Exacta Perfecta. I'm a wheel man, and I'm gonna crack your freakin' mob fix if it's the last thing I do on this bent earth. I figure if I bet enough on the key nag after what you duke me, I'll beat the show. I'm wheelin' it for the longshot.

"Send it in, baby. It's your dime—you're down what, like 70 large?"

"One hundred large. Got a thing for binary debt."

"You talk a lot of shit, DQ, and come up on the wrong end of the zeros, you know that, Motherfucker?"

"You gonna tutor me now, Croky? I shoulda given you my Harvard scholarship when I had the chance."

"That really true?"

"It's as true as you and the nurse scoring med supplies for that twisted fuck Cousin It."

Crocus, a balding man with a boyish face and rat-dark hair (hulking compared to Null) body checked Null up against the counter and grabbed the collar of his St. Vincent de Paul salvage rain-beaten leather jacket. "Don't fuck around, DQ. Don't you ever, ever, bite the hand that feeds you. You know It holds the paper on you—you and your impossible-odds one hundred large."

"Take it easy, Croky, I know. I was just sayin."

"Well don't fuckin' say."

"Okay, okay. Everyone knows you and Missy are the salt of the earth. Ease up. We all gotta do stuff we don't love to get by. Me included."

Crocus let him go, just about cast his skinny frame down to the seedy gray linoleum. But that would have been too easy. Null was such a lowlife and thought he was so high and mighty, you could see in those calculating eyes. He almost fell down anyway when Crocus released him.

"You smell like shit, Null, like stale old vomit. Why don't you clean yourself up or something?" Crocus made a face.

"Like that'd do any good," said Null, fighting for equilibrium while rescuing betting tickets from random shoes. He smiled and showed bad, brown teeth suffering the usual mope's neglect.

"You're a fuckin' junkie. I don't know what the fuck they see in you."

"Same thing they see in you, Croky. Some grab-ass lackey who'll do what he's told and keep his mouth shut about it."

Crocus's face went red as he smacked Null down to the linoleum, then threw a thick, yellow brown envelope down with him. "You're sayin' you're like me, you dumb fuck? You scumbag addict? If they didn't want you for something, I'd stomp you down to the little shit stain you already are."

Null struggled to get up. "That's a tautology, but who gives a fuck. You're not like me, Croky. You're a better class of mope." He slipped the envelope shakily into his inside pocket. "They got better things planned for you than they do for me, Croky, but you're not made and you never will be, so you're still just a mope. Remember that the next time you kick the shit out of me."

"You want I should tell you what to do, DQ? Or do you remember it?"

"I got a neuron or two still fires now and then."

"Yeah, I have to remember to duck. Same old DQ, just cannot win—bets the short price winners but can't catch the long shot to bump his wad. Plays the Perfecta, and then fuckin' wheels it!

Schmuck! Don't you fucking know the wheel always comes back flat! You are betting every horse to place. Fucking addict."

"I'm not a fucking addict, Croky. I don't pull scores to get high. I just like coming high to the track. Makes the fantasy of it all so much more surreal."

"Shut up and do what you're supposed to. That way, Gomez'll let you keep running up that one hundred large into the outer limits, where you already fucking live anyway. You box today or what?" Crocus laughed.

"Hey!" Null said, almost fuming. "There's nothing funny about boxing the Perfecta."

"Are you fucking kidding me? One horse to win, any to place, the one horse to place, and the whole field to win? Why don't you just give me your fucking money? I wanna put a down payment on a spread in West Newton."

"Sure, Croky, and why don't you ask Missy to score me some morphine while we're at it?"

Crocus gave Null a lame punch in the mouth, but it sent him reeling, nonetheless.

"You got a better shot askin' Morticia for a date. In fact, why don't you? She'd probably whack you out just for fun and then we could all have a laugh."

"Why not? You fucked her and lived, Natty, so there's new hope for the dead." He wiped the blood from his mouth and breathed sourly right in Crocus's face. "I only lose it on the track, Natty, but we know where you lose it, don't we?" He made a move to smack Null, who put up his hands and shouted, "You really wanna do that? Throw me a beatin' so I can't do what I gotta do? You better kill me then, because I'm gonna explain why it didn't get done. Fester won't like that, Nat. He might want you to do a little confessin' too, if you know what I'm sayin'."

Crocus turned away and waved his hand in disgust. "Always a fucking pleasure, DQ. Always a fucking pleasure." He walked off, leaving Null to collect himself just in time for the box to come apart at the seams on the cheesy TV screens just above the windows.

The key nag went dead last, the losing tickets still prized tightly in his hand like the vain hope of the big win was prized in his mind.

Null patted them into his pocket gently, not missing a beat to spin his wheels, and homed in on the board to study up for the next play of the wheel.

———

"It looks bad, Kay, and no denying."

"So, you can't do me this solid, after what I did for you?"

Dr. Crotchet fidgeted with sweaty hands on the oak desk in the serene, faux antique intake room of Charles River Hospital, nestled in cool woodland and rolling grounds of plenty just off the campus of Wellesley College. It looked like a private estate, a cliché from an old movie, the Sternwood estate from The Big Sleep, or maybe Roger Wade's seaside place from The Long Goodbye. The façade fireplace churned out centrally heated air tinged with wood smoke perfume for the soothing touch.

"You did it for my wife."

Kay stood, coloring up.

"I did it for you. You know Sylvia doesn't care about anything anymore. You know this better than anyone."

"I know you have the shakes, Kay." Bitter.

"I need a drink, Don."

"Yes, you do. My wife doesn't, though. She doesn't need a drink. She doesn't need anything at all anymore."

"She's here, isn't she? In her own private sanctum?"

"Where else could she be?'

"She could be in a public hospital, like Selwyn Blunt."

"Yes, but not in the security wing—he's a frequent flyer by now isn't he?"

"Considering how many of the other inmates have had him down in Walpole, his frequent flyer miles are getting pretty well used up. Soon he may not fly at all."

"Deft how you did that, putting baby raper on his jacket and leaking it to the clerk trustee. Labeled him instant ass-party for every stand-up convict right away, didn't it? They hate rapists—pedophile rapists especially. Makes them feel morally superior—fucking virtuous outlaws they are, with their own special code."

"They still remember mama, I suppose. But you agreed it had to be done—a fin for what he did wasn't enough. Was it?"

"It was a catastrophic joke."

"But it's enough this way, isn't it?"

He stared at her with a conscious effort to empty his eyes of anything she could read.

"If he survives his term, it'll be with full blown AIDS. It's what he deserves—for destroying Sylvia. Once she was my world." Then he muttered, "Maybe she still is."

"You wanted justice, right? Needed justice?"

"Like you need a drink?"

"Worse. Can you sleep now? Can you live knowing that Blunt paid for what he did to Sylvia?

"No. But when I lie awake, it isn't as bad as it could be."

"How will it be when I lie awake?"

"Bad, but you know that. The shaking is getting worse. It's been, what a day?"

"Twenty-two and three-quarters hours. And I need you to admit me."

"Your insurance is the way to go, and not this kind of clandestine, under cover of darkness—"

She leaned into him, fixing glassy eyes on the indirect glare of his trifocals. "I need a contradictory thing. I need you to admit me without making a record of it yet draft me a letter saying I went through detox successfully."

"That's ridiculous and bordering on the stupid."

"That's pretty much police politics. I want proof I'm back with the sobriety program to satisfy the boys club and no researchable record to screw me in the press. Now, can we do this?"

"You're asking for too much."

"You're the one who asked for justice, remember? You know what that was asking for?"

His mouth twitched. Once.

Later that night in her room, whacked on her back as flat as she could be on Dalmane, Quetiapine, Ativan, with a hydrating drip of glucose, 100mg thiamine, 2gm magnesium and multivitamins, Boyd thrashed about as well as she could in her Humane

Restraints, envisioning her children, husband, and the long fall to the street.

And, wracked with suppressed guilt as she was, she sweated bullets, envisioning her favorite waking nightmare.

It ran through her mind screaming silently. The creation of a soulless monster named Null.

THIRTEEN

"Lady, get the fuck away from me!" shouted DQ Null as Detective Specialist Lieutenant Kay Boyd sat down across from him at his favorite table at Kelly's Diner in Somerville. He stood up as if he had just been doused in hot soup by a clumsy waitress who nearly fulfilled the prophecy with hot coffee instead.

Boyd calmly checked her watch, flipped her badge, and bid him sit back down with the quiet forbearance of an elementary school teacher. "Can we skip the preliminaries? You're supposed to be a bright guy, so let's get to it."

Null flapped his arms once to show his grudging complicity and plopped back down to his chair. "Your dime."

"Fifty cents now, thanks to Verizon and their area-code-every-fifteen-steps program."

"You can put that away now, as I am not disarmed." He spun his finger about in the air. "The happy horseshit routine."

"I didn't think you would be. Buy you a coffee?"

"I'm already drinkin'—look, you're getting in the way of my research." Null's cigarette ash cascaded down onto the misfolded pages of that morning's Herald overlapping onto the Racing Form.

"Nags?"

"Ponies, fucko."

"That's Detective Fucko, DQ. Try not to forget that and keep a civil tongue in your head."

"Well, Fuck off then, Detective fucko."

"Okay. I thought Crocus was the tout, and you were the wheel man."

"Gee, you're good, detective! Know how to tell time too, do ya? Okay, let's get it over with. I am not gonna be your CI, no matter fucking what! I may be a gambling addict and skin pop heroin, but I don't have a death wish."

"Keep racking up the losses, DQ, and they'll be one in the same."

"It's a point, I grant you. Look, no is no, so get offa me and let me get back to my decoding."

"Decoding?"

Null grumbled and sighed at the same time. "Everybody plays dumb, but okay. They fix the races, you know, mob, outfit, family, whatever. Then they put out a code for those in the know to make their bets. I crack this every so often. When I do, I whack a chunk off my losses and vig."

She accepted coffee from the immaculate waitress done up in the style of fifty years ago, drank it hot and black, her arm rock steady. Null almost chuckled, detecting the strong fumes of that morning's gin not too carefully hidden under a Listerine gel strip. "And they call you DQ because…?"

Null flushed a bit and his eyes narrowed on a face that would have been handsome if it were less lined, less sallow from drugs, the hair less matted and cheek and chin not lost in a perpetual twilight of stubble. "It's from when get I too close and they have to change things, do a new code, work around my winning."

"DQ?"

"Disqualified. They fuck me by disqualifying the horse so I get nothin'. It's my punishment for breaking it and trying to play at their level. They don't miss a trick."

"But they let you win sometimes."

"Sure, if they don't see me yacking with Boston's bull dyke answer to Eliot Ness." He gathered up his papers and stood up to leave. "Okay, that's it. I'm gonna have to work damage control now since you got me splattered with cop taint!" he shouted madly to the patrons of Kelly's and back into the kitchen so even the Guatemalan dishwasher could make him out. "I don't got nothin' to do with this OC Twat—this Estrogen Detective! I don't know nothin' from her and I don't want to know nothin'!" Louder still. "I don't know nothin' from nothin'!" He tried to bolt then and there, but a surprisingly spry Boyd barred his way. He pushed her aside and moved toward the door.

Boyd spun about with creaky deftness and gave Null a stiff yet heavy sap to the back of the neck, knocking him right to his knees.

He knelt there quivering, refusing to fall, his eyes fighting for focus, his hands grasping for purchase at smoky air.

"You think I'm asking you to be a CI, you miserable prick? You don't have a choice. I could bust you right now for whatever heroin you're holding. Bust your ass for being the hopeless degenerate mope you are."

Null rose groggily to his feet and fumbled back into his seat, resigned to finishing it with her. "Do it, I'll plea it down and be out in a week."

"That's right, king of the plea-down, aren't you?"

"Better king of somethin' than schmuck of nothin.'"

"I could bust you right now, but I'm not gonna. No, I'm gonna let you do something you're not used to doing."

"Fuck you. Bust me already."

"Think!"

"Thinkin' is what's telling me you're blowing smoke up my ass."

"They're doing KP, Null. Tell me you don't know what that is."

"It ain't kitchen patrol."

"But they're dealing in meat just the same—little kids. You know what else they do? I bet you know, you hopeless fucking mope."

She lit up a smoke, sucked in and blew out hard directly into Null's wan and sallow face.

"After they use these twinkies up on film, fuck the life out of them, they sell them off for scrap, ship them out of the country so we can't prosecute. No victim, no crime. Little kids wind up fluffers for some fucking sultan of untouchable oil wealth, disposable toys for third world princes. We're talking kids, mope, little ones, toddlers not teens."

"Remind me to cry you a river sometime about that. It's a world of shit and sorrow and I'm just doing my part to not drown in it. Why the fuck brace me?"

"Because, as they say, you are the weakest link."

"I'm telling ya, I don't know nothin' from nothin. And if I did know, I'd be shipped off somewhere as processed sausage quicker'n you can say Kennedy-Patriarca. You don't even joke about screwin' with these people, but you already knew that bein' OC, am I right? You know what Cousin It does, Uncle Fester—maybe they'll call in that nightmare Thing LeCoeur to tidy things up. Guy skull fucks dead horses, for Christ's sake! Open your fucking eyes! If you know about it, so does every dry humpin' bitch tryin' to make his nut out on the street. Ain't nobody gonna give you the time of day on Family business, least of all me. I'm gonna be lucky to survive this encounter. Now can I go? Or do you want to cold cock me with that lead dingus one more time for good measure?"

"They all said you have a brain Null. Ever try developing a heart?"

"Like I said, Detective, I don't have a death wish."

————

Joseph Xavier Null moaned loudly from his cot in the den of Missy Crocus's condo.

The moan startled her, not because it was loud, but because it was so conspicuously a moan of pleasure.

He remembered what it was like to feel the obliteration of all feeling—not the absence of feeling, but the release from feeling. Sense-memory, they called it, recollected cognition, a ghost of registered experience was all Null had left of feeling. And in his comatose state, his unconscious running as free as a toddler before the inevitable fall, he was almost able to capture what it was like. A white moth too quick for fumbling childish hands.

Heroin.

The white moth spread huge wings over oblivion.

Null was enfolded and weak with pleasure remembered.

He moaned and sighed again.

He was letting the needle "register," playing with blood mixed with heroin solute, pumping it in and like a liquid yo-yo, the main vein of his wasted forearm pulsating like a worm in the sun. Propped up in bed in his Andrew Square 3-bedroom digs above Parnell's Karate Studio, Null was too blissed out to notice or care that Fester the Confessor just kicked in the door and was lumbering toward him.

He had the grace to slide the needle out and let the rubber tourniquet fall free from his arm. Null watched Fester and his trumped-up anger of threat and control just as God would—with the hint of a smile.

Null never braced himself for the kick to the solar plexus, just sighed and took it with seeming ease.

"Fuckin' flake, just hit up, dint ya?"

"I need to warm these old bones, Fester." His body was wracked with coughing, but he himself was not. He vomited though, as a matter of course. Heroin users were always vomiting.

"Degenerate gambler smack addict." Fester grumbled, clearing a path through the debris on the floor with little kicks of frustration.

"You gonna kick the shit outta me too, Fes'? Don't bother. I won't feel it till Tuesday."

"What's the point? You're gonna do what you want, no matter where it gets you. It's either kill you or deal with it." He tossed a package that landed with a slap flat on Null's thigh. "You'll be killing yourself soon enough."

"What's that? A tip?" Null was having trouble keeping his eyes open. Figures the giant clod would have to pick now to roust him.

"How can you live like this?" Fester lit up a smoke to kill the odor of vomit by the bed.

"It reflects my inner calm and order."

"It reflects a drugged-out mope on his last legs. Better get it together DQ, before there's nothing left to get."

He picked up the yellowish, hastily sealed package and waved it in the air. "Just for the milk run, ya. We need those shipping containers handled just so. In there is your emolument plus a generous spread of buck notes for them dusky stevedores."

"Oh, you big time gangstas are so generous!"

Fester pounded the headboard of the bed with his fists, flicked his cigarette onto Null's sunken chest. It lay burning for a moment before Null brushed it to the floor and Fester stomped on it so hard the walls shook. "You stupid mook! You tryin' to burn to death?"

"No, but it's a way to go, and that's a fact."

"You oughtta be on your knees in gratitude we don't take everything and make you a galley slave till that hunnert large is paid off, deadbeat fuck."

"Let me win a few more, I'll pay it off."

"Want the moon, don't ya? I'll say this, mook, balls you got. Pity they're so far up your ass they do you no good."

"I get down on my knees, you might think I'd be suckin' you off like one those Family boys. I don't bet I'd get anymore winners from the system you made guys are into even I was on the made track."

"You wouldn't 'cause you're too much a pussy. Now don't let that horse you sponge up into your veins fuck things up for us on the waterfront. We need you down at the wharf makin' sure it all goes nice and tight."

"My kingdom for a horse! If wishes were horses, and oh are they in my case! God, are they!"

"You're hallucinatin'"

"I'm not hallucinatin' that if I get busted, I wind up dead in custody courtesy of a friendly officer. Which is why you trust such a mope as me with Family business."

"You're a pussy, Null, nothin' but a fat-mouthed pussy. Just keep to the job, put your back to it and stay alive." He spat on Null.

"What would it be like, Fester? Just imagine for a sec, what would it be like."

"What would what be like?"

"Me trading places with you. I get to be the inhuman homicidal maniac. You get to be the mope lost in a funk of drugs. How would it be, Fes'? Could it ever be? God's a funny fucking guy, got a hilarious theater of the absurd sorta streak goin' on there, oh ya."

"I would never be you, DQ. I'm more of a prick, not a pussy like you."

"Gender-bending then? Tricks get laid, made and played, ya know."

"Be a fucking nightmare nobody'd wake up from. What the fuck do you care? As long as you can shoot horse and bet horse, you're all right. Stay on the point, motherfucker. Just remember, almost goin' to Harvard don't count any more than it does in freakin' horseshoes."

"Truer words were never spoke, Fes." Null retrieved his works from where they lay beside him on the bed and wiped the needle clean with his shirt. "Wanna hit up with me, Fes'?"

Fester scowled and clomped from the room, cursing.

Null laughed a dry laugh and took another long pull of freshly cooked heroin into his arm, then vomited.

He nodded off, looking like a peaceful child, the needle still in his arm.

———

Down by the Charlestown Shipyard was where Null broke down with the sickness, caved in just like the pussy Uncle Fester made him out to be. He fought it, but it was no use.

Everything was fine. The juice was spread about in just the exact packets Gomez himself had specified. No hitches, no heat, nothing obvious to even the prying eyes of the petty professional informants, the wino scum half-passed out in the shadows. It was a milk run, getting the containers loaded, and the wheels greased.

It was a gray morning, scented heavy with machine oil mixed with tide death, rotted periwinkles and eels, beached jelly fish and herring gull offal. It smelled of sweat and whiskey and of the distaste of the sea kissing urban land.

The usual creaks, crashes, and splashing could be heard, the catcalling and purposeful bleats of the low men of the semi-legal sea.

Then it happened like science fiction special effects, the huge metal cube suspended in mid-air from the unlikeliest, ungainliest of cranes suddenly broke free and floated.

There was a crack from the busted chain.

Then the huge boom of impact and the pained metal groaning.

Then the softer, high-pitched squeals and whines. Hysteria: shrill, squalling, drill-like.

Null grimaced but felt secure—the container's breaking free and smashing on the jagged shoreline wasn't his responsibility. Not his fault; sure, they'd rag on him, threaten him, but facts speak loud, even to paranoid thugs. Null had nothing to do with it.

Still, there were precautions to take; perhaps taking back the money until matters were rectified, or at least making the overt gesture to do so. Covering your ass when the Family was involved meant not losing it. Extra precautions were normal precautions.

He made his way down the sloping grade from the gray wooded antique docks. Then he saw it—them—writhing like injured white worms. Excited maggots in the heat. Some ran, others crawled; others twitched hanging limp in the wreckage.

Now the black-side merchant marines and their hod carriers came running to catch the ones screaming an impromptu getaway. A pain hit Null that stopped him on the grade and made him fall back to his heels and slide down until he sat in the ashen sandy filth-flecked earth.

Little girls.

Naked, feces-smeared, bloodied, half-starved little girls—eight, nine, maybe some were an unhealthy twelve or so. He would have been sick if there was anything left from the heroin to be sick with. Precious cargo, the leavings of KP sold like sea urchins to the Japanese at a price. So what? So fucking what?

Missy heard him say the name loud, not like that of a lover, but certainly that of a lost love.

"Cassandra!"

The sound of it was so mournful it chilled her and she almost began to pity the monster lost in his hopeless delirium as the fever ate his life away. It was a toss-up as to whether the infection would kill him, but as long as she was seeing to it, death would have the edge.

Fuck the Family and anyone in with them.

"Cassandra!"

Null mouthed it, watching the filthy girls flee, all white, all early puberty or before, all a sort of "girleen," as Nabokov put it. Little licentious Lolitas shipped off to Dhubai at a bulk price. They could be bought and sold, just like his sister, first raped by a worthless father, then sold off by a worthless mother.

Just another AIDS death of a whore. No one ever connects the dots in the early tricking out of innocence. No one connects them to the hard bitch spitting blood dying in bleak defiance on the charity ward. There was always a buck to be made off the lowborn meat.

Now Null was making a buck off of her too.

When there was no mother, her hands washed him.

When there was no mother, she cooked, fed and put him to bed.

When there was no father, she taught him how to fend off shakedowns and gangs

Here she was again—the whore, the slut—moral core of his being.

Sweat with perhaps some tears ran in rivulets down his unclean face as he stood, watching all the savage merchandise scatter. The workers from the illegal side of the sea just weren't numerous or fast enough to run the panicking children down. He watched the boatswain trip and fall, lunging for one, the cargo mate fumbling in the dank oily sand for another.

He went down the grade to the quay and collected back heavy grease from the rogue merchant marine, first from the mate, then from the others, watching Family juice sink into their brains. When fear registered, payment was made. Null was at eighty percent with this, which wouldn't be much to cry about to Fester and Gomez. The stragglers would make their amends on the next run, or in some other way. Gomez made a hobby out of running down Family chump money, and the chumps who wanted to hold it. Sometimes Gomez would visit them personally with his specially trained muscle bitch Helle and dish them out some macho humiliation while dishing out their pockets.

Every man to his taste. Right now, Null's taste was feeling a hard pang for the swift running of the horses.

The merchantmen laughed at his heroin shakes, his jumpy manner, typical junkie; they'd have given him a beatdown for sheer fun had he not been steeped in the juice of the Family. So, they just poked fun at his sickness instead, slapped him with irrelevant laughter.

But the shakes weren't from heroin, at least not directly. They weren't from that type of need.

Before giving Fester the bad news, he stopped off at a payphone and dialed a number he memorized simply as an exercise, a minor precaution.

Kay Boyd's cell.

"It's me, Joey X," he whispered. "Your CI."

FOURTEEN

The side of his face hit the brick front of the rehabbed warehouse with a vengeance and efficiency usually reserved for loan collections. But this was no collection; it was, improbably enough, a reward.

"Fuck!" Null coughed on impact.

There was a growl of laughter.

"Easy there, Hortense!" came a gravel voice seasoned from the street.

"Yeah," came another. "Don't do nothin' might cause accidental damage or nothin'.'"

Null twisted away, scraping his face against the bricks and swung out, managing to connect with a wild blow. The impact bloodied his knuckles and made one of them flail backwards for a moment.

Detective Bim Hundertwasser laughed when Sergeant Grant Monad body-checked Null with effortless cool, spun him about and cuffed him with a succinct ratcheting sound as crisp as the early morning winter air.

Null was shrieking like an offended college student.

"This is a fuckin' roust! Go-Go Gomez'll have me out in two hours with an apology. You can't pass this crap off as caramel custard even to a judge at Suffolk."

"Guess again, Stephen Freakin' Hawking – we're not readin' you no rights and you're gonna go along and cop to the charge. This is a brief history of your time."

Hundertwasser bounced him off the side of the cruiser, more from habit than vindictiveness. Monad prevented his head from smashing against the upper rim of the cruiser's body as he shoved him in the backseat.

"What charge, for fuck's sake?" Null shouted with mock reason, as if making an appeal. "Pickin' my feet in Poughkeepsie? Wipin' my ass in Wappinger's Falls?"

"Nope," Bim Hundertwasser grunted jovially. "Mopin' in Massachusetts."

"You fuckin' jokin'?"

"Yup. Gotta love it. But every word is true, sonny boy. Mopery is still a misdemeanor in the Commonwealth. And you've just had your ass busted for it."

"Jiggery Pokery is too, but you don't even know what the fuck that is!" cried Null.

"Maybe not. We know what the fuck you are, Joey X."

"Do we ever," added Monad.

Null laughed and clapped as they weaved off Storrow Drive, circled back on the turnaround by Mass. Eye and Ear and Mass. General and approached the division down by Government Center through a series of cavalier jerks through traffic. "Here it comes! We get personal to hurt my little feelings. Degenerate gambler, fuck up drug addict, cheap ass bagman, faggot, whatever."

"That's not what you are, Joey."

"Not at all," echoed Monad.

"No, no—heaven forfend."

The cruiser lunged down the narrow ramp into the precinct garage, jammed to a stop in semi-darkness. "Welcome to Mope-a-Dope, date bait. Better pretty up, the woman upstairs hates to be disappointed."

———

They booked him, printed him, but did not throw him into holding.

No, they took Null straight back through the "authorized personnel" area to Boyd's office, uncuffed him and offered him coffee and a sandwich, which he declined, already feeling the light dry heaves of dope deprivation beginning to crease his stomach. One of the young pup ADAs was standing fidgety by a weary seeming Boyd slugging cold coffee. Null chuckled dryly—he heard tell from Fester she was a stone lush.

Hundertwasser took some passing joy in shoving Null down into a chair waiting for him in the cramped office jammed with case files, papered and confettied with tracking data on bulletin boards of various crime crews, with blurred and smudgy looking photos hastily tacked here and there. Papers were everywhere, barely hiding the old-time grim gray institutional linoleum floor and her desk was a gun metal gray bureaucratic disaster dating back to the White administration. Hundertwasser left with an informal wave at Boyd.

The ADA broke the ice. "So, you're charged and on the docket, Mr. Null, but don't worry, we'll let you pick any date you like for your arraignment, then for pretrial." His voice was high, thin and reedy.

"I'm supposed to be grateful?"

"We're the grateful ones, Mr. Null," said the ADA with an absolute lack of conviction.

Boyd wiped her mouth on her sleeve, sighed, and propped her head up on her elbows. "Look, Joey X, you know why this happened, right? Do we have to explain to someone as bright as you?"

"Tell me so I know, just in case."

"Cover," the ADA grumbled with a voice that threatened to climb to a falsetto on the very next syllable.

"They can't know we're not charging you with anything for real, so we pepper you with a bunch of harassing misdemeanor beefs and let their defense counsel Ophelia deal with it. When she gets it tossed, they don't bat an eye—just the usual hammerlock to get you to testify in the KP boondoggle."

"Oh, that's gonna go down good after your table hopping me down at Kelly's."

She guffawed sloppily. "Oh, don't worry. The whole Family knows we want to turn one of you lesser mooks. That's why they pay you and scare you. That's why we slam you with blowjob busts." She was always proud of her correct and unfeminine mastery of the profane patois of the street.

"I'm going to be the Commonwealth's nasty ambitious wire-haired terrier nipping at your heels—"

"That's right, and down the line, we'll feed him to Ophelia. Meantime, we'll get it bumped, delayed, back-scheduled until you dig something up for us." Boyd smiled.

"What am I digging for? Am I gonna wear a mini-cam like in a reality dating show on cable? Get you some titty shots?"

"No, you'll just get me time and place, who, when and where."

"What about the what?"

"Oh, we have that already. You can go, Jeff. I think Null and I will be fine from here on end."

The ADA flicked on an over-the-counter whitening strip smile and bowed out both speedily and deftly.

"Two things I want, Joey X, and two things only."

"What, a fifth of Jack Black and the company of one of the calendar cops?"

"No, Gomez Gomelsky's ass and enough evidence to shove right up it till he bleeds from his mouth."

————

Boyd was throwing up nothing in an isolation room at Charles River Hospital. Once things had seemed more in control, as if a promising outcome could have been coaxed from chaos like an image from marble, just from work and will.

She let out a cry, wiping her mouth as she fumbled her way back to the bed.

The first day of detox was always the worst. She knew this cold, and it would help her through this day the way that Gilbey's gin had helped her through the night, which at the time seemed so very nondescript.

Things were going too well, so it was bound to happen. Rookie Detective Third Grade Nick Andromeda was working his way into the Family under the Vitti Vittorio identity out of New York. The real Vittorio was in the Federal fink program, turning all his New

York friends for a new lease on life at minimum wage in Lincoln, Nebraska, rather than winding up dead in his hometown of Chelsea, Massachusetts. The vitiation of the murder, assault with intent, extortion and various lower muscle charges made the switch worthwhile, while he informed on remnant Gambinos, Bonannos, and Castellanos to the Feds and learned to sell shoes at Walmart. Andromeda slipped in with fishy creds from the New York espresso-sipping dacoit assassins, but since there was no love lost between them and the Family, this worked as part of Andromeda's calling card seeking entrée into this skew faction of the Boston mob.

This was working fine.

Boyd had an infiltrator in the Ork, someone who had actually had a sit-down with Malek the Mallet and lived to tell the tale. Malek was like Vlad the Impaler—difficult to see and once seen difficult to survive. Quick disappearances, quicker reappearances, generally as a floater with a bashed in skull were common. Sometimes they were found with their heads nailed to the boards of the docks off Congress.

Nobody saw, nobody knew.

Now, maybe OC would know and get Malek his overdue lethal injection. Malek, unfortunately, was down on the list. He was just into murder and drugs, but hadn't tapped into the KP thing yet. Nature abhorred a vacuum, so she knew once they cracked the Family wide open, Malek would slide right in with the muscle of the Ork, tamp down the Dorchester Gangsta Boyz and run KP for himself, tap the secret slap shot studios down at FPAC for production, and make a bid at squeezing out New York through New England and the Tri-State area, Kennedy-Patriarca style.

She'd crack them too, front and back end, informant, undercover, then the timely raid.

The next thing was to work in another informant, someone a little savvier, a little more stable than Joey X.

And work him before they all got the fear from Joey X being thrown to the dogs.

She didn't want to think it through. Joey X was going to be a casualty.

He already was one—a casualty of the street since his teens.

Was it really true he could have gone to Harvard?

It was a pity about wasted life. She was an expert in wasted lives. She used to nurture and coddle them, like an idiot. But now she knew what you do; you set it back on its course and snuffed everything out. It was the only way.

Guilt was the price you paid and gin let you make those payments on the installment plan to get you through another day.

It was a bad day today, and she was watching the clock so she could permit herself the flat pint of relief.

They were so close, they nearly had the time and place, but Hundertwasser put in the report anyway.

Joey X's last phone communication was cut in mid-explanation —sounds of a struggle and a voice that chuckled the confirmation, "Fuck you!"

———

Null moaned in memory, sweating with broken fever, as he remembered the small room off the library of the North End building that housed Family Capo Cousin It's playpen. Instantly his nose was hit by a faint, dank smelling human odor, something cheesy like a compost heap, yet metallic, coppery. He couldn't be sure. It made him nervous. He hadn't been roughed up much, though, just the perfunctory punching and elbowing to the face and whatnot before they threw him into it and bolted the reinforced door. They fed him something from Il Panino and Cousin It himself joined him and gave him wine. "Just tell me everything you told them and we'll find a way out of this for you," he had said. "Leave out no detail—nothing's too small. Do a good job, and you'll keep all your fingers, I promise you, on the lives of my children."

He didn't seem too bad, Cousin It. Reasonable. Null said he'd do his best. Then they threw him in this room until tomorrow.

They had taken everything from him, wallet, keys, useless betting chits from Suffolk Downs. He found something in his pocket—a packet of something.

He ripped open the paper taped about whatever it was and revealed a familiar-looking street baggie. So, this was supposed to be heroin. No fit though, he checked all his pockets thoroughly for works, even his shoes. It was probably poison, meant to be sniffed.

He tasted it.

Whoa.

That was the shit.

The wheels began turning, and he began to get it. And he didn't like it.

He liked it less when a section of wall began to rise, revealing slowly a cell the size of a closet. The odor was now overpowering and made him gag. In the center of the dank cell, lying panting and legless on the floor, was what was left of Nat Crocus. Due to the blood and disfigurement—the face had been sliced, ears removed, one eye was a nebulous mass of injury. Null wasn't sure who it was until he heard the voice, which said simply, somewhere between a wheeze and a scream:

"Kiiiiiill.....me! Please....Kill....me!"

Null knew everything now.

He wanted to reach in toward Nat to comfort him, but he was afraid to touch him. He didn't see in the half-light that he couldn't. The rusted wire mesh between them was honed razor sharp to cut them both up.

"Nat, hold on. I'll figure a way to get you out of this," he lied.

Crocus laughed and cried at the same time. "You were...always...a fucking failure on the short con..." He lost himself for a moment, then came back, gulping, "Just kill me!"

"I can't."

"Put your hands through the bars and strangle me." He was gargling blood as he spoke. It was a struggle, desperate, but this moment was his make or break to get the torment to end. He had to come across. "They're watching, idiot!"

Null noticed he had the shakes again. It was time for a little hit of the horse.

I got the horse right here!

It was the pure stuff, no doubt, enough to last until tomorrow—potent shit he could still get off on even without a fit just by sniffing.

That was the idea.

Of course, they were watching, and this was the warm-up for the show.

He could save it and use it to numb his own pain, take a temporary escape, slake his shakes and use the whole bag, or....

Crocus was weeping like a girl, unashamed and naked in his agony and—worse!—in the full, yielding knowledge of his agony. Null didn't feel ashamed for him; he couldn't imagine even the hardest muscle off the street not blubbering like this, ripped apart and left semi-dead in wracking agony just as Crocus was. He was brave in his way.

Coward or not, though, there was no way to survive this; there was no way to go out in such anguish with dignity, no triumph, no moral victory. They knew this, Cousin It and his crew. They had experience; they had seen into the mists of suffering and come out with blazing truth. Men broke easy—all men, every man. All you had to do was go beyond mean civilized restraint—do things unthinkable even in a context of war or terror. Easy as a child's game of action figures; hard for a man to do, sure, so you had to be a rare type of man to go so far, to hunger and will to go so far. That man was now running the show. Cousin It had the rep of enjoying the many ways a man could break; he catalogued them all, honed methods, made a study of the process and applied the results over time.

He took his time, as death was never the point. Death was the timekeeper.

And Null was next.

The rule is when tortured to play along and give them what they want, and the design here was one dead, one tortured, or two tortured, both living. This was the only way it could play; and it was set up this way to paste an approving smile on Cousin It's face.

He couldn't let him know he knew.

Null's hands shook with need. His mouth was dry.

He never thought of himself as addicted, but here were the signs—fuck! They all knew but him; he thought all along he was chipping, dabbling, but they knew from his street buying habits just where he stood. This fact galled him yet tickled him at the same time. They really did know him better than he knew himself. It was the accidental truth.

It wasn't just the dying fear smell coming off Crocus that was making him dry heave.

It was the onset of withdrawal.

Came the whimper while he was on his knees in the corner imagining the laughter.

"O-o-o-o-oooooooooooooooo!" like the wailing of a movie ghost which died off into a crying jag.

Null failed at vomiting.

"Dooooooo something, for Christ's sake!" Crocus lay propped up, sniffling in blood and his own filth shadowed in the cell revealed to the room behind a rusted low carbon steel mesh. His torn and bloody cheek was pressed against it. There was no doubt of the hope that Null would slice up his hands trying to get to his—what was he? Friend? Crocus was as close to a friend as someone like Null could ever have had. He was part of the buddy system of the street; they each let the other know when the shit was coming down. But whatever he was to Null, what was between them now was meant to cut Null up good and proper.

Null looked stupid and pathetic, as he was thinking. Deep thought can give you that appearance.

"Natty, can you use your fingers at all? Ya got one good hand?"

For a second Null thought it was a coughing jag, but it turned out Crocus was laughing. He held up an obviously broken arm, bloodied and cut up so half hardened strips of newly scabbed skin hung loose from it. The thumb and index finger were all that was left on the hand.

The other arm was gone, hacked off sloppily from the shoulder. The sloppiness was deliberate for a maximum of agony. Crocus' mouth had been cut apart so badly on the left side that it was now set in a permanent skeletal grin.

"That'll do," said Null.

"They left me my tongue so that I could beg," said Crocus.

"Good," Null said, angling for his voice not to crack with emotion. "We're going to need it."

Null crawled over to the mesh and looked into the ruined, one-eyed face of Nat Crocus. He slid the packet of heroin under the gap between the cage and the rug. "Take it," said Null. "Force it up your nose and down your throat. It'll put you out pretty quick."

"How——?" He struggled for his voice to function. "How the fuck long for?" It was like a belch.

"With luck for good. It's pretty pure and you never had it before."

Crocus wept and sniveled again, which took some time to be decoded as laughter. "Clean living is my friend!" he screamed, then struggled to get all the packet up his nose and mouth and sucked and sniffed and gulped in the half-light of the adjacent cell like the caricature of a fiend. It was wet, sibilant, desperate. Null wasn't sure he'd be able to ingest it all, get enough in him, but it turned out he did a pretty good job. Licks and smacks echoed in the cell.

Then it stopped.

Crocus fell back from the mesh and went over with a soft thud.

Null heard the sound, like a tire deflating at the corner gas station in deep cold. *"Sssssssssss!"*

Crocus was cooled now. A lump of empty refuse in the filth.

Null's lower lip trembled and his eyes welled.

He suddenly came upon a way of saying goodbye. It was to imitate something he never really was at all. He stood up shakily and turned about slowly, spreading his arms apart like Christ on the cross, addressing himself to each and every corner of the room, to any place where a camera lens might be set to pry, screaming at the top of his lungs like some mad and ancient shaman.

"Alright you motherfuckers! Let's get to it!"

FIFTEEN

They let him out after that, right into the library, whereupon they gave him a drink, which he didn't refuse—some Scotch Null would never have spent the money on. They were all there, with non-threatening smiles and genial attitudes. It was like they were about to forgive him. It was like watching Crocus die was punishment enough.

Belief is the creed of the torture victim—hope at all costs.

Grasping at and clinging to the furthest flung possibility of relief, of fairness, reconcilement, escape is how the torture victim may survive past the break when surrender is all that's left—a surrender that fell on deaf ears as the juggernaut demiurge of meta-pain persisted courting death, the timekeeper, to call it quits.

Null didn't know that then. All he knew was that there was room left to play.

Morticia was there, and flirted with him, threw herself at him and he responded, weakly, with wary eyes on Uncle Fester and Cousin It.

She put herself against him, head back, chest thrust out for the touching, one leg curling itself round his waist.

His hand trembled, spilling the Scotch, which Cousin It promptly refreshed.

All he had to do was tell everything: who approached him, which agency, local or Federal, was RICO involved? Did he talk about the upcoming shipment? Were the KP studios compromised? They just needed to know. After he told, it would all be okay.

He could keep his fingers. His feet, even.

All the extremities, in fact—not the slightest harm would come to him. They would let him live without further pain, maybe even a measure of greater responsibility.

They'd give him better tips on the ponies.

No more blood cloth gambits.

As Cousin It hyped him, he felt as if he were having an out of body experience, a premonitory response to what was to come.

And he knew it would come despite Fester's breaking in to clarify.

They couldn't go round killing all their best help, Fester explained. He'd make a great example of the forgiving power of the Family; you make a mistake, you get a break if you show real remorse and repentance and do your very best to undo it. They had to off Crocus. After all, he was low man on the witness list, the weakest link.

Thinking of Nat Crocus, Null wanted with all his heart for it to be true.

But he knew it wasn't.

This was just to get the lowdown up front so that for Cousin It, that sick fuck, the torture that would follow directly after would be all gravy. Purity of destination; a defined goal would only screw up the art of the thing, he was known to say.

Null swallowed hard, sweating against Morticia's skin as she pushed herself away in a teasing dance. He wanted to give it all up.

If it were anything else, he would have done it, death and torture to follow or not, at least it might improve his chances.

They had him cold on a monitored call, so it wasn't a matter of needing an admission. They knew! He'd been too clever in circumlocution over to a clean cell phone for them to get much else.

No, they just wanted to do damage control. Millions were at stake against Null's rotten life. Once they knew what they had to know, he'd be dead, or within the long preamble to death that Cousin It specialized in and Uncle Fester so doted on.

There was no forgiveness, there was no slack, only calculation and advantage.

And there had been Cassandra.

His younger sister.

Children construct the most marvelous illusions, the most elaborately improbably, half-baked and wonderful explications for the obvious and grim. It never occurred to Null and his sister that they were white-bread Dorchester Shawmut Ave. poor trash, living in a half-gutted tri-decker their drunken contractor father never could get a handle on.

When Dad was hauled off by the cops for disciplining mom, it was because he was working with them. When mom brought home Uncle Jimmy, it was to protect Cassandra and Joey, though Uncle Jimmy had Joey out on the street delivering baggies of horse for pocket change and started doing Cassandra as soon as their mother was passed out on the couch in front of some game show.

Joey X caught on and tried to stop him. That was his first drug beef, age eleven. Uncle Jimmy had friends on the force—and why shouldn't he, as a drug informant? They picked up Joey X and sent him to juvenile detention for a few days where he barely avoided being raped himself, courtesy of a knife slashed deep into the heel of his left sneaker.

When Joey was released, Jimmy wound up his guardian thanks to his mother. So, Joey X, aged eleven, learned the street from a bagman's eye-view and learned to ignore what he had to ignore, even to the point of other fathers and uncles doing their own little girls at various points around Blue Hill Avenue and Grove Hall. It wasn't that rare—they tried to get it in his mind that it wasn't that abnormal, Uncle Jimmy and his cronies, when they plied him with beer and dealt him into their poker games.

They'd fuck anything that moved.

And Joey X got nervous when jovial, plump, balding rough and tumble Uncle Jimmy started to refer to him as "that li'l piece o' chicken." It wasn't too long before he surrendered himself to the youth home—"The Home For Little Wanderers"—and tried to live an actual life, go to school, be a kid, before the big crash, the final crash over failing to rescue Cassandra. The crash that blew Harvard to hell and set him on the street scraping up money to save her, to get her out—all too late.

All for nothing.

He should have known.

She had long since given up, and after the final crash, Joey finally understood that she was right.

But she shouldn't have been right.

He was bucking the fact of her being right even now.

No, if he could help it, she would not be right—never be right!

So, his answer was the lie they wanted to hear; that he told them nothing, that he was shining them on to get CI dope to turn for Gomez. They bought this exactly zero.

Fester threw him a long beating, warmed him up for what was to come.

Morticia clawed his face good, kissed him deep and hard as if to suffocate him while Cousin It and Lurch strapped him down in the specially retrofitted dentist's chair. Lurch went to work on his ears while Cousin It, with the skill and focus and ruthlessness of craft of an old-time clock-maker, went to work on Null's hands—the sensitive joints, the sublime weakness of the metacarpals.

Though he refused to do it, Null screamed and screamed and screamed. His mind didn't stand a chance against his body, despite all propaganda to the contrary.

That was when the screaming really began.

Even to his own ears, however, his screaming was drowned out by their bellowing laughter.

———

They all had a go at him after that, touching his blood, getting right up next to his pain and spitting on it. All of them were jolly about it, save Cousin It, who was reverent about working on Null. So far, he hadn't gotten what usually came within the first 10 minutes, after the sinking of the power drill into the chest and the reinflation of the lungs. They were working on day two as it stood, and there were no signs of getting the information required.

If he couldn't extract it within the week, they would have to shut down and presume even the local law knew about it to make the intercept that would jam them all up and cost them near a billion.

Better to sacrifice a few million and ramp up in a month.

Cousin It would make sure that Null would be alive to know about it; rub his failure in his face like a fat lump of dog crap.

Lurch Luchese urinated right into the open sores on Null's battered chest.

Morticia lapped blood from his face and tortured his testicles, nearly sliced off his penis.

Grandmama carved the Family name into his thigh and spat in his face.

Gomez went at him with a straight razor for laughs, took his right testicle.

He would have taken both, but he needed to leave a little something for Morticia to work on.

Uncle Fester went at him long and hard. Cousin It had to stop him, let his subject stew with some synthetic mescaline to keep his neurons piqued in a recuperative lull so that he could go at him again later and not outright kill him.

Wednesday snapped his humerus.

Pugsley sliced off the right pinky for a souvenir.

For a capper, Cousin It tore off all the toes of the left foot. It was done beautifully and with a minimum of mess. Morticia actually cheered, watching, awed.

Cousin It whistled the Rodgers and Hart tune "I Could Write A Book" as he went the full catalogue of Null's wounds, stanching some, bloodletting others to keep them fresh. There were some days left yet to extract the hard kernel of information from the surprisingly stubborn shell of the soon to be broken street mook.

He poured vinegar in his eyes.

With a remote electrical unit strapped to his genitals, Null was made to race down the hall, groggy, weak and hamstrung – literally. A lateral incision just about severed that particular muscle from the bone.

Some of his teeth were extracted and the nerves stimulated to achieve maximum response. Null bucked up hard, strapped in the dentist's chair as if he were having a heart attack.

Cousin It marveled that he didn't, as he worked on further widening the vistas of agony his subject Null was so lost in.

There was a special art to cracking the hard ones – and it was so elegant and gorgeous when they broke. The nanosecond of it was like the kind of orgasm that could make you weep. All Cousin It had to do was keep up the harsh, calculated variegations of continuous, round-the-clock torture.

All he had to do was lay siege against his humanity.

———

There came a point when he was almost able to tell them.

There came a point, but it was weeks ago.

It was when the pain and the non-pain were still clearly demarcated.

He could almost reach for the death they would allow him like black, succulent fruit ready to drop from the vine at a touch. He could almost taste it, like a dream. It was there, fragile and pendulous, big, thick and promising.

Then bang.

He dropped it and they dropped it.

Suddenly, the subtle nuances of manifold pain bled in on him. Null dimly began to understand that there was enough blank non-pain for him to register the full depth of every diverse injury inflicted on what was left of him.

This was in the lull when the shutdown hit, when the shifting of film, DVD and streaming ops began; when the waterfront clean-up of the export of special KP feature players hit high gear.

It was a question of manpower. They had no time, having to beat a guesstimated raid that would jam them all up. Even Cousin It and Uncle Fester had to roll up their sleeves and load the trucks with servers, papers, props, cameras, writhing, screaming, little ones bound for the special care of Grandmama.

Grandmama had a little cellblock set up with cable TV and dollies and sweetheart jammies for the little girls to keep them primed and pink for use. Now, it was going to be standing room only in the basement cellblock.

So, he was left neglected, with IV's pumping in antibiotics and lactate of Ringers to keep him at the threshold of death and health so as to guarantee his remaining sensate to the pain.

There must be no sensual blackout to the pain.

The huge, engulfing, all-swallowing whale pain left, only to be replaced by piranha pain, biting tiny bits of Null at every conceivable sensitivity.

The pain was set to eat away at him by degrees while they covered their collective asses against the raid that would never come.

But fucking them over and costing them upwards of a million five in lost revenues didn't bring a smile to his face.

The pain was busily eating him.

Of course, something happens when pain is sustained over long periods of time along with calculated incessant and yet intermittent trauma.

You begin to eat the pain.

You begin to live off the pain.

Shuddering cold and naked to the agony, sensate with calculations of care, left on pause and yet to replay and replay again the remnant diastole and systole of pain. Within this sustained vibration of misery comes an opening in the stony quiet. Each drawing of spindly, agonizing breath makes the tentative opening that much larger.

A clear, idyllic window at the base of the breaking mind, creaking, creaking, creaking.

The window opens slowly, but it opens and doesn't stop until there's enough room.

Room for what? You may ask.

Why, for God to crawl in, calm as you please, for a visit.

————

The coppery taste of his own blood brought Null around. His clothes were brittle about him and cracked with the dried blood, sweat, excreta—the fluids of surrender and injury.

The catheter itched, and the surgically jerry-rigged colostomy bag ached and burned enough to be perceived through all his other bodily miseries.

Someone was touching his face, slapping it actually.

Null spoke, and it felt like coughing razors. "Batman it's you!"

The dark figure in the cold shadow of the torture library strode closer, threw its shadow cape away from the square-jawed, cowled face.

"No, I'm not Batman. I'm God."

"You're fuckin' with me."

"This is true."

"You're here to help me escape, aren't you Batman?"

"Yes, but I'm not Batman and you're staying right where you are."

"Please, God!"

"Oh, I heard you, don't worry. I always hear; and I grant you Joseph Xavier, this looks pretty terrible. You know, in many ways it's worse than some things I've seen in Bosnia-Herzegovina, Iran, El Salvador and China. And it's so long and drawn out. Many saints didn't last as long you did before I took them."

"Take me then, please, oh lord God Batman! Please!"

He touched his filthy blood and tear caked cheek. "But I already have, Joey. You're mine now, and on a course for me."

"Please God, let me die, help me die!" At this moment, he cried as tenderly as any small child.

"No, I'm going to help you to live."

"Please, save me from the pain."

"All your pain will go away, Joey, all of it."

"Thank you, God, can you do it now, please? Please?"

"I can, but I won't."

"Why not? The real God wouldn't do this to me."

"The real God is just like Batman, beyond your logic and belief, he seems to have a life of his own."

"God is a trademark?"

"Of a kind."

"I'm insane now, aren't I?"

"Yes Joey, you are and no denying."

"But if I have the capacity to actually doubt my sanity, can I really be insane?"

"Why not? There are no hard and fast rules in these things, you know—unless of course I decide there are."

"You're a mean, rotten, heartless son-of-a-bitch, aren't you?"

"Right on every count but the last. I'm the son of nothingness. Now, life—all life comes from me and, let me tell you from what I know about it, life's a bitch."

"Your sense of humor sucks too."

"Maybe, but I like it. It tickles me."

"You're fucking me over, aren't you?"

The gloved hand stroked the ruined brow. "Joey, Joey, Joey. I let my own son die in agony on the cross with spikes hammered through his ankles and wrists, then get stuck in the spleen with a spear from a tormenting soldier. Meanwhile, you and me, we're not even related!"

"That's an old joke, fucker."

"Well, wit is the epitaph of reason. Freddy may have even said that hugging the horse before they took him away. I'm not exactly sure. You're right. I never had much of a head for amusing anecdotes.

"Why are you here?"

"I always visit the holy places, Joseph. And this place is most holy; you can feel it like electricity buzzing through a wire. The power here is off the charts, Joey, I gotta tell ya."

"What's holy about this?"

"You, Joey."

The black shadow passed as the first faint light of dawn seeped across the rug.

"Please, my God, don't forsake me! Don't leave me alone! Please!"

His tears were dried, dabbed away by an expert hand.

"Don't worry, Joey, I won't."

The harsh dental light snapped on as Cousin It sank the squealing power drill back into his thigh all the way up to the collar of the bit.

Uncle Fester, standing at the doorway, laughed and laughed.

"Batman," he said.

SIXTEEN

Boyd was sweating and cursing, trying to block it all out but standing no chance without a bottle of Gilbey's to back her up. She was fighting the trivial urge to somehow sneak just the smallest drink by making the whole thing seem much more important than it was.

It was all so petty, yet pinning everything on a single drink kept her from leaving her voluntary committal at Charles River and seeking out one down the road in snotty Wellesley.

She had to force her eyes to stay open. Otherwise, she'd keep seeing it.

The horror of the past.

The pleading faces of the dead.

The horror of Null.

Boyd felt she had been sweating it out for at least a week, though it had only been hours.

Boyd had been sweating it out over the Ork when it all fell in her lap.

A series of connections lumped together by the magnetism of fact and she was up and out of the stakeout suite in Lynnfield where she had been surveilling Malek the Mallet's chief narco lieutenants. She didn't stop for a second, no explanation, just buzzed for backups headed for the North End. Screaming into the handset, she wanted two tactical teams, one for a big town house at the corner of Salem and Parmenter right over Polcari's Coffee, a townhouse where Ignazio Cavilli kept his private professional enclave. And one for the disused Coast Guard slip across Boston Harbor in Charlestown.

Coordinated on the back-end by the rising thug undercover Andromeda, Hundertwasser, Monad and the rest of the OC task force's on-call personnel were all mustered up through a skeptical Captain Parseeman and assembled by patch link for a nasty-boys-style raid on Cousin It's Playland, as well as on that certain water-front location, the one Boyd had doped out on the line. Boyd was frantic to get there first, put the red and blue pie-plate on top of her unmarked BMW yup-mobile to skip traffic hurdles.

It all had come from an errant thought—

The last joke from Joey X. Null, made on the fatal phone call where his decoy status finally paid off—ass piracy on the low seas, he had said. Ass piracy on the low seas. She didn't get it the first time, didn't even hear it at first, but oh, she heard it now.

He was being coy, smart. As if he were a real CI, instead of meat from the jump.

It meant they were using Coast Guard decaled boats out of the abandoned quay off Charlestown on the other side of the North End.

And the date of every shipment he had said was always the same. Today's date, in fact!

It all rolled around in her head and clicked just as Malek's boys were picking up phony bags of Fang (fentanyl) off the Lynnway. It all clicked with the clockwork snapping of the date in her mind.

It was a slight relief of her guilt to know that Null wasn't snuffed in vain as she took to the street in a panic, screaming into her cell phone.

She blocked off traffic, flashing her badge at the pissed off vehic-ular unfortunates stranded now in the narrow maze of North End streets as the tactical officers used a battering ram to clear the doorway of Cousin It's townhouse. They came in from the room, from the back of the basement, and splintered the high gloss oak front door.

They didn't hear it in the basement where Grandmama watched over next month's cargo, fattening them up on McDonalds, and convenience store apple pies.

They didn't hear it right away upstairs in the library, where Gomez, Lurch, Cousin It, Uncle Fester and Morticia were assembled with some soldiers, partying, celebrating the renewal of the shipments of KP movie stars and of the revitalized KP op's restored under new management on Albany Street in the South End. Boyd followed them up into the library, where it was a crowded scene.

When she got in the door, Gomez Gomelsky was still working over what was left of Null's face with a straight razor.

She tore him away from Null and the dentist chair and a burly tactical guy in a black flak-padded jump suit grabbed him from behind. She nodded for the officer to release him.

It was like 30 years ago for the crew on the street corner—nobody knew/did nothing. Playing innocent with shifty, parodying faces, like it stood even the slightest chance of flying.

Lurch Luchese actually whistled until a short tactical guy in a black mask cocked a snub nose to his jaw and calmly waited.

Cousin It filled the void with a statement like the punchline to a half-heard joke. "Guy never broke. I thought he'd roll and flip you in ten minutes, but he didn't give nothing up. Goddamn inspiring heart check, you ask me. It's the electrodes to the balls what separates the men from the boys, ya know." He laughed at the taunt.

Morticia punched him hard in the arm to shut up.

Everything in the room stopped when they all saw Null, when they finally took in the full measure of him, strapped in the dentist's chair and wearing a pointed, pom-pomed party hat and fright wig like a clown.

Gomez stepped back, and they all got the full view of Null.

Boyd almost doubled over when it hit her. What she was actually seeing.

He was still alive, after a fashion—what remained of his lips trembled. The eyes were wide, wild and as actively disconnected as those of a chameleon, rolling every which way. Blood dripped into him from a bag and seeped out of him in various degrees from a ridiculous catalog of wounds. He had been catheterized and colostomied. His body was wasted down to bone, stuck within dried, caked rags of what had once been slacks and a shirt which now just seemed another injured, deadened layer of skin for him to molt in his mindless misery

He was something out of a splatter punk nightmare, out of a grade-Z horror flick made flesh.

They had gutted him and his intestines were exposed, left hanging over his crotch.

They had drilled holes in his skull exposing parts of his brain.

Trepanation, Cousin It called it, to open up his secrets. Aerate his mind.

He was forced to smile with huge gouges whacked out of the sides of his mouth, exposing broken, hammer-shattered teeth.

Boyd hopped back a single step, as if she had moved too close to something burning.

In truth, she had.

Anguish was coming off Null in palpable waves, like car exhaust on a sweltering summer's day.

Boyd looked behind her and all she could see was her people staring at Null in disbelief for seconds of the heaviest pause she had ever known—so quiet for that moment she could actually hear Null breathing. The silence was broken by the sound of one tactical man heaving violently on his knees in a far corner of the library.

Uncle Fester let out a chuckle and found himself twitching on the ground after receiving a quick jolt from a nearby stun gun, anonymously delivered and shoved hard into his left kidney.

She saw tears flooding down the face of one young nasty boy who couldn't have yet been twenty-five, his assault weapon cocked and moving up and down in his arms with the shifting of his feet. She doubted that Null was long for this world, daring to look at him again, despite how much it hurt her stomach, made her knees quake and her eyes feel suffused by an aureole of holy fire.

Gomez sneered to break the silence. "So, read me my fucking rights already and do what you gotta do, so I can get out in time for the Homeless Assholes Association Charity Ball tonight, or whatever the thing is. St Francis Of Assisi House or some shit. Make it fucking snappy; I got a hot date."

Boyd turned to Gomelsky, adjusted the lapels on his Hugo Boss jacket.

Her voice quavered and sounded thick. "You're going to pay for a long time, Gomez. This time we got you and everyone else. It's gonna be a steeplechase to see who gets the deal that fucks you. But I'm gonna stump for no deal for you. This time you're as over as freaking Vanilla Ice."

"Yeah, sure thing, Lieutenant. We'll just see what kind of a circumstantial dismissal our ten-million-dollar defense fund can't get us. Stupid bitch, we buy our justice by the pound, in bulk. It's a volume business and don't forget it. Meanwhile, make sure you don't mishandle the chain of evidence, or fuck nothin' up. Okay?"

Boyd sighed wearily, her guts roiling and wrenching at glimpses of the amazingly still-living Null—an explosive pain built in her head, forcing her eyes to see.

It came out raspy, like a whisper, but clear. "No, I won't be mishandling anything."

Nobody saw it coming.

Her arm went back in an arc and came forward again with a ruthless follow-through, cracking directly into Gomez's face with the butt of her Sig-Sauer. It made a sharp, slogging crack.

Gomez hit the floor hard, like a bag of sand cut as it hung from a proscenium, like a flounder slapped down on the counter at the docks for weighing. Panting on the floor in blood and spittle, he whined, "I'll have your badge for that lieutenant! Fuck if I won't!"

Boyd knelt down and patted his head as the blood continued pouring out his nose and mouth.

"Fuck if you won't, Gomez. And you're gonna want it known down on the block for the day or two I'm gonna manage to keep you there that you let a fucking woman break your face? You do that, honey, you're gonna have more hot dates than you'll know what to with. Go tell 'em a woman broke your face—hell! I'll tell 'em for you if you want."

"Urrrrrgh!" Gomez moaned while Fester still twitched as he

seized on the ground. It might have been a no, but no one could really tell.

She kicked Gomez hard in the groin to shut him up and addressed the room before heading down to the other moaning that came in off the radio now hanging from her sidearm holster. "Get this man fucking med-evac'ed to Mass General, and I mean now!"

They all heard Null manage one word as the young, wet-eyed nasty boy tentatively drew in closer to unstrap him from the chair.

"Muvva!" he cried.

"Muvva!

———

They pulled twenty-eight young girls of various races and ages from the cages in the basement where Grandmama would read them bedtime stories, fix them up with plushies, throw in the burgers and pies. They were clean and pink, even the dark-skinned ones, and all in their jammies awaiting the magical trip to Dhubai, Brunei and wherever else Gomez had brokered them out.

Parmenter street was jammed with news trucks, blue beat cops, black tactical, suits, galoots, grips, bindlestiffs and social service types crawling all over the town house like ants in the clear, frigid afternoon. It made all the national feeds and evening editions of the Herald, Globe, even the Globe's parent company, the New York Times.

Quizzical faces of rescued girls huddled into special trucks made teasing news posters and blue screen newscasts nationwide.

The core crew of the Family was arraigned by nightfall, and each freed on astronomical seven figure bail payments awaiting trial. The KP cash cow started mooing again down in Lowell in a resold U Mass dormitory building, underwriting the burgeoning defense expenses.

Boyd was lauded by Mayor ArtyMarty whatsisface in a hulla-baloo ceremony pivoted hard on the ascendancy of women within the Boston Police Department, though she would continue to spend her career on the outskirts of it within her for-the-moment well-funded OC task force. There was cake and politicking. There was coffee and connivance. There were noises of warning coming off inspector LaCuna and from Parseeman. She took the cues and knew what counter-noises to make to play along.

Anything to get the scum off the street, even if that scum happened to help populate the department.

When Null was triaged at the E.R. and sent up to med surg, the surgical resident refused to go along with any plan to work on him. As it stood, Null was a parody of what a grown-up male human being was supposed to be. He looked like he deserved to be junked.

The chief resident was a stressed-out pup—Indian hip out of Louis Prang, Harvard and the teaching hospital at the Beth Israel. "Jesus fuck, this guy's a death burger well-done on a bun. We can't do shit for him but maybe serve him up to the morgue."

Boyd was there to give that little "extra" she was so famous for. It was a lame kind of payback, but the best she could come up with. "Sure you can. We both know you've dealt with worse."

"This guy's toast, Lieutenant, and he's an indigent—no insurance. DNR, I think."

"It's on the city. Just make sure he doesn't die while we're arguing about it, or I'll fucking arrest your ass for manslaughter."

The resident gestured dismissively for his staff to cart Null away and prep him for surgery.

"So, the city's footing the bill for this hopeless cause du jour? And what, praytell, did, he do to deserve such largesse? Get somebody reelected? Provide a smear?"

"He's a fucking hero, so just make sure he gets through. Arty-Marty himself says he's a hero," she lied. Everyone knew ArtyMarty would say anything to anyone as long as the cameras weren't running at the time.

"You're telling me this fucking deathburger's a hero?"

"You wish you had a tenth of this guy's nerve." And I fucked him over, she thought, possibly right into the grave.

The hero.

"I guess this is why nobody wants to be one anymore, isn't it?"

"It's something you don't come back from," she said without thinking, often how most deep thoughts are arrived at.

Null made twenty hours of surgery at Mass General, infarcted twice, crashed hard and resuscitated. He made nurses station and resident locker room gossip round the clock until his last surgery left him almost whole, although entirely lost from reality. Even in his mercifully dissociative state, they arbitrarily added another ten hours of plastic surgery, just in case there was any hope of rehab down the road.

For a hebephrenic disconnect—
For a catatonic maladaptive—
For a man-made schizophrenic catastrophe—
For a vegetable.
For a hero.

Boyd went to see him in the ICU, where he lay bandaged, catheterized and colostomied just as he had been in the dentist's chair in his pom-pomed party hat during the celebration of his near murderers. He looked both spastic and blank, his eyes rolled back in his head and fluttered dreamily even as an anti-psychotic was added to the mix of his drip on the line-in.

He was still surpassingly ugly, due to the wounds of beatings, breakage, mutilation and a straight razor to the face.

He was still surpassingly out of it, even though the anesthesia was said to have worn off.

Boyd kept popping in and out, during and between shifts, hoping at least he'd reach some order of consciousness, get something back so she could take the weight of at least the guilt relating to him off her plate. She hoped for this, but it simply wasn't happening.

A voice jarred her.

"You a friend of this guy's, Lieutenant?"

She exhaled, holding in the tremors.

Another psych guy come down to monitor the freak, read the chart, check the dilation of the pupils.

"I know him."

"Too bad this one's got no next of kin."

"Why's that?"

"Because he's headed for a lifetime of maintenance at Arbour, that's why. Only with him the lifetime won't make a decade."

"Why's that?"

"Schizophrenia, the deep kind. The kind where you live in your own little world and never come back. The kind we don't really understand."

"So? Maybe he built a better world than this?"

"Odds are he didn't. Descartes noted you make your fantasies up out of bits of reality. Indeed you can't make them up any other way. We have some idea as to what this guy's reality was. The ones who helped make that reality with him wrote it all over his body."

"So, he could be rewriting it now."

"Or reliving it."

"What's the point?"

"Point is, this was a drastic altering of basal brain chemistry through persistent trauma, which could be altered more easily than endogenous development of the same disorder. Joseph Ledoux has monographs on this fact, and along the lines of the cognitive altering of brain chemistry."

"I don't get it. So what. You're quoting psych' theory."

"No, I'm quoting science fact."

"So, what if you are?"

"Makes no difference. This guy can't give any permissions, sign any waiver in his current state. And there's no next of kin to sign one for him."

"Sign one for what?"

"For a course of therapy, I'm developing. For some trials I'm putting together in a bid for Federal funding and private sector grants. This guy's the best candidate I've come across yet evincing imposed, intervening psychosis."

"Course of therapy...?"

He shrugged. "Might bring the guy back."

Boyd blew out a breath, folded her arms and crossed over to the foot of Null's bed where his chart hung in a plastic pocket. She whipped out a pen from the inside pocket of her blazer, grabbed the chart and scribbled on some crumpled form several leaves into it. Boyd went over to the resident and stood in front of him, dead-expressioned. In a sudden, sucker move, she pushed it fast at the resident's chest so that he had no choice but to reflexively grab the folder to him.

"What the hell's that for?" he said, bent over, as if recovering weakly from a punch in the stomach instead of just a manipulated reaction.

She said with narrowed eyes and a cold, small voice, "I'm his next of kin."

SEVENTEEN

Null was screaming in a distant, dispassionate tone of observation that was for some reason urgently loud. Missy couldn't hear it. She was pulling a double at the Mt. Auburn Hospital E.R. She figured Null being left alone couldn't do much harm to her place or get very far in his current condition and she was right, yet at the same time wrong.

Wrong because the neighbors heard the wailing, pathetic voice. Condos above and below resounded with banging and vengeful voices.

Null was lost in some twilight remembrance; fever dreams of septicemia eating into his brain like worms.

He couldn't hear the knocking and shouting.

It didn't stop him from crying like the amplified announcement for local street cleaning.

"I can't feel myself anymore! I'm not in myself anymore! Nothing matters! Nothing!"

On the verge of a laugh and a cry, the voice settled into a clinical monotone. "I am no longer alive!"

Then came the shriek that was more an experimentation than an expression. "I am no longer alive!"

Null tore at the air to get out of something he simply could not touch. A veil that closed him off from the world.

Boyd screamed too, and loudly.

She was screaming for a drink to relieve the itching under her skin, screaming for anyone anywhere at any time to come and let her out, just for one little miserable half pint of Gilbeys for God's sake!

She cursed everything, God, her life, the quid-pro-quo of underhanded justice that got her in here, low and under the radar. She stopped just shy of cursing Null, though.

No, she was far too late for that.

It had all happened rapidly for patient Null, Joseph Xavier, Jr. He was fast-tracked in a quick and uncontested disposal to Lemuel Shattuck State Hospital in Jamaica Plain, the low end of the custodial for the indigent and the insane. The only thing lower was "Titticut Follies" down in Bridgewater, where they kept the old deadlosses living on borrowed time like Albert DeSalvo, and Theron "Thing" LeCoeur. LeCoeur himself had barely survived, hiring himself out to both guards and convicts as the cheapest hitter down on the wards. Thing wound up being released by administration ahead of sentence, out of fear—there were too many bodies and, having buried most of them himself, he knew where to dig them all up.

And he was the one who did all their killing.

Under recommendations from the psych resident and using some of her old Social Services pull, Boyd got Null admitted to Arbour, where the psych resident from Mass General had the ability to enter him in the first trials for a new anti-psychotic drug series interpolated with a biofeedback/behavioral conditioning program. She figured she could assuage her guilt with this, let the long slow rehab take its course and let him suffer with the best chance while she worked with the wreckage of the Family to tidy them up off the street.

The problem was, the more she tidied, the more they absorbed her time, Gomez and company. And the more her time was absorbed, the messier her tidying made things.

Evidence was lost.

A key witness had gone missing.

One confidential informant was on the MIA list and unlikely ever to be seen again.

Another—a decoy—was, well, that was Null. Pointless to pursue his testimony when he couldn't even use a knife and fork yet.

It had been months again since the drop-off at Arbour, where he had been strapped down raving in the locked ward, narcotized by the first wave of drugs and phase one of the psychosurgery.

So, Boyd made the call and set up a visit, from the next of kin.

———

The months had passed in a whirl of seeming seconds for Null, awash in dreams that lasted years within minutes and a month that went by in a single, untenable sigh.

He ran through tawny fields of green rushes and lush swamps as a four-year-old. Building snow forts, tree forts, forts for protection that all crumbled down under the heavy brogan shoes of Uncle Jimmy.

He suffered drug overdoses as a young man in his twenties and the innumerable pangs and pains of sexual liaisons gone horribly wrong.

He molted his own skin –

Peeling off and stepping out of himself—

And stepping out of himself.

And peeling down to more of himself, out of which he no longer so much stepped as ran.

Running into nothingness.

And running into a corner whereupon he met and was covered up by all the dark, dead faces, as if brackish masks made of entwined, writhing leeches, then by a darkness itself so dark it obliterated everything to an empty white.

At times Null would wake from this and just stare into the middle distance, no longer moving, no longer blinking as the dust settled over the corneas and irises of each eye. Itching without scratching; sweating without wiping a rivulet running down his face away. Heaving without vomiting. Hungering without wanting.

Tearing up without crying.

One thought kept thundering hard through his mind. One thought: "I have no reason to breathe."

He made his heart stop for a full three minutes then calmly started it up again. He was as disinterested as if he were testing a frog he was in the process of dissecting, instead of himself.

He stopped breathing for five minutes to prove the point, then let his autonomic nervous system ride it out, succumbing to the spasms of life sustaining respiration—the drowning reflex that made him buck in his bed like a mechanical Bull.

"I have no reason to breathe!" he said aloud again, without urgency.

"None."

———

Boyd couldn't quite catch herself or her breath when she walked into the door-less wardroom at Lemuel Shattuck and saw Null sitting on the edge of his bed in his hospital johnnie, as light and quiet as a bird. He was mottled purple with bloody scars and suture tracks rolling over him like cartoon centipedes, hunched over and pensive. His face was tight, but everything else hung loose. Null didn't seem to notice her, so she knocked.

"You're already in," he said evenly.

"Nothing to keep me out."

"Looking for testimony?"

"They said you made good improvement. They weren't lying."

"Depends on what you mean."

Her hands were shaking, she realized, so she covered this by reaching into her purse for a pack of cigarettes, which she thrust at him.

"They don't let you smoke in here."

"Fuck what they let you do in here. You probably need one."

"No, I'm cured of that."

"Really."

He looked up with eyes both clinical and blunt. "Yes, that part of my brain was sacrificed during one of the procedures."

"You had psychosurgery?"

"More like psychotropic lavage."

"Brainwashing?"

"More like brain showering, but why not?"

"You don't seem too bad."

"No, I don't, but I'm worse than bad."

She cocked her head; his responses were almost comically mechanical, like a stilted parody of human conversation. A sarcasm of accuracy. Was he baiting her?

"No, but when you were unresponsive and psychotic, you were bad. Very bad. Now you're just, um, unresponsive."

"Not just—almost entirely."

"My heart bleeds. So tell me, are you feeling up to testifying against the fuckers that did this to you, or do you want to whine some more?" She had sympathy for him, sure, but that wasn't going to stand in the way of her nailing every last member of the Family.

"Decoys don't usually survive long enough to give testimony, do they?" He looked at her as passionately as a fish. "I mean, aren't they generally too stupid to do it, right?"

Boyd sighed at the expected obstinacy. "We take what we can get. And you did survive. We can help you continue that."

"I doubt that you could, but you're working from a false premise."

She shrugged and lit a cigarette. "I don't get it," she said, chewing on the filter. What do you mean?"

"I didn't survive."

"Very funny."

"I'll take your word for it. I wouldn't know anymore, you see, I just can't feel anything."

"That's why you're complaining?"

"Just reporting. Nothing registers, nothing evokes any response, though injury makes me feel puzzled as to how best to handle it."

"Stop blowing smoke up my ass, Null. I know you're not yourself. Who could be after what you went through? But you have a real chance here to strike back at the sons of bitches who, who-uh, who—"

"You mean the ones who hamstrung me? Who severed my Achilles tendon? Removed my right testicle? Plucked the toes off my right foot one by one? Eviscerated me, and then decorated me with intestines like leis from Hawaii with a clown's hat?"

Boyd shook with rage, maybe guilt, certainly disgust.

"Shut the fuck up! Just shut the fuck up!" she shrieked.

Null looked inanimate and cold.

She drew deeply on the cigarette, killed it and lit another. "I don't need an itemized list."

Null seemed to be reciting rather than speaking. "You may not need one, but I do. And even though it helps me remember, I just can't get at all that it matters, that I should care, even could care!"

"Don't give me that."

"I have nothing to give you, and you have nothing for me that I want." He made a noise—an aborted laugh? "Except maybe the ability to want anything."

"You're making jokes."

"Only by accident. I'm like a prop corpse in a black comedy—incapable of laughing at the butt of the joke. Me."

"The chemicals, psychosurgery, the conditioning—"

"Left me clean as a whistle." He pointed to his head. "But I have an aftertaste of something in the back of my mind, a fading image, a slight suggestion. It's stamped on my brain like a boot print."

"What is it?"

"A memory. Tickles in the back of my brain yet I can't laugh."

She puffed out a gout of smoke and suffused her face with it, closed her eyes. "I know that – that's what all that means. But of what?"

His mouth hung gaping there for a moment as he sat immobile at the edge of the bed, weighing, considering. "It's the after image of the last thoughts and feelings of the late Joey X, of the departed DQ Null."

"You're being poetic—you're right here in flesh and blood."

"No, I'm being accurate. Joey X was tortured to death by the Family. I'm what remains, that's all. That and the little imprint on my mind. Just a little tickle."

"Of?" she challenged.

"Hatred," he said coolly, checking his fingernails for dirt, then blinked. After that, in a rapid, broken gesture almost too fast to see, he grabbed the cigarette out of her hand, stubbed it out on his tongue and swallowed it hard. He was as expressionless as a lizard and as motionless as if he were made of plastic when he repeated the word in a puff of smoke.

"Hatred."

———

She stopped him in the hall, sad, blasted, but still showing a weary, hangdog poker face. She said it, tiredly, and he laughed.

"Doctor, I get the feeling that maybe you should be in with your patients."

"I get the feeling you're right. But you saw him?"

"I did. And it was a failure, your little trial."

"I see." He rubbed his snub little nose. "Tell me, did he know who you were? Who he was—where he was? Could he tell you what happened to him?"

"Yes, but he's insane."

"Okay. Granted. He is. But a different kind of insanity, a new kind, in fact. A sort of endogenous sociopathy, psychopathology down to the chromosome level like Asperger's syndrome, a discreet form of autism."

"He says he can't feel anything."

"Well, he's wrong."

"How could he be wrong about how he feels?"

"Because he doesn't understand how he feels. It's a side-effect, nothing more, nothing less."

"Some side-effect."

"But he really *can* feel. The nerves, CNS, and autonomic all work just fine—the trouble is in the solution. The amygdaloid nucleus of the brain—the site where electrochemical exchanges register and transmit emotional responses. To flatten those responses was a way of defusing his schizophrenic dissociation."

"You're telling me you erased his emotions."

"To give you literary license, yes. And no. It isn't that we wiped them clean, we sort of dismantled the means of production. For example, he can feel hunger—it just doesn't matter enough to make him eat. He can feel pain, but it has no context, no meaning and therefore no impact other than to be distracting or confusing."

"And this is a success?"

"Resounding!"

"He was better off insane, in his own little world."

"I don't know. I never asked him what it was like. But now that he can tell me, I will. And he'll be honest down to the last detail."

"Why do you say that?"

"Well, he has no use for lying anymore. Lying is a remote function of self-preservation. But that basic impulse is as gone as his ability to feel happy or sad. He just doesn't care. In fact, at the neurochemical level, he simply can't care. He has no reason to lie; there's nothing at stake whatsoever."

"You lobotomized him!"

"Different, more crude surgery; but you could say the side-effect is that he's been lobotomized from all emotional response.

"What makes you better than his torturers, doctor?" She was red-faced, spitting imperceptibly as she spoke. "Tell me, what the fuck makes you better!"

"That's an easy one. I took away the pain. Probably forever."

"Terrific."

"He's not dead, and all cognitive function has been restored. He's lucid, grounded, practical, able to perform in the world, if he so chooses. He really is a new beginning for those castoffs in the living hell of stage three psychosis, catatonia or hebephrenic schizophrenia."

"Yes, but how can you choose to do anything, to perform, when you don't feel enough to care? When you don't even have the will to live?"

"Poetic, aren't we? But you make a very compelling point. In any case, I don't think he's going to be with us very long."

"I guess not. No will to live."

"Exactly. It's like lacking a component of the immune system. Opportunistic viruses and conditions creep in. He'll have no resistance, and none of the fight we have seen statistically save borderline patients from failing. He probably would have lived longer, left in his hebephrenic trance state. But this way, he makes it possible for others—"

"You're a first-class fucking bastard, aren't you doctor?"

He chuckled and shook his head. "No, Lieutenant Boyd, I'm not—"

She slapped him once hard across the face, turned on him and lurched away.

He finished his statement, calling behind her in the echoes of the secure corridor of the isolation wing. "—I'm not the first-class bastard."

Her high heels echoed in the corridor and faded.

"Medicine is."

EIGHTEEN

Everything in a city screams, even in a city as minuscule and cozened as Boston.

Screams come in the street, in the quiet desertion of the corner wino, the crack boy and his boom box, the arguing marrieds, the gay significant others hissing, college lovers capering, pederasts, short con jobbers, nickel baggers grasping.

Thugs converging for a score. Union workers scamming back-hours.

The wind screams in empty lots through burned out buildings, clouds of urban dust and street debris.

The greed screams out from business district authoritarians coaxing money from their legitimate scams, warring against sense, grasping at the short term, phones and headsets pressed against malevolent, child-loving faces. A loud tension in the streets.

The screams come from behind hospital walls in detox.

The screams come from secluded rooms in rehabbed housing for poor workers of fifty years ago, loaned, re-sectioned and jacked up for the poorer yet more richly skilled workers of the enlightened age. The new jack condo mortgage slurbs.

The screams come loud from behind private walls, dissipating like a bad smell.

Empty, endless, irrelevant in the human scheme of connivance and hiding, the screams die and renew, die and renew.

Null as the fever broke.

Boyd as the petty need turned back upon her flesh and tore her up.

The screaming of the phone.

Then the quiet, monotonous voice at the other end making its report.

"He's dead. Pneumonia."

She slammed down the phone and felt a silence apart from precinct business and hubbub close in on her hard, smother her like a filthy blanket. The Gilbeys came out in full view of the task force. No one said a thing as she drained the last from the half pint, lobbed the empty into the mouth of her purse on the floor.

The squad room called her into a meeting on the intercom from her plastic phone console lying skewed like a toad on her cluttered desk. She just sat there and stared ahead thoughtfully.

"Hey, LT, they're calling for you!" This from an eager beat cop transferred to research detail.

"I know," she said. "And very likely they'll get me."

––––––

Southern Mortuary by Boston City Hospital is a spotlessly ancient institutional hole that only recently upgraded from state of the art 1928 equipment to that of the mid-seventies. The refrigerated slab units are a sullied white enamel, speckled with black chips, with covered, vented coils raised on top just touching the dried, smeared and painted-over plaster of many mayoral administrations ago. The implements and even the examination tables seem to be the relics of defunct, consolidated public high schools, cast-offs recycled by the city for one of its least important functions—forensic medicine.

Suffolk County Medical Examiner is more or less an honorific title bestowed on some department head at one of the many given prestige hospitals dotting Boston and its outskirts, and the staff, more or less ambitious volunteers. All were of course paid part timers, and the chief M.E. no doubt took out his rubber stamp at least several times a week to earn your standard blue collar annual salary, but the hands-on autopsies, postmortem exams, and all pathological verifications or denials of the need for an inquest were handled by doctor specialists trained doing rotations or working on staff in everything from dermatology to plastics, but almost never pathology.

Today's expert, or should we say tonight's, since no one could abrogate a sacred day shift at a prestige hospital merely to clear the county's business of a postmortem on an indigent, was an ophthalmologist trying to beef up his resume in hopes of landing a gig at a teaching hospital in Hawaii. This was years down the road, as the favors he had to pay back just to get his small corner office on staff at New England Deaconess would keep him an indentured servant until the power players that he owed in senior administration moved on first.

Anything he could do to help them move on, he would do.

This included cutting up the abused and burned out remains of Null, Joseph X., Jr. to determine direct cause.

It looked like the usual mercy DNR of a street casualty carried off by the old people's friend. But there were mitigating factors in the chart. In fact, there were some questionable transfer papers and DRG forms that were, well, wrong. Approvals for drug "cocktails" no conservative Boston hospital would ever allow—combinations of unlike phenothiazine tricyclics, psychotropics like Paxil, Zoloft— even the outmoded imipramine hydrochloride—as well as a compliment of atypical antipsychotics. It was a loaded laundry list: aripiprazole, risperidone, clozapine, olanzapine, quetiapine, and ziprasidone. It all looked funny. Worse, some resident was making authorizations department supervisors would have had trouble with, never mind senior staff!

The whole thing had a bogus feel to it.

Fuck it. Let sleeping corpses lie their asses off. No one ever thought twice about a post mortem on an indigent. Especially one with no next of kin. No, wait.

Some joke!

There was a next of kin listed—the head of the Boston Organized Crime Task Force. Next of kin in a pig's eye.

Let the papers fall where they may.

Dr. Norm Schwabbel did the usual morphological examination

and shuddered with a sharp frisson of disgust. Not the revulsion for wounds, scars, or damage of any type—this sort of thing even the most mediocre doctor had moved beyond. It was instead the unique physical revulsion born of the moral knowledge of a depth of wrong, the sinking recognition that with deliberation, even care, a human being had been subjected to brutal acts of calculated horror. War victims are blown apart, gutted with indifference, gross trauma reducing them to pieces at a remove, under exigent pressure, in the heat of battle, left to languish and die ignored, even interrogated ruthlessly and torn to bits, then slain.

But this man wasn't a war victim, wasn't a casualty amid the surge of troops. Oh, no. Someone had in fact been very peaceful and labored about it, almost taken his time.

Whatever marks of violence there were (and there were many) were focused, patterned, organized.

This man wasn't a reckless expedient of war, a passionate victim of rape and revenge. He had been worked at like a business.

Worse, on closer inspection from the remarkable detail of injuries—

He had been done for pleasure.

The keloid scars were everywhere, and only small, sensitive parts of the man were missing, not the larger extremities—none of them with clean cuts. None.

Jesus Christ! What hadn't they done to him? Whatever wasn't removed was broken or damaged, whatever looked whole, was actually far from intact, damaged perhaps to better than half function if he could completely heal. Not much chance of that now, though. He recoiled, dropping the toe-less left foot of the emaciated and grayish naked form back on the examination table.

Whoever had done this—had worked on this man, for lack of a better term—well, he hadn't finished.

He had been interrupted, stopped presumably in the middle.

Schwabbel let out the sigh he hadn't realized he had been holding in.

Interrupted with a bullet, he hoped.

With a near sadness he hadn't felt since his first med school cadavers, Dr. Schwabbel, made the first cut of the Y-incision from groin to torso. It went fine, smooth—then a fluke! Blood flowed out of the wound as if from a pumping heart! No, he must have hit a hematoma or something, a pocket—

Something!

He couldn't breathe. The scalpel fell and bounced off the table as his panic began.

His airway—blocked! Instant panic.

The gnarled, surprisingly strong fingers of the corpse were around his neck.

The thing sat up, naked, sunken chest bloodied, the face sallow leather stretched over a human skull. A grinning, perhaps grimacing, skull. Dr. Schwabbel flapped his arms as he saw the fist coming.

Then he saw nothing at all.

————

The doctor was hobbling in the street in a soiled lab coat, ambling like Quasimodo in search of sanctuary. Having been hamstrung once made it forever a chore to walk, much less run. He lumbered across the city in a perverse crawl amid the shadows all night long, the misplaced intern or resident who walked like a crab, like the subject of a hazing prank separated from the guffaws of the group, impaired and wandering aimlessly, lunging fitfully without purpose, sick and drunken in aspect.

But the aspect belied the fact that the slumped figure in the lab coat and permanent-press clothes that hung on him like a punctured balloon over a twig was walking a walk not of confused hopelessness, but one of stilted, injured memory. The crabbed creature huddled in the lab coat knew exactly where he was headed—

Gethsemane.

Not really so much a garden as a cemetery.

On his way, he found himself bounced up against a wall by some Snoop Dogg types in chains, truncated dread locks, baggy prison-wear jeans, and the dull glad rags of the Blue Hill Avenue set. They played street corner pin ball with him—"pimp ball" one of them called it. Though it was cold, they dressed as if they were stylin' in LA, rolling down Sunset instead of marking time on Columbus.

"Axe him for cash and if'n he don't put up, cuz, we introduce him direct to the Boston beatdown!" said the leader in a black and silver do-rag.

Before he could protest, the gang laid Null flat, and collectively sank to rifle through his pockets and pick him clean, all but the tallest, weaving back and forth to loud rapping in his head, smug.

They were too late.

He had already been picked clean.

And yet there was another disturbing fact they weren't privy to.

The late Joseph X Null, Jr. was, postmortem, no longer much of a victim anymore.

When the first of them went down, the recognition of this went up.

They scattered fast, but it didn't take. One stood his ground in slack-jawed denial.

"Shit dawg! It's like punchin' smoke!"

That was the first and last thing the tallest and most stooped of the gang-banging Gangsta Boyz from the corner said, making a pitiful lope for freedom before Null slit his throat with his own discarded blade.

Shots were fired in rapid report and died.

It looked like the shortest, stubbiest of the chain-wearing Gangsta Boyz was going to make it before Null dropped him with a broken corner piece of cinderblock rebounding off the back of his head.

He lay writhing for purchase in street debris. Null cranked over toward him with unaffected slowness.

"Why, dawg? Why?" Pained, panting.

To his surprise, Null answered, almost friendly-seeming.

"It's as easy to as not, and dead enemies never come back. You can't have too many dead enemies."

"Yo, listen Dawg! I am not your enemy!"

"That won't matter in a minute."

"No! Unfair! Unfair!"

"I said the same thing when the Family ripped my fingernails off one by one."

"I'm sorry, man!"

"You know the Family?"

"I have a family!" Sweat, tears, thrashing.

Null shrugged, thought for a moment, then broke the boy's neck, twisting it the way he had seen it done in the movies. Like most of the commonplace fantasies taken for granted in movie-land, it took several takes to get it right and was hard work, and perhaps a little more messy than one might have deemed tolerable.

But when it was completed, the effect was both final and agreeable. He nodded once.

"Either way, it's unfair, alive or dead," Null argued to the slack corpse of the gangsta boy. "But this way, it's more orderly."

Null wiped his sleeve and rose, lurching his body further west, stepping over the hip hop corpses of the Boston Bangers as he made his way. Then he stopped sharply, as if gripped by something.

After holding himself frozen for a moment, he spun back toward their scattered bodies, and walked over to each one, standing over each, kneeling down as if to ask forgiveness, or perhaps to pray. What he was actually doing was picking them clean of anything useful from inside and outside pockets, fanny packs, pokes. He took cash, jewelry, drugs, a Glock Nine Millimeter and a Colt Thirty-Eight Semiautomatic. He tossed the cheap Pakistani and Chinese steel knives into the gutter.

Then he spoke to the echo of the deserted urban street.

"One man gathers what another man spills. The Grateful Dead said that. I'd be one of them, if I could feel gratitude. Oh well—"

He shuffled on.

"You can't have everything."

He cocked the Glock, which put one slug in the chamber, and held it tightly in the pocket of the lab coat.

Just in case.

———

Gethsemane Cemetery was in that part of Boston where West Roxbury crosses into Newton, the suburb just after Brookline, an intersection of privilege and privation, prosperity and poverty, where squalid Huntington Avenue and Mission Hill kiss the riches of

Route 9 and Chestnut Hill. Right where the VFW Parkway's winding, hilly rushing traffic heads off the Arborway toward the strip malls, car lots and cheapjack warehouse outlets of Dedham. You'd miss it if you didn't dare impede the pinched, angry flow of cars on the parkway and look down clear-cut green slopes on the right to at least glimpse the vacant, juxtaposed histories of John Elliot's Pulpit Rock and Brook Farm.

Cemeteries of a kind.

Pulpit Rock—a giant natural headstone where the Reverend Mr. Elliott force-fed the gospel to the Wampanoags, translated scripture into Algonquin and managed to live long enough after to found Roxbury Latin. A feast of lingua franca! Meanwhile, fifty yards away from this naked place, in a forgotten view, lay the stone piles, well ruins and dilapidated gray barns of Brook Farm groaning perpetually in the wind. Brook Farm held the remains of America's first failed writers' utopia/commune. Hawthorn immortalized it at the center of his "Blithedale Romance" only for it to be almost entirely forgotten but by put-upon college students—a place where Emerson, Dana, Ripley and a gaggle of Harvard divinity students all wallowed as au courant communards of Fourierism.

Until the bills fell due.

The first hippies, elite, contradictory, sherry tippling and opium huffing transcendentalists.

But some expenses can't be transcended.

Meanwhile, around all of this, the headstones and mausoleums of the less exalted immigrant working stiff soldiers dotted the landscape, grew and bloomed.

Less exalted, yet better known.

Now only Gethsemane Cemetery claims your consciousness—just another bone yard built for the war dead of the last century. Should you take the right and head down Baker Street for a closer look, it's all you get on either side. Cemetery sprawl. Even the signs for years on the VFW Parkway trumpeting the historic spots Pulpit Rock and Brook Farm have long ago rusted and fallen away, leaving only dull pointers to the Garden of Gethsemane.

Gethsemane, last lying place for the first betrayed.

Gethsemane, where Null found himself at the end of his crawl.

He limped in from Brook Farm, kicking aside some ancient sign promising restoration of the historical site, negotiating headstones homing in on a squat building just past that. Here he would actually have to avoid the impedimenta of security—scrubbing a guard or cop would cause more trouble than it would be worth. He assessed that he was too clumsy and graceless to avoid detection, but there was nothing for it but to try.

Null skirted intermittent lighting and overt motion detectors, making his way toward a grounds equipment storage and administration building. Sprinklers played across the graves in staggered order, dancing high, like silver daddy-long-legs spiders. He smashed the light over the door with the butt of the Colt. Not being so tall, he had to spring up as clumsily as a frog to do it, freeze for motion detectors, which shone a harsh spot right on him. He fingered a keypad by the door as if he had always done it, let himself in as the dead bolt at the knob shook with a jarring snap. Far from jarred, and as cool as a company employee showing up at the same old job at the same old time, he drew the blinds, turned on the lights and made for a first-aid kit under the sink in the kitchenette.

He booted up the nearest PC, switched on the Wi-Fi and went to establishing pop mail and surfing accounts wherever he needed them, drank a coke from the machine as he did, and dressed his minor wounds and scrapes from the kit in between. The suture line at his upper chest was still pumping out blood and decorated Schwabbel's Brooks Brothers nerd shirt with a stain of heavily darkened scarlet running down the front. He unbuttoned the shirt and tossed it in a corner, pouring Betadine over the wound and taping gauze pads across it blotting up blood.

He knew where everything was—the place was just like home to him.

In fact, from now on, it was going to be home.

NINETEEN

"Who the fuck is Dr. Benway?"

"There is no Dr. Benway."

"Fuck if there isn't!"

"They explained it to you down at administration—this is surgical specialties and we simply have no Benway here."

"He did psychosurgery on this guy! Arranged for it! Put him in trials, for God's sake!"

"I saw the paperwork and the name—no one knows him and he's not on the payroll. He's not on any list but the list for the floor and the E.R."

The pinch-faced, dry-skinned haggard yet freakishly youngish senior resident smiled at Boyd with vacant sweetness. Her hair was rat gray and her lab coat buttoned up to the neck, covering her stiff, bony frame. She towered over Boyd and made her feel fat.

"But he was here! Chief resident from Psych!"

"Psych says no. Sorry."

Boyd was sweating now, with a hot need for Gilbeys and cold comprehension. "I can shut this hospital down while I investigate it for criminal malfeasance."

"You'd have a better chance shutting down Harvard University on the same premise—mid-semester." She gave the smug in-the-know glare of an alumna.

Boyd glared back, street style.

"Do you know how many criminal acts this Benway, even if he's a doctor, inflicted on this man, and on this hospital? And even then, the entire hospital is an accessory before and after the fact, by statute."

"Read the law, Lieutenant. We're fully indemnified on charity work. And from what I can see, Benway only helped him. Mr. Null was at death's door when you bullied us into taking him."

"Well, if he was at the door, you carried him across the threshold, because he's sure as fuck dead now."

"His prognosis improved—"

"I could have done an icepick lobotomy on him, for Christ's sake, and his progress would have improved. So what?

"So, of course Benway's a doctor. How else would he know about procedure here and in surgery? What would explain it?"

"Plenty of criminals know police procedure. Doesn't make them cops."

"Forget it Lieutenant, I'm sure it's just a case of misplaced paperwork—"

"And you'll find it if you have to fabricate it, won't you?"

The senior resident smirked and went behind the Ikea desk in her single-windowed office closet at the head of surgical specialties. She sat stiff-backed in her cheap swivel chair as if ensconced upon a throne and with exactly that attitude. "I know we'll find the entire personnel file and all Benway's records. That will satisfy you, and then maybe you'll think twice about foisting off indigent death burgers on us. Won't you? I'm out of time, by the way."

Boyd broke into a laugh she couldn't contain, as if a coughing fit from a gob of mis-swallowed food.

"Are you alright, Lieutenant?"

Boyd sank into a chair and made a show of recovering her composure. "Sure I am, but you're not. You're going to have a tough job ahead of you, resurrecting a concrete professional history and track record out of transgressive fiction and beat postmodern prose."

"I don't follow."

"No, I don't suppose you do. They really don't so much educate you anymore as process and certify you, do they?"

"You're being insulting."

"You're lucky I'm not being arresting."

She arched a ratty eyebrow, as if to say, "How sophomoric." But her eyes told the story. They always do.

"It just dawned on me where I know the name Dr. Benway from."

"Okay, so you know he exists then, and not as just some rogue crypto-medico."

"Oh yes. Sure. He definitely exists. He's a pillar of the medical community alright—"

"I already knew that." More smug tautness to the face—a preamble to dismissal.

"But you didn't know he was a fucking character out of William Burroughs' 'Naked Lunch,' did you?"

———

Null sat and didn't move for two days flat. Same chair, same position.

He had previously thrown all the blues CDs he could find into the carousel of the CD changer. The task force guys liked to have all the comforts of home where they worked. He ignored the metal, oldies, punk and pop and went only for the blues. He remembered that was the music of pure emotion, the cry of corrupted gospel soul straight through the wounded and irrevocably damaged heart. He reasoned that perhaps if he surrounded himself with naked emotion, he might spark some kindling of the same within himself.

This went nowhere.

Leadbelly's "I'm On My Last Go Round" was screaming.

The morning sun greeted him through the one blind he neglected to close, just as the moon did through the clear sky over the graveyard. A fly licked his nose. Dust settled on his unblinking eyes.

He was reviewing, considering.

Getting in had been easy. When Joey X was alive, he would have been too flooded with impulse and scattered thought to have remembered the existence and location of the special investigations safe house for narcotics and vice. The Family laughed about it, particularly Fester. He even knew the pin code for the alarmed entrance.

They had a man inside, of course. They always did—as many as could be bought.

There was always an underlying level of paid information flow at the base of the pyramid of ranks that kept The Family in business. The good cops gave it up for the bad to make the dollars work in the plan for what counted most—The Soft Life.

The easy ride to the end.

All this meant the corrupted safe house was safe precisely because it was corrupt. Why should the Family venture in where they had already intruded? And why should vice come around to a safehouse in a graveyard when there was no active task force in play for drug investigations in the dead of winter, when the traffic was at its lowest?

Maybe to party themselves, maybe to fuck an indebted whore, a tryst on the side, gay, straight or bi?

Maybe for a score?

There were cameras to prevent that, surveillance feeds, seven generations out of date.

Null had looped back the tape to the cameras from a VCR first thing—set it for continuous repeat. They do this all the time in the movies, but who'd bother in real life?

Someone with literally nothing better to do.

The irony of the graveyard was not lost on him yet meant nothing to him.

Graveyards had sexual allure for the young, sure, but those past a certain age felt the taint and intrinsic foreboding of taking sinful pleasures so close to the dead, especially in a Catholic town like Boston. The Jews were even worse about it—wetting their hands this way and that—while unbelievers were the most fearful of all.

The graveyard was the place where rejected belief might most betray you.

The Family paraded all these concepts before Null, openly discussing all their business before the dying, tortured mook. Tantalizing him with inside knowledge laid bare. It was the honorific insult.

Let the CI know everything and never be able to do anything about it.

Let him die included and close to the Family as one who's excluded, frustrated, impotent.

You can always trust a corpse in training.

No, for now, he was truly safe in the safe house. In a day or two he'd move to the groundskeeper's house, then from there to a squat outside Mattapan where he could pirate electricity, make a base and mime comforts he couldn't appreciate anymore. Act as if he could appreciate them, be moved by the small simple pleasures of freedom to resurrect what was.

Sentimentality versus biological mutilation—no promising outcome there.

It was all by rote, the last circuit of a habit vanishing slowly from his brain.

He had eyed a rotted-out mausoleum slated for refurbishment as a possible way station. He evaluated the merits of that. It should be an unlikely place to find him—very much out of old-time comic books and immune to the touchstone of criminal reality.

He could take it over; bribe the groundsman.

Kill the groundsman.

Become the groundsman.

It was all the same.

One graveyard was as good as another.

And that was the fact that kept him immobile, firing neurons furiously.

Why do anything at all? Why bother?

Even when dead happens to be sentient and ambulatory, dead is dead.

A rat ran across his unresponsive foot. Null didn't even shift his eyes at the perceived pressure of the weight on his shoe.

The light took hours to move across his scarred, lean, impassive face. A vein in his massively sutured neck pulsed tremulously, like some time-elapsed amoeba, distinguishing him from stone.

He weighed and considered, reviewed, plotted, rejected, posited and deconstructed.

Then suddenly, right after day one, in a clear voice unaffected by the dryness and disuse, Null spoke.

"Just because I have no will to live doesn't mean I have no will at all."

It was there in him, an unapplied and perhaps inapplicable capability—like a powerful engine sitting with no one to operate it—it existed inert, lacking the impetus to move, an operand without an operator.

But what if he insisted upon an operator—willed for there to be one so as to move him, apply his will to purpose as if he could will the existence of God from chaos?

Big if.

He would still lack a reason to live, a meaning. Most just had an impulse, an irrational need to live—a feeling like a flame licking under the heart and guts.

Logic was a machine driving to the end of a question, whether one cared or didn't.

He was a corpse in a box of logic, albeit an incomplete corpse able to act, yet the box was open.

Did will have its own inertia? Once applied, would it imply the next question in such a way as to drive inexorably toward it?

Which would be the driving force, logic or will? Causality or casuistry?

Prior humanity was a ghostly recollection, a series of flash images in memory, vivid but disconnected, divorced from any but the most a priori meaning for Null.

Yet there was a sense memory of a type, the device an actor has and makes use of to place himself within a scene, to affect a character, a pose, an approximation of what any audience would know was an emotion, that rapid staccato salvo of feelings and responses that makes the dead page live.

A tickling at the back of the mind, an irritant.

Hate.

Lurch Luchese pissing into his wounds. Morticia O'Doyle almost slicing off his manhood, licking his blood and sweat. Fester beating him.

Gomez working his face with the straight razor.

Hate.

Or more precisely, a memory of hatred.

It was at the end of the second day that he spoke again and nonchalantly shot the rat dead as it wobbled across the room carrying the top of a discarded seeded burger bun in its jaws.

"I can make decisions and abide by them. A decision, the act of choosing, jump-starts will. And the cause of the decision is the tickling—this is the laughter response of my inability to laugh." He paused and his lips smacked unconsciously. Conclusion:

Punch-the-fucking-line!

"I will kill them all."

He stood and almost fell over due to the fact that both feet were asleep, as were his legs for having sat in one position for so long. He steadied himself against a room pillar and spoke again as if ordering himself, commanding himself to be set to the task.

"I will kill them all, but for one. And for that one, I have a special place."

'Why bother?' came an even little voice in his head that balmed the tickle against his mind as effectively as anything else. He stood stiffly and walked over to the kitchenette in search of nourishment, vitamins. There was now a purpose in preserving what health there was.

"To make a point where there is no point."

"See that my grave's kept clean!" Blind Lemon Jefferson moaned at top volume.

"And for the memory of Joseph Xavier Null."

TWENTY

Dorchester is as unforgiving as Roxbury, and Mattapan makes these two former places look like gardens of hope, broken and spacious with the debris of forgotten houses, disused apartments, bombed-out blocks—the unrehabbed South Bronx of Boston. The shadow of the now defunct Met State Hospital consumed much of the spirit if not the skyline of this urban community of drug thugs, crack whores, old-time bookmakers, older-time alcoholics and real-estate grifters touting gentrification projects on the short con for the long green. Debris.

The debris of hatred and frustration dominated every street as did the storefront windows blocked by perma-filth of merchants both failed and failing, the shill fronts for crime crews, crack and skag dealerships, alky and shooting galleries for the old timers, fuck pads for Gangsta Boyz hot on the pimp and cowboyed up for whatever street action could be copped in a zone that made the Boston police nervous, not because it was so foreign to them, but because it had touched them so deeply and one way or another, they were all from it.

It was never very far from the truth to make the old time Boston Police observation. "The cops are the robbers."

Of course, poor families still strove and struggled along, having no other means or understanding of the Boston system of privilege and patronage, being ignorant, fugitive, illegal immigrant or fresh off the boat, a green card amnesty win or lottery victory at the beginning of their woes. Some were fifth generation underculture who just couldn't catch a break in the stratified Darwinism of the criminal street. They had children, most of whom couldn't grasp the fact that things in the street debris were as bad as they were, and beneath the sooty rapacity of the roving posses of tribal bangers, could in fact get worse without warning.

It was in the twilight realization of children playing that the Ford Galaxy—a junker if ever there was one—rolled up close enough to catch that painterly tableau: lithe, twisting bodies of black, Hispanic, Ukrainian and "multicultural" waif-lets in the early afternoon sunset playing kickball. Innocence screaming delight and fury.

A fight broke out over the ball between two young teens, little girls trying to get in on the action and connect miniature punches and clumsy kicks.

Theron LeCoeur let his arm hang out the window and his twisted lamprey-eel sucker face twisted into a smile. His eyes misted over.

"What now?" asked Wednesday, grumpy and uncomfortable, cramped as she was into the entire backseat of the Galaxy.

"Just wait, precious," soothed a fidgety Pugsley. "Thing knows what he's doing."

"As long as he's clear on the split."

"He's clear," Pugsley said, watching Thing watching the children.

"I don't care who makes the killshot, we split fifty even and you two can work out your own details past that."

"But you said one third each!" Wednesday protested.

"No, precious, he didn't, and whatever split he wants is fine. We won't argue."

"Either way it's fine with me," Thing said with absent dismissal. "We argue, I take it all. So make a decision, and while you're deciding, look out the window and tell me what you see."

"Kids playing and fucking around on the corner by that back yard and broken building lot, two of them fighting."

Thing LeCoeur breathed evenly, said nothing.

"What the fuck are we doing here, Peter?"

"Rein her in, Pugs. Or I will." It was hard to ignore the disturbing sibilance of his deformed mouth, and harder still to say anything about it and emerge unscathed.

Pugsley remembered clearly watching Thing LeCoeur tear off some wise ass soldier's lower lip for just giving him the acceptable level of shit. He handed it back to the guy and challenged him to a debate right then and there, not breaking a sweat.

The guy fainted.

"What the fuck are we doing?" Wanda "Wednesday" Impetigo screamed.

Pugsley leaned over the seat toward her face to clamp his hands over her mouth before she did more damage, but Thing stopped him with one arm, pushed him back up front.

He was deceptively strong, like a fat powerlifter in baggy sweats.

"You're a dead shot, Pugs?"

"I do all right. Better with a knife."

"What the fuck are we doing here?"

This was so loud that the children outside heard them and stopped for a moment to size up the Galaxy, instinctively seeking weakness like young pack animals. The white faces inside were a tip-off and they all slowly approached, the older ones first.

Thing smiled so broadly this time there could be no mistake about it. He handed Pugsley a Glock nine millimeter outfitted with special rounds—armor piercing, Teflon filled dum-dum style copper-stoppers.

"What the fuck is this for?" asked Pugsley.

"Yeah," echoed Wanda. "What the fuck—?"

Thing clamped his hand over her mouth with genial firmness, put his finger to his lips. "Shhh," he warned.

The tallest boy at the front of the gang of kids approached them the closest and hailed Thing through the open driver's side window of the Galaxy. "Yo, you lost or sump'm?"

"No," said Thing. "We're good." He turned to Pugsley, still smiling. "See them all nice and clear, Pugs?"

"Sure, I—but why?"

"If you see them, do your job then."

"What job?"

"Yo, dis ain't a cool place to stop, homes!"

"Do it now, I said!" Thing sprayed him with saliva.

"Do what!"

Thing sighed and shook his head as the group approached even more closely and the lead kid was bearing down on the car.

"Gun them all down," he said in a clearly perceptible whisper. "Please."

Pugsley sweated, swallowed hard and did exactly as he was told, popping off the last little girl as she tried pathetically to run away, her pink shirt nearly riding up over her head as she died. You did things like this in the Family when they came up. You didn't question and you didn't hesitate. If you did, you never made another move again.

Pugsley got out of the car and finished her off as she lay squealing on the ground. Then he hit them all again with the Glock until the clip was empty. Thing wheezed with satisfaction, thought about it for a moment, then got out of the car.

Reading him, Pugsley handed Thing the Glock with fresh rounds and watched him cross the broad, chopped up street until he reached the two winos adding their commentary to the rumbling urban undercurrent of noise. They were laughing and talking trash. Thing gave them each a five, then, as they slobbered gratitude, blew their heads off, each shot sinking into the ancient brick behind them.

He crossed back and stood over the children, surveying them.

They lay in a bloody, twisted heap of immature and gangly limbs.

Thing made sure to put a bullet in each of their heads just before the Galaxy pealed off and drove away.

———

Null and Boyd left together but separately.

Boyd was released from her private hospital stay after completing the inpatient phase of Detox. She would follow up with outpatient treatment at Charles River under Dr. Crochet. The one file pertaining to her medication and inpatient therapy remained sealed in his office and secured as unavailable in the electronic patient file queue. She had lost ten or so pounds and her hands shook more than ever, but her eyes were clear. Her complexion went to a tone of gray no amount of makeup that she applied could conceal, or even ameliorate. Rather than going home, she went right to work, or more precisely, straight to the Ashburton Place office of Inspector Phillip LaCuna.

She waited two hours to see him, opening and closing her fists with a faded issue of *Woman's Day* magazine in her lap.

LaCuna lumbered in from a meeting, eyed her wearily and gestured for her to follow him into his office after doing the secretarial stroke and cursory message check with his receptionist, the niece of a city councilman. "Word gets out, doesn't it?" He kicked the door shut with the side of his shoe and it made an unexpectedly resonant slam.

"It always does. So, you know I'm dried out? I don't have to show you my paper?"

"Oh, by all means!" he said clapping his hands and sitting back in his chair, leering at the picture window view of the Boston afternoon skyline behind him. "I would never deprive you of the opportunity to lay more paperwork on me."

Boyd thrust it at him and he laid it unread upon his desk over a clot of files.

"So you know then?"

"Pretend I don't."

"Okay, ArtyMarty just appointed himself a nice, female-friendly police commissioner, which means you get to get away with more whiny power plays. The mandate is a "tie-goes-to-the runner" attitude, Boyd, your favor. Think of it as found money."

"I'm reinstated."

"The paper says you're clean and sober, for today, at least, so how could I not? The new commissioner will be relieved to hear that Boston's first female OC Task Force head is back in her respective saddle."

"Don't be such a sore loser, Phil, I'm not so bad. Don't take it so hard."

"I don't take it hard, Lieutenant, but you will."

"Why should I? Things are getting back on track."

"Indeed they are. You're now lead on the homicide investigation regarding our mystery perp likes to whack out members of the Family."

"Well, that makes it easier."

"Or not," countered LaCuna. "You didn't hear?"

"No, I didn't hear. I was in detox at Charles River until this morning."

"You're gonna wish you stayed. Seems your dead guy perp took out a gang of neighborhood kids last night."

"That's not like—"

"Know anyone else uses Glock nine millimeter rounds, Teflon-filled copper stoppers? Armor piercing, the kind that explode and leave some ugly holes like these?" LaCuna tossed crime scene photos in an ugly spread across his desk. Children—mutilated, blown apart and ripped up wherever the rounds hit just like the soldiers of the Family.

Boyd jumped back, repulsed. "Oh, God."

"Welcome back, Lieutenant."

————

Missy had finished sponging down the emaciated Null and frowned at him. He looked gray and deathly, only the keloid scars, all of which were pinkish, showing any kind of vibrant life. Yet he was as assured, alert and rested-seeming as a professional baseball player fresh from a massage. "You should probably stick around for at least another day, not that I really want to have you."

Spindly, swollen hands with crabbed, uneven fingers traced his injuries, checking the integrity of his form. He was silent for a minute, checking, visibly processing.

"No, I'm fine. Ready to go."

"It's your funeral and I see you're in a wicked hurry to get there."

"I was once. Now I'm taking my time sending those there who need to go."

"You're not dead, so I don't get the drama."

Null stood up and did his strangled walk over to his clothes, removed an object from the inner lining pocket of his overcoat. He loped back to where Missy was sitting, grabbed her hand with a strength that shocked her and pressed it into her palm. He withdrew his hand and she examined what looked like a folded piece of paper.

It was a folded, crumpled picture postcard, from Tahiti. It had been rough-handled, dog-eared, spider webbed cracks and venous wrinkles worked all through the once tawdry brilliant photo emulsion of beach-scape rendering the image garbage. She carefully smoothed it out, sensing it might be some kind of precious artifact.

It was.

Missy looked at it, her head bowed in concentration, reading what must have been writing.

Her head hung there long after reading, as if she were still trying to make it out.

Moisture dripped from her face as her head stayed where it was and her body refused to move. Droplets came down fast off her nose and chin.

Tears.

The postcard read, roughly, in a personally unpolished scrawl.

"I can't do it! I WON'T do it! There is a way—"

Way took up most of the card.

The rest was saturated by a dank brownish rust color.

Blood.

"Not his last words by any means," said Null, naked and unfazed. "I believe his last words were, and I'm quoting verbatim. 'Clean living is my friend.'"

She looked up, trembling, puffy-eyed and suppressing sobs. "What the fuck does that mean?"

"It means he had no tolerance for heroin, so I could use the bit they gave me to cool him out permanent, put him out of his misery like a damaged racehorse."

"You fucking killed him!" She didn't charge at him but remained in the chair facing the cot with its IV setups where Null had lain for at least a week.

"You know better than that. You know what the Family does. There wasn't much left of him when I gave him the stuff. It was his choice. He wanted it and I helped him. Euthanasia, they call it."

"You're lying!" Now the tears came down and she didn't even bother to wipe them away.

"Do you want me to describe how he looked with one arm ripped out of its socket and his legs cut off—"

"No!' She screamed this standing up, "No, don't!" then took a breath, recovered hard and asked, "Gomez—he's the one gives the orders, the one in charge."

"That's true. He makes the decisions." Null grabbed his clothes and dressed slowly in the oncoming shadows of the dying sunset, the Boston late fall bloody-corpse sky.

"He's the one ordered Nat dead."

"No one else would have cared."

"Fine," she said, getting rid of the IV set ups and stripping the cot. "I helped you, so you can help me."

"Don't ask for the moon, Missy. People around here have a tendency to do that, until it comes crashing down on them."

"I'll ask for anything I fucking want!" she shrieked.

"So ask then."

"Gomez, I want him. I want you to give him to me. Alive. That son of a bitch is all mine."

"You want to kill him?"

Her glazed eyes hardened and locked. "Bad."

Null froze for a moment like a stalled animatronic mechanism, his face leering distorted in the shadows like a dented plastic Jack o' Lantern.

"Deal," he said, and it was almost as if he had smiled.

TWENTY-ONE

The wind blowing through the cracked-open streets of Mattapan smelled like sour milk yet was icy. Chalk lines, crime-scene tape and a surly uniformed detail adumbrated the latest disaster of poverty, neglect, social stricture and rock-ribbed American tribal primitivism at its most complex. The entire block of Walk Hill Street heading to Babson Street across Blue Hill Avenue was demarcated by beat detail uniforms marking time until ArtyMarty could come and give a unity speech, heading off potential looting and rioting Haitians, Barbadians, Dominicans and the lumpen racial underclass quotient herded to live the way the Irish lived in South Boston over a century ago. District D-83 was always a problem, with its drugs, gang-shootings, random rapes, drive-by's and silly cacophonies of muddled and often lethal violence.

Now it was a liability for the mayor, who had set up a meet and greet with the denizens of Mattapan, replete with security snipers where he would further trumpet the appointment of the new female-friendly commissioner, known now amongst the ranks as "Buffalo Bill."

Boyd had until noon the next day to work the scene, get it canvassed, and lock it down for the "community healing" ceremony.

Even Mattapan residents weren't slow to use the outrage of a gang of murdered kids to suck funds off an already strained fiscal budget for the city. And the bad part was, nobody would blame them, at least for a few weeks. Lawsuits were looming and the press was already happily gunning for ArtyMarty but had yet to make a move on Buffalo Bill. Even the Herald was playing it cute, looking for the best time to rip up the city's new no-longer interim commissioner.

Boyd had a laugh at that, having known Buffalo Bill from her own academy days.

Bill had teeth, no fear of using them and a fair set of brains behind the teeth that set them hard with a mechanistic ambition that had come up from the street. He had ripped more than a few in his time and weathering the Herald's Murdochian hype-o-smear was nothing compared to greasing and pleasing the backchannel ward-healing machinery that got him where he was today.

Bill and ArtyMarty still set the agenda.

The quicker the case was cleared, the quicker and more pain-lessly those weeks would pass. What could be better than making the thing less about gangs and more about organized crime, espe-cially when the head of Boston's nationally known OC Task Force was a woman—a woman of whom it could be said had paved the way for more women of command rank on the force?

It don't get much better, thought ArtyMarty, as he put the squeeze on the seniors just below the new commissioner.

"Come to gloat, have we?" This from a dour Byron Wurdalaka, standing by with Yonah Shimmel and his scurrying band of crimi-nalists.

"You bet your sweet ass we have," Boyd said, humorless.

"Look at me," he said, indicating the diligent forensic crew with a sarcastic sweep of his arm. "I'm the Pied Piper of freakin' Hamelin!"

"Stop blowing jazz then and tell me what you know about rats and children," said Boyd, grateful they had cleared the corpses away, dismayed by the stink and the stains. Her eyes were watering.

Shimmel exchanged glances with Boyd, working like a demon on his knees collecting shell casings.

"So, you're in charge now—it doesn't matter. This case sucks and if I could get off it, I would."

"Sour grapes, Byron. You know it's got career-maker written all over it and if you could knock me off and run the case into the ground in your usual cronied-up hack-like way, you would."

"You act like being cronied up is a bad thing when everybody's cronied up, LT, including you, as we can see from the incoming commissioner."

"That's right, Byron, stick to what you know and who you blow. And who you can't. So what do you say happened here?"

"I say our boy has branched out into drug revenge slayings. You don't do an execution in this neck of the woods without it being all about drugs. And you don't do kids like this unless it's payback for a serious burn. I'd run down mommies, daddies, uncles and such."

"Nice of you to finally admit it's OC."

"Gang-related maybe," Wurdalaka grunted.

"Fiddlesticks," Boyd countered.

"Guy was seen too. "He pointed. "Took out two winos suckin' sterno over there across the street. Had no problem whatever doing even crappy potential witnesses to make his life easier."

"Why wasn't it two guys?"

Shimmel piped up: "Kay, from the amount of shell casings, it could have been three or four. Whoever it was, definitely was into overkill, same as the other times, sure, but with one essential difference: no bruises, no marks of impact whatever, just exploding Teflon dum-dum rounds. The postmortem wounds to the cranium are interesting. A new wrinkle if it's the same guy, because our guy never left a scene without getting in a little hands-on action with at least one of the vic's."

"So, you got precise headshots through front of the skull, targeted. It's not like it means anything."

"But he didn't do that to the winos, did he?"

"Well, they wouldn't resist as much as kids, now would they?"

"No," said Boyd thoughtfully. "Maybe as much as dead kids might, though. Remember, he shot them postmortem."

"What the fuck difference does it make? It's the same guy who's doin' the family. He just widened his field of victim selection is all." Wurdalaka's rum-blossomed cheeks were flushed pink with exasperation.

Shimmel looked wan and somewhat lost in his expression as his words, aimed straight at Wurdalaka, found their mark. "The traces say otherwise, Detective. He was correcting the other guy. Doing clean up."

"Leaving this many corpses ain't too clean."

"Cleaner than you think," Shimmel parried, trying to sound assertive and failing. "There were less rounds fired into the winos than into the kids and none of them fired into the winos weren't killshots. The rounds that went into the kids—they were all over the place like the guy was nervous and maybe only half-looking. What does it tell you?"

"It tells me one of them was an apprentice, or an assistant of some kind," said Boyd. "He was correcting the work of the trainee."

"Exactly!" enthused Yonah, at the top of his game, doing what he did best, showing up an abusive Boston PD thug with science and reason. "We can all agree that no one walks away from a properly delivered headshot—survivability is nil. So, it's an educated guess that the assistant did the kids, the maestro took stock then grabbed the gun from him and ran across the street to silence the winos he caught out of the corner of his eye. Then he hustled back and planted definitive killshots in the frontal lobe of each of the kid's brains to make sure the apprentice's work stuck."

Wurdalaka eyed the criminalists wearily, as they snatched and bagged every candy wrapper, cigarette butt, wad of chewing gum and any detritus they came upon within the yardage of killing. Effeminate, emaciated Yonah Shimmel almost looked smug and Wurdalaka almost caved in his face for it. "Listen, LT, why don't you get Buffalo Bill to give Shimmel here his gold shield so he can take this case and I can finally go off shift and get some sleep?"

"Because the world's an unfair place, Byron, and even political appointments won't change that."

"Okay, I know you're right because I still wind up working for you."

"That's right, and since you do, you're going to have to help me reconcile the fact that somebody who would allow himself to be tortured and nearly killed all to make sure we would have a decent shot at rescuing a bunch of kids from the clutches of the Family's KP set-up suddenly turns around and murders a fucking group of them for no apparent reason!"

She was breathing hard, letting the adrenaline block the urge to vomit.

"I don't work from the theory that it's your dead guy, DQ whatsisface. I don't do science fiction."

Boyd studied his haggard, defiant face. She knew he just got off pulling a double and so, regrettably, this was the time to hit him, like that first opportunity to lock eyes with an unruly pet dog.

"You work from any theory I tell you, or your career's science fiction. So, find me a reason why this fits."

"You're good on politics, Boyd. How's this for a reason: This embarrasses the city—the Mayor's office and the PD—a guy we can't catch up 'til now doin' our policing for us goes and whacks uninvolved kiddies in the most politically embarrassing neighborhood in Boston."

"I'll bite, Byron. Why does it fit?"

"It fits where it always fits. Who benefits? The Boston Redevelopment Authority's urban *greenscape* push, stalled but now gets big momentum, the Mayor's umpteenth new urban outreach program has a purpose, lawyers for lawsuits, the press—they all get their piece. But who really takes it on the chin?"

"We do," said Boyd, grasping it. "BPD."

"That's right. LT, we're being spanked."

"Punished?"

"You know, with all this politicking going on, reminds me about what my father said about Nixon. I used to laugh at it, but now I don't."

"I don't need folksy wisdom, just an investigator with a brain."

"He said, 'Whenever you finally get a handle on whatever sneaky low shit the Republicans are up to, they always cry conspiracy theory. Those are the magic words that make any complicated intent disappear'—well my father was a Democrat and a cop, so was his father, and so am I. And I'm telling you, I know a blowjob when I see one, and this definitely has the look of major league blowjob."

"You lost me."

"Whether you like it or don't, LT, I'm workin' Family ties on this one, and that means the department's included. Whoever pulled the trigger and placed the shots, this homicide's payback for a Family double-cross. Somebody somewhere didn't hold up his end."

"This is a different direction than I see the investigation heading."

"Maybe. But you don't have much better to go on with your dead perp theory, do you? It ain't washing too good."

"You're saying this is a police corruption case?"

"You're being naïve. I'd never say a thing like that."

Nausea and need suddenly came thundering down upon her and she blurted it out, weathering a wave of unexpected pain. "So then, what the fuck are you saying?"

"LT, LT, I figured you'd at least get it by now, being you got that woman's sensitivity/intuition/moon goddess thing going for you." He drew satisfaction from the imminent cloudburst darkening Boyd's face and smirked, telegraphing who was really in charge.

"I'm saying your dead guy isn't coming after the Family at all."

"No?"

"That's right, LT. He's coming after us."

———

Ophelia was in the bathroom off the master bedroom of her Federalist three-story on Belmont Hill off Pleasant Street, putting on her elaborate KISS-style rock-club face when she thought she heard a noise, then dismissed it.

Blonde, pale, thin yet shaped hard, Sophie "Ophelia" Thalberg was an astonishing surgical bombshell who, despite compounded surgery upon surgery, simply could not remove the look of surprise from her face. She covered that look with layers of makeup and the overlay darkness of the rock clubs on Lansdowne Street. She was a Geri-Goth, a club cadet pushing fifty with the shape and aspect of a college kid and the penetrating sense of purpose of a trial lawyer, which she also was.

She had that dogged commitment to false premises that produces the absurd conclusion that did nothing but benefit guilty clients and confuse even the most politically jerry-rigged Suffolk

County Superior or District courtroom. As a criminal defense attorney, she was a resounding success. As a person of the type she experienced every day in her mind's eye, she was on her way.

Finally, after twenty-odd years of struggle, she was going to get her twenties down right. She was going to live the life she watched the privileged live while she slaved away her twenties and thirties positioning herself to be what others simply were by birth and luck: a hip, hedonistic glam-rock personality living the high life surrounded by the right elements of the low life.

She had everything but the rock, and she would get that soon enough.

The Family was muscling her into the media distribution end and she was taking night classes in entertainment law at Harvard Law, which itself comprised its own body of entertainment law. Gangsters, groupies, guitars and glamour—this was the blood and substance of Ophelia's life and her recipe for storming the rock and roll world. Criminal law was just a day-job, a gig, the means to an end that would have her living the glam rock life somewhere in Europe as the presiding Hecate-like eminence over a brood stable of cavern-chested skank boy rockers, the kind she liked to frolic with in bed.

And she could, in that well-ruminated upon dream scenario, squawk the lead song in tortured histrionics onstage from time to time as her skank-boys wailed.

Ophelia had begun life on the hopeless boulevard of the busted, the Lynnway in Lynn, (Lynn, Lynn city of sin, they sang). Unwanted as are so many, she was used and exploited by damaged parents, Lou and Clio, failed beatniks and maintenance substance abusers awash in drug sales and the loose under-culture of its true-believing middlemen. Plain, quiet, fearful and as shyly conservative as her parents were boisterously Bohemian, Sophie grew up working. She was cook and laundress at home, class grind at school, maniacally fighting for the business of grades, and typical teen slave at a myriad of part-time jobs where she was distrusted and given only the most demeaning of tasks. There was a younger brother who never had to work, who was better loved than she and so, who predictably enough died when she left her teens of a well-precipitated speedball overdose that froze his heart and fried his brain. Being loved less had saved her life—her parents simply didn't consider her worthy of joining their special privileged lifestyle that eventually landed them in a drugless Boise, Idaho rental in the WITSEC, the Federal Witness Protection Program after finking on every heavy supplier they ever knew.

All this was explained to her by a Federal Marshal named Tote Fearing, with her parents' contact specifics left out. He had put his job on the line to do it, but he was old school. You just don't leave your daughter permanently without some kind of explanation, a word of goodbye. The explanation was both general and real as the word of goodbye and tearful wishes was too specific and entirely fabricated.

Ophelia, twenty, slaving her way through the accelerated program at U Mass Boston, to somehow claw her way into a better school, seduced him. She took the older, hard-bodied, grizzled Marshal, by way of experimentation, reward, and to settle some of the urgent Daddy issues looming over her nearly untried sex life. It was as if she knew exactly what she was doing, her instincts were so strong at that moment.

She was telling her parents in no uncertain terms to fuck off.

It wasn't too long after that both parents were executed with shotgun blasts to the face on an Idaho drug burn they compulsively orchestrated somehow gone wrong.

What had gone wrong was the long memory for faces of the network of suppliers.

Then Marshal Fearing introduced her to the secret places, private lofts, VIP settings, the after-hours nightlife beyond the transitory rock clubs for kiddies, and to Gomez Gomelsky, who always had an eye for talent. Fearing handed her off to Gomez—partial payment for some service Ophelia already surmised—who then set her up with a nicer apartment, a better monthly income, and more parties than she could conceive of there ever having been in dowdy, conservative, thug-drunk cozened old Boston. All she had to do was hold her breath for a few minutes once a week and have sex with him.

It was Gomez who financed Villanova Law School, lubed up the leverage to dunk her into the Harvard Law program, costing her the two years credits she had there, but gaining her something else: She no longer had to fuck Gomez for her basic comforts.

All she had to do was represent him.

And now, that's all she did.

That and her weekend clubbing, her coterie of starving feral rock 'n' roll leather boys, logboy rejects from the past made bad, just how she liked them—convenient toys for her as she had once been for Gomez, but they lacked the true fire she had possessed from day one to parlay being a toy into a game all its own. She would run the game before she was through, no matter how funny the balls rolled.

God, however, has a sense of humor almost no one can appreciate, as we are all ultimately the butt of it.

Ophelia didn't know it yet, but the time had come for her to quit.

She should have known it when she looked up and saw the overcoated figure with the damaged face staring at her from her bathroom doorway, but it just didn't sink in.

"Going out?" asked Null.

TWENTY-TWO

Ophelia went for her dignity against the terror that the scarred and repulsive figure at the door had anything at all to do with her day gig, that he was in any way connected with the stone criminal freaks she had to defend to make her nut. Look at him, though—the scars, the utter cold set of the vacant eyes and chin! How could he not? Ophelia trembled at the sink and let limp hands with black enameled nails drop her eyeshadow applicator into the copper basin.

"I asked you a question," Null observed. He was covered with sweat, his face had little bloody scrapes and was flushed, but his breathing and expression said dead calm.

She was in a black lace camisole that would have looked so come hither beneath her taut-waisted open collared plastic leather tunic and matching toreador pants, had she made The Roxy earlier. Now, caught half-dressed in panties and camisole at the sink, she looked improbably vulnerable—a hard, aging Barbie gone wan and pallid with fear. She froze even as Null seemed frozen.

She had spent vast sums of money to possess the perfect décolletage, the cleavage of the ripest 23-year-old at age forty-four, and she wasn't going to ignore any chance to work it, even at this suspect moment. She flashed Null, feigning icy allure as her mind raced to find a path to safety—a way to remove herself from what was coming.

Null blinked once, looking like a disinterested lizard in the desert.

Ophelia's eyes darted about, assessing a move to make, a chink in the situation through which she might crawl. She stopped when she noticed Null was watching her eyes, somehow evaluating and anticipating her thoughts. Her skin crawled when she thought, *He's comfortable with this. He's done it many times before.*

"This is breaking and entering," she exhaled affected smoothness, resuming her make up after fumbling in the sink for it. She did her eyes with quick, little stabbing motions.

"No, I just walked in."

"Burglary too."

"I didn't take anything."

She sized him up and let out a scream she thought would put him off balance. It didn't.

"Anton!"

"I don't think he heard you."

"He heard me alright. He takes his time, does Anton. A pro never rushes."

"He's your security?"

Calm slowly flooded back to her like the blood to her cheeks. She would leech away control of the situation in the next few minutes. Meanwhile, she let her considerable chest fall a bit with a sigh of relief. This one was probably gay anyway. Not the rarest thing anymore, gay hitters.

"Oh, he's more than that. If you knew who I was working for, you'd be on your way out the window about now." She smiled, taking the upper hand. "Know anything about guns?"

"A little. I'm new to them. You aim, point and shoot, allow for kickback, don't miss."

"Well, Anton carries a forty-four Magnum Desert Eagle, the largest, most powerful semi-automatic in the world, cocked and locked. And if his aim isn't always the best, he likes to get up close enough to you so that doesn't really matter. You know, you have to ask yourself: Maybe he's standing behind you right now?"

Null shrugged, leaning against the doorjamb, experiencing the cool of the paint without feeling it. "Maybe, but he isn't."

Wild-eyed and lustful with unease: Now or never. "Turn around and look!" she screamed to jar him into a false move, get him to lose focus on her so she could twist away. He cocked his head thoughtfully.

As if reaching for a cigarette, Null pulled the Desert Eagle from the inside pocket of his overcoat, extended his arm and nudged her cheek with the muzzle. "Now you know I can't turn around and put this gun to your head at the same time, right?"

"I can't—"

"Can't what?"

"—Can't argue that." She began to shiver and not from the draft or her state of semi-dress. It was the knowledge of what was coming next.

Null pressed the gun hard to her cheek to confirm this. "We're at condition zero. Did Gomez teach you what that was?"

"I don't—"

"I do. I'm new to guns, but it goes something like this: Condition One is cocked and locked; Condition Two is hammer down with a round in the chamber; Condition Three is a loaded magazine, empty chamber; Condition Zero, though, is as close as it gets: a round in the chamber, hammer cocked, the safety disengaged." He made an impression on her cheek with the muzzle of the gun. "That's where we are now."

"And where Anton is, is dead, right?"

Null reached behind and dragged the body into the bathroom, dropping it by the scarlet painted toes of her pale bare feet. "He's right here." Anton's body left a skid of blood that beaded up on the tile. He made it look like the two hundred thirty-pound thug was a straw dummy.

Ophelia jumped back on the edge of the sunken bathtub. She had instantly been transformed into a gangly, knock-kneed teenager with a desperate urge to pee. She danced nervously in place.

"He made mistakes, a few bad moves. He wasn't really ready for serious security for the Family's lead counsel. But then, it wasn't necessary for him to be any good, was it? Who in their right mind would go after a defense attorney, a civilian? But then, as you know, I'm not in my right mind."

"Who are you?"

"The last of Joseph Xavier Null, Jr."

"I don't know you."

"Of course you do. You know who I am and why I'm here."

Unselfconsciously, she removed her panties, sat down and peed. Null evaluated every move and allowed her to do this without asking, it being the natural thing to do in a bathroom. She watched him watching—abandoning with a sigh the tiny hope that he would avert his eyes the way all these parochial criminals did. It wasn't happening. The story was right there in his eyes: dead, slightly dusty lenses in a surveillance camera set-up, missing nothing.

"You take liberties."

"If you're going to kill me, at least I can get some relief before or during or whatever."

"There's no if about it. Mistakes have their price. Anton would tell you that. If he could."

She pulled up her panties, stood and flushed, then ducked beneath Null's arm, stepping into the huge master bedroom with the picture window and patio balcony. She tripped over Anton's arm and went tumbling forward. By the time she stood and righted herself, Null was there with the gun at her neck.

"I don't know anything, honest! Please! I'm just a lawyer. I do court stuff! That's it!"

"That's enough." He coaxed the gun into her weakly unwilling mouth. "You keep getting Gomez, Fester and the rest of the crew off with every trick at your disposal. You'll do anything and they make you rich while you do it. You're an invaluable help to the Family. You coordinate their overall defense and they gave you a three-shift law firm all your own in Back Bay with which to do it. You're a phenomenal legal linchpin that needs pulling to crash the Family wagon. So, I'm pulling you."

Null thought about it, removed the barrel of the Desert Eagle from her mouth and pushed her away toward the four-poster bed of wrought iron, muslin and a black satin reverse duvet.

"You're going to kill me because I'm good at what I do?"

"Yes. Now get dressed, and not in the gear you were planning to wear. No clubbing for you tonight."

She did a strip tease in reverse for Null, starting with a wonder-bra, working her way up to boots, black denim jeans and a blinding white starched riding blouse buttoned up to the neck. Ophelia added the schoolmarm touch by putting on her distance glasses with the Louis Vuitton frames. She felt this might drive home the helpless victim role enough to give her an opportunity to either bolt from him or somehow stick a knife into him. She was ticking off locations of convenient weaponry in her head even as she was changing. Ah yes, she remembered as she was forcing on the right snakeskin Nocona boot. The left one had a nice, long protective stiletto in a pocket of the lining. All she had to do was bend over and thrust up at exactly the right moment. Goody.

"Why kill me?"

"It's more orderly. Final. That's all."

"I believe you. I don't think you do it because you like it, you do it because you determine it's necessary to achieve an effect, get a result."

"You could say."

"So, cut to the chase, Mr. Null. What's the result you want?"

"The result I want is what life would be like if you were dead."

She was sweating but at the same time getting it. "You want me unable to represent the Family—to just disappear. In a word, default."

"That would be the point. Unable to conduct Family business ever again, even if you wanted to."

"End my professional life for good."

"That's right."

"How about I end yours instead?" She ducked down in a clumsy spasm and went up at him with the blade as fast as she could, but the knife wound up flying to one side of the room while she flew off to the other when he knocked her flat with a savage backhand. Null stepped toward her and lowered the gun to her face for a clean head shot.

"No!" she screeched. "I'll do it, I'll quit. I won't be an attorney anymore!"

"Really."

"Yes, I'll default at the next hearing without filing for an extension or even leaving word with the clerk's office. I'll just fucking vanish. It will be exactly as if I had died suddenly."

"You'll leave town—the entire east coast, in fact."

"I will."

"Tonight. Now. At this exact moment. No packing, no preparation, no goodbyes."

"Just my car, wallet and keys. Hit, git and split."

"Don't forget your credit cards."

"What? Why the fuck do you care?"

"I want them to track you and know you fucked them over. I want bench warrants issued against you in this state."

"If I disappear the way we're describing, you'll get them."

"I'm killing your career, but you get to live."

"That's about the size of it."

"Interesting. What will you do with the rest of your life?"

"How the fuck should I know?"

Null fired three rounds abruptly into the wall next to her. "This is a rock 'n' roll weapon, I think. Loud, fast and out of control."

Shivering and covered with plaster, wood splinters and bits of paint, Ophelia sobbed.

"I think you should work with kids. Daycare maybe. It doesn't pay much, but they say it's rewarding. Maybe you'll try that?"

"I will!" she screamed with penitence that started as trumped up and ended genuine. "I really will."

"If you don't, I'll have to fix the mistake by fixing you. And I will find you. I'm funny that way, you know?"

"I—I'm not laughing. No—I'm not."

Null fired all around her again to make his point, emptied the clip, tossed the Eagle aside, crouched down to her level and said, "Laughing? You should be leaving."

She stood as if in a dream rather than in shock. "You're right. I should be. Thanks." She remembered to grab her wallet and keys. She turned and stared at him, confused. "Why didn't you kill me when I went at you with the knife?"

"It wasn't the best moment. You could have had things to tell me I might need to know. Like where the Family's new KP set up is."

Without missing a beat, she replied, "It's in Attleboro, on the third floor of the same warehouse across from the PD where the *Paddleboro* sex club was busted. They're working a lightning strikes theory there backed by payouts."

"You're useful. I should keep you around."

"No, you were right. I should be leaving."

"Just as well. This practicing having human feeling, affecting affect, is physically taxing. I think I might actually be tired."

"You don't know?"

"No, and the only way of finding out is to make a mistake with you. This makes killing you more attractive."

She shook her head slowly, 'no' like a contrite child.

Null removed a tin of charcoal starter from his coat, squirted it about the room quickly and liberally. He tossed a match onto it and the flames bloomed wildly.

"Are you insane?"

"Yes. Clinically, I think."

"What the hell are you doing to my home!"

"Removing temptation. I want to make sure you have absolutely nothing to come back to."

They had to both leap from the balcony to keep from being engulfed by the fast spreading flames. Her house was like a giant red carnation blossoming against the sky.

And even though she had broken her leg in the fall, Ophelia crawled to the Lexus and didn't stop driving until she hit Brownie, Kentucky, where she had to pull over because a tire blew in the midst of a speed trap. The officers ran her and—to her relief—she found that she had managed thus far to outrun a five-state bulletin. They helped her change the tire.

Otherwise, she would have kept on driving.

In her mind's eye, she still saw the shadow of Null stretching long across her lawn.

Watching.

TWENTY-THREE

The middle-aged, stooped-seeming figure in the Burberry trench coat huddled to itself in the gray cold morning as it approached the main entrance to the vast, squat, pavement gray James Michael Curley Senior Residences and Community Center. The figure had no problem getting through security and one of the jeans and pullover sweater psych major types cheerfully showed him where he could find who he was looking for.

Sure, their faces registered a hesitation born of disgust, but Theron LeCoeur always liked to look on the positive side that his warped looks were "striking."

He wasn't wrong about this. He was so striking in the ugliness of his leering deformity that he had become known as the face that confused a thousand sketch-artists. ID-ing him seemed beyond most Identikit men, as no one could agree on just what he looked like and what precise shape his weirdly unsettling visage took.

They saw him coming in, so they'd be sure to see him coming out. And why not? He was always especially calm and serene after a job. No need not to make a relaxed exit if he did what he had to do correctly. In fact, it was essential in remaining unmemorable.

He pressed the button, which produced a poorly simulated recreation of an old-fashioned doorbell. An old guy, pushing seventy or eighty, in a maroon cardigan sweater, slicked back yellow silver hair, jutting belly standing over six feet even with slumped posture, filled the doorway after abruptly yanking the door open. Thing smiled, which made his face look like a parasitic sucker in search of purchase.

"What the Christ do you want—? "The man stopped himself and whispered: "Jesus, Mary and Joseph, what the hell do we have here?" not caring if the shorter figure before him heard this or not. "What can I do for you, boyo, you collecting for something? March of Dimes, Jerry's Kids? What's the tragedy of the week?"

Thing's eyes narrowed.

It was clear beneath a lisping sibilance: "No, sir, I'm just looking for a friend. You know Joey X, right?"

The flabby, florid face puckered into a sneer. "Oh, it's like that, is it? Well, I can't help you."

"You're Eamon Cuchulainn aren't you?"

"I said no sale buddy boy, so blow." He was about to shove the heavy pressboard door closed until Thing dangled a fresh hundred before him. The man snatched and pocketed it in the twinkling of a brown toothed smile.

"Can I come in, Mr. Cuchulainn? Please?"

"Of course, boyo and call me Jimmy. Everyone around here in this god forsaken place does."

It was the impoverished apartment of a drunken old reprobate underwritten by the Commonwealth. A discomfort zone of newspapers, magazines and The Racing Form draped over every piece of old cheap matchstick furniture, which also served as the resting place for an assortment of coffee cups, whiskey glasses and plates chock-a-block with the stale debris of old food. The place had the stench of beer-soaked loneliness and cigarette infused brooding. "Take a load off, boyo and sit ye down. You a drinkin' man? Care for a tall, cold one?"

"No, I'm fine. You go ahead." He stood sizing up every corner of the dumpy living room, checking behind the doors of the other rooms as Jimmy rooted through the refrigerator in the kitchenette at the far end of the room for a beer.

"Just as well," said Jimmy, his head still stuck in the refrigerator. "I think there's only half a one left anyways."

The bedroom and bathroom, filthy as they were, were clear. The half-room off the kitchenette was stocked too full with clutter and busted up baseball and beer promo memorabilia for him to be concerned about. Jimmy stood up from the refrigerator with a grunt and downed a half-filled bottle of Carling Black Label. He plopped down into a threadbare La-Z-Boy set before an old, obsolete Zenith TV.

"Okay, laddy-buck, what can I do you for? Are you going to introduce me to our friend Benjamin's brothers and cousins and if so, who do I have to kill for you to do it?"

Thing laughed and Jimmy joined him, connecting. The grim day was looking up.

"I just need to know about your nephew, Joey X."

Jimmy frowned and spat. "That miserable shite—he ain't my nephew. Just the son of some drunken whore I used to waste me time with. Now there's an apple didn't fall very far from the tree."

"Fall?"

"Sure, he hit the pavement of Grove Hall when he was old enough to walk and kept right on runnin'—runnin' his mouth, runnin' lookout, runnin' drugs."

"Were you close?"

"I tried to be—tried to steer that boy in some direction."

"But he was a problem."

"Destined for failure, that one, despite my best efforts."

"Mind if I confirm a few things about Joey X with you?"

"You're no friend of Joey's are you, Mr.—"

"Just somebody who pays to know. No, I suppose not. And I see there's no love lost between you and your nephew as well."

"That boy was never my blood. He's trash." Cuchulainn tossed the bottle into an empty box of six pack cardboards with a threatening thud. He eased back in the Lay-Z-Boy for the ride.

"So, now that we have some preliminaries out of the way, can I confirm a few things with you?"

"And why would you be wanting to do that?"

"You know the bible, Jimmy. Know thine enemy?"

"So, it's like that, is it?"

"Yes, it's like that."

"Well, sonny boy, we can go on talkin' like this, but you'll be havin' to duke me another hunnert before we do."

Thing flipped open his Versace wallet, slipped out another note and pressed it hard into Uncle Jimmy's thick sweaty, flaccid palm. Uncle Jimmy held it up to the light, snapped it hard, and cackled before shoving it in his back pocket.

"You moved in and had a thing with Mrs. Null, correct?

Uncle Jimmy blew out his cheeks and shook his head gravely. "No call to be vulgar—it wasn't quite that way, and in this neck of the woods back thirty year-ago single mothers didn't last long without having some kind of man around to fend off the wolves and wild things. I was doing a service—"

"You fucked his mother." LeCoeur let his sucker mouth leer a little and Jimmy caught it. He knew the time for gilding the lily, glossing bullshit on top of pure shit had come and gone. It was pointless and might actually impede another Benjamin falling into his pocket.

"Alright, I'll play. She was a good lay, when she was sober. When she wasn't, well—" Uncle Jimmy chuckled.

"There was the daughter, then."

"That's right. Young and not so fucked up all the time on beer, not so bloated-faced and fat-bellied. You want to measure me Johnson too?"

"Just keep it in your pants for the time being. So, the brother tried to stop you?"

"Little pussy he was—there was I gettin' him the best gainful employment on the street and he wants to bust me wide open for baggin' a little something he himself couldn't get."

"She was what, 11-12?"

"Well, boyo, we don't start 'em much earlier than that."

"No, you have to draw the line somewhere."

"Just so."

"And where did you draw it?"

"Well, discipline must be maintained, and a child needs to know who's in control."

"Meaning? Be clear here, Uncle Jimmy, and the Franklins keep flowing, but I have to be kept satisfied. Know what I'm saying?"

"I helped the boy in a little donnybrook with the law."

"Try that again, Uncle Jimmy. You were running drugs for the Winter Hill gang."

"So I was. Statute of limitations long past, boyo."

"Keep going, Jimmy." LeCoeur's eyes were hard and knowing, mirthless.

"I had the tot busted to keep his ass quiet. I had been a CI myself when DiGrazia was running the show. You make friends, develop longstanding business relationships."

"You were one of Whitey Bulger's fixers, weren't you? Police liaison?"

"When did this suddenly become about me, I wonder?"

"When it became about DQ Null."

"I did nothin' but good for that boy, damn near put his sorry ass into Harvard, and what thanks do I get? He jams me up, kicks me teeth in and runs off with his sister."

Thing's eyes burned and reflected the heat. "So, he loved his sister?"

"Didn't we all, boyo, didn't we all." He started to push himself up from the La-Z-Boy, grunting, "That last little drop was barely enough to wet me whistle. Shall we continue this on the way to the corner package store?"

Thing shoved the big man down hard at his sternum with one arm, standing. "Sit tight, Uncle Jimmy. You can drink your brains out when we're done." He let another hundred feather down to his chest and Uncle Jimmy crossed his hands over it like one of the dead.

"How did you get DQ into Harvard? Full scholarship."

"That bank, The Boston Five—Suffolk Franklin, long since swallowed up, funded the program for underprivileged kids. Underprivileged! Now there's an absurd lie if ever there was one! Anyway, it was Boston Latin that done it and I pushed him into that school, made him study, put his punk ass on the bus every day and picked him up after, all while his drunken mother was runnin' round on me."

"You mean when you were banging her daughter, who acted as a second mother to the kid and was the one put him on the Harvard track. She was a National Merit Scholar before you put her out tricking, right?"

Uncle Jimmy frowned and pouted, sucking the neck of the empty bottle. "You could tell it that way, but I never would. He blew off Harvard for the ponies anyway."

"What about the sister?"

"She died of the AIDS, poor thing. I was so worried I got meself checked and would you believe it? An old scoundrel like me clean as a whistle." He chortled at fate.

"I heard he ran away, started working bagman for Gomelsky's family—"

"Then it was the O'Doyle before that kike came in and fucked it all for fair."

"Right. Anyway, he did that to support the sister in a hospice, where she could die comfortably."

"That's the idiot boychild right there—always looking down in the street hoping a twenty'll blow by, not that he'd ever be fast enough to catch it."

"No, not that he would be."

"Imbecile gave up his life for the dead and dying."

"He was a sentimentalist, you're saying."

"I'm saying he was a stupid, ungrateful cunt, what more do you want?"

"He loved the sister."

"Dead and buried."

"No love lost between you and him though."

"It's all on my side—that little bastard only loved what he couldn't fuck." Uncle Jimmy's face turned red and piggish as the eyes narrowed and the sacks beneath bulged. He threw his head back and laughed in such an incongruous way it almost made Thing jump. "He certainly fucked me, and that's a fact!"

"I had an Uncle Jimmy too, once. You don't really remind me of him, but you're a lot alike."

"Fancy that. Would ya look at the time?"

Thing unfolded his wallet yet again, licked the corners of another hundred-dollar bill and pasted it to the forehead of a smiling, dreamy-eyed Eamon Cuchulainn.

"Oh, you're a card you are, Mr.—"

"Let's keep it anonymous."

Uncle Jimmy hefted his huge flanks up and slid the hundred into his back pocket. "You're paying for the privilege."

"Okay, so we have determined that Null hates child abuse—this is why he's taking out the Family's KP operation."

Uncle Jimmy went white and shot forward in his chair. "He's doing what? I thought he was dead, and you were just too dumb to know it."

"So, you were ready to take money for giving the 411 on a dead guy, when the guy paying you thinks he's still alive?"

Uncle Jimmy shrugged and sputtered a bit. "Well, you never specified."

"True," said Thing. "And we have also determined that, though you're Null's closest living relative of sorts, that he can't stand you. Loathes you, in fact. Wouldn't mind seeing you dead."

"It's a mutual understanding between us. Almost as strong as a blood bond."

"So I gathered."

"Is that it then?"

"Yes, it is. And it's very disappointing."

"That's not my fault."

"No, it's not. And I have to tell you I'm saddened by it."

"You pays your money and you takes your choice in this world."

"Ain't it the truth."

There was a vacuous, discomfiting pause.

Uncle Jimmy, several savvy expressions of wary comprehension traveling across his face at top speed, pushed himself up and forward from the chair, nearly crashing into Thing, who pushed him back effortlessly.

"Stay put, please."

"You're a lot stronger than you look, boyo."

"They tell me that, yes."

"Saddened, you said before? Saddened by what? That you gave me all those hunnerts for essentially nothin'? Well, you won't be takin' 'em back now, you know, so don't try."

Uncle Jimmy, who towered over Thing and outweighed him by

eighty pounds or more, took the same fighting stance as an outraged bull after having confronted the picadors.

"No," said Thing softly, kicking the legs out from under Uncle Jimmy, landing him right back in his chair, blocking his mouth and nose with a small flat square of flexible rubber he kept in his pocket for the purpose. He did this with one hand as he gently pressed down on the carotid artery of Uncle Jimmy's neck with the other. Uncle Jimmy kicked out comically into empty, stale air, which then died away even as Jimmy himself died away, making barely any noise at all, except for a muted, babyish gurgle.

"No," said Thing again with real remorse as he gently removed the hundreds from Uncle Jimmy's pockets. "I just hate giving away a freebie."

TWENTY-FOUR

Sally Wroth was a haggard beauty whose face had been brought down one step lower by the gravity of the situation, or to be precise, the gravity of Wanda "Wednesday" Impetigo demolishing her kitchen.

Wanda's husband, Pugsley, watched, leaning uneasily against a bilious yellow asbestos-tile wall as he picked his teeth with one of his wide, palm-sized throwing knives.

"Stop it," the woman pleaded. "You don't have to do that! I don't know anything."

Wanda heedlessly smashed a pile of mismatched china, sweeping dishes, cups and plates off the lower shelf of a thickly painted open cupboard in an alcove too cramped to hold her entire bulk, making her struggle to reach. The woman sobbed and shakily tried to light a cigarette. Meanwhile, Wanda's immense arms wobbled furiously about the small expanse, taking clocks, pots and cheesy dingy bric-a-brac down to the floor and her rampaging feet.

The cigarette trembled in mid-air, unlit in the woman's pale fingers.

Pugsley lit it for her.

She inhaled deeply and shut her eyes, vainly wishing for all of this to go away.

"Bullshit, Sally," shrieked Wednesday, further trashing the kitchen that the woman no longer wanted to know about. She averted her eyes to the gray Formica of the ancient kitchen table. "You still love your ex—everyone says so. I bet he even comes back here for a little of that dried out old cunt of yours."

Sally stood to argue, but Pugsley knocked her back into the kitchen chair. "You'll sit there first and tell us what we need to know, then you can get up."

"I—I have to pee," she stammered.

"Then do it where you're sittin' in the chair and on the linoleum. Go piss on your own kitchen, because, missy, you're not getting' dick till we know where the scumbag you've been boinking is hiding that soon-to-be-corpse of his." Wednesday frisbeed a dinner plate directly at her head with serious intent. The miss occurred solely due to Sally's twitchy reflexes; the hyper-vigilance of the abused saved her for the moment and for that moment only.

"Close call," observed Pugsley, nearly drowned out by the plate smashing into flinty shards against the circa 1940s double-basined porcelain-enameled sink. She caught it though, just as she caught the throwing knife spinning in the air and landing smoothly in the palm of Pugsley's hand. "Wanda may miss, but I never do."

Sally Wroth stood up, shaking and defiant, angry. She knew no one was coming to pull her out of this one; there would be no last-minute rescue. Why should there be? There never was before. To make matters worse, she had picked a house rental on the outskirts of Medford in the type of neighborhood where everybody had to work, and so nobody was home for blocks and blocks but the insensibly drunk and the hardcore unemployed, like her.

Her roommates all had jobs, but she was a victim of the Bush downturn, of terrorism, globalization and urban class. Her job as a production word processor for a downtown investment bank had been shipped off-shore. Expediency had economically nullified the bridge between a late-30s business degree and the first break to start the course of her professional career.

And the Bush types don't give bridge financing to rehabbed women from Andrew Square.

She had come from where Null had come from—the ossified society of inbred crime and graft, of the street deal and the cheap basic hustle to stay halfway comfortable and intact. She had loved

Null, cared for him after Cassandra died, did scams and scores with him, did drugs with him, married him—

Sally even acquiesced when Null dumped her and pushed her into going back to school, joining the "barney" square-johns of over-earning privilege.

(The barneys were the yogurt and granola fuckups from the suburbs who now ran the entire planet. Rich kids come to Boston to party down and get richer. Moneyed crap artists like Bush.)

Gutter rat, scumball Null was her personal savior.

Null drugged out, doing papers for her, coaching her on assignments, she still didn't understand though she finally got the degree. Null doing half her assignments half in the bag and getting them right.

And now she would rise in the world, albeit late, very late, perhaps in vitro fertilization late, while Null himself would likely sink and die.

If he wasn't already dead. She'd heard the bad rumors and ignored them. Either way, Null was gone so what did it matter?

She knew he wouldn't care if she betrayed him. Hell, he would have insisted upon it. He was that type; dramatically noble in a place and time where only the smooth and the slick using a noble act for self-advancement could be recognized as such.

Wanda smacked her angrily in the back of the head with an immense beefy arm that trembled like jelly when it sent her reeling face first into the stove.

Sally spun about, bloody lipped and dead-eyed, charged into her attacker's immense bulk and began punching away. Wednesday just stood there, shaking her head and looking bored.

"You're gonna need a lot more muscle than that if you want to get a rise out of me, babe," said Wednesday sweetly, then grabbed her arm and threw her into the wall as if playing with a small child. On impact with the wall, Sally dislodged a clock and a large trivet depicting the serenity prayer that exploded on the floor next to her when it hit.

Pugsley poured himself some coffee from the drip maker and made a face showing that it was beneath his taste, though he downed it anyway. His face and protruding ears, slicked back nearly nonexistent hair and small chin all gave him a rat-like aspect as he sniffed at his Museum of Fine Arts mug of coffee.

"If you want to survive this encounter, Sally, you'll hook us up with your ex-hubby and you'll do it sooner rather than later."

"Fucking cow'll do it now or I'll snuff her ass."

"You're a fucking 600-pound horror and you're calling me a cow?"

"I'll be calling you side of beef in a minute if you don't give and give now, bossy."

Pugsley stepped over to where Sally sat splay-legged and dazed on the floor. He nudged the exposed arch of her foot with the steel toe of his motorcycle boot.

"I'd do it if I were you, honey-bunny. I've seen Wednesday like this before. And I can tell you this—someone always gets hurt and hurt bad. And it ain't never Wednesday."

That being said, Wednesday knelt down, smiled, made a move that seemed as though she was about to help Sally up, but punched her in the face instead. It was a massive punch, and it nearly put her out entirely.

Sally wet the floor.

This meant only one thing. Wednesday and Pugsley had to stand there in that grim, now demolished kitchen and mark time waiting for her to recover.

Bored, Wednesday walked over to her husband, hugged him so hard she seemed to be absorbing him with her imposing mass just as an amoeba absorbs some bit of inoculum for sustenance. "This gets me so hot!" she exhaled into his ear.

"I know, pumpkin, but first things first. And remember: Thing is right outside."

She released him with a glum, if not sullen expression, and pushed him away so that he nearly lost his balance as he flailed backwards, barely catching himself. Wednesday was too preoccupied to notice. "Fuck yeah, I forgot that fucking toad was outside. Everything's a pop quiz with this guy. I feel like I'm back in high school."

"I know it sucks, darling, but if we pass, there's a lot of money to be made, so let's make sure we do this one right."

"Because if we don't pass—?"

"Then we'll have to flunk him first before he does the honors on us." Pugsley picked his teeth nervously with the knife.

Wanda's plump face split into a grin: "Well I have a simple plan for him, sweetie, something you like very much that will have him crying for mama and beggin' for mercy."

"Simple plans are best, sweetiekins."

Sally moaned sickly from the floor.

"Oh goodie," squeaked Wanda excitedly, making the room, if not the entire house shake, as she did a little hop up and down, crying, "Party time!"

Pugsley's teeth vibrated.

———

She couldn't take much more, she knew. It seemed that the fat pig had been slapping at her and punching her for hours, if not days, even though it had only been fifteen minutes. Still, fifteen minutes is an awfully long time when you're being persistently beaten by a frowzy, frizzy blonde behemoth in a huge muumuu saturated with the world's loudest floral pattern whose every punch was backed by her 600 odd pounds of blubber and the muscle necessary to heft it all.

"Orchids," she thought when the last punch landed in her face, showing off comets just inches from her corneas. "Psychedelic orchids."

"Tell us, Sally," Pugsley said, dabbing at her face with a napkin. "Where's the fucking mutt?"

Wednesday leveled a punch to her gut, and she heaved over, vomiting bile on the linoleum.

"That's enough, precious."

Wednesday pulled her up from her doubled-over position and slammed her hard into the back of the kitchen chair, which produced a little gasping sound.

"We're not getting anything here, lambie, are we?"

"So far not." Pugsley paced idly about the debris. "Ask her again."

Wednesday shrugged. "I don't think she can take it.

Sally nodded avidly. "He has a place down at Andrew, over Parnell's Karate Studio."

"Been there, trashed that."

Sally looked up, panting; Pugsley held a glass of water to her lips and gave her a drink. She spoke quickly in between panting. "That's all I know. We stopped seeing each other when I started school. Northeastern." She had the urban Boston honk deforming her speech, pronouncing it "Nawth-east-en."

"You loved him so you know more than that."

Sally spat in disgust. "Love's nothing. It fades like a dream. Good for kids, maybe, but that's all. But one day you find you're not young anymore, and then the truth comes home. Love gets you nothin'—that it's all about money, and what it brings you: security, a warm, clean, well-lighted place to be in with a minimum of worry. Compared with that, love just ain't worth a shit."

"Bitter, bitter," laughed Wednesday, giving husband Pugsley a peck on the cheek.

"Fuck you. Love's for the rich and fickle, the well-heeled—fodder for the long con and that's all, brother. Only good thing about it is it makes the lives of the Kennedys miserable, and that's fucking it!" She suppressed a sob and cast her eyes maniacally about the room for any chance, any opportunity at all, that might get her out of this. All she saw was Wednesday's chunky, pallid face blotting out her view. "I don't fucking love him anymore!"

"So we hear, but I bet he still loves you, though, wants to, umm, see you, maybe?" teased Wanda, kissing her cheek.

A tear slid down Sally's face. "I don't know what he does anymore. He left me. Was a time I would have gone with him anywhere—even to detox. Anywhere.

"My fucking heart bleeds."

Sally stood up abruptly, jerked away from the table. "Look, I haven't seen him for years. Joey's small time, he's not in your league, he's just a loser at the track and a family all-purpose short-con bagman. If it wasn't for Joey, I'd be a dead hooker like his sister." Cyanosis had already begun to make a purplish creep across her face from all the previous impact. Her head throbbed with rage and pain.

"Maybe you still will be," leered Wednesday.

"Maybe," she said. "But if that's the case, I can still take one of you with me."

"The fly always does its bravest buzzing stuck in the web. Is that what you want, fly?" Pugsley shook his head, bemused.

"That's what I want," said Sally, and pulled the surprise move of stabbing Wednesday in the ample gut underhand with a serrated steak knife from the last of the Five and Dimes where everything was priced at ninety-nine cents. She fell back, and the chocolate brown handle stuck out from the left side of Wednesday's abdomen like the joystick for a video game, looking to be a seamless part of her until the blood started oozing.

Her face betrayed confused astonishment.

In two steps, Pugsley grabbed the knife from his wife's abdomen. Blood jumped from her in a spurt and Wednesday released a low bellowing of pain.

"Kill the bitch!" screamed Pugsley.

Sally bolted for the door, but Wednesday tackled her to the cluttered floor, grabbed her legs and pulled her beneath her, even as she clawed helplessly at the linoleum to get away. There was no chance. When Sally was finally dragged underneath Wednesday's jiggling mass, and her screams muffled by the enormous weight of her billowing flesh, Wednesday hefted herself up then let herself crash back down hard onto Sally, allowing the full effect of her weight settle in all over her.

Sally was completely engulfed in Wednesday's bulk so you couldn't even see her feet.

Wednesday pressed down hard on Sally, making a high-pitched squeal not unlike the prize pig whose neck is rubbed in a certain way to produce such a whine of delight.

You could see Sally struggling with the rising and falling of Wednesday's body.

She kicked into spongy flesh with an insanity of purpose, as her muffled screams became muffled grunts. Sally was literally gagging on Wednesday's flesh.

Wednesday held firm, keeping herself limp and relaxed, pure dead weight upon the hapless woman.

No doubt from underneath, Sally clawed, bit, punched and

elbowed. No doubt it was like using a hammer trapped inside a huge foam mattress.

Wednesday relaxed entirely, despite the sharp discomfort of the knife wound. She let her body do all the work and soon the struggle was over. Yet Wednesday was sweating, shaking, her leviathan legs shot straight back and flexed stiff for a moment.

She let out a series of short yelps, spasming where she lay as if in a seizure of some kind.

Pugsley knelt down beside her. "Did it happen again, pumpkin?"

"Yeah, it did." She breathed heavily. "Tough little bitch."

"Was it good?"

"Yeah," said Wednesday, limp and exhausted. "I came."

"As long as she's dead."

"Oh yeah." Wednesday closed her eyes dreamily. "I doubt even you could have survived that, sweetiekins."

"Might be interesting to try."

"Oh, no. I don't want to go husband hunting again at this late date." She sighed. "Now help me up, for God's sake!"

Pugsley did his best, but the effort landed him against the wall and Wednesday smashed the chair as she leaned against it to help push herself up. They both stood shakily, the bloodstain now huge against Wednesday's muumuu and Pugsley eying it worrisomely. "Is it bad, do you think?"

"Nah, just a flesh wound." She smiled broadly to show its lack of consequence, though it pained her badly to fake it.

"Missy will fix you up down at Mount Auburn, don't worry. No questions asked." He knelt down to the crushed ruin that had once been Sally Wroth Null, felt her neck gently for the carotid with two fingers.

Nothing.

Pugsley straightened up warily and began compulsively wiping surfaces down for prints with a handkerchief, just in case. His nervous mind set to work: They'd definitely have to loot the place to make it look like a standard break-in before they left. Nice little profit on the side, with any luck. Could be good if Sally's roommates were for real college students, and not late-life rehabs like her. Real students were always careless about leaving daddy's money and other valuables around.

"Well—?" Wednesday asked impatiently.

"That's it for her. You don't get much deader than that."

"Good," Wednesday said, adjusting her bloody muumuu, wiping the sweat from her glistening jowls. "Then she can join her husband." She shifted her girth toward the door. "Because they don't get much deader than him either."

TWENTY-FIVE

The worst that could happen is matter-of-fact in a city, even one on the verge of becoming a minor theme park, like Boston. The worst that could happen is an everyday affair, glossed over by the disaffected malaise of the workaday. It's something you half-hear if it isn't you, and if it is you, you're far too busy dealing with it to be able to judge it for what it is. The worst that could happen is run-of-the-mill, a normal state of affairs like a nerve-jangling headline you pass in the street that dawns on you later just overshadowed your life.

The story was leaked, dolloped, and lobbed lowball to all the right contacts at all the various network affiliates and few dailies remaining in the state.

"Gang Assassin Shoots Kids—Five Killed," was the inescapable result.

The twist was the addition of the Identikit sketch of Null unofficially submitted to all the conduits of the news. Dead bang, it was Null, yet since Null was declared dead, the image was simply identified as the composite police sketch of the unidentified perp.

It was absorbed out on the street like money fallen to the gutter.

So was the blood of the two cops, Hummel and Howe, that Thing shot point blank in the face with Teflon-filled copper stoppers, asking for directions in Hyde Park off the avenue. That got sucked right up with cries for more.

Thing neither smiled nor frowned when his face was splattered with their brains. It had to be done that way, for effect: Two nice-guy, youngish jock-cops, who liked to swagger and be "good guys," thick guys loved to be the ones you had to knuckle down to and serve their petty, God-given authority to either pat you on the head or kick you in the ass. Happy to roll down the window and receive your toadying respect, or the quick flash of the muzzle of a Glock firing right into their dull eyes.

Thing made sure to leave plenty of Glock casings in the squad car to make the message plain. Next he phoned it in off a stolen cell phone to make it even plainer—a phone he took off the pocket of the oldest of the Mattapan kids he had to blow proper holes in after Pugsley's clumsy job on them.

Now the flak-jacketed extraneous details were out in force. Extra foot patrol, extra mobile beat teams.

The crime killer was now a cop killer and, whereas before he was a curious nuisance bust way down on the list, he had become a priority bust of utmost contemptible urgency: You don't go around murdering the blue image and symbolic virtue, even in a town like Boston. It's worse than killing ghetto kids.

It can't be tolerated.

So now the Identikit image of Null was everywhere, yet there was no one close enough to him to give him up, and not nearly enough people knew enough about the allegedly dead low-level bagman mope to bring him back to life.

Ceremonies and press conferences came to Hyde Park. Arty-Marty handed it off to Buffalo Bill, who handed it off to Boyd, who slathered on the approved line of community policing, neighbor-hood watches, prudence over vigilantism compounded and some-what contradicted by the addition of a reward.

The city now seethed for a dead man.

The criminals all wanted Null, and the law wanted Null.

They had to get past the fact that he was dead; the accepted, accomplished, entirely untrue fact.

Not nearly as dead as his ex-wife, Sally, though, whose murder went down on the blotter as an unsolved burglary mistakenly walked in on by some lower class, white trash bimbo who should have been working. Damn near served her right, shame though it was. This was a true death that, like her life, might just as well have never been, Boston-style.

But Null of course had had neither proper life nor death so now he was the center of it all.

Only it wasn't him. It was someone like Null. A Null copycat clone. This was the type of quantum doublethink that went down smoothly through the ranks of the Boston Police. Boyd knew it and sent it down with a smile just as she sent Byron Wurdalaka down into the street to work point, coordinate the details and flanks combing the back alleys and burned-out slurb zones for Null. Monad, Hundertwasser, Andromeda and ten newly selected members of the OC task force went hunting for the one criminal in the city Boyd knew they'd never find.

It was all a stall for time, until she found him.

She wouldn't have to look too far, she knew. He'd come calling for her. She had a place in his pantheon of retribution – he'd made this clear. And now that he'd come upon a reason for living that included her, there would be little else for him to do but to come for her.

As long as she was open to the moment, she would find him, waiting for her, waiting for his justice.

Then she would take a copper stopper and place it squarely in the center of his damaged brain.

————

Fester wobbled into Mass General, bloody and beaten, reeking of rum, though he'd barely taken a drop of wine to steady his nerves. The whole bottle of Bacardi had been poured all over him as he was being tossed and flopped about his Kenmore Square condo like a wet rag doll. He didn't even fight it anymore, just went limp when it came, tried to curl himself up into a ball and protect himself until it stopped. The time before—just a few days prior—he had made the mistake of reaching for his gun. He squeezed off a few shots before nearly being beaten to death with it.

That time he was so bad off that he couldn't even drag himself to

Mass General, never mind cab it. This time, he left the gun alone and remained ambulatory.

Fester wound up in a private room with the lights off after a full range of scans, PET, CAT, EEG and a caveat by a smartass resident to stay out of barroom brawls.

How could he protest this when that's exactly what his bearing and appearance stated loud and clear?

Big-time-bar-brawler-former-bouncer. He reeked criminal and thug even more than he reeked of the 151-rum poured all over him and lit up as an accelerant, melting his silk shirt to his barrel chest.

Lying there in bed, third-degree burns on his stomach covered with layers of pigskin, Fester blubbered like a baby.

The fact that Gomez Gomelsky walked in with chocolates didn't stanch the flow of tears one iota.

Fester's swollen face was lit from the wayward fluorescence of the corridor and from the ambient glow of sharp urchin-spiked street lighting just outside the open blind of his window. Gomez threw the box of Godiva Truffles on the bed between Fester's legs and slumped back in a semi-comfortable visitor's chair. He was dour and reluctant in his manner.

"Hurt that much, does it?"

Fester's catcher's mitt face sniveled, slick with tears. "Fuck yeah —several freakin' nights a week." He looked like a penitent special effect from an old TV show. 'Lost In Space', maybe.

"So move."

"I did. He found me anyway. I need more guys, Gomez! I need more guys!"

Hopelessly eying the smoke detector and sprinkler sensors in the ceiling, Gomez lunged forward and savaged open the box of chocolates, which Fester ignored.

"You're not getting 'em. He keeps killing every solider I post near you, Fes. I can't afford the attrition anymore." Gomelsky popped a chocolate in his pouchy mouth and chewed vigorously.

"Then he's going to kill me! I know it!" He framed this statement with a heaving full of liquid sobs.

"Nah," Gomez said, a thick chocolate cud on his tongue, "he ain't gonna kill ya."

"How do you know?"

"Because from what I seen, if he wanted you dead, you'd be cemetery mulch already. This mutt's got plans for you."

Then his eyes went wide. "That—that could be worse!"

"You could be right!"

"What are we fucking gonna do?" Fester's hands trembled, and he was fumbling for something—a cigarette of course. "What am I gonna do?"

"Uh-uh, Fes—you'll set off all the bells and whistles and make a rainstorm in here if you light up that cancer stick." He swept his arm in a pass as if performing magic.

"F-F-Fuck if I care!"

Fester found what he was looking for and clumsily stuck a half-ruined Marlboro in his mouth, poised a book of matches between stumbling outsized fingers, and struck them feebly.

Gomez slapped the smoke from his mouth and the matches from his hand down onto the bland and colorless rug. "You're pathetic, you know that, Fester?"

"I know," he wept, "I know! I don't care anymore!"

"How can one guy do this to someone like you, a fucking made man, yet? This is just one guy, for God sakes!" One guy that was taking out most of his crew with no end in sight. One guy—right. Like Attila the Hun was one guy.

Fester sobbed and stammered: "F-fucking Null!"

Gomez stood and began gearing up to repeat a carefully prepared speech he had in mind. You don't just leave a made guy twisting in the wind without looking beneficent as shit and invoking some ceremony. Before you cut him loose. "Look, enjoy the chocolates and rest awhile, okay? I gotta go see to some of our more urgent problems here—"

"Like Ophelia running off and disappearing? Like her fucking defaulting on a case could put us all away forty fuckin' years apiece?"

Gomez stamped the floor once for attention and raised his voice, almost choking with exasperation. "No, like most of the top members of our thing being killed off, you strunz-y goddamn bastard!"

"I'm sorry!" Fester whined and continued weeping. "I'm sorry!"

"Sorry? You're fucking pathetic. Get a fucking grip on yourself, *stugotz*!"

Fester wheezed, shut his eyes and lay there, limp and enormous, like a beached manatee. "This Null. He's on me, beats the fuck out of me, whacks out every guard we post. He's fucking torturing me so I can't think straight anymore. I can't take it. I'm breakin' apart here. Nothin' I do stops this shit psychopath. I can't raise a fucking hand."

"They all say he's dead."

"Maybe they're right! It's like dealing with some fuckin' horror from beyond the grave, but he's alive."

"Not for much longer, he ain't." Gomez reached over and grabbed a chocolate from the golden box, sucked a white truffle slowly.

"Like you can stop this monster."

"Like I can't? I'm using one monster to annihilate another – with any luck they finish each other off and I get less headaches."

"Thing? That sewer-faced creep?"

"That's right. Set 'em against each other, I can get rid of the both of them."

Fester began blubbering, "But what's left after—tell me, what's left?"

"Just because we lost our top people don't mean they can't be replaced, maybe with less colorful types. Truth is, everyone at the top tier was getting smug, complacent. It's time to drive in some new ambitious blood. We still got talent in the rank and file, and a booming KP enterprise to run. Plus, the waste-management end, the up-market hooch, the book. The court thing just means shelling out more money for another shyster and stalling for time legit. We didn't default, that cunt Sophie did. All that's just a setback."

"And you got me, remember."

"Oh, do we ever! Which brings me to my next point. Fester, I think you're gonna take a leave of absence for a while, get away from this Null fuck till we can burn him down."

"I'm under indictment. I can't leave town."

"I'll fix it so you can."

"That would make it permanent then."

"Maybe, but you're not doing either of us any good in your current condition, you know."

"Kick a man when he's fucking down, you piece of shit!"

"Look at it this way: think of it as retirement, that's all. How many guys you think get to retire from Family business and live to tell the tale?"

"That would be none, cocksucker."

"Wrong, numbnuts. Now there's you." Gomez pointed at him solemnly.

"You're fucking killing me, here!"

"No, I'm lettin' you live. It's just best we sever ties for a while, at least until we get a new defense team together, get our ducks in a row with what's left of our thing, personnel-wise, know what I'm sayin'? Maybe Null will ease up on you if he knows we're on the outs. Think of it as a temporary thing."

"Yeah," he chortled grimly. "Temporary as breathin'."

"I'm pullin' the soldiers off you as of this minute, Fes'."

Fester bolted up from the bed and grimaced with agony as he did, folding the patch of pig skin. "Don't do that! Don't. He'll take it as a sign! It's like painting a bullseye across my balls!"

"Not like there wasn't one there before." He checked his watch. "Your floor is clear as of now, Fes, and every soldier we got is gonna steer clear of you as a fucking kill zone till further notice. Capisce?"

"Wait, you could use me as bait to kill Null. Fucker won't let go of me, comes around my place more frequently than a freakin' high-end hooker!"

"No, too much could go wrong. I thought about that. Null's got way too much control of you and where you live, Fes. Besides, I think he expects it. And when Null expects something, the body count starts climbing."

"You're throwin' me to the fucking ghoul! Givin' me up like a party favor!"

"That's one way to look at it, I suppose."

"It's what it is."

"Okay. Maybe so. But you got more of a shot this way than if we were to handle you in the old-fashioned way, *verstehst du*?" He pointed his index finger like a gun and let his arm drop. "Besides, you have an excellent point about laying bait for the fucking mutt."

"Well, you're laying me already, so I might as well be the fucking bait. I tell you, I can help you jam this motherfucker up."

"You've done enough as it is on that. No, we have some other bait in mind, don't worry yourself."

"Yeah? And who does he want dead more than me, pray tell?"

"Oh, some police official, my sources tell me. That and the fact that he likes little children."

"Jesus Christ, so he's another one of them, a fucking chickenhawk?"

"No *sceccu*—I think he'd like to rescue all the meat from our little freezer before we can export it to market."

Fester grunted like his old self. "Big dream to be a fucking hero. Anyone knows anything knows the world shits on fucking heroes. Shits and spits."

"Yeah, but he really doesn't seem to know this fact. Makes him an amateur, a kid. Besides, it's his fucking fantasy to be a hero, and if you know anything about us, you know we're in the business of making fantasies come true. Now ain't we?"

Fester's swollen face went slack for a moment, then twisted into a smile. "Ya know, I'm beginning to feel better about this already. So, you're telling me that the rat bastard gets his fantasy, gets to become a fucking self-sacrificing Jesus-weeping hero after all?"

"That's right, Fester," said Gomez, getting up to leave. "He'll be a hero alright—the way most of those who want to be, get to be—"

They locked eyes in the darkness and froze there for a moment in a terrible gaze of mutual understanding; a tacit connection.

"—By dying for it."

Fester clapped.

Gomez murmured something incomprehensible to himself, then turned his back on Fester like he was nothing at all, walked off slowly down the hospital corridor without another word.

The last thing he heard pacing away was Fester's insensible laughter choking off to a long, violent sob.

TWENTY-SIX

"You're a good boy, Nicky."

"I try," said Nick Andromeda, squirming in his seat. He had no desire to be where he was at that moment, much less facing the man he was facing. It was a bright office as high as Boston could bring you in the Harbor Towers, overlooking the seemingly endless slag and detritus of the Harbor Tunnel project. It was a CEO's office with picture windows, embarrassing yardage of waste space, boasting comforts irrelevant to the pursuit of business and an imposing oval onyx desk where he guessed no paperwork had ever been done.

The envelope rode across the icy smooth surface of the desk and stopped at the edge.

It was a showoff office meant to put an interviewee off balance, awe him with the indifference of power and prestige. Maybe this office was used three times a month—the rest of the time this sort of business would be conducted in a North End club, maybe a South Boston squat, or a dark restaurant where the food and liquor was the cover for something less savory. Someone on the long-con no doubt rented the place the rest of the time.

Andromeda's hands twitched toward the packet on the edge of the black onyx desk.

"Just the beginning, Nicky, you keep doing what you do."

"Might be the end."

"You nervous about being here? Why should you be?"

"Guys that see you on a regular basis wind up not seeing anything at all."

"You don't have to worry so much," said Malek "the Mallet" Turbot. "Just do what I say, prosper and live. You're a special boy, Nicky, you know that."

"Short bus special? Because I'm not feeling too bright right about now."

Malek laughed, trying to sustain an outward appearance of good humor while his diverticulitis was acting up and already his gut was beginning to claw its way through his chest. His bad eye was hidden behind wrap-around mirrored visor-style sunglasses. "Oh, we all know how bright you are, Nicky—everybody. Maybe one day you replace Buffalo Bill, but meanwhile being bright can blind you to your own survival, know what I'm sayin'?"

"I was headed there before you started talking."

"You know what I expect, then?"

"Yes, I do."

"What you've heard is right. I don't disappoint well."

"I heard you were a stone psychopathic killer who murders routinely to be on the safe side when any situation presents a toss-up."

"This is a world for big boys, not little pipsqueaks. Don't get emo all over me, okay? This suit's expensive." Not that expensive— gangster Gucci off the back of a truck.

"You want me to do your killing for you?"

"Of course I do. I don't like to get messy and I'm in a position where I don't have to."

Andromeda stood and was about to slide the packet back across the desk.

"Now wait, Nicky, you don't have to do much but what you were supposed to do in the first place. Stop that fuck Null. Just like your boss wants you to. I'm just saying you stop him with a bullet, make a definite kill out of the confusion when it all comes down."

"You want more than stray shots, you want a killshot pattern placement. What will the BPD firearms discharge review team say?"

"They will say whatever my little fucking packets tell them to say. I'm telling you, I want a dead zombie, Nicky, dead as the Family is when he finishes with them. It's not as if anyone wants to try the fucker and it's not as if he don't deserve payback of the kind he's been visiting on poor Gomez."

Andromeda paused, gazing at the packet, the money, the promise, and bit his lip. He had suffered for nothing; he could certainly do the right, easy thing for an exorbitant payment. Make a good kill and put the mope out of everybody's misery. "I can group shots in chaos, I guess."

"Such an all-American boy, Nicky. You can group shots! I am loving that."

He grabbed the packet and shoved it into the inside pocket of his Hammacher-Schlemmer period bomber jacket. "Yeah, it's all about the love."

Malek smacked both palms down hard on the flat, glassy onyx. "What I ain't loving so much, Nicky, is LaCuna making sure evidence gets lost so Family members can walk just to get mowed down by that zombie Null. I want any survivors picked up by the state. You tell that greedy fuck we pay better at Ork and no cop is untouchable, am I right Nicky?"

"I'm not so sure."

"Be sure, Nicky. At Ork we don't care about your quaint social taboos—uniform, cassock, strapless gown, flesh and blood is only that. Take it to Phil. Tell him it's juice or muscle, he can have his pick, but I'm going to have my way, be sure."

"I get extra for this?"

"You already got it, special Nicky. You get to leave intact." He spat that last syllable so moisture hit the back of the chair where Andromeda would have sat like a shot. "Burn a votive candle to God for this."

"Fine." Sweating, Andromeda turned to leave. He just now was delivered the realization that when he was trying to infiltrate the Family, they had already infiltrated One Schroeder Plaza. The betrayals were just too opaque to track. He began to feel dizzy, wondering if the surgery and hospitalization had been nothing even before Null showed up.

"And don't wait for the zombie to whack out Gomelsky before you do what has to be done. When Gomez is stripped naked, neither he nor we will know for sure from just exactly where the deathblow came. And there's going to be more than one of them, I can tell you that."

"You'd be the one to know." Andromeda uttered this by rote, his thoughts elsewhere.

"Of course I would." Malek's amblyopic left eye looked crazy, going off to the wall as he removed his wraparound sunglasses to glare at Andromeda. "After all, Nicky—"he winked—"I set them all up, didn't I?"

———

It was a dank space with cages and hay in the grim, antique industrial congestion of downtown Attleboro. A center for New England redneck reactionaries, Attleboro was a troubled town, with a bible study group gone wrong called "The Body," depriving its youngest members of proper medical care, and with the Paddleboro illicit sex club arrests of 2000. The Foster Building where the party was held is located kitty-corner to the Attleboro Police Department, and in a roomy loft once used for the manufacturing of soap and for the counseling of alcoholics was now where the cages were, along with armed guards, Grandmama Gomelsky sucking her cigarillo and pacing up and down nervously, checked her Rolex.

Tripods, lighting solids, controllers, decks, Ikegami video cameras with complex lenses and rolled up backgrounds lay and leaned spidery with shadows on a pallet off to the side. The jumble in the inadequate lighting looked like an immense bug at rest.

Only two small children huddled naked in one of the cages—the others were empty.

They were like dogs in a pet shop, hopeless and hungry-eyed, wary of what was going on beyond their restricting walls, barred so sight and sound were not restricted.

Armed thick men sat and shambled idly about the space. They weren't there for the two in the cage. They were there for the group that was on their way.

One sat in the corner on a stool wearing an Armani suit holding a Colt revolver and rocking back and forth to the tune of his iPhone —twenties maybe.

An older guy reclined against the cage making faces at the children inside, two girls too traumatized to be terrified anymore, half naked in scraps and rags and filthy, both white.

White was always at a premium in Dhubai.

Grandmama checked her watch again while a soldier in his mid-thirties made coffee across the expanse in a small kitchenette. She flipped open her cell phone and pressed to connect when out of the corner of her eye she caught a flash—like sunlight glinting off a shard of glass or a strip of metal. It was nothing.

"We're gonna die," the younger girl in the cage said to the older.

"No, we won't, but we're gonna wish for it soon just like when we made the movies."

"Shaddap," said the older soldier who had been teasing them. "Keep quiet or you get no bath."

The bigger of the two girls smiled cheerfully and hocked a gob of spit in his face.

"Fucking cunt!" shouted the soldier, shaking the bars of the cage as she cowered by instinct, grabbing the younger girl and huddling in the corner.

"Oh, leave them alone, Nast, for god's sake," groused Grandmama, still trying to connect with her cell phone. "They'll have enough on their hands when the new girls get here. Maybe we can keep them from tearing each other apart, huh?"

"Do 'em fucking good," grunted Nast.

"WAP technology is for shit," she mumbled, clicking shut the cell phone and shoving it into her bag.

"We're gonna die!" the small child whined.

"No," came a hollow voice. "You won't, but they will."

The world for the two girls seemed to stop on its axis at that moment.

Grandmama heard this, as did all the soldiers but the one with the iPhone in his ears who rocked on in his mind. With the others, the sound registered hard, like an old-time air raid siren, yet also like a whisper at the finish of a ghost story. She turned to watch the flash and heard a soft trundling sound—the head of the guard who a moment ago was sipping coffee in the kitchenette came rolling fast toward her across the floor.

"Null!" shrieked Grandmama. "Null! Kill the fucker! Kill him now!"

The older guard at the cage was next and spattered the two squealing girls with gouts of blood.

"Keep screaming," Null advised the children calmly, a shadow hanging from a chain sliding madly on a track from a pulley across the ceiling. "It distracts them."

They obeyed, hysterically.

Both remaining soldiers strafed the ceiling, one thick number with a scarred, pitted, puffy face and a snub nose 12 gauge took out chunks of wood and plaster, pumping furiously.

Null took out puffy face in a single sweeping motion, hanging upside-down from the ceiling like a bat – twisted up in a chain on a pully riding a disused industrial track, sinking a machete right through his Bill Blass tie into his fat, barrel chest.

The guard in the Armani—a baby-faced twenty something— came up with the Colt and dropped it just as suddenly, coming back down with the barrel of an upside-down Glock in his face. Null hung down in front of him, eye to eye. The guard flinched and quivered. He had heard about this hitter, this freaking ghoul. He was killing them all and so far he could not be stopped. It was dumb-stuff, comic book hype and delusion; Hollyweird melodrama.

But now he had a conversion to the faith of staying alive, which meant terror.

Terror in the face of Null.

What made him tremble and sweat was that Null's attention was fixed squarely on him, the bloody machete in one hand, the Glock in the other, hanging upside down in front of him like a bat. What made him sweat and tremble was the undeniable knowledge that he was near death.

"You wouldn't expect to find a machete in Boston, but the gang bangers use all sorts of creative weaponry stashed in the squats of Mattapan. I found this one in mine after I cleared them out. Works good."

He back-swung it and the guard threw up his hands and wailed, "Please!"

There was a clicking sound and without seeming to turn or look behind him, Null shot Grandmama dead in the arm with the Glock. Something went flying off and skittered over by the cage where the two girls sobbed and cowered.

A chromium Ruger twenty-two.

Grandmama slumped down into a battered chair and lit a fresh cigarillo as shock set in indomitable and cold. She had to struggle to keep her head from bobbing down and from burning her wounded shoulder with the red end of the cigarillo.

"Please don't kill me."

"It's more orderly if I do." He raised the machete. Predictably, the guard went for the gun and Null shot off one of his fingers. "Like I said—"

He leveled the gun at the guard's neck and smoothly entered condition one.

Then the soldier had an unexpected reaction: He began to cry.

Unrestrained, unembarrassed child's tears; tears of shame, tears of regret.

"Don't!" cried the twenty-something, suddenly reduced to a teenaged-something or below by his crying. Fallen to a heap with a bleeding finger stump, he was now a vulnerable boy in a grown man's suit, clothes that, though tailored, were far too big for him now. "Please," he slobbered. "I'll quit! You'll never see me again. I'll go back to school!"

Null poked him in the arm with the tip of the machete, drew blood.

"What will you do, become a lawyer? I don't think we need any more lawyers. Adds to the confusion."

"Psych-Psych-*chology*. Maybe—social work! That's what I did before, when I flunked out of UMass Boston." He was buying time, saying anything not to wind up dead yet. Anything.

"Try UMass Amherst next time. I hear it's nicer."

"Y-you went there?"

"No. I never went nowhere." Null slid over to where the boy lay in a heap, lowered himself down and touched a gleaming teardrop, hesitating on his pink cheek with a finger, examining it.

"Please!" the boy soldier shouted, recoiling from Null's touch.

"What must it be like to be so terrified and to want to live so badly with hardly any reason to go on but the brute fact of it? They're real your feelings by the way; very deep and very real, and I think you mean them. The tears look authentic."

Sensing hopeful purchase, the boy soldier revved up his song and dance, threw himself whole into it whether he meant it or not. And as he did, he began to feel that he did in fact mean it: "I swear! Tomorrow —first thing—I start auditing classes! I'll spend all my time getting ready to enroll for the next semester! I'm serious—really!" His breathing was sharp and spastic, lending a queer staccato quality to his speech.

"After a little trip to the emergency room, of course?"

"I'll say it was an accident. I did it myself, I'll tell them, fucking around with guns."

"Tell them I did it, for all I care, the fucking around with guns part. I don't mind. Go and file charges. Trust me, they'll get lost. Just like you."

"No, I won't. I'm done with all this. You'll never see me again."

Quietly, flatly: "Okay, you can go then."

"What? Y-y-you—?" He was sure he was hallucinating.

Toneless: "Get up, leave the gun, unlock the cage where the girls are and exit."

The soldier stood shakily and began doing as he was told.

"Be sure you never see me again, soldier. Make sure you stay away from anyplace I might be."

"B-but how will I know where that will be?"

"You'll know. You know exactly where. You know every inch of the place and it's those inches that now make up the boundaries of your life."

The guard stared at him, frigid, perplexed, his mouth slack. "Thank you," he managed, suppressing a sob. "Thank you!"

"Just make sure I never see you again. Because if I do, you'll be sure to see my face—"

"I know, I know," he broke in, clumsily unlocking the cage.

"—the moment before you look upon the face of God."

The guard couldn't get the cage door open fast enough. When the lock finally sprang, he kicked it open, lurched up and fled wildly, praying all the way he wouldn't get a bullet in the back right before he burst out into the cold dank air and diesel smell of the soot-flecked Attleboro afternoon.

His prayers were answered.

He had left his iPhone behind on the chair and Null grabbed it up, examining it with interest. Null pocketed the thing.

There was a scuffing across the floor and Null was on it before he had a chance to see to the girls cringing away from the door in the now open cage.

The scuffing was the dazed and wounded Grandmama dragging herself across the floor to get to her Ruger 22. Null swung by and kicked her in the face, still holding the machete, the Glock now pocketed. He dropped down from the chain and dragged her up from the floor with his free hand, gazed into her murky eyes.

The girls were huddled tightly together and whimpering in the back of the cage, sure that their lives were lost.

"How dare you beat up an old woman?"

"Do you think they're more afraid of you or me, Grandmama?"

He holstered the machete behind him underneath the overcoat.

"You of course. You're a monster!" She raised her good arm and smacked him one, albeit ineffectually, on the right side of the jaw.

"Doubtless, Granny, doubtless. But they don't know much from me but the blood of one afternoon. You, on the other hand, they've known for weeks, months, blood or no."

"I've taken care of them. I'm like their own dear Granny."

He held her up, staring blankly into the fuming hatred of her expression. "You shoved them into live porn feeds with logboys, made them do each other in orgies with old men on video and now you're selling their flesh to third world presidents, sultans, sheiks and grandees—shipping them in containers like beef. I don't even think they think this makes you their grandmother."

She burst her lips apart. "I'm the closest thing to any kind of mother they have ever known or will ever know. You understand nothing."

"I understand you trick them out like whores and sell what remains like high-priced caviar."

"When you're starving in the winter, you eat rats to survive."

"You're not starving and they're not rats—just little children."

"You have a soft spot for them?" She leered with a smirk of triumph. "Good to know."

"Get all the ideas you want, Granny, they're going nowhere."

"No, you're going nowhere. You think they're coming here with more girls? Making shipments from here? No, my friend, they're coming for you. And soon. Meanwhile, those girls are going where they're going and all you can do about it is to suffer and bleed worse than you did last time. If any survive, and you can be sure you won't, *petuh*, they might work out a great life as courtesan to some military strongman or sheik. One or two could rise in the world to power. You have no way of knowing what God intended."

"And you do?"

"Feh! You talk about God, but you don't know anything because you believe in nothing, you embody nothing, all you do is kill. You have nothing to do with God, but everything to do with death."

"All a point to consider, but as the song says, it ain't necessarily so." Null shoved her down to the ground, cranked his odd walk over to the cage and soccer-kicked the gun into the furthest corner of the loft's expanse. He twisted down by the open door to his knees and called to the girls inside. Neutral, monotone: "You kids have to go now. Seriously. This is the time to make your break."

They ignored him, so he crawled into the cage and tossed them out the door like unruly cats, and like unruly cats, they hissed at him and squalled and clawed at him with ingratitude and fear.

He imitated the voice of the Wizard of Oz, both booming and bogus. "Get the fuck out of here!"

Half-naked, squealing, they scurried toward the door, Null up and kicking after them.

They made it out, a spectacle in the Attleboro streets—a police blotter news item in the making.

"Attleboro's finest will be here soon."

"Then do it and go."

"Do what?"

"Me, you stupid insignificant piece of shit. *Pidar gnoinyj!*"

She forced herself to stand, bloodied and shaking, her wounded arm limp and swinging as she walked toward Null, lopsided. Null stared vacant, waiting in one place by the cage. She went at him with her good arm, putting everything she had into it, landing one good punch in the center of his face before he grabbed her arm and held it, just held it, without twisting it or squeezing the wrist too tight.

It was as if he didn't care.

She spat at his face and missed. "Fucking *petuh*—you don't get it. This was supposed to be where we finished you. But it's not over yet, no, you'll have to go where they'll be shipped from, and that's where you'll die, not that you even care."

Null let her go and she nearly fell over.

"Then you have to tell me where to make that happen."

"Of course, fucking *petuh*." And she told him. "Now you can show an old woman some mercy. Be grateful I send you to your death to save the precious little children from whose bones I bake my bread like fucking Baba Yaga!"

"Mercy? I suppose that would be human. Compassionate."

"It would. I'm a wounded, sick old lady. Show me some."

"God's mercy, perhaps."

"It is from him that all things come. Even you."

Null strode over to her, bore down upon her without touching her.

"Sweetness, innocence, playfulness; doing something for someone else just for pleasure; maybe even doing something right, not because you understand that it is, but somehow know that it is. Children do evil just like they do good because they feel it. They don't understand it, yet they all have compassion. The will to save a cat, a bird, even a small frog."

"That's right."

"So, tell me, Grandmama, what are you left with when you take the little girls in the cage and rip all of that away from them. When you crush them until if they aren't dead, then they might as well be. What happens after you use their bones to bake your bread and you eat that bread to the last crumb? Just what's left? Can you tell me what's left?"

"I don't know and I don't care."

"But I think you do care."

"Feh! Why the fuck should I, *petuh*?"

He grabbed her, unsheathed the machete from the scabbard across his back, and took her down to the floor with precise silence.

Then Null whispered in her ear, close, so that she would finally know:

"Because…I'm what's left."

TWENTY-SEVEN

The names of God.

They tried to suppress this, make it something only the doer or perp would know.

Tried and failed.

It was just too good, too fancifully extreme amid the grim panoply of death left behind in the Kattleboro Kiddie Porn Loft (as it was nicknamed by the press).

Attleboro's finest took a worse reaming from the press than they did under the ungainly specter of Paddleboro.

But the headline that stood out was simply "Names of God," stark and bold.

One freakish murder to the press outshone and overshadowed the wholesale abuse and flesh peddling of small children.

And indeed, in its gore, it had more spectacle than the empty, foreboding cages and the half-clad urchin girls screaming maniacally down Main Street.

Called in on a consult, it was the only time Yonah Shimmel ever lost his lunch.

As many of them as could be remembered, phonetically, and spelled out in the original language—Greek, Hebrew, Latin, even Sanskrit—were there, deep and plain.

Carved hard and sharp into the withered, wrinkled flesh of Kostianaya Noga "Grandmama" Gomelsky in big, final welts were the names of God. It was neat, painstaking work, you could see, when all the gore was washed away; you could see and read them clearly.

Much more clearly than the name "Gomelsky," somewhat hastily inscribed on Null's thin and wasted thigh, which could be read with effort.

It was to teach her the final lesson of what God can mean.

It had gone statewide now: bureaucracies of city government and police force liaisons and paycheck double-dipping coordinating details forming a vast clusterfuck rolling across the state, all seeking the man who was not Null.

The man who Kay Boyd believed was Null.

The scumball who took out a gang of kids playing on a street corner and two good-guy cops in their patrol car, not so much the psychopath taking out the entire Family, bit-by-bit.

It was a none-too-subtle manhunt covering Dorchester and Mattapan, Downtown Boston, down Tremont heading through the South End run out of the mayor's office, sanctioned by Buffalo Bill and through Kay Boyd as lead shill. The OC task force automaton of overarching politics. It galled her, but it went without argument that ArtyMarty had to make a showing and prop up the new commissioner without setting him up to take the fall should ordinary failure occur.

She saw the logic. Failure to clear OC cases was more the rule than the exception. She was meant to absorb it and make those above her look good while she did. As always in Boston politics, the success would be theirs, the failure, hers. It was the deal you made to be effective.

It was the deal you made for your own agenda.

And Kay Boyd's agenda included a new item: Get Null alive and get a confession.

Something that Benway had said: "Well he has no use for lying anymore. Lying is a remote function of self-preservation. But that basic impulse is as gone as his ability to feel happy or sad. He just doesn't care. In fact, at the neurochemical level, he simply can't care. He has no reason to lie; there's nothing at stake whatsoever."

LaCuna gave the news from Buffalo Bill. "Kay, with the flack you're taking on this recent murder spree, you're slated for reassignment we don't clear it soon."

Boyd adjusted graph paper and thread connecting pictures, bios and "sheet" printouts in a twisted genealogy of local gang crime. "Ain't it hilarious how 'we' always translates to 'me' taking the fall."

"You know how it goes, Kay. We serve the public. They don't get whatever they think they want, blame and penalty both wind up in the lottery of internal politics. Or infernal politics, if you like. Besides, it'll blow over and you'll be rotated back to some special function or other. Buffalo Bill has a shine in his eye for you and no mistake. You fit his agenda, personal and professional."

"He doesn't swing that way, Phil. We weren't rivals at the academy. He just wants potential enemies as close to him as his friends. So, where does he plan to dump me if I don't clear this?"

"Public relations," LaCuna murmured, almost sheepish, his jowls reddening a bit

Boyd belched plosive laughter like a feather stuck in her throat. If she had been drinking anything it would have come out her nose. "Fuck—! Is it sadism or dada-ism, Phil? You tell me."

"Oh, some of both, I imagine. Anyway, I came here to tell you to abandon your resurrection theory as to the family gang slayer."

Climbing down from the chair she was standing on to secure torn and imperiled branches of her OC Family tree, Boyd sighed wearily. She went to her steel desk overburdened with accordion files whose stubby legs were all but bereft of their original gunmetal gray paint and punched the intercom on the speakerphone.

"Okay Byron, get in here. Time for your song and dance. Do it good enough I'll slip a buck in your undies."

Wurdalaka swaggered in without knocking. "Hardee-frickin'-har, LT."

"You speak the language, Byron—give it to Phil the way he likes it."

"Phil, we've reached a consensus."

"Oh, I always like that!" LaCuna said, beaming with honesty.

"We thought you and ArtyMarty and his highness would all do a backflip at that."

"Get to the point, Byron, would you please?"

"Comin' round to it, LT. You have to excuse me. I got caught up in the niceties and all. Okay, we think it's a Family struggle from some united lower soldiers, like a worker's rebellion. They're trying to take over the KP op's by holding their own secret putsch and lay it off on a dead guy. They smelled weakness at the top, so they took their shot."

"Simple answers sound best," said LaCuna agreeably.

"That's right. They used the Null CI disaster as a smokescreen under which to whack out the bosses and pass it off as non-OC."

"Smart game," said LaCuna with unreadable disbelief.

"Typical power play from semi-smart thugs."

"I suggested Homicide and OC coordinate some details to all known Family locales and make some busts, then we play tiddly-winks to see who flips whom when."

"Exactly," said Boyd. "We turn 'em like the tube-steaks they are, hot off the grill."

"What are we leaking to the press? And when do we do it? For the requisite impact, I mean. You obviously need to milk the scatter effect before you round them up."

"You would have to ask me that, Phil. This is standard gang-war stuff. They'll show themselves no matter what the fourth estate gets wrong. Let the Globe and Herald spend a few bucks playing catchup with real police work."

"Andromeda's off your roster for now, if you make these busts. His undercover will be compromised."

"No, he's on the list, Phil. There's no investigation left to compromise anymore since most of the principles are dead, and I need every available body I can bring into this that knows what it's doing."

"He'll make their list if any of them recognizes him."

"Who gives a fuck? When this is over, most of them will be in Walpole and the rest dead. They're cop killers now, Phil. The slow approach has been over for days now. Fuck, the streets are running with blue to catch these mooks!"

"It's your show, Kay, barring approval from Billy and ArtyMarty, of course, but knowing them, they'll let you hang yourself at this juncture. You're destined to be leaking more facts to the press I fear."

"Phil, you don't want me dealing with the press. I may be too honest to do it."

LaCuna's face creased with mirth. "Kay, Kay, perish the fucking thought. There's no one in city government from here to Bullfinch Place thinks that!"

———

The safe house in West Newton had gunsels up and down its three stories, none of them facing directly the grayish white schizoid afternoon of fair and foul weather. It was bad enough that a few major crime figures were known to own large housing tracts in the posh, old money suburb of Boston, where stodgy wealth and prim manners still held sway—Junior League, SPNEA, Porcellian, Skull and Bones. To see crime boss lackeys brandishing an arsenal of long and short firearms would have been infra dignitatem, not to mention cause for the calling in of favors to select state and local authorities, which would have been inconvenient if not outright suicidal.

The gunsels had made themselves scarce combing and recombing every inch of the fine old historical-society-endorsed rehabbed Federalist manse, avoiding balconies and picture windows.

Gomez Gomelsky sat sullen and brooding, Helle, his female bodybuilding consort collapsed on a daybed, her arm set in a heavy cast with a metal cage about the shoulder at the site of dislocation and her massive jaw wired shut. Gomez was licking the rim of a thick tumbler of grappa, lost in thought, seeming to entirely ignore the supplicant before him.

The supplicant was a highly animated, somewhat toad-like Theron LeCoeur, pacing before him in short little steps like a student before the principal.

"You killed two citizens, you killed two patrol hacks, you blew away a bunch of kids and now the street's just about earnings-fucking-free thanks to you and the super-sized presence of the big blue boy scout brigade. And I pay you for this shit?"

Thing's face flushed with anger, which he refused to show in any other way.

The sweat beaded then ran across his brow and his fists clenched in his pocket.

Otherwise, he almost looked calm in a masterful parody of standing loose.

"Yes, you pay me and no complaints there. Speaking of which, you really shouldn't complain about my work before you know, I mean really know what I'm driving at."

"What you're driving at. The streets are running cold with blue and the infection is growing like algae into every backroom thing, every show we got goin' in this fuckin' town, from Revere to freaking Allston/Brighton, earnings are strangled by pissant police paranoia and you're sayin' I shouldn't complain? You deformed little wiseass fucker!" Gomez sprayed grappa at Thing as he sputtered with rage. "You're hurting me worse than that scumball zombie ever did."

"You're talking about the mutt did in your own mother."

"Fuck my mother! I'm talkin' profit and loss here!"

"That's wrong, Gomez."

"Wrong is it? I'm hemorrhaging cash here and you're telling me I'm fucking wrong?"

"That's no way to talk to someone like me," whispered Thing.

"You'll suck my cock in hell before I change my tone with you, pally." Gomez threw the tumbler at Thing's head. He twitched aside but was a hair off—the heel of the glass glanced off the shiny smooth skin of his forehead and left a red mark.

Thing drew his Glock from his inside jacket pocket and dove at the snickering Gomez who didn't bother moving from his chair. Nor did he stop snickering.

He didn't have to.

Three gunsels, all plus-sized men, were on Thing instantly as a single blurred and swooping shadow, holding his arms, cocked automatics pressed to his skin, not uttering a sound.

"That was brisk," said Thing, calm, unblinking.

Gomez smirked and dangled a palm-sized device before Thing's cloudy corneas. "Panic button. I saw this thing on TV where the president's daughter had one of these doohickeys. Presses it once, the Secret Service grunts come busting in all jacked up, take out any mope dares to touch the protected presence. Fuck me running. I'm at least as good as the President's daughter in some jackoff TV series."

Gomez nodded, still snickering, and the shadows released Thing, moving back away from the windows.

Thing stood up slowly, spoke evenly, rubbing his hands to direct his tension away from his rage. "It plays like this: the kids and the cops both give the fuzz another angle and focus. They don't think you're whackin' out your own crew, so they don't think these tie-ins relate to you. They're typing this Null fuck for this – or the clever mope passing himself off as Null. You're in the clear, and now they have a compelling reason—"

"Fuck your compelling reason, you walking suppurating mutant blowjob! Turning up the heat doesn't take it off of us! And then two fucking citizens—"

"Both not connected to you in any way."

"Yeah? Well, not for long, asswipe. This Boyd fuck doesn't rule anything out! And now that the cunt is running the show upstairs, she has even more power. I pay heavy to get evidence lost, interrogate and dispose of CI's, seal leaks permanent, and she still gets the fucking goods. By the time I get a new lead counsel in place, she'll for shit sure have enough on us for a fucking case again!"

"You're saying a woman cop is too effective—I mean, just because she broke your jaw with the butt of her gun?"

Gomez chuckled at that remark as if to say "not bad, kid." He had respect for anyone who could find a way to give him shit and remain standing. "I'm saying man, woman or chick with a goddamn dick, this shit just can't go on, know what I'm sayin'? Do you feel me, or fucking what?"

"I feel you," Thing said sotto voce, secreting a low sustained growl beneath.

"This whole thing has got to be kiboshed, and I mean fucking yesterday, or nobody gets, paid, including you, Tweedledumb and Tweedledumber."

"Oh, well, I have a plan for that too."

Thing explained to Gomez his planned sequence of events, turning on the charm as hard as possible, fighting hard to avoid as many sibilants as possible along the way to minimize spray and the dreadful sucking sound his twisted lips could so easily fall into. And while his busy mind was managing that, he was busier, still marking a date in his mental calendar when he would at last be taking his time cheerfully breaking Gomez's wattled, scrawny neck.

TWENTY-EIGHT

He was a weedy little man in black shirt and jeans, motorcycle boots strapped with chrome steel O-rings on either side of each ankle and a leather vest that made him look like a shoemaker. He wore a long-horn skull bolo tie surrounded with mottled turquoise on which the skull was set. Slicked back thinning hair, virtually chinless, a nose broken so many times it was little more than a carbuncle in the center of his gaping face, he radiated street sleaze.

The nervous workings of his face gave the overall effect of a weasel whose snout had been pushed flat.

He had a nervous smile flashing on and off like a cheap beer sign, a tic that showcased spectacularly bad teeth.

Life had hardened him into a brutish caricature beyond humanity.

Hence the tic.

They brought him right into the taskforce bullpen and sat him down in Boyd's office. There was going to be no mistake with this one; two uniforms kept watch on the mook as he eyed the files that threatened to swallow up not only the battered metal desk, but the entire back end of the office. The near-chinless, weasely man licked his lips as he thought of all the information he could score and squirrel away right off the OC task force honcho's office at One Schroeder Plaza. All he needed was a good ten minutes alone with it.

He could taste it in his mind and frustration rocked him like a wave as he sat there and sweated and did a little hop in his seat, as if waking abruptly from a dream.

"No need to get up," said Boyd, coming in with Wurdalaka and Andromeda. The uneasy peace between she and the homicide detective was as apparent as the sly servile look in Andromeda's eyes. The room had suddenly become thick with outsized men.

"I thought wonder boy here was in lock-up," said Wurdalaka out of the corner of his mouth.

Boyd sat behind her desk and put on a pair of reading glasses, punching at a computer whose top-heavy monitor threatened to teeter off the edge of the desk and come crashing to the floor. "Peter, Peter, Peter, why are you here and more importantly, why are you still at large?"

Pugsley started to stand and one of the uniforms pressed hard on his shoulder to keep him down. "You wanna remain seated, pally, if you wanna know what's good."

"That's right, Pugsley, take a load off, relax."

"Listen, go check my fuckin' BOP so we can get to the point. I don't need to sit here and be treated like this when I came in of my own accord—"

"Yeah," Wurdalaka snarled. "You do need to sit there and be treated exactly as we're gonna treat ya."

An amused, dismissive wave. "Oh, I know your fuckin' BOP by heart by now, and the rest of your cronies—28 counts of child endangerment, molestation, pandering and kidnapping. It's a marvel of modern perversion that you're out on the street instead of having your own butt party in lock up."

"My bail was eight hundred thousand dollars plus, paid in full."

"Sure it was, Pugs. With kiddie porn money."

"Prove it, fuck-o."

Andromeda chuckled, shook his head and nailed Pugsley one solid drive to the solar plexus. He folded immediately and a small silver knife clattered to the floor and slid over by the toe of Wurdalaka's shoe.

"Looky, he's got a prize inside," chimed Andromeda. "Like a box of stale Crackerjack."

"I thought we had metal detectors for this," Boyd nearly mumbled.

Wurdalaka looked professorial in explanation. "Fucker must keep a lead-lined sheath in his shirt. Remember, Nicky, he's a pro with the knives."

"Okay, can we end the machismo comedy hour now?" Boyd said, half-yawning. "Officers, kindly bag that knife for me and put it in evidence locker under the Impetigo section of the Family KP docket? You can also go. It's getting hot in here again. Just too many bodies."

They did as she asked with good-natured subordinate grunts.

"F-f-fuckers!" Pugsley hacked and heaved, struggling to catch his wind. "I come in alone, no lawyer, no friends, not even my goddamn wife, and you show me the fuckin' goldfish!"

"Now there's a term I haven't heard before."

The phone bank intercom bleated mournfully; Boyd elbowed a button on the console to quiet it.

"He's being cute, is Pugsley, Wurdalaka explained. 'Show him the goldfish' is old time jargon for the rubber hose treatment. For torture, in fact. Pugsley knows a lot about torture, doncha, Pugs? I mean, you were there for that masterwork they did on Joey X, weren't you?"

"I had nothin' to do with that. That was all Cousin It, may he rest in peace."

"Of course you didn't, Pugs. After all, it wasn't like it was some special Family collaborative effort, which would be why he'd be whackin' you all out."

Pugsley stood up and shouted and found himself shoved down again by Andromeda just as quickly. "Dead guys don't whack out nobody!"

"Bullshit, Pugsley. We all know he's not dead. So, why are you here, anyway? You want protective custody? We do that, you know you're gonna wind up down at Suffolk bitin' the pillow."

"Why the hell would I need that?" He flashed his bad teeth and almost enjoyed Boyd's struggle to hide her disgust.

"Because everyone knows you sliced off his pinky for good luck. Maybe we'll find traces of his blood on your knife. Ya think?" She leaned back in her chair and made a hollow whistling through her teeth.

"Yeah, Lieutenant. Sure. I got his finger right here in my fucking pocket, just like a rabbit's foot. A lucky, fucking rabbit's foot, and before you have lover boy over here crease my gut again, lemme tell you somethin'. You're not gonna take my good luck charm from me. You're gonna gimme back my goddamn blade and I'm not going into lock-up. No way, no how."

Andromeda grabbed him up from the chair and slapped him open-handed double time.

"Let's just see about that, Petey."

"Ya, we'll see about it, putz. You'll be off-duty sometime, then we'll see. I may not look it, you know, but I'm bigger than you."

Boyd put on institutional indifference. "Okay, Pugsley, that's all the time we have for you. I've got meetings to sleep through and cases to clear." Her phone bank intercom emitted a sustained and muted moan. She ignored it, despite what she had said.

Andromeda threw the little man squirming back into his chair.

"This is gonna take precedence, what I have to say here. So, screw your meetings and your cases! And if you fucking touch me once more, you won't get bupkes!"

"Uh-huh. Fine. Sure." Boyd cleared her throat and bellowed sharply: "Then fucking say it already, before I throw you to the boys in gladiator school, for God's sake!"

"No need to get pissy about it. What I'm gonna do is, I'm gonna take you straight to the one guy who can I-D and deliver you the fucking hitter been takin' out the Family, those ghetto brats and your two bush-league beat cops."

Boyd and Andromeda just stared in a sort of dreamy stupefaction, which was both capped and protracted into dead air by Pugsley's concluding statement:

"And I got a surprise for yez, I'll tell ya right now—it ain't your dead fuck Null!"

———

One Boston Place at the end of Washington Mall and kitty-corner to the old State House and Center Plaza is a swanky address for investment banks, brokerage houses, real estate boiler rooms and shady civil attorneys basking in the glow of workaday greed. One Boston Place is where sleazeball hitter Pugsley took Boyd, Andromeda and a Detective First Grade Baptiste Protiste to ride shotgun. Boyd put Wurdalaka up to fronting the charge of the extra street patrols in what they mutually conceded was a vain political effort.

Wurdalaka had cracked that this was reminiscent of the time the whole department wound up being the tool in some furrier's murder plot back in the eighties.

Nobody laughed at the crack.

The Charles Stuart race card misdirect had the whole department jumping to overrun Mattapan and Roxbury in search of a black banger suspect who didn't exist. It's what politics demanded at the shooting death of a rich white suburban lawyer chick downtown —Stuart's wife.

Stuart winding up as the shooter tossing himself off the Tobin Bridge.

"Sounds like Null, don't it?"

Boyd produced a dulcet grunt at this and let it go.

Pugsley took up the slack, making random stabs at chatter all the way downtown and on the elevator up to the nameless suite of consulting offices where the meet was to take place.

Boyd told Pugsley to shut up in a burst of frustration and he apologized officiously, grabbing yet another tack and tangent for more of the same as they strolled through the lobby.

They ultimately let him ramble, noting how hyped up he was.

His nerves made them, in turn, nervous, put them on their guard.

The hallway from the lobby was long and paneled in burnished cherry. It ended at a vacant reception enclave behind a high, wide glass façade in which were set doors and inch diameter peg holes for the once impressive lettering of a now defunct firm. It was plain nothing was happening at this location, meet or no.

Pugsley pushed in anyway and Protiste drew his gun.

So did Andromeda.

"Guys, guys—it's cool. No one's here but the party to whom you will be speaking."

"Casualty of the Bush freebooting," murmured Boyd. "You'd think set ups like these would be the ones that wouldn't get hurt."

"Yeah, well it was an import/export racket," said Pugsley. "Cover for something else."

They all knew what that "something else" was and said nothing. Protiste whistled with dry naiveté.

A low, loud whisper of a male voice: "Send her in alone, Pugsley."

"I can't. She brought her friends."

"They want the information, she comes to meet me alone – they don't, they can pound sand."

Protiste and Andromeda scoped the place out with efficient silence, looking for private elevators, vents big enough to exit from —any means of egress—and found none. They wanted to see the room and pat down the hidden figure whose shadow and fleeting glimpses of black bedecked pink flesh could be seen through the hinges and gaps of the semi-closed door.

It wasn't happening.

The guy didn't want to be seen.

"Just send her the fuck in, Pugs, and have them go whistle it if they don't."

Stating the obvious, bad teeth gleaming in the office light and late sun of the unobstructed windows: "Standoff, boys. What's it to be?"

Andromeda said it low: "Guy's got a gun, he's got a great hostage."

Protiste hummed it after a fashion. "Got a gun maybe, but with two detectives calling for backup, how far can he go?"

"I'll tell you how far," said Boyd. "He kills me then goes out himself. So, I'm going in."

"Fuck that," Andromeda said. "I'm coming behind you anyway. All god's chillun got guns, even you LT."

Boyd shrugged, walked down the hall followed by Andromeda, guns no longer drawn, but surely gripped, while Protiste spread

Pugsley up against the wall, kicked his legs apart, pressed the barrel of the Police Special to the back of his neck.

"You guys always gotta be assholes, don't ya?" Pugsley sneered.

"Tit for tat," said Protiste and engulfed Pugsley's face in the smoke from his freshly lit cigarette. Then he brought out the cuffs.

———

"Christ," said Andromeda, "this is what the secrecy is all about? A fucking retard in an expensive suit?"

Boyd lit a cigarette herself, nothing but sweat on her brow to betray that she wasn't as impassive as she looked.

"She was supposed to come in alone."

"Well she didn't. So stand the fuck up and be counted." Andromeda did the pat-down, tossed the desk. Nothing. The funny looking, pink-skinned little man in the suit spun about awkwardly, his squid-sucker face telegraphing benign bemusement and nothing else (and that was a guess—really, it was like interpreting the expression of a tropical fish).

"You guys are a hands-on bunch, aren't you?"

"I'd rather use tongs, but the department hasn't approved them yet."

"Do I know you, detective? You look familiar."

"Yeah? They say familiarity breeds contempt. No, I think I'd remember a puss like yours—unique to say the least."

"Yes, you cut quite a dashing figure yourself, Detective. Just let me know when you're done."

Andromeda slipped a wallet out of the man's suit and, seeing he was off balance from his stance, gave him a light, cruel push that sent him back down into the chair, which nearly tipped over backwards when he landed in it.

"I'm done."

Boyd took the wallet, flipped it open, fingered about 700 hundred dollars in fifties and hundreds, a bunch of credit cards and the all-important Commonwealth Driver's License before lobbing it so it flopped open onto the desk and spread some of its contents about. She took out her tablet and made notes with the stylus. The names on all the cards matched with some slight variation of the middle initial. The last name on the Triple A and hoary Blockbuster Video rental card were both misspelled the same way.

"Okay Mr. Inverarity, let's have it." She clapped her hands twice. "Hubba, hubba."

"Please. Call me Pierce, Lieutenant. And you can have it when your handyman here makes himself scarce."

"I'll be outside waiting in what passes for reception, LT. Give a holler if we have to come sedate the beast."

"Oh, he looks pretty much subdued as it is. We'll just let him tell his story and see whether we take him with us when we go."

She jotted something down on a pocket steno pad, tore out the sheet, and slipped it to Andromeda on his way out.

"Run him," she said.

Andromeda put his index finger to his eyebrow as he took it and left.

"You won't find anything, Lieutenant."

"Oh, I'm sure not, Mr. Inverarity. Now, shall we get to it please?"

Theron "Thing" LeCoeur folded his hands behind his bald and shining pate—bouncing back a blast of sun from the shadeless window—leaned back and answered her with a smile that was so broad and from the heart that, even on his deformed face, it actually looked like a smile.

TWENTY-NINE

Kay Boyd was on top of the situation.

More precisely, she was on top of the scumball in the fancy suit with the deformed face.

It hissed at her—the face of a suckerfish or lamprey eel!

First, she drew down on him with the Sig-Sauer, then jumped him with shocking speed before he could contemplate his first move, screaming his name.

Thing was genuinely impressed at this, as he let her take him down, went with it to see where she'd go and how far she would take it.

He always liked to know this about a woman when he could.

And since this wasn't a catered affair, different rules applied and such things were both possible and desirable.

She drew down on him in the middle of his ridiculous proposal, not that it was all that transparent in and of itself. From her perspective, it simply must have seemed solid. What provoked her to slam into him was the same thing that always did.

His fucking face.

"Christ!" she had shouted just moments ago. "I know who the fuck you are."

He stood up smoothly, seeming as relaxed as the CEO who had once occupied that office. "You checked my ID already." He made his way toward her with low grace, dripping seeming uncertainty.

The sight of the Sig-Sauer's blind-eye barrel stopped him. "Easy, Lieutenant, I'm unarmed. Your boy checked me out already."

"He's still doing it so we'll see what your alias brings up."

"You want your information or not? You're going to feel stupid when this dead-ends."

"I feel stupid enough as it is not having doped this out before dragging my sorry ass in here."

"I'm not dancing with you, Lieutenant. If you want to go, go. No harm, no foul. You're holding all the cards anyway, what with your guys outside and the Sig in your hand and all."

"Oh. no. It's been more than twenty years, and you've managed to avoid anything but the worst of necessary institutional photo shots, I grant you. But there's no mistaking that face. There's no getting around that."

The Sig-Sauer wavered slightly in the air and Thing's murky eyes caught it, noted it.

"Isn't it a bit cruel to make fun of how I look?"

"Theron "Thing" fucking LeCoeur—ace family hitter numero uno. Up and coming New York mob contractor, Boston ties still intact. Face only a mother could love."

His face was serene, boyish. "I can assure you she didn't. My mother didn't love much of anything." The suckerfish lips twisted into some kind of expression Boyd was unsure of.

"How many warrants out on you? How many skip-traces?"

"How deep is the ocean?"

He stepped closer but stopped when he heard the hammer cocking back. He read her eyes and they told the story:

Boyd was close to cracking.

The suckerfish lips twisted harder together—pinkish slugs.

You don't move when a cocked Sig-Sauer shakes in your face. You keep it low-key.

"Easy," Thing lisped almost inaudibly. "Stay loose."

She obliged him by lowering the gun and spinning slightly to the right to get behind him while reaching for her Smith and Wesson high security cuffs, black. A light sweat peppered her face and neck.

The cold ran across her body. She knew exactly with whom she was dealing. Thing's resume was one of the worst in the system and the proof of that was that it never once left her mind.

That sad, wretched face.

The sad and wretched acts at the beginning that mutated into the hard, undeniable acts of the professional hitter at the end, framed by peripheral atrocities of violence for pure release! These were the ones cataloged and photographed. These were the ones with the warrants defaulted on. Mistakes of impulse and immaturity that had diminished over the years.

"Nick! You and Protiste, park that cretin and get the fuck in here!"

Lips twisted like copulating worms. The cloudy eyes narrowed. Thing's succulent breathing filled the gap of silence for a moment. Then he mouthed the words articulated solely by the shaping of his breath. "They're dead."

Boyd jabbed his jaw with a roundhouse swing and together they went down.

That's what brought her to her current position, which didn't last.

She thought she had him when she was forcing the muzzle of the Sig into his mouth, grunting with struggle, but he yanked it out, chipping a tooth, and slanted it up so that he got powder burns on his face from the flash when the first round fired.

He was deceptively, unbelievably strong—just about broke her wrist before she had to let go of the Sig altogether.

In a pro move, Thing slammed her gut with a targeted punch so extreme it brought her right up off his chest, then back down again to her knees.

In spite of herself, she produced little whines of pain, panting like a woman in labor.

Thing stood up, unruffled, uncocked the gun and brushed the dust of the scuffle from his Gianfranco Ferre suit, concerned for the fabric.

It was over. He could see that in her eyes too.

A cell phone had fallen by her feet and she darted down to pick it up before Thing could decide to shoot her. At the touch of the keys, the face lit up and displayed a number. She read it and sagged with the weight of new knowledge.

"You're the fuckin' shooter took out the Mattapan kids and Hummel and Howe!"

With a slurping sound like a dentist's suction hose, Thing patted her face with ersatz affection and said almost sadly as she fought to get her breath back. "You know, Kay, you're much better at this than you need to be."

———

"Okay Andromeda, it's story time." Byron Wurdalaka honked in outer Boston high ward style. "Make it good, because if it ain't, I got Family ties issues to address with yez."

They had rushed Andromeda through triage and the cacophonous E.R. of Boston City with a gaping abdominal wound, broken ribs and uniforms flanking the gurney. Now he had that most exalted of premiums that a hospital could offer—a private room. He had been surgeried and stitched up less than five hours ago, and groggy as he was, the questions were coming and LaCuna and Parseeman were both there, letting homicide hack Wurdalaka ask the point and shoot questions.

He brought them up to the point where he left Kay Boyd in with the informant.

His speech was slurred, thick with Demerol, but they got it steno'ed and recorded, nonetheless.

When he reached the stripped-down lobby, he saw Protiste lying flat on his front, the lax and drunken look of death on his face, drooping lids, drooling mouth, wayward tongue. Red blossomed beneath him into the rug like lichen; oddly beautiful. Andromeda took the stance and drew down on exactly zero with his Walther PPK non-police issue. He danced the kata of the gun about the space, ready to fire.

There was a suspicious pause for something wrong. He didn't breathe, listening to the buzzing of the low-yield lights, trying to catch it.

Whatever it was, it came fast. It glinted sharply at the edges of his vision and rapped his knuckles hard when it hit, breaking his hold on the weapon, which fell down to the rug and abruptly misfired.

Before he could look up from where it had landed, he felt it overtake him, claim him, make him ridiculously frozen mid-motion.

Fire in the belly.

He had been knifed.

In shock and unsure what to do—remembering not to yank it out—he suddenly saw a wild Pugsley bearing down on him, scream-ing, "Fucking amateurs! I hate 'em!" Pugsley put his skinny, wiry arm around him firmly, smelling of sweat and tooth decay.

In a lightning motion, he yanked the knife out from Androme-da's gut and this blacked him out down to ground level, but only for a moment.

When Andromeda at last surfaced, the blur came over him like fog hanging low to the earth, revealing the secrets of the low ground in grades and depressions.

Voices.

Pugsley talking angrily to a giant fat woman towering over him. He watched him get up on his toes and punch the woman in the face. While they were distracted, he dragged himself to the gun, lifted it, tried to bark out a command but only really coughed it.

The eclipse fell upon him fast, the heaviness like sleep, the deep, bruising pain.

He shrieked when it came down to his previously injured and now knife-torn gut. The weight and force.

Shame was as far away as hope. The shrieking was involuntary.

He was dying.

Wednesday Impetigo was crushing the life out of him.

"So then what? The cavalry comes?"

"No. Security doing the rounds"

"The other dead guy, you mean."

"Ya." He choked off into a spasm of pain, taking him like searing heat. "The—another—one."

"You're a lucky guy, Nicky. You know that."

"Yeah," he grunted, shame now close to him in his mind since hope had returned. "Dead lucky."

If a face can ever have been said to have flashed from green to red and back again, it was Boyd's. The wind and cold running through her hair and down her back made her sweat stick to her like a cold paste.

The rush of air was deafening in her ears.

It was her anger that kept her warm.

They had her at the very prow of the MDC maintenance tug as they churned out of Boston harbor south toward the Islands. She was kneeling, ankles bound to wrists, some kind of plastic boating rope locked to her own security cuffs. Spray dappled her face and created an illusion of tears as Thing idly played with her hair.

Pugsley put his hand on her ass and she elbowed him. The knife came out, but Thing grabbed his wrist. The twisted slug smile said, "Patience."

The tug was full of large, thick men. Armed men, the last of the family soldiers. The weaponry was badly hidden under overcoats and by the onset of darkness, but she got the sense there was a great deal of it. From what she knew about LeCoeur, he wouldn't have had it any other way.

At the stern sat Wednesday, her full ballast seeming to tilt the boat toward her enormous ass. It didn't help matters that she wore a down jacket she couldn't possibly zipper closed at the front that billowed and threatened to spill off the boat.

In the cold clarity of the afternoon, Boyd was getting it, and she didn't like what she was getting.

They were heading for George's Island.

It was obvious what Thing wanted.

It was all about the fucking fort!

What she knew was this.

Georges Island was the transit center of the 34 mini-islands dotting the water off the Boston coastline. This was because it had the best and largest dock. And since the island was situated at the entry point to Boston Harbor, a fort with high-powered guns had been established there, ostensibly to secure main shipping channels, but really as an early step in the preparation for civil war.

Fort Warren.

Grim, gray and cut under the land in long squat buildings, the fort served as training ground and patrol point for the Union army, but soon it settled into its main purpose as it became clear no real action would test its fortifications—a prison. It turned out to be somewhat the reverse of Andersonville, actually earning a reputation for humane treatment of its Confederate prisoners. Regardless, the place reeked of an undeniable inhumanity. A misty patina of bleak anguish hangs over the place still, unseen but inescapably felt.

Fort Warren was decommissioned in 1947, left to rot until it was acquired by Boston's Metropolitan District Commission for historic preservation and recreation in 1958, never quite completed.

The grim, gray place has been rotting intermittently since then, even in its most recent incarnation as a part of the National Parks Service. Somehow, through the magic of Boston-style political intrigue, the very much non-Federal MDC still services and maintains the fort after a fashion.

As always, hurting for money.

The thought intruded in Boyd's mind that the Family juiced the city wherever it could.

Why not the under-funded work-a-mopes of the MDC?

Fort Warren had enough history to be a lucrative tourist spot, despite the need of a ferry, tug or dinghy to get there. Edgar Allen Poe haunted the Fort during his short, moribund military career, pulling sentry duty as a corporal. They say that an actual ghost (if there can be such a thing) haunts the place to this day. "The Lady in Black," spectral remains of a Confederate prisoner's wife, sentenced to death (they say) for aiding in her husband's escape, summarily hung in a black robe hastily made from the drapes of the mess hall to fulfill her last request of dressing in a lady-like fashion when executed. She still walks (they say) the gun emplacements, bastions, parade grounds and footpaths of the fort. Why she would choose to stay, no one could say.

There wasn't much of an allure to the Island, especially for a ghost, as the place was always underattended. Only the most naïve tourists didn't shun it.

The problem was that the place was ugly. The entire twenty-eight acres of the island was foreboding, often treacherous to traverse, shelter from the blistering sun and burning wind being minimal, and recently constructed, and many buildings closed off, though what was inside mostly duplicated the sparseness of the open buildings. Even Alcatraz had more charm.

Fort Warren now amounted to little more than a fifth-string historical monument, amongst the crush of more convenient historical monuments in Boston proper, and a less than inviting picnic ground for families, meaning specifically children, who had an average of a half hour's wicked delight in the fort's having been a Civil War prison before descending into fits of petulant, noisy boredom.

And it was too soon in the season for children, the "park" not opening this year officially until late May due to maintenance work on the hazardous drop offs in and around the prison structure Bastion C. Insurance liabilities due to prior neglect being a yearly battle as pitched as the one for funding.

No, the only children on the island right now were in cages.

She grasped it, finally. The Family was shipping off the KP discards in MDC boats for pickup by a special yacht. Or two.

The dead-end set up of the stockades and bastions of the fort would be the perfect place to cut off an attacker, hold court with him until he was over and done. If you were of that particular mindset and had a small phalanx of shooters along with you to pull it off, well—

It might be the perfect set-up for settling up with Null.

They were laying for him and she now understood her place in the scheme of things. She was to be a prop in the coming showdown. A distracting complication to allow them to whack him out more easily.

The anger rose from her stomach like bile, but instead of cursing, she laughed.

They didn't understand that you can't distract a man physiologically unable to care. They didn't know what Null was. All this time, and they just didn't know.

She laughed harder and Pugsley nailed her hard in the arm with his fist to shut her up.

The bored grumbling of the soldiers behind her and Pugsley and Thing was as low as it was contentious. They moved awkwardly with the tossing and wallowing of the tug.

She baited them. "You'll never lure him there, you know. You'll never get him where you want him to whack him. If anything, he won't even show."

"I'm not worried about him showing, Lieutenant. Zombie-fuck knows all about it, down to the timing."

"Really? And how do you know?"

"Ol' Granny gave it up to him right before she gave up the ghost. And we gave Granny up to Null as a little bonus to make sure he'd bite."

"Gomez's idea?"

"No, but he approved it."

"So, you're gonna just lay there and wait for him."

"No, Lieutenant, sad to say."

"Why sad?"

LeCoeur sighed wearily, cupping his hands around a cigarette to light it.

"Well, I'm pretty sure he's already there. Waiting for us."

THIRTY

It came smoothly and in stifled quiet like a dream, distant and easy —the tug docking, the men debarking at the beachhead, two of the hugest of them stinking of beer, cheap aftershave and their own feculent sebum hoisting Boyd aloft. It was these two, one on either side of Boyd, who bore her up the uneven terrain to the barracks of Fort Warren. She shivered, not so much with the pummeling wind off the choppy harbor, but with frustration. Ever since the long, impossible night that had remade her life with the death of those few she loved most, she hadn't been in such a helpless position.

And she hadn't been completely helpless then, just too late when she finally took the worst of the motherfuckers down.

So she thought.

But now she struggled stupidly against the arms of the big men, who held her without difficulty, unable to do even a suicidal move.

She ran over what she knew in her mind but was too furious to make it work for her.

It seemed Fort Warren was like a magnet for events like these.

The fort was really more a type of defensible depression, the big twelve-foot guns and Rodman cannons having long since been removed, and all the long, squat buildings, stone gray and lozenge-like, assembled in a closed, almost star-shaped pattern at the center of which was a flat parade ground. Beneath this was "The Corridor of Dungeons", which was just what it implied, shadowed, dingy and cramped cells following the length of the lozenges that closed to make a wall within a wall, the prison within the fort. For a tourist spot, it was a far from cheering sight.

More than by any history or spirit, the place felt more haunted by the lingering presence of a palpable fear and its accompanying despair and woe, no doubt as much now as it had ever been then. To Boyd, it was as if these things stained the very earth beneath her.

Dusk was coming, and the only sounds other than the herring gulls of the harbor, the unimpeded wind and the slopping of the waters was the low assent of the soldiers replying to the succulent commands of Theron "Thing" LeCoeur.

Wanda and Peter Impetigo, Wednesday and Pugsley, brought up the rear, Wednesday's stertorous huffing and puffing, nearly swallowing the rush of wind.

It felt like a long hike to the large, flat open parade ground defined at its edges by the ancient gray prison buildings, before they came in through a sally port with the name of the fort and its founding date of 1850 over the entrance. The barrack buildings and walls cut the merciless wind, which was a relief. She was hoisted up high over thuggish, knotted shoulders, feeling the unevenness of the ground rip into her. After they had skirted the trees and had entered onto the parade ground past the powder house, she saw how it was going to go down:

The kids were caged in the overlook building, the watchtower above the yard and the prison barracks. A row of soldiers would aim down from the tops of the main barracks building in front of the watchtower on one side, by Bastion C, and the remainder would snipe at him from the old, empty gun batteries on the opposite side. Null would be shot to pieces, caught in between, while snipers took potshots at him from the doors and windows of the barracks at ground level just to make sure.

No doubt he would keep going regardless until Thing deemed it safe enough to come lumbering down from the overlook position where the main load of kids was caged, and personally and precisely took the time to blow his brains out.

And she knew there wasn't a thing she could do about it.

What she didn't know was why she wanted to do anything about it at all.

Her main worry was survival. She should stick to that and stop thinking about the twisted, ruined fortunes of Null.

This only made it worse, of course, and she thought about it all the more. Thought of Null and his queer mission to avenge the death of his own flawed and largely worthless humanity.

A fragile humanity snuffed out like the last candle in a prison cell.

This thought was interrupted by her being thrown down on her side, stuck painfully in a reverse of the fetal position on the dried, earth-caked floor of an ancient prison cell; her joints inflamed with oozing, electric discomfort; the skin of her wrists and ankles abraded raw, burning angrily. She lay next to two hefty metal dog crates of torpid, filthy little boys, some of them still in their KP movie costumes, clothes of exaggerated style and cut to exaggerate certain fantasies, objectify them as willing and easy, weird adult designer ensembles now soiled and rank and revealing PVC sex-wear. Boyd glimpsed this and shut both eyes tight in revulsion.

Some were giggling, others were fighting, one or two were sobbing.

There was no point in uttering words of comfort in her position and into the cages.

For them, it would amount to another unreal bit of play-acting, with the usual conclusion looming ahead. It was all in the movie.

And this time she couldn't be sure that the conclusion wouldn't be worse.

Then she heard the dull crackling of gunshots from above and knew it had started. She could almost smell the powder.

Biding her time, lying there in ancient prison stink and the odor of fear of small boys too terrified to speak, her own pain and terror being willed away into a dull distance, she knew that Null had come.

This made her toy with the belief that somehow he would get her out of this.

And she tried to be grateful to God for this delusion.

Voices were shouting wildly; there was a long, unrestrained screaming.

"Please," she sighed softly. "Please."

———

What Boyd had to miss in the gathering darkness above her was that Null was in fact coming, and coming fast right out of the trees. He came brazen in his overcoat and hat, heading directly toward Battery Jack Adams by Bastion B as if the fort and the island were already his. If she had seen this, she would have lost a heartbeat in despair.

Had Boyd seen this, she would have choked back on her hopes, seizing up in spasms of woe and gulping hard for air.

Because the last chance was as dead last now as a blood-cloth nag at Suffolk Downs. A no win.

Maybe she would have been one of the few to weep for Null.

Null waved his arms as if wanting to be seen, squeezing off not even a single shot.

Thing roared down from the overlook to "execute the motherfucker."

In seconds, Null exploded ruefully into splashes and patterns of blood, wailing incomprehensibly.

It was overkill, like in a bad, high-concept action movie.

Not Tarantino or Woo, but some anonymous hack who shot his wad and was now working in his father's brokerage firm.

They pulped Null's body but good with a wild blistering of bullets long after he had been flattened and shot to immobility on the ground.

Finally, it stopped.

And the shooters went down to gloat and joke about the lack of necessity for this gambit.

"Shit!" a voice echoed off the long barracks buildings, "one fucking bullet in the back of the head would have done the job just as good!"

Thing gazed down critically from his position in the overlook building, smirking with smug calm (if you were adept at interpreting the behavior of his lips) at the corpse on the parade ground. A horror crawled up his sensitive back, and he abruptly screamed at the soldiers to get back into position. He screamed so loud that it exaggerated his lisp and distorted the enunciation of his words beyond the comprehension of his men.

The horror was simple enough to grasp from the overlook. The shots at Null were all fired from one side only.

The soldiers on the quiet side were still standing, but there was no action. They weren't doing anything.

The answer to this was the horror that had crawled up his back like a tropical millipede.

A very simple thing:

They were all standing there propped up dead and Null was what had killed them.

Before the men down in the parade ground could reposition themselves, or even scatter—right when finding out that the man that they had just shot was simply another of them with duct tape over his mouth already beaten half to death, his ankles tied together in Null's coat and hat—they were cut down, headshots all. Fucked into decoy status by the actual Null.

Null, who was firing high-powered rounds down upon them from the roof of the prison that now housed Boyd, doing his own brand of targeted overkill.

They had fired back, too late and far too scattered. And now they just lay there. Forced to move only by points of impact.

Their massacre was as quick and dirty as what was given to one of the line of men Null had shanked so very quietly and efficiently as they waited for Thing's high-sign to whack out the fucking mope when he emerged. Thing had been right—Null had been waiting for them, and in fact had already taken the fort from them by the time they believed they were taking their positions.

When really, they were just taking *his* positions.

Null, automatic rifles now in each arm and wearing a flak jacket, looking small, dried up, even vulnerable without his coat and hat, descended the long concrete steps to the parade ground to wipe out the remaining snipers firing at him from the barracks as Thing LeCoeur made rampaging, incomprehensible noises from the tower above. This was because Null was out of his range, for the moment.

Null blew off the jaw of one of the soldiers sniping at him from a prison window; two others simply cut and ran when they saw him coming. There was a strangeness coming off him in this attack that hit home. He was like a walking black hole, his own event horizon:

Dead calm.

Unhurried.

Long guns blazing without a miss.

Exhibiting a terrifying cool.

Death's favorite.

———

"Don't pray," said Null, cutting the waterproof nylon boating rope from Boyd's ankles and helping her to her feet.

"This whole thing is to whack you out—you shouldn't be here," she said stifling a shudder.

"No, it's for them, not for me. They just don't realize it yet. Do you have the handcuff keys?"

"LeCoeur does. They're in my purse along with the Sig-Sauer."

"You have something against holsters?"

"Senior police staff, especially women, don't use them as a rule."

"Bad policy. These are High Security, which means they only work with the keys they came with. No generic handcuff key will work. We'll just have to get them back so you can help pitch in."

"Why are you helping me? I'm not on your side, you know."

"You are for the moment."

"True. But when it's over, I'm going to put you away."

"I'm counting on it," said Null, reloading each gun with 7.62 × 39 mm rounds from his pockets. "You are my reason for living."

"We need to get to the tug and get the fuck out of here."

"You go ahead. I have a little cleaning up to do."

"You're set on killing each and every one of them, aren't you?"

"Just about, Lieutenant."

"They still have you out-manned and outgunned."

"Not by much." He locked in the clip of the Kalashnikov Type 2 assault rifle, did the same with the Chinese AK-56 and, one at a time, rotated back the bolts, which pumped up a shell from each magazine with crisp mechanics, then looked up into Boyd's eyes with empty indifference. "I'm not worried. I can't worry, really, no matter how hard I try."

The rifle flew from his hands like it was struck by lightning and Null jerked back as if he had caught something coming at him.

He did.

It happened too fast for Boyd to see at first, but she was able to see it now:

A gleaming knife sunk deep to the curve of its hilt just below Null's left shoulder, a rivulet of dark blood flowing down.

A voice bleated from the doorway, breaking into a whine on the high end:

"You should try harder, Pally. You need to be worrying, and I mean a lot!"

Pugsley.

THIRTY-ONE

The kids ran out screaming for freedom, not realizing they were stuck on a cold, foreboding island. Not realizing much of anything but the will to run. They wriggled fast past Pugsley's legs and he let them go, having no ostensible reason to stop them.

They wouldn't get far.

The joke was that when you were out of the square-john system, the island—as it was once meant to be—was a prison within a prison. Always a joke with the jokers doing none of the laughing.

Boyd had bloodied her wrists, opening the cage trying to buy a few minutes.

This failed.

Thing elbowed Pugsley aside, his face too distorted to determine just exactly what his expression meant.

Then he raised his *Heckler und Koch* M-16 knockoff, which projected his attitude where his face could not.

"Boom-boom, Mr. Null."

Boyd rushed him and Pugsley kicked her smoothly to the floor, chuckling. She fell over sloppily and made an unconscious whimpering noise when she twisted to get her shoulder to take most of the impact of the fall. The noise embarrassed her and she wished she could have taken it back.

This is how it is near death. The inconsequential and trivial matter as much as life itself.

And then it dawns on you that it *is* life.

The cries of gulls mixed with those of the little children, caged and not. Boyd hoped the boys were still able to be boys enough to find good hiding places on the island. She hoped she would die well and not like a pussy.

"So do it, Thing. You win."

"It was inevitable."

Pugsley was already up with the next knife aimed straight at Null's solar plexus, but Thing signaled him urgently a firm "no." So, he just waited there, his arm up, fixed, poised and ready to throw.

"Fire down, Thing, or I'll just take my rifle back and get back to killing you."

"Tell me, Joey X, have you met Wednesday yet?"

"She won't fit in here."

"I know. We're going outside."

Wednesday was waiting for them under Bastion C in the parade ground; a huge, black shadow standing like a heap of mud. Service and maintenance spots glimmered down on them like spiky miniature novas, timed from when Thing had louvered the junction box and set the mechanism back at the ranger station. He was still certain of being a few steps ahead of the game, though he was perplexed about the terrific loss of men from this skinny insect.

It was an apt metaphor.

Null really was like a type of bug in his robotic movements, his stalled-out mannerisms. If Thing didn't know any better, he would have considered him mindless.

But mindless creatures just don't kill soldiers this efficiently and keep right on killing. No. Null was as exacting to his purpose as Thing was to his. He knew it was going against better judgment but dispatching this gypsy hitter needed to be done just so.

He had to make the client Gomez happy before shooting off his nuts for good and all.

You delivered the contract first, then took care of any personal beefs with the client directly after.

They would appreciate that in New York; it wouldn't interrupt the continuous flow of work there as long as he handled Gomez properly. More important than squashing a bug like Null, establishing the mark of a professional.

The unwritten laws of conduct from the bottom defined the lives of the hitters at the top. This was the weird alchemy of the streets that made success out of failure in America.

Pugsley dragged Null out rough, trying to torture him with the knife by pushing the handle back and forth as he did. Null simply went lax and allowed himself to be brought along. Boyd was allowed out on her own, bloody wrists slick under the lights and flat black cuffs.

"Now we have enough room," Thing observed, not a trace of malice in his voice.

"For what?" Null asked dully. "Morris dancing?"

"No, dickweed, so you can dance with me," Wednesday squalled.

"Wednesday's a talented girl." Thing squinted into the light, blue dusk fading to purple.

"I remember," Null said like it was nothing. "She broke my leg once."

"Fucker, I can do more than that."

"Go girl," said Pugsley. "Show him!"

"Hey Null, this is how I killed your wife!"

Null took a step backward as the shadow descended upon him.

Too little too late.

Wednesday was on him, bouncing up and down like an inflated parade float in the wind, kicking her legs and making small noises of triumphant struggle.

She kicked her legs.

Thing abruptly grabbed Boyd by the shoulders, leaving his *Heckler und Koch* assault rifle on the ground, pushing her up against the wall. "You're gonna bring me everything I need to own Schroeder Plaza, you annoying cunt and you're gonna do it while you die slowly as I fuck you."

"Eat shit and die, creature-from-the-fucking-black-lagoon." She spat in his face and reddened with frustration when she realized he enjoyed it, licking his pinkish slug-like lips.

"Ah, my little police pet, I haven't decided whether I'll fuck you before or after. It's a tough choice, because in order to do it, I have to make you go away. Then you can be the fort's Lady in Blue—ha! Ladies in black and blue like a bruise!" The deformed face creased and crinkled at this.

Wednesday made loud noises and produced a single hideous keening squeal.

"She's coming!" screamed Pugsley excitedly. "She's coming!

Wednesday shivered and shook on the ground, presumably smothering Null, breaking him, killing him with her crushing weight, giving him the final suffocation of her all-encompassing flesh. She bounced up and down violently for a few seconds, making a low, juicy growl, then sagged motionless, spent.

Her enormously thick neck was covered with light pin-pricks of sweat shining like dots of mercury in the light.

Pugsley was almost afraid to go near her. "Jesus. That must have been a whopper!"

Thing was distracted from Boyd and looked on slack-mouthed.

It was almost beautiful to watch the way Null was dying, or had already died, under the formidable behemoth of flesh.

Then Wednesday rose, making an eerie groan that was in no way reminiscent of anything human, much less animal. It was like some ghastly, greaseless machine.

The front of her muumuu was soaked and black in the light with blood.

All eyes turned to the ground in front of her.

Thing managed to get this out before it happened. "Where the fuck—?"

Where was Null?

The question was answered with horrific speed.

Null cut his way up and out of Wednesday's enormous and now quite dead body the same way he cut his way in, with Pugsley's knife jolted from his shoulder. He was coated with blood and darkened bilious gore like infantile vernix as her corpse fell away from him like a gruesome mantle or rubber sumo-suit parody. It made a loud, soggy plop on the ground.

Pugsley was so stunned he couldn't move for a moment, his

body locked up with emotional conflict, stymied by a quick-mindedness that was just too slow for the events unfolding.

Null sunk the knife into the right side of his neck, which sprayed out blood like a fire sprinkler as Pugsley sank down to his knees and summarily died.

Thing pushed Boyd into the wall of the bastion so that she bounced off hard, dove low for the rifle, rolled toward it, grabbed it up and pointed the barrel directly at Null's bodily-fluid glistening chest as he lay on his back. "You're disarmed."

"For the moment," said Null, just before Thing pumped the entire magazine of five shells directly into his torso. This knocked Null flat on his back, coughing, kicking, and struggling like an overturned turtle.

After fussing with Pugsley's corpse for a moment, Thing strode over to where Null lay with supreme confidence. He calmly staked Null's open palms into the ground with two of the late Pugsley's throwing knives, a single sure motion for each.

Now only his legs kicked as coughing continued.

"Look at him kick, Lieutenant. He really is just like a bug. I wonder if he even really feels any pain from this."

Boyd pushed herself up against the wall of the bastion, still cuffed and bloodied. "Oh, he can feel it alright, LeCoeur—he just doesn't care."

"I'm going to give him a few things to care about before he dies."

"Well, he won't be dying from the shotgun blast, since you spent the magazine into his metal reinforced, Kevlar flak jacket."

"I know. I only wanted to break his ribs, mess him up inside. Knock him down a bit. I want him to see me do you before I correct his brain damage the way God meant for it to be corrected."

"You don't get it, do you?"

"I don't have to since you're both going to get it first."

He had her against the wall, undid the high security cuffs, spread her arms and held them, pressing his body against hers, letting his loosened pants drop to his ankles.

He forced himself between her legs.

"Null may not feel anything, may lack affect, but I'm the best of both worlds—I can turn it on and off when I please. Like a button in my mind. I can murder cold and fast without a thought, and turn about and be sweet and tender, just like I'm going to be with you." He sighed deeply against her. "Before I gut you like the fucking sow you are."

She could feel him throbbing against her and her nausea rose along with black bile in the back of her throat.

Thing gloried in her scent, lay his weight into her.

She roared inarticulate protest, wrenching her face away.

Thing licked her neck, said, "You know, this will only be my second time having one still able to reject me." He paused and added, "It's just as exciting as the first."

It was just as he was fiddling with her skirt that he felt a blinding pain in his leg; at first like the searing bite of a deerfly, then like the savaging from a wolverine.

He released Boyd and fell back to turn and see the bloody Null standing there, Pugsley's knives still sticking through each of his palms

Thing realized he was bleeding; felt dizzy, even weak, as he fought not to stumble with his trousers about his legs. He brought up his hands from the site of injury and they were coated with blood.

Boyd had meanwhile sagged down, now looking up, grateful with relief.

Cries of gulls; maybe the cries of children.

Null stepped right up close to Thing, toe-to-toe, looked him in the face with nothing behind it and spat a projectile into his eyes.

Whatever it was bounced off him and landed in the grass of the parade ground. Thing did not dive down for it but gave Null the fisheye back instead. This look changed directly after Null spoke:

"That was a bit of the skin of your thigh I just spit in your face. I had to bite it out of you so I could rip into the femoral artery, which, judging from the amount of blood coming out of you, I'd say I did."

Thing swung at him and missed, woozy, almost falling over with his pants tangled about his ankles.

The eyes told the story:

Worried. Frantic.

"You can do many things, LeCoeur. You're a versatile guy. Not like me. I can only do one thing. Just one. And now I'm going to do it to you."

Thing screamed inarticulately, forced himself to get up and fight but fell over again as Null dodged him neatly.

"You have a couple of minutes left, Thing. But you're not going to die easy."

Thing wailed, choking with panicked disbelief. "This can't be happening! I'm—too good—for this! Not—fucking—*me*!"

"I know all about you, LeCoeur. You were born under punches. So, it's really only appropriate that you go out the way you came in. Under punches."

Null dragged Thing up by the collar of his shirt, brought him up to his knees. Thing gazed up into Null's eyes as if there might be something there. Mercy maybe. Anything!

Those eyes were open, clear and focused.

They told the story—absolutely nothing.

Then Null started punching at him evenly and repeatedly like a metal stamping machine, kept punching until the last few minutes had elapsed and Thing lay there like a soiled, foul-smelling rag doll, with his pants down, dead.

Null kicked him clinically and there was nothing from him, not even the death rattle that his insistent blows must have drowned out entirely.

Boyd approached Null, eyes welling.

Like a cat grooming itself, Null tugged the knives out of the bloodied palms of his hands with unsettling calmness.

A voice came fifty yards down on the parade ground. "Give it up, Null! Stand away from the Lieutenant."

Andromeda.

His gun was raised and aimed right at Null. It was obvious to Boyd he was about to shoot him and go for the killshot to the head. She could feel it. Her eyes saw the telegraphing of it, the hitching of the shoulders in the sparse, hot light, the widening of the legs, the attitude of the gun.

She got there first, grabbing up and firing Null's Chinese AK-56 type 2 knockoff right into Andromeda's shoulder process.

He dropped down when the shell hit, shouting, "LT! Fuck!"

He rolled about on the ground in pain and oncoming shock as if he were putting out a fire.

"You fucking shot me!"

This from Monad at the top of Bastion B. "Hey! LT! What do you think you're doin'? You can't do that. What the fuck is wrong with you?"

Boyd shouted back, "Fuck you guys! This is the other set of rules. You know what they are."

Hundertwasser shouted down from Bastion C. "You can't shoot a fellow officer!"

"Can and did, boys. Bring me up on charges later, if you have to, but you know what the rules say about that too. The real rules. The ones that keep you alive on the street!"

Andromeda was livid: "Fuck you, Boyd! You almost killed me!"

"Don't be a drama queen, Nicky. I'm way too good a shot to kill you! I goddamn firearms qualify every year!" But not with an AK-56 knockoff, she forgot to say.

"Cuff that fuckin' mutt, LT! We're comin' down!" Hundertwasser.

She ignored them for a moment, touching Null's scarred and bloodied cheek with her fingertips as he stood motionless, almost in a caress. She said it softly, no artifice in her voice, just a faint tinge of incipient grief. "You poor thing. You poor, poor thing. It's all gone, isn't it? There's nothing left inside you anymore, is there?"

"No," he replied, his voice more a vacancy than a presence. "Nothing at all."

With a jerky motion, he reached into his pants pocket and removed a crumpled, decades-old wallet photo and pressed it tightly into Boyd's hand.

She smoothed it out, saw within the faded colors of the aged emulsion the oval face of a somewhat buck-toothed girl posing shoulders up in a traditional parochial school dickey and blazer, a mischievous innocence in her eyes as well as a hint of unknowable sadness.

Cassandra Null.

Boyd had no idea who it was, but she pocketed it carefully.

"You should keep this. I have no use for it anymore."

"What is it?"

"When I had a heart, this is what it looked like."

Her fingers curled around it. A tear rolled out of her eye, glinting sharply in the emergency lights like an icicle. She fought to clear her throat and her mind, shouted to break through: "Now—"

Flash viewpoint: It was plain to her then that his eyes were dead.

"—Get the fuck out of here!"

Null took off.

Monad and Hundertwasser passed her by moments later, giving hard chase. They ran Null down to the docks where the MDC dinghy that got them there was moored, only to watch him drop down fast like a herring gull in a dive for food, an awkward weight that fell into the sea.

POSTMORTEM

The shrieking of a minor city cannot be expected to tell the story anymore than the eyes of a madman can, yet they both do it well and completely, even though both are far too terrible to face. It seems the duty of the professional news media is to offer the ever-hopeful public an acceptable alternative.

The dailies and affiliates carried the story with smarmy omni-science.

It never made the national feed.

The story did hit the front page of the Herald for one day's edition, then was relegated to the unread back-end filler you'd find on the floor of a bus, the subway or blowing down the street in a crumple, same day of publication. It wound up beneath the fold on page two of the Globe.

The Patriot Ledger and the Springfield Union gave it quarter page space also below the fold, but at least on the front page, abutting the usual stock story about a quickie visitation from a Hollywood celebrity stumping for Podunk movie ticket sales.

They all ran the same photo.

Boyd squeezing out a cheesy stifling smile clasping hands with ArtyMarty under the aegis of a beaming Buffalo Bill at a lectern with the BPD insignia on it backed by detectives Andromeda and Hundertwasser and beat patrolman Monad, now bumped up to task force status. Andromeda was in a shoulder cast and didn't smile, a dour contrast to the lewd and knowing grins of Hundertwasser and Monad.

The dailies all sang the same song in unvarying rinky-dink news-ese.

Theron "Thing" LeCoeur, 38, of Brockton was killed in a shootout at Georges Island with two other as yet-unidentified accomplices. LeCoeur had been lead suspect in a rash of mob-related murders of alleged crime figures, all of whom were facing racketeering and kiddie porn charges out on bail.

According to Organized Crime Task Force Leader Boyd and backed up by a few award-winning investigative spotlight-hot seat-action news reporting teams, LeCoeur was staging an internal takeover of the vice operations of an organized crime group known as "The Family," including a lucrative kiddie porn set-up run out of Attleboro. It was Boyd's theory, supported by the BPD and by a coterie of stalwart, uncompromising journalists, that LeCoeur had shot a group of children in Mattapan who may have been potential witnesses, as well as two street persons who witnessed that shooting.

Boston Police ballistics specialists pointed out that, patrolmen Hummel and Howe were shot by the very same gun as the Mattapan victims, and to clinch things, a cell phone belonging to one of them was found in LeCoeur's pocket after he was shot resisting arrest, which in this case meant firing on Boston police officers, wounding and nearly killing Detective Andromeda.

LeCoeur's accomplices were believed to be Wanda and Peter Impetigo of Ashland, a husband-wife team of Family enforcers, but positive ID had yet to be made out of the coroner's office.

There was no mention of the children loosed screaming from their cages.

There was no mention of the removal of the twenty odd bodies from Georges Island.

There was no mention of Null.

The front page of the Herald wound up framed on Boyd's wall: "SHE'S NO POWDERPUFF!"

("That's Why The Lady Is A Champ," was her other favorite, followed by "She Shoots, She Scores!")

More importantly, she kept the damaged photo Null had given her in her wallet, near the pictures of her dead children.

The Boston Basilisk filled its ongoing highly editorialized news gap of front section column inches with the exclusive truth of "Boston's Secret Crime War." The paper's hard-hitting probe told of how Theron "Thing" LeCoeur staged a coup within the Gomelsky Family for the sole purpose of muscling in on the Mattapan drug trade, taking it away from the Gangsta Boyz crew of Mattapan, who in reality were dealing meth to their own in a grass roots effort to effect social change.

The story—recommended by its diminutive publisher for the Pulitzer Prize—showed that Gangsta Boyz gang-banger-in-chief, Alphonse "Heavy Cheese" Petomane, was funding half-way houses and a Roxbury women's shelter with some of the proceeds of his "enterprise," quoted as asserting, "It ain't all about the bling-bling, yo." The two-part investigative piece took up two complete, consecutive news sections of the weekly tabloid.

Almost unnoticed, the under-circulated grunge competitor to the Basilisk, Boston's "Weekly Dig," ran a short, fanciful account about how an unnamed Boston mob torture victim came back from the dead to wipe out the rising crime crew called "The Family." The story raised questions about a surplus of bodies removed in secret from Georges Island, but nobody bought this; nobody at all. It was considered more of the attention-getting apocrypha of an upstart weekly too in touch with the vagaries of the youth market to ever be in touch with reality.

Gratuitous sarcasm wasn't journalism.

At least not this year.

———

Null staked out international departures at Logan for two days straight, his long shank under his topcoat, face shaded by a new slouch hat bought for fifty cents at one of the Saint Vincent De Paul thrift shops dotting East Boston. The shank had been cut down from the ultra-sharp machete he had used to inscribe the names of god on the flesh of Grandmama Gomelsky. Cut down and honed long and slim. For two days, he waited silently at the Delta terminal where Gomez had racked up all his frequent flier miles off an Internet free-airline-ticket scam, looking like a stooped little old man, harmless if not on his last legs.

Gomez sauntered down the concourse without a care, Helle showing off her bulging arms in a Gold's Gym muscle tee, carrying his luggage surrounded by three tall, thick overcoated gunsels. The first one to relieve himself in a nearby men's room never came back. The one who went to fetch him died with more difficulty, squeezing off a single muffled shot as Null gutted him up from pretending he was tying his shoe. It didn't raise the fuss and attention Null thought it would, simply swallowed up by the mid-range ambient cacophony of Logan Airport.

The third and last had some kind of an attack in line and Null called for help from security personnel.

Helle dropped the baggage and bolted for the ground transportation exit, her triceps and trapezius in exaggerated bronze relief as she disappeared.

She didn't look back, and she didn't say a word, which would have been difficult anyway, owing to the fact that her jaw was still wired shut.

Gomez saw the shank under Null's coat and went along, recognizing just how quickly the thing could kill him before he could pull his pudgy girth away and make a scene. He was too fucking old for this and he knew, since he wasn't dead yet, that there was a deal to be made. Null, in his spidery fashion, wanted something, and this turned out to be true. Gomez led him out to his BMW in central parking ahead of security and well ahead of the BPD, who might have wanted to talk to them had they stuck around.

Gomez unlocked the door and Null clocked him unconscious from behind.

When Gomez awoke, they were speeding down Storrow Drive, and he was bound in nautical rope with duct tape over his mouth. Null had a short conversation with him before they reached their destination.

"You took my left testicle, Gomez."

Muffled protest.

"By rights, I should take yours, both of them in fact. It's what the law you follow says, I should do. Am I right?"

More of the same; bound legs slamming the driver's seat.

Null swerved jaggedly, narrowly avoiding corner crunches and sideswipes with the other cars.

"But I won't do it. You always thought you had balls and where you're going, you're going to need them. You'll want to keep them as long as possible."

Gomez grunted throatily.

He pulled up in front of the E.R. entrance and left the BMW in an ambulance zone, where it was sure to be towed.

A prim and crisply dressed RN helped Null put Gomez on a gurney while he struggled, grunting until she put a gas mask over his face and he was out quickly, forced to inhale solely through his nose. Gomez was triaged through quickly while Null left like an incidental shadow.

Missy Crocus looked up from her patient to say goodbye, but Null just wasn't to be seen.

Gomez awoke stripped naked, tied down in a windowless lab somewhere in the bowels of Mount Auburn Hospital. Fresh duct tape covered a piece of foam rubber stuck in his mouth. He couldn't move and he couldn't scream.

But he could listen.

"Welcome to pathology, scumbag."

Gomez was squealing now, shrill beneath the gag.

His arms and legs, wrists and ankles, were tethered together flush with the underside of the table.

"You know who I am, and I know who you are, and you know why, don't you, scumbag?"

She bent over him, looked in his eyes, even mopped his brow.

He squealed, knowing.

She let a tear splash down on his face. Then another.

Missy could make out the broken, muffled distortion of the words under the tape. "I'm sorry

She patted his cheek and whispered to him. "I believe you. You can apologize to Natty yourself, when you see him in hell."

The grunts, squeals and bleats became incomprehensible as he spasmed back and forth frantically within the quarter-inch of give his bonds allowed him, trying to wriggle out. This wasn't happening. To do it, he would have had to move the burnished steel pathology table, which was rooted securely within the old, glazed concrete of the floor.

"I studied how to do this, but bear with me in case I make any mistakes, okay?"

Gomez produced a high whimper through his nostrils.

"As standard procedure, we begin by lifting the brain from the cranium to establish its weight, mass and morphology, but I think I'll save that for last. We'll start with the internal organs first."

With that, and without a second's hesitation, she made the long Y-incision from pelvis and scrotum up to the clavicular head at just the right depth and attitude, with a minimum of bleeding. It was so perfectly executed that the procedure made her feel a faint bulge of pride in her breast, as she folded back the flaps of skin and adipose tissue to remove Gomez's liver.

———

Visiting hour at Lemuel Shattuck Hospital in Jamaica Plain, the high security in-patient ward. The big man wore the customary hospital johnnie of humiliation under a lush and sash-less Ralph Lauren terry robe with the only slippers they'd permit him—the cardboard kind. His hair was mussed and his face was flushed. He looked pouty, puffy and drugged, shambling off to the common area in a depressed torpor.

His cardboard slippers scuffed the floor and never once lifted.

There was no one else in the plain airy, greenish Naugahyde-cushioned, white-walled and natural wood-trim common area accented with framed seascapes on the immaculate paint job—he had pulled the last of his strings to get these sessions alone, one hour, once a week. And he was grateful for this last bit of wise guy *noblesse oblige*. It was the only thing keeping him alive in this sterile, hopped-up pit.

This was the only thing left.

His visitor was late, and he both hated to wait and luxuriated in the waiting, lighting up a cigarette, as he always made sure to take his visit in a designated smoking area, with suction fans for ventilation and closed doors. His hand shook even after he lit up the smoke.

Where the fuck was he?

"Right here, Fester."

"Jesus fuck, stop doing that!"

"All part of the program—your program."

"Fuck you, Null! You took money from that jag-off Malek the Mallet and don't say you didn't!"

"He was paying me to do what I was going to do anyway."

Fester stood and banged the table, towering over the sunken Null, waving his fists. "Bullshit! You took one-hundred large for a hit on the whole fucking crew! Chump change! I'll fucking quadruple it if you get out of Dodge and don't come back."

"I like our original deal better."

"What fuckin' deal? You whack me out when I least expect it right here at the fucking laughing academy? You just come at any moment and shank me like a piece of meat in my bed, unless I meet you once a week and—"

"And what, Fester?"

He hung his head, standing there more beaten than contrite. "Confess my sins."

"Fester the Confessor."

"Confess this. You took one hundred large to do this, you prick."

"No, I took one hundred large because that's the debt I owed you from my action at the track. From every fixed race, one hundred large of hopelessness, one hundred large of entrapment. One hundred large of fear. That's what I was owed in owing you. That's why I took the blood money."

"You say you're fucking dead, not fucking human anymore, and I definitely can see that. What the fuck you need one hundred large for?"

"Funeral expenses, burial costs. It's not cheap being dead these days."

"Well ya got no fucking sense of humor, I'll give you that."

"We share that, don't we? We have a bond you and me—torture, despair, humiliation, death."

"Fuck this shit, Null, you and your pissant drama show. You're as dead as I am!"

"No, Fester, you're much, much deader." Null nonchalantly stuck the barrel of his Glock in Fester's stomach. Entered condition zero.

"Fuck your mother, I am!"

"It'll happen soon, but only when I decide it's right and when you won't know."

"How the fuck—?"

"You think you're the only one here afraid of me?"

His eyes teared; the fat lower lip trembled. "No."

"Good—you're learning."

Fester tried to stand it off, keep the grim poker face of the shake-down, but he said fuck it and crumbled, collapsed back down into his seat.

Abject, sniveling, he said, "Please don't kill me. I'll pay you—pay you big!"

"You already are, Fester. And that'll do for the time being."

Null secreted the Glock back under his coat. Stood and turned his back on Fester. He started walking down a long-shadowed corridor.

"Please, tell me!" Fester raged, then his voice grew small. "I have until next week?"

Null didn't turn, just kept on walking. "Yes. You didn't make your confession this time. And I want to hear everything. Before you die."

Almost happily, somewhat craftily, Fester said, "So, I got at least a week?"

"At least," said Null, and disappeared.

Fester stood up, dried his eyes on his sleeve, adjusted and hiked his open terry robe, revealing sweat-dank paisley pajamas. "Thank you!" he called into emptiness. "Thank you."

A grin played across his sodden face. He had another week to get together a strategy to whack out Null and get a foothold back in the scene again. Take care of that fuck Malek too. He could do it. All he had to do was be a good boy, bide his time and convince the shrink in charge that he was a world-beater again, rarin' to go!

Shouldn't be too hard. No, not hard at all.

He scuffed back to his room—one of the myriad afternoon judges was on the idiot box, maybe even Judy! Oh, that bitch made him laugh till he pissed himself. Who said justice wasn't a laughing matter?

They were watching from a door left ajar, the two men, both thirties and slender in a compact, nervous way, each with a somewhat hungry look, one in bewildered wonder and the other in amused resignation. The first, a clean-shaven food service maintenance guy in a navy jumpsuit named Olson, turned to the second, a white-coated lab tech and male nurse with a full reddish-brown beard named Johnson, and said, "What the fuck was that? What the fuck's the big goon doin'?"

Johnson put his finger to his lips and dragged Olson back from the door.

"Guy's lost it, permanent."

"No shit, Sherlock."

"Don't be so loud. He might get violent if he overhears."

"Well, this would be the place for it, wouldn't it?"

"Way I heard it, it goes like this guy used to be some Mob mucky muck. Instead of goin' away for forty-somethin' years on a kiddie porn beef, he decides to go round the bend instead. Do his tour of duty here."

"Decides. So, he's sane and faking it. Good plan, buddy."

"No, I don't think he's faking—no one around here does. You see that fuckin' routine?"

"That's some crazy shit man, I admit."

"Paranoid schitz', the doc's say. And a few other things to boot." Johnson played with his beard unconsciously.

"So what was all that for?"

"They don't know. Guy insists he go out alone to the smoking area of the visitor's lounge once a week so he can fucking sit there for an hour, light up a smoke, and talk to his 'visitor'."

"Visitor? You gotta be fucking shitting me! Guy was yelling at a fuckin' empty chair!"

"Yeah, it's way fucked up. Alls I know, he doesn't do this, they gotta keep him sedated and isolated from the other residents."

"Crazy shit!"

"Did you see the guy's eyes—even from here?"

"Yeah, man, scary."

And the eyes tell the whole story, if you take the time to read them.

If Olson and Johnson had looked into Fester's eyes—really looked—they would have seen. They would have known.

The story was right there.

A simple thing he now knew:

Death and terror are always and solely a friend of the mind.

———

Don't miss out on your next favorite book!
Join the Melange Books mailing list at
www.melange-books.com/mail.html

ACKNOWLEDGMENTS

The author hereby wishes to acknowledge his small band of supporters:

Nancy Pepin, née Durocher, who's with me in all things and in everything that matters.

Scott Oddo, for his friendship and keen intellect; Jen Davis, for all she had to put up with; Marc Songini, for his wit and his literary japing; Huntley Dent, for all his help; Steve Dooner, for his astonishing breadth of cultural literacy, abstruse and not; Kate Nicholas, for her sharp wit, bordering on slight insanity; Susan Gambrell Reinhardt, whose sweetly acid commentary is always inspiring; Glen Dansker for being a mensch and Joe Schatzle for always knowing how to crack me up.

This parvum opus is for you all.

THANK YOU FOR READING

Did you enjoy this book?

We invite you to leave a review at the website of your choice, such as Goodreads, Amazon, Barnes & Noble, etc.

DID YOU KNOW THAT LEAVING A REVIEW...

- Helps other readers find books they may enjoy.
- Gives you a chance to let your voice be heard.
- Gives authors recognition for their hard work.
- Doesn't have to be long. A sentence or two about why you liked the book will do.

ABOUT THE AUTHOR

Gary S. Kadet has been a journalist, covering various beats for the Boston Herald, Globe and even Playboy Magazine, which also published his fiction. He was a contributing editor for the nationally-read Boston Book Review where he covered crime fiction in his "Trouble is Their Business" column. In the 90s, he was a trailblazer on the Internet, running the 10th largest adult website in the world, appearing on MSNBC commenting on the future of adult material on the web. His novel "D/s - an Anti-Love Story" was the first novel to portray the real-world BDSM scene without prurience or sentimentality and was a Book Of The Month Club main selection.

He is also the author of "The Ogre Life" (Ukiyoto Publishing, 2021) and the upcoming novels "Violent Mind Candy" and "High Body Count" (Melange Books, 2022), "Mens Rea" (Foundations Books, 2022) and "Viral Load" (Yard Time Publishing, 2022).

GarySKadet@protonmail.com

facebook.com/CleverNovels
twitter.com/GaryScottKadet

Printed in Great Britain
by Amazon

74000260R00177